TALIESIN

CHIEF OF BARDS

Alexander Corby

This book is dedicated to my late father and my beautiful daughter. No sorrow in my life will be greater than the thought that two such brilliant souls will never meet each other in this world.

Special thanks to everyone that helped make this book possible. Specifically, I'd like to thank my wife, Mumu, for her patience and love, my parents for their unwavering support, and my friends Dano, Jess, Anthony, and Shawna, who helped encourage and motivate me, whether they knew it or not.

Extra special thanks to Sam Kifer for her scrutiny and meticulous attention to detail.

Lastly, I would like to mention all my teachers and mentors from fifth grade, through college, and physical theater school. Their praise and encouragement stayed with me during the hardest moments of this long process.

Alexander Corby

CONTENTS

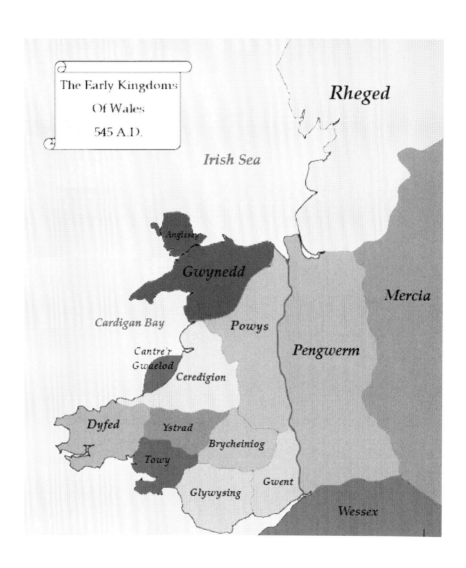

The Early Kingdoms
Of Wales
545 A.D.

Irish Sea

Rheged

Anglesey

Gwynedd

Cardigan Bay

Powys

Cantre'r
Gwaelod

Ceredigion

Pengwerm

Mercia

Dyfed

Ystrad

Brycheiniog

Towy

Glywysing

Gwent

Wessex

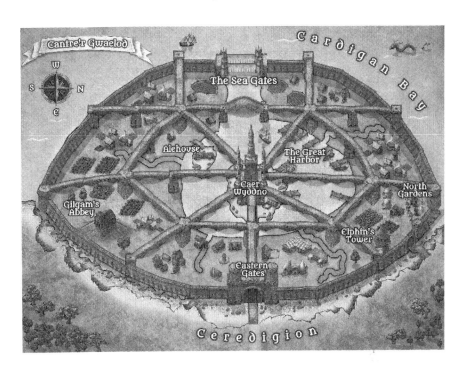

Author's Note

The following piece is, first and foremost, a work of fiction. While several characters have their place in the annals of history, it would be a gross injustice to presume their portrayals here are accurate representations of their actions or circumstances. While researching material for this project, it became apparent that the term 'dark ages' was a far more fitting description of this era than previously believed. Records of sixth-century Britain are conflicting at best and practically non-existent at worst. Several motifs and images, namely those of the mythical kingdom of Cantre'r Gwaelod, were inspired by poetry contained in the thirteenth-century manuscript, *The Black Book of Carmarthen*, while other snippets of the Arthurian pantheon were taken from Geoffrey of Monmouth's *Historia Regum Britanniae*. It's worth noting that both works were written several centuries after the events they describe by authors who could never have had first-hand information about the people they were portraying.

Even Taliesin's own poetry comes to us from a manuscript, the *Llyfr Taliessin*, that has been dated only back to the early fourteenth century, although it is accepted that many of the poems contained within do originate from the mid to later centuries of the first millennium A.D. Ultimately, the only first-hand account of any of the characters of the following narrative come from the monk Gildas' *De Excidio et Conquestu Britanniae* where he offers a thorough, and often scathing, account of Maelgwn's reign over Gwynedd. Whether the modern age can take Gildas' report as historical fact or merely personal gripe remains to be seen. It should be enough to say that Maelgwn was a genuine Welsh king who acted questionably enough to draw the ire of the clergyman, but the rest is left to speculation.

The uncertainty revolving around this particular period of history became more of a boon than a curse to the author. It permitted certain adjustments and liberties to be taken for the sake of a smooth, coherent plot. For instance, even though several accounts of Taliesin's life describe him as a bard in King Arthur's court, the author felt it more compelling to place Arthur's reign several years before the birth of Taliesin. The territory known as Ceredigion was also expanded to give more weight to Maelgwn's bid for extra land. It bears repeating that these details, as such, are only included for the sake of the story and should not be referenced in anything other than a pseudo-historical sense.

The scarcity of historical records of post-Roman era Britain can be attributed to numerous factors, not the least of which is the sheer volume of time between these forgotten centuries and the present day. Another glaring reason for the lack of written accounts is the supposed illiteracy of the general populace. It is well known that the only people empowered to write and record events of the sixth century were monks, such as Gildas, and other scribes of the church. Unfortunately, this tempts the researcher to regard the early Brythonic people at large as barbaric and incapable of meaningful culture. This assumption would be a grievous fallacy, however, when taken into consideration that most rural communities most likely kept their histories and stories as part of an oral tradition, passed down from one generation to the next.

The benefits of keeping written records for future generations to explore are obvious and have allowed us to expand our present knowledge of history and humanity. The author would also submit that there are various benefits from keeping an oral tradition as well. This concept is briefly discussed in chapter thirteen where the character Bryn defends the benefits of adhering to an oral tradition, claiming that such practices allow the individual to gain a visceral understanding of the past and present rather than just a cerebral one. This rings true here in the twenty-first century where there appears to be no limit to the amount of written information at one's fingertips and yet, despite this fountain of knowledge, we are left thirsting for a deeper wisdom.

The story of Taliesin, steeped in myth and fable as it is, is ultimately a tale of our own potential for this divine, visceral inspiration. Albert Einstein phrased it concisely when, referring to his imaginative thought experiments that led to his theories of special and general relativity, he described "a storm that broke loose in my mind." Taliesin's most recognized poem, the *Cad Goddeu*, begins with a similar ecstatic leap of consciousness when he personally identifies with timeless images of the natural world that transcends the confines of the individual. The goal of this work is not to convey a historically accurate sequence of events as much as it is to prompt the reader to consider a deeper, timeless truth inherent to all thinking and feeling creatures. It is a truth that we need only to delve into the limitless potential of our minds and souls to grasp and bring forth the divine inspiration of *awen*.

Notes on Pronunciation

This book makes use of several names and proper nouns in the Welsh Gaelic language which, like all forms of Gaelic, follow its own form of pronunciation different than those modern English speakers are typically used to. Rather than *anglicize* such names, which would constitute nothing short of a shocking betrayal to the culture this book pays homage to, I have chosen to keep these names in their Gaelic forms. I have summarized the main differences between English and Welsh pronunciation for the words that are most relevant to this work below. For a complete understanding of Welsh pronunciation, it would be best to consult a thorough study.

Anglesey – ANG-guhl-see

Bryn – Brin

Caer Wyddno – Kar withno

Cantre'r Gwaelod – kantra g-WHY-lod

Ceredigion – kerr-a-DIG-ee-on

Connwn - A fabricated name that should be pronounced KON-nin

Cunedda – kun-EDD-a

Dyfed – du-VED

Enid – EE-nid

Gwyddno – Gwithno

Gwynedd – GWIN-eth

Lunantisidhe – Irish name originally, pronounced lun-an-TEE-shee

Maelgwn – MY-l-gwin

Powys – PAU-is

Seithenyn – Sith-en-in

Taliesin – Tal-ee-EH-sin

PROLOGUE

Arthur's reign had passed. The stability and peace that his rule brought to Britain had burnt out like kindling spent too soon in a fire. With the great King's disappearance, warlords and tyrants again vied for dominance in a dark age renewed. Despite this tragedy, several pockets of safety and prosperity dotted the landscape of medieval Britain and Wales. One such refuge was known as Cantre'r Gwaelod, or the Lowland Hundred, ruled over by King Gwyddno Garanhir.

Easily standing six feet tall and pushing into his late sixties, Gwyddno was a legend among the Cymry, the people of Wales. Tales of his exploits with Arthur or his excursions to the lands of Annwn billowed around him like a cloak wherever he went. For all his fame, however, Gwyddno would seldom elaborate on these stories. The King of the Lowland Hundred was a practical man who liked to keep his focus on present concerns. Presently, the King was very concerned about another miraculous event that had arrived earlier that day.

"You swear that everything you told me is true, Elphin?"

The King sat at the head of a modest wooden table in a bare, slate stone room atop the highest tower of Caer Wyddno castle. On his right sat his oldest son Elphin, his head wreathed with thinning red and gold hair and his face flushed red. On his left sat his second son Seithenyn, whose dark eyebrows creased together over a stern

1

face. Across from the King against the dark gray wall, stood Bryn, the King's bard. When the court wasn't in need of the bard's stories or songs, Bryn accompanied the King on his every appointment, keeping a mental record of anything that could have any impact on the kingdom.

It was late on the first night of May, and the crash and rumble of the nearby ocean filled the gaps in the King's conversation.

"Upon my life, Sire! And on my honor, and all the ancestors," Elphin replied. "It's a miracle of a tale to be sure. If I hadn't been in the thick of it, I don't know if I would believe it myself."

"I hardly believe it because you *were* in the thick of it, brother," Seithenyn spoke up. The younger man was smartly dressed in black robes to match his darker head of hair. Many women in the kingdom considered the King's second son a handsome man, but the fearsome sneer he wore contorted his face into an uninviting mask. "We all know your tendency for 'fish' stories."

"We all saw the same miracle just now," King Gwyddno reminded him. "That was no 'fish' story. I don't see any reason to think that Elphin is not telling the truth. The more important question here is what does this mean?"

"I believe it means trouble, for us and the kingdom, father," Seithenyn replied. "A newborn babe, who is capable of all that, and found the way he was? This spells disaster. No doubt he is a changeling from Annwn or a curse from some wild sorcerer. He will bring ruin to us."

"He is only a babe!" Elphin insisted. "The child is the picture of innocence. You heard him. What if he was sent by heaven as a gift to us? Think about what glory he could bring to the Lowland Hundred."

"You've bonded with him too readily, Elphin," Seithenyn chided. "I know how much you've wanted a child of your own, and I do sympathize with you, dear brother, truly." Seithenyn dug a finger into his ear, wiping away an unseemly gob of wax. "But we cannot allow your desires to lead us to catastrophe."

"Never mind my desires!" Elphin kept his voice low but failed to stop his face from flushing a deeper shade of scarlet. "The boy is clearly a wonder. What if we bring catastrophe down on us by rejecting him? You haven't considered that thought, have you?"

"Depends on how we reject him," Seithenyn replied. "Perhaps if we treat him well but pass him on to some hapless widow farther south?"

"Bah." Gwyddno waved his hand dismissively. "The boy clearly came to us. That's not how things work. If we toss him out, he'll surely make his way straight back to our gate and probably the less fortunate for us. It might be the safest to end him, but for his tender age, it would be a barbarity. It is a tricky spot we're in." Gwyddno sank back into his chair, searching for answers in the cracks on the stone ceiling while raking through his beard with his hand. At length, he addressed his bard.

"Bryn, what do you make of it?"

The tall man, dressed in his colorful jacket, plucked absently on the strings of his small harp and sucked on the inside of his cheek. He was used to recounting stories and historical lineages, but he was seldom asked to give his opinion on matters so important. He waited for the howling wind to calm down before he gave his answer.

"As your Majesty knows, I have traveled to many lands across Britain and have witnessed many strange sights, but I must confess that I have never seen such a wonder as what was brought to your Majesty's court this evening," Bryn spoke cautiously. "In my eyes, I cannot see any evil in the boy, but many things can deceive the wisest men. I would volunteer this compromise." The three other men in the room turned their heads to the musician. "Let Prince Elphin adopt the child as his foster son and raise him here in Cantre'r Gwaelod. Give him thirteen years to prove his powers for either good or evil. When the boy's nature is made clear, then the King can decide to permit him to stay in the kingdom or banish him if he deems necessary. "

The other three men furrowed their brows and scratched at

their chins as they considered this option.

"If the boy wants to do us evil," Seithenyn spoke at length, "then he may do too much damage before we could put a stop to it in thirteen years' time."

"And if he brings us good fortune one day," Elphin countered, "then thirteen years may not be enough time for him to prove himself."

"And if the babe's gifts are nothing more than a passing spell of madness," the King said, "and he is indeed just a simple boy, here to live like the rest of us, then thirteen years should be enough to tell. It is a choppy plan, but I don't see any other path that makes more sense."

The King's voice carried a tone of finality. Seithenyn's face curdled into a frown, but he kept his mouth shut, knowing better than to press a futile case.

"Where is the babe now?" The King asked Elphin.

"I gave him to my wife to look after. She put him to her breast and the lad fell right to sleep. He's barely stirred an inch in the past few hours."

"Not so impressive as he was when you first brought him, eh?" Gwyddno shrugged. "It figures. We'll have to wait until the whole affair runs its course. Go then to your wife, Elphin. Tell her that the child is yours now; what will you name him?"

"The same thing I named him the first second I saw him," Elphin mused as he picked himself up from his seat and stretched.

"We shall call him Taliesin."

CHAPTER 1: Elphin the Misfortunate

Midwyv Taliessin.
Rhy phrydav y iawn llin
Parahav hyd ffin
Ynghynelw Elffin

I am Taliesin
I sing of true lineage
I will continue to the end
in the pristine service of Elphin

~ *Cwyndawd, Llyfr Taliesin*

Of any marvel in all the world, few compared in scale or beauty to the kingdom of the Lowland Hundred. Known to the people of medieval Wales as Cantre'r Gwaelod, the vast walled country covered thousands of acres. The royal citadel of Caer Wyddno boasted castles, courtyards, elegant shining towers, and impenetrable walls and turrets.

Every square foot of stonework, cut from the slate of the neighboring hills, glittered with jewels, pearls, and treasures from foreign lands. Even so, the true wonder of the Lowland Hundred was not its wealth, but its unique location. While the eastern facing border of the kingdom hugged the concave shoreline of Ceredigion, the westward facing wall sat twenty miles out in the middle of Cardigan Bay. The whole kingdom of Cantre'r Gwaelod had been built on a dry seabed and the inhabitants protected from the raging waves by a wall as strong as a mountain.

The sea pounded and roared relentlessly on the slate walls of the kingdom, never ceasing its bombardment. Many years ago, stonemasons and craftsmen from Ceredigion dealt the sea a crushing defeat. During one fateful low tide, the men heaved the monstrous stone blocks out into the water and erected their unconquerable fortress and inner harbor.

According to legend, the men also had help from the mysterious good folk of the hills. It was said that in his youth, Gwyddno Garanhir had paid visits to the mystical world of Annwn and had won favors from the King of the Fae there.

Now the people of Cantre'r Gwaelod and King Gwyddno enjoyed the fertile green land that before had sat at the bottom of the sea. For ships to leave or enter the kingdom, they needed to pass through the monumental floodgates that stood guard in the very center of the thirty-mile wall. Since the day of the sea wall's completion, all the marauding waves of the tide could do was crash deafeningly against the unforgiving stone and wait.

The people of the Lowland Hundred depended on the sea as much as they feared it. In addition to the green pastures and farmlands, the kingdom also enjoyed an endless bounty of fish, mussels, clams, cockles, and seaweed from the cold waters. Gwyddno also commanded an unrivaled armada of ships feared by even Saxons and Norsemen invaders. The home of this fleet of ships and fishing boats lay behind the sea walls in the great inner harbor of Cantre'r Gwaelod. The harbor filled in the very center of the kingdom and surrounded the King's tower of Caer Wyddno as a moat would surround a castle.

Every day at low tide, the monstrous sea gates would open and allow the gentle ocean currents to carry the fishing boats and passenger vessels into the harbor. As high tide crept closer, the sluice gates would drain, and the metal gates would slowly close with a clang that echoed throughout the whole country. Gwyddno's greatest fear was that one day, the sea gates would fail them and allow the rushing waters to overtake his beautiful kingdom, dooming it to a watery demise.

While the beauty of the kingdom could be appreciated from almost anywhere, the inner harbor just before sunset held a certain beguiling charm. The sea gates would open, and golden sunlight would flow in and reflect off the rippling water, creating a moving tapestry of gold and amber rays of light that painted the gray stone of Caer Wyddno. It made the whole city look like it was made from living golden glass. The young boy, Taliesin, admired the rich sight as he paced up and down the piers of the harbor one late November evening.

Taliesin kept his gaze set on the open sea gates and into the bright sunlight. The sultry beauty of the harbor did little to ease his anxiety. He paced restlessly back and forth on the wooden pier, occasionally reaching down for a stray stone and skipping it across the rippling water.

At twelve years old, Taliesin was lanky for his age. Though fit and agile, his body lacked the lean musculature that the other boys typically showed off. Sandy-colored hair framed his angular, sharp face with wide intelligent eyes that looked as though they could pierce through solid stone. No one in the whole kingdom would describe the youth as anything but handsome, but very few dared to say so to his face.

As the sun inched closer and closer to the horizon, more ships trickled in through the open sea gates, some richly decorated with ornate embroidery adorning their sails. Others were plainer and modest in size, but Taliesin could make out the shapes of fishermen on these boats, laughing and cheering themselves over the size of their haul of fish. With every ship that passed Taliesin by, the boy became more anxious. He impatiently swept the horizon with his eyes, searching for one particular sail. The sun had nearly set, and the sea gates were about due to close when Taliesin finally spotted it.

A medium-sized boat with a single, light blue sail drifted towards the pier. Taliesin's foster father was already a day late coming in from sea. The unfortunate law of Cantre'r Gwaelod dictated that any ship that did not pass through the sea gates before the tide began to rise must wait outside in the bay for the next low tide when the gates could be safely opened again. Depending on the weather and the height of the water, a ship could be waiting for a day or longer. As the gates finally closed for the night, Elphin's ship arrived at his pier.

Ropes were thrown over and the ship's crew fastened the vessel firmly to the dock. A ramp was lowered, and Taliesin saw his guardian carefully step down off the ship.

"Well, isn't this just the grand welcome I was hoping for," Elphin said with a wide grin as he watched Taliesin run up.

"Welcome home, dad!" Taliesin wrapped his arms tight around Elphin's shoulders. The older man returned the embrace warmly. He had been at sea for a week and the boy had sorely missed his foster father.

"I hope that you've taken care of the kingdom while I've been away."

"Everything's running smoothly, I've double-checked. Although mother was rather concerned that you missed port yesterday. She's in a bit of a state, just to warn you."

"Mmm…" Elphin nodded, fixing his gaze on the barnacles glued to the wood of the dock. "I was afraid she might be. I thought that it would be best to try my luck closer near Ynys Manaw. There were reports of great schools of salmon and mackerel there last month. It took me a bit longer to return than I thought." Elphin shook his head and looked back towards Taliesin. "Well, we best head straight home and try to assure her, can't keep her worrying after all."

Elphin made to leave hastily until his foster son stepped in front of him.

"I think that has to wait. I went to see Grandfather earlier today and …well… he wanted me to tell you that you are to appear before him immediately, as soon as you arrived."

Elphin did his best to stay neutral, but Taliesin could see some of the color drain from his ruddy face.

"Has he?" Elphin asked. "Well, I suppose we must accept our King's invitation. He didn't happen to mention what he wanted to see me about?"

Taliesin shook his head.

"No, only that it was most urgent."

King Gwyddno was celebrated throughout all of Britain as being one of the most gentle and sensible rulers of his day. Some even went so far as to compare him to Arthur Pendragon himself, although Gwyddno would wave his hand dismissively at such comparisons. Nonetheless, the King had standards to keep and was not above dealing out punishment, not even to members of his own family.

As the two of them began a brisk walk towards the throne room of Caer Wyddno, Taliesin inwardly braced himself for the question he felt he already knew the answer to. "Dare I ask, father, but how was your catch during the trip?"

"My what?" Elphin asked, distracted.

"You sailed halfway to Ireland and back," Taliesin pointed out. "Didn't you catch any fish while you were at sea?"

Elphin scratched at his receding hairline and let out a strained laugh.

"Wouldn't you know it, boyo?" he said, jocularly. "It seems that the damned Irish already took our share of the fish."

***

"And wouldn't you know my bastard luck, looks like the damned Irish had already taken our fair share of the fish." Elphin had just finished relaying his story to his father, seated on the throne. Unlike Taliesin, Gwyddno was hardly amused by his son's excuse.

"Prince Elphin! Take heed what words you use and what they imply of our majesty, the King." Abbot Gilgam reproached him from the throng of nobles standing to the side. The paunchy bald abbot had no tolerance for obscenities or of any talk that went against the teachings of the church. The King, generally more permissive, waved off Gilgam's objection, although his face remained stony.

"You're telling us that after a week sailing from here to the Isle of Man and back again, with a crew of thirty stout men and just as many fishing nets, you returned to us a day late without even a single mackerel to show for it?" The gruff voice was Seithenyn's, the sea gatekeeper, standing at the right side of the King's throne.

"You can ask any of my sailors. We cast our nets diligently and in good faith, just as any ship here in Caer Wyddno. Sometimes the sea favors you with her bounty, and sometimes she's stingy. You would know that if you ever thought to use that barge of yours that's collecting barnacles in the harbor," Elphin retorted.

"Hah, you know my duty prevents me. Who else would the people trust to open and close the gates? If it wasn't for my diligence and perseverance, we'd find ourselves tending a godforsaken swamp."

"My father has never given you grief about how to run the gates," Taliesin stood just a little behind and to the side of Elphin. He typically refrained from talking out of turn but his uncle's attack on his foster father provoked him. "So, I don't think he deserves criticism from a man who never sails."

Seithenyn fixed the spry boy with a menacing glare. "I know how to sail and fish, and I also know how to sire my own children, rather than fishing out some jetsam brat from a shipwreck."

"I'll make jetsam of you and your brats, you drunken sot!" Elphin cried, abandoning all composure. The whole court then erupted into a cacophony of discordant arguments and thinly veiled threats. Seithenyn's cronies rallied behind their benefactor, while several knights yelped half-heartedly in Elphin's defense. Father Gilgam turned beet red and began sputtering his reproaches at no one in particular.

Only two mouths remained shut throughout the orgy of vehemence; the bard, Bryn, whose wide eyes took in every detail they could, and the King, who sat heavily on his throne peering in disgust at his unruly court.

The King rose to his feet. The room immediately fell silent. Gwyddno allowed the stillness to hang for a moment, gathering his authority out of the thin, cold air.

"It appears there is a misunderstanding," he announced, his ire dripping from each word, "I did not summon Elphin to this hall over who knows how to sail or sire children! The next man who speaks out of turn will receive twenty lashes on the spot!" He paused to allow anyone who would dare test the King's resolve to show themselves.

They did not.

"Moving on," the King continued, confident that he had restored order. "I believe you, Elphin, when you say that you tried sincerely to make your catch and found no luck. Also, that the winds were not with you on your return, making you late."

"Thank you, Sire," Elphin replied, cautiously.

"It wasn't a compliment," the King said with a frown. "I believe you, because in the twenty years you've been sailing for the kingdom, you routinely have had the worst luck of any sailor I've known or heard tale of. You push your sailors to the ends of the earth looking for schools of enchanted salmon and every time without fail they return home with nothing but worn faces and empty bellies. Your consistency is nothing short of astonishing, so bravo!"

The King smacked his hands together furiously in mock applause.

"By Annwn and all the stars, if it hadn't been for you

delivering the finest catch this kingdom has ever seen, I would have had your ship burnt to cinders long ago for fear it would bring enough bad luck to sunder the levies."

Elphin kept his head bowed low and all the court, except Seithenyn, took pity on him.

"This dismal pattern, be it your fault or not, must cease, or I fear it will rear its head for generations to come. Tell me," Gwyddno inclined his head at Taliesin. "Has your son taken any interest in the sea? Has he shown any more competence than yourself in operating a ship?"

Taliesin felt slighted for not being addressed directly. He had helped his father and grandfather countless times by pointing out the best spots in the harbor to pull up mussels and shellfish. Sometimes, he would advise when to plant or harvest the grain out in Ceredigion's fertile plots. He should be allowed to speak for himself.

"He has a fine head for sailing, " Elphin replied in a loud voice, but with his face still turned down. "But he still has a few summers before he will be ready to command his own excursions. I aim to take him on several voyages and teach him first-hand."

"No. I forbid it," the King said with a disgusted snort. "The last thing I'd want is for him to pick up on your worthless habits and bad luck. I shall consider one of my master fishermen to teach some sense to the boy."

"If you feel it wiser, Sire." Elphin deflected the hurtful criticism.

At this point, Taliesin dared raise his hand.

"Begging your Majesty's pardon, but I don't see any bad habits that I would pick up on a ship that I don't see enough at our house," Taliesin said.

"Trust me, lad, there are many," Gwyddno responded with an amused smile.

"I could sail with Elphin and help us find the best fishing spots. I already help you with the cockles and the grain."

"But can you tell us how you know where to dig for cockles

or when to harvest?" Gwyddno asked the young boy. He rested his chin in his hand, looking like he was playing a game with a toddler.

"Uh…well…I just look for where I imagine there are the most shellfish. It's really as simple as that, I would just do the same for the salmon."

"Is that so, then?" The King traded a knowing glance with Elphin. Seithenyn shook his head. "Well, I may consider the idea come spring season. That would be your…thirteenth year, am I correct, Bryn?"

Bryn the bard jumped and bowed formally and held his legs in a deep bend to keep himself lower than the King. The bard was strikingly tall, which had earned him the nickname 'Bryn' which meant hillside.

"Yes, Sire! This coming May marks the thirteenth year since young Taliesin was…brought to us."

"Well, we will consider it, but in the meantime, it would be good for you, Taliesin, to try your hand at a trade. Such a clever youth as yourself would surely excel at something marvelous."

"If I may be so bold, your Highness," Father Gilgam interjected from the right side of the throne. "But the young boy has shown great promise in penmanship and writing. It would be an honor to admit a page boy as sharp as Taliesin to the abbey."

Taliesin held back a cringe at the thought of spending hour after hour in the stuffy old abbey. Gilgam was telling the truth. Taliesin had far surpassed any of the other boys his age in reading and writing. Along with that, while the others quietly groaned and rolled their eyes to have to listen to the scriptures, Taliesin drank in the strange stories of far-away lands and odd characters with a ravenous curiosity. What turned Taliesin off to the proposal was the thought of having to sit through Gilgam's lectures all day. The clergyman had a talent for turning the most exciting stories about Samson and Daniel into dry, unliving morality lessons.

If Gwyddno heard the abbot's suggestion, he didn't show any reaction. He only dug his fingers into his beard absently as he stared off in deep thought.

"Perhaps it is time to try the young lad at horsemanship, Sire." The voice that spoke was Enid's, the chief guard. A broad-shouldered woman in heavy armor stood forward, her braided dark hair streaked with silver. "Taliesin may be a young bean of a boy now, but with proper training, we could make a fine champion out of him, yet."

Again, the King dismissed the suggestion. "Taliesin's natural talents seem to lie more in his head than his body. If he was prone to horse riding, sailing, or fighting he would have shown it by now. And, if he desired, he could go copy scriptures in the abbey whenever it suited him, so I see no reason to restrict him to the abbey." The King threw a sidelong glance to Father Gilgam.

"Rather," he continued, "I think that Taliesin might be suited to train in a position of serious responsibility and one that would make use of that fine head of his. I would like to see Seithenyn train the boy on how to operate the sea gates, should we ever need a second gate master in the future."

The announcement stunned the court, but nobody more than the King's two sons.

"Oh, well, Sire, I'm not sure the boy's mother would approve…" Elphin stammered.

"You see, your Highness, I was hoping to take one of my own sons as my apprentice," Seithenyn explained hastily.

"Actually, I was just thinking that the abbey might be a fine spot to busy myself during the winter," Taliesin added.

King Gwyddno only chuckled as his three family members tripped over themselves.

"No, I'm afraid I've already given this more than enough consideration," the King continued. "I can't have my two sons at each other's throats forever. This is a marvelous opportunity to strengthen family ties. Taliesin will spend the next six months apprenticed to his uncle and that is my final word on the matter. I see that we are already closer to this goal of unity, as I've already accomplished the daunting task of putting my two sons in agreement with each other."

Under the music of the King's hearty laugh, the two brothers exchanged mutually sour looks. Taliesin himself anxiously bit at his thumbnail, a habit he'd had since childhood. His mother had reproached him countless times to abandon his nervous tick, but he found it compulsive during stressful times.

At last, the King composed himself and turned his attention back to his oldest son.

"Now, my poor Elphin, we still have to decide what to do with you."

Elphin's face turned a shade paler, dreading whatever retribution his father would cook up for him.

"This is an uncertain time for the Lowland Hundred. With Arthur gone these last twenty years, the Saxons and Norsemen are becoming bold again. And instead of looking to defend Britain against these invaders, we have kings and warlords throwing their weight around trying to sure up their own kingdoms and declare themselves emperor of all Britain. Instead of uniting the land, as Arthur would have done, we stand at the brink of catastrophic war!"

"Does your Majesty refer to Maelgwn of Gwynedd, my Lord?" asked a grey general with an overdeveloped sword arm. Connwn of Powys, one of the King's oldest allies, was a renowned fighter and had a tactical mind as sharp as the sword that hung from his hip.

"Aye! The Dragon of the Island." The King spat out the words. "He's either bought off each of the primary nobles on his spit of land with his dragon's gold, or he's ripped them to shreds, one by one. He's been sending envoy after envoy to our walls as 'signs of good faith' and 'steps to forge a lasting friendship with the kingdom of Garanhir'. But these messengers and diplomats he sends smell like spies and brown-nosers to me. And at the same time, I have to listen to reports of his sycophants wooing some of my own allies up north with the same empty words."

"Powys has seen dozens of such messengers, my Lord," Connwn confirmed. The kingdom of Powys lay east of Cantre'r Gwaelod and shared a border with Maelgwn's territory. "Maelgwn must certainly be getting desperate to appeal to my countrymen. He knows we've supported the Lowland Hundred since the fall of Arthur."

"Do you suspect he means to attack us, your Highness?" One of the generals from Dyfed spoke up. "Who could possibly throw in their lot with such a tyrant?"

The King shrugged. "His neighbors to the north might see more reason in supporting a local tyrant than a distant king," he pointed out. "And quite a few have yet to weigh in, should it come to war between Gwynedd and Cantre'r Gwaelod. The Picts are always an unpredictable group, and then there's Rheged."

"If Maelgwn is gathering allies to attack us, why not strike first?" Enid called out.

"Because even though we'd likely win," Connwn explained, "we'd surely be severely weakened and vulnerable to the Saxons."

"Besides, Maelgwn isn't ready for war yet," the King said, "He means to use us to help him rein in the whole of Wales and then stab me in the back when he believes he can get away with it. He just doesn't know how to get a handle on us yet. We're far too prosperous for any of his bribes to mean seal shit to us, so he's trying to flatter and impress me into doing his dirty work for him. We'll bide our time for the moment, and hopefully, some jealous lord will oust him before we have to waste our time dealing with him. But, until then we'll have to play his game of false diplomats, which brings us back to you, Elphin."

Gwyddno paused, checking to see that he had his son's attention.

"Some days ago, one of Maelgwn's sniveling riders arrived with an invitation to his midwinter feast. Nearly every lord and king in the isle will be there to enjoy Maelgwn's hospitality. I want you to go as my representative, Elphin, and gather as much information as you can without raising hostilities. Let him believe that he may strike an alliance with us yet, maybe try him for how much gold he'll cough up, but nothing more. That should be a simple enough mission for even you to accomplish."

The proposal was so unexpected that nobody in the court room dared speak. Finally, Seithenyn broke the silence.

"With no doubt to the wisdom of his Highness, but do you truly think that's the best course of action? Such an important mission should be entrusted to someone with more reliability. I volunteer to go instead, father. Why, I'd do wonders for the image of Lowland Hundred."

"Oh, I'm sure you would," the King said with a sneer. "At a feast overflowing with libations, I imagine you would give us quite an image indeed. No, your greatest contribution lies here, Seithenyn. Your expertise is needed for the sea gates and hopefully, you can pass on some of that expertise to your nephew in the coming months. Elphin, on the other hand, has had almost no luck on the sea, so we shall let him look for it on land."

Gwyddno sat himself back on his throne, signaling that his decision was final.

"You will leave here for the Dragon's castle in a fortnight. Go and make yourself ready."

***

"What did grandfather mean when he said that you had brought in the best catch the kingdom ever had?" Taliesin pressed his foster father. They were both riding Elphin's horse as it clopped along the stone causeway that led from Caer Wyddno to Elphin's tower. The acreage of the Lowland Hundred was so densely populated in some areas that the King had built several raised causeways over the kingdom, allowing easy access to and from the central fortress. Elphin's tower stood a few miles down the northeast-running causeway.

"I suspect he was referring to you, my boy," Elphin returned. "You know how fond your grandfather is of you."

"Why should that be, didn't you find me on a piece of driftwood from the wreckage of a pirate attack? I may be *your* best catch, but hardly the whole kingdom's. Surely I'm not as valuable as a barge of fine salmon."

Elphin tugged absently at his beard. "Maybe to the King, you are! You certainly are to us, you know! Anyone can see that you got a good head on your shoulders, a smart lad, like you."

Taliesin let the matter drop and hugged his rough wool blanket closer to himself. The early winter had brought icy gales that cut through the very rock of the sea wall. Near the center of the citadel, in Caer Wyddno, the heat from the village fires wafted up from the hollow of the levied seafloor below. It would spiral up the slate towers and eventually favor all the halls and chambers of the castle with a warm draft.

The causeway that traveled from Caer Wyddno to Elphin's tower passed over hog farmers and blacksmith huts. To their right, on the eastern border of the kingdom, a turreted stone wall ran along the coastline, protecting the city from any attacks by land. As they drew closer to the tower, Taliesin felt a stinging gust of frozen air cut through his clothes.

"It's just as well I won't be out fishing these coming days," Elphin mused as they came within sight of the tower's front door. "It's going to be a cold couple of weeks now, I'd say. I could use a change of pace."

"I don't suppose you'd like to take my place with the gate master the next few weeks then, would you?" Taliesin joked.

"Hah! Not on your life, boyo, not on your life," Elphin laughed. "My condolences by the way. Aye, maybe the King's right though. Maybe your uncle will come around to you once he sees how clever you can be."

"I get the feeling that's exactly why he's so brutish with me." Taliesin saw how his uncle liked to present himself. Whenever a dilemma arose, he was always the first one to offer obvious advice dressed as gifted insight. Taliesin couldn't remember a single interaction with his uncle that didn't involve the prince droning on and on about how much intellect and knowledge was needed to operate the levies and how concerned he was for the kingdom once the time came to choose his replacement.

"He's brutish towards everyone, Tali." Elphin tried to console him. "He spends far too much time in the alehouse after his shift, he gets hardly any rest and takes his misery out on all of us. No, you can keep your time with him, thank you very much."

"I should have pressed grandfather to have Bryn give me music lessons, that might have served me better."

"Aye, well you may be right there," Elphin admitted, as he led his horse around the landside of the tower towards the modest stables they kept in the back. "But you were wrong earlier, you know, clever as you are."

Taliesin cocked an eyebrow at him as Elphin extended him a hand, helping him dismount the horse.

"I'm afraid you were not the best catch of my life, boyo. That will forever be my fair and gentle Crissiant."

Elphin, typically a modest man, had every reason in the world to brag about his wife. Crissiant's stunning beauty was celebrated, and quietly envied, in every household in the Lowland Hundred. Some had even suggested that the lady was a gift from mermaids to Gwyddno's son, such was her otherworldly beauty. She boasted delicate features, crystal blue eyes, and radiant red-gold hair that shimmered like the sea at sunset. However, while most would fawn over her looks, those who loved her were taken by the lady's gentle heart. A bright star that could guide a soul through the most violent storms, she was a pillar of refuge, love, and, above all, patience.

But even saints have their limits.

"I don't understand, Elphin." Crissiant kept her voice low, but her words were terse. Taliesin could see her lips pressed into a thin line, which told him she was doing her best to control her temper. After embracing his love, Elphin had tried his best to tip-toe around the subject of his fishing venture. True to his reputation, he did not succeed.

"I'm sorry, love," Elphin said sheepishly. Taliesin noticed that his foster father showed even more humility to his wife than he did to the King. "I thought I could catch schools of salmon up farther north, I thought the winds would be with me."

"And that's the reason we had to wait over a week for you to come home? Come home empty-handed still?" Crissiant went about the room fixing and adjusting this and that. She moved quickly and carelessly, obsessively smoothing out the wrinkles in the hanging curtain that covered the bare walls.

"No man can see his own future," Elphin said with a shrug.

"No fisherman dares come back to the city with nothing to show for it!" Crissiant countered. "What else do you get up to when you're away? Sailing off to Gaul? Courting some sailor's tart?!"

"Now, my treasure. You know I could never-"

"I don't see why you should be off fishing every other week if you are never going to bring home any fish!"

"Oh, you won't have to worry about that, Mam," Taliesin chimed in. "Dad will be off for Gwynedd in a fortnight for King Maelgwn's Christmas feast, he won't be getting back on a boat until spring, it seems."

Crissiant was mad at her husband, but after hearing her foster son's announcement, she turned livid.

"You're off to WHERE?! After you only just come back?!"

"It wasn't my choice, love. This order came from the King."

"It's true, Mam," Taliesin said, regretting that he had even brought up the subject.

"All because he wants his son to finally achieve something for him, make him a proud father! Where is the consideration for your home, your family, your wife?!" Crissiant abandoned the pretense of tidying up the house and laid bare her full displeasure before Elphin.

"Uhmm, Taliesin, perhaps you'd best run off to bed, it's

running late enough already. And you'll be needing to see Seithenyn early in the morning," Elphin directed his foster son.

"Oh, gracious! You'll be off to see who?" Crissiant demanded. She brought her arms up to hold her disheveled hair in place as she slumped onto a bench, near exhausted. "Am I to be the last to know about everything that happens to this family?"

"It wasn't my choice either, Mam," Taliesin said as gently as he could. "I don't have the slightest desire to learn a thing from uncle, but grandfather insisted. I'll have to apprentice with him for six months. I offered to do duty in the church instead, but Gwyddno decided against it."

Crissiant softened. "Aye, I'm sure you did Taliesin, my darling boy. It's cruel of your grandfather to subject you to that horrible man, but we'll have to bear our misfortunes."

"Indeed, we will, Mam. All of us," Taliesin added hopefully.

"Well, off to bed with you." Crissiant gave him a warm kiss. "Remember that you are to meet with Father Gilgam tomorrow when you're done with the gatekeeper."

"Oh?" Taliesin tilted his head quizzically. "What for, then?"

"Regarding those dreams you've had of late. I asked the abbot to counsel you and ask the Lord for deliverance."

Taliesin managed to turn his audible groan into an exaggerated yawn, at least enough to cover face, and then excused himself up to his chambers. On his way out of the room, his mother called back to him.

"Make sure to close your door, love. Your father and I still have more to discuss."

Taliesin wasted no time climbing the spiraling staircase that led to his modest bedroom. After changing into a nightgown and rushing through some of his prayers, he buried himself under the thick blankets. He grabbed a down pillow and pulled it tight over his head to drown out the din of the argument still simmering downstairs.

"A fine thing for a prince to be sent away from his wife and home like an errand runner! And after you've just come back, too!"

"Even a prince can't disobey his king."

"Why couldn't a prince get someone competent to do his fishing for him? Why couldn't he find some useless business here in his own country at least?"

"Ah, dear! I'm doing this for the good of our house just as much as I am for the King. For your sake too -"

"My sake?! I've become a pariah in the court for your sake, Elphin! No one will come near the wife of the King's black sheep of a son!"

Taliesin tossed over to the other side of his bed and tried to listen to the distant murmur of the sea. He could feel exhaustion liquify his muscles. He tried to savor the final moments of the night before he had to wake up and face his two least favorite people in Cantre'r Gwaelod. Gilgam was bad enough during his Sunday sermons, but Taliesin positively dreaded having to tell the old zealot about his dreams. He doubted the abbot would have anything promising to say about them.

As long as Taliesin could remember, the night would bring strange and enigmatic dreams, some more frightening than others. Sometimes it would be something as innocuous as imagining himself as a soaring bird or a fish in a stream. Then, bit by bit, the dreams began to change into nightmares. No matter where Taliesin pictured himself, there was always the dark shadow of a hunter or some dreadful monster just behind his shoulder.

Once he dreamt he was a free and wild hare bounding effortlessly across soft green pasture. Then a snarling hound would spring out of nowhere and thundered after him. There were no trees, no holes to dive into. He could only pivot and swerve away from the beast as he felt his hot breath and spittle run down his back. Some nights he might dream he was being chased by a ravenous hawk, or a giant cat with teeth the size of daggers. As terrifying as getting chased was, the last phase of his dreams would turn his blood to ice.

Occasionally, his dream self could no longer keep the

monsters at bay and they attacked, but instead of waking up with a start, Taliesin would find himself in a frigid cold, pitch dark space. He couldn't move, couldn't breathe, and couldn't wake himself up. When the dream void finally released him, Taliesin would wake up in his bed shouting at the top of his lungs and bawling his eyes out like an infant.

It was after one of these episodes, when his mother found him on the floor in such an inconsolable state, that she ordered him to see the abbot.

CHAPTER 2: The Sea Gates

Py gynheil y byt
Na syrch yn eissywyt
Neur byt bei syrchei
Py ar yt gwydei

What supports the world
That it falls not into vacancy
Or if the world should fall
On what would it fall?

~ Canu y byt bychan, Llyfr Taliesin

Taliesin arose early to find his father sleeping at the head of the dining table snoring loudly, his head buried under his arms. Shaking his elder awake, Taliesin asked what happened. Elphin mopped up a bit of drool from his chin, bleary-eyed.

"Your darling mother and I had a disagreement over who should rightfully sleep in our wedding bed," Elphin answered

"Well, it's both of yours, isn't it?"

"Not when she's the only one home to use it, is what she'd say."

Taliesin helped his foster father clean himself up, scarfed down a modest breakfast of porridge, and then began jogging down to the sea gates. The sun was just coming up over the hills east of Cantre'r Gwaelod and the morning sea air was crisp and cold. The sea gate stood about ten miles from Elphin's tower if he cut over and headed south along the top of the sea wall. Taliesin kept himself moving at a brisk pace, partly to make good time, but mostly to keep himself warm in the icy air.

Taliesin had covered about a third of the path when he heard the clop of a horse gaining on him from behind.

"Oy there, Cuz!" a boy's voice called out. "Care for a lift?"

Taliesin turned just in time to see a brown mare nearly on top of him. Tudno, a skinny boy no more than eleven years old, sat rigidly in the saddle with a death grip on the reins. While Elphin had only one fosterling child to call his own, Seithenyn boasted seven sons, the youngest of which was Tudno. Taliesin never bonded well with his uncle's children. They typically treated him with jealousy and suspicion. Tudno, on the other hand, was used to being excluded from the rowdy activities of his older brothers and developed a fast friendship with Taliesin, who was closer to his age and temperament than any of his brothers.

Taliesin looked up, amazed at his cousin. In all the years they had known each other, Taliesin could hardly remember a single time he had seen Tudno on the back of a horse, let alone in control of one.

"I've been taking lessons with Cherno!" Tudno explained proudly. "For practice this morning I'm to take Lilypad here all the way around Cantre'r Gwaelod. I can help you along to wherever you're headed if you want."

"I'm not sure I'd take my chances," Taliesin teased back. "What's to stop you from driving over into the ocean?"

"You mean besides the solid stone wall? Give me some credit, Tal. I told you I've been taking lessons!"

"For how long? A week?"

"Well, if you prefer to walk…" Tudno said, making like he was about to gallop away.

"Right then, right, I was only teasing now. Help me up then."

Tudno stretched out his hand and helped his cousin onto the back of the saddle. The older horse whinnied at the extra weight. "Take me over to the sea gate if you can."

"Hah! About to spend the day with my father, are you?" Tudno cackled as he pressed his horse into a forward trot.

"So, he told you, did he?" Taliesin felt patronized.

"Huh? No!" Tudno said with a shock. "I was just having a laugh with you. You're actually going to spend time with him?"

"Yes! He didn't tell you? The King assigned me to six months' apprenticeship with him."

Tudno looked back, aghast, and took a moment to listen to the distant crash of the ocean waves against the slate walls.

"Sorry, Tali," he said sadly.

***

At the very center of the ocean wall, where the lush fertile plain of Cantre'r Gwaelod pressed furthest out into Cardigan Bay, stood the sea gates. Boxed in by four towering spires, the gates were more of a giant hallway framed by two massive bronze doors on either side. Incoming ships would be corralled into the passageway between the two gates. Once there, water could be drained out or let in to match the level of the Lowland Hundred's interior waterways before allowing the ships to continue to the inner harbor. This system carried the unspoken advantage of providing the gate authorities ample opportunity to collect due tariffs on foreign goods or question visiting ships as they waited for the sluice gates to open. With the capacity to hold several vessels at once, the sea gate was a monstrous structure dwarfed only by the castle of Caer Wyddno itself.

Tudno allowed the horse to saunter up to the triangular

courtyard that preceded the gates' towers before yanking her to a quick stop. Taliesin carefully swung his leg over the back of the horse and hopped down.

"Do you think your dad will be in a good mood?" asked Taliesin.

Tudno shrugged. "It's hard to say. He was out late again last night, but he didn't get into a row with anyone at home. That's sometimes the most I can hope for."

"Any advice?" Taliesin asked hopefully.

"Don't ask too many questions," Tudno replied. "And don't go offering any opinions unless he asks for them, which he won't." Tudno shot a glance at the near tower, scanning the windows for signs of his father. "Really, it would be best to do what I do most of the time. Don't speak unless you're spoken to and stay at least an arm's length away." Tudno turned his head down and absently rubbed at the side of his face.

"Right, well thanks, Tud. See you afterward maybe?"

"Sure, I'll be at the abbey a bit before dinner. God save you!" Tudno pressed his legs hard into the side of the horse. The beast whinnied in protest and then made its way up the ramp that led to the single bridge that passed over the sea gate along the interior wall.

Taliesin made his way to the imposing oak doors decorated with bronze on the side of the tower. He quickly saluted to the two guards that stood at the gate's entrance. They nodded back to him and lifted the heavy iron latch securing the door. As foster grandson to the King, Taliesin was used to being recognized by the guards and pikemen that patrolled the Lowland Hundred. Taliesin entered the gate's hallway, then turned on his heel and addressed the guard closest to him.

"Pardon, but where should I go to find the gatekeeper, Lord Seithenyn?"

"To your right and up the stairs, boy. He keeps watch on the northwest tower."

Taliesin thanked him and began to trudge up the stairs. "And

I'd take care not to wake him if he's sleeping!" the guard called after him.

Taliesin immediately noticed that despite the immensity of the gate, there seemed to be very few men operating the heavy doors and machinery. As he ascended, the stairs took him by strange metal wheels the size of carriages and lined with square teeth. The strange wheels were of various sizes, but the smallest was still the size of a full-grown man. Many were coated with barnacles and thick rust except for on the inside of the jutting teeth. On closer inspection, Taliesin noticed that the teeth of each wheel fit perfectly into the teeth of another.

A thundering crash startled him out of his reverie. Taliesin looked up, fearing that some metal fixture would collapse on top of him. The violent noise sounded again. This time Taliesin recognized it as the thunder of the waves on the bronze sea doors. As a passenger on Elphin's fishing boat, the boy had passed through the sea gates dozens of times, but he had never actually ventured inside the gate towers. He found the whole experience mystifying and wondered how he never asked himself how the great gates were built or how they operated.

Following the twisting stairs up to the top of the tower, Taliesin arrived in front of a heavy wooden door with a brass latch. Lacking any alternative, Taliesin rapped his fist cautiously against the door.

"You're late!" a rough voice answered from the other side. "Well, come in already! I don't have any time to waste." Taliesin pushed open the heavy door to see a small chamber with open windows lining the walls. Seithenyn stood propped up against the low window ledge that looked out over the sea. He held his head in his hands as if he was afraid it would roll off his shoulders and into the churning sea below.

"Good morning, Uncle," Taliesin said with a polite bow. He could at least try to foster a cordial relationship with the gatekeeper. "Pardon me for being late. I didn't realize how far the sea gates were along the wall."

The gatekeeper only winced in evident pain. "I will overlook it on two conditions," he said, keeping his eyes clamped shut. "One: that you don't let it happen again now that you understand the distance, and two: that you don't talk anywhere near as loud as that for the rest of the day. I had a long night last night and I'm not the least bit interested in listening to your voice."

Taliesin bit back his retort and waited silently for his next command. Seithenyn kept his forehead plastered to his hand as he rested against the window arc. Finally, the bloodshot-eyed man snapped to attention and fixed Taliesin with a puzzled face that quickly turned into a frown. He jerked a thumb at a bucket of water draped with torn, rust-colored rags.

"The first thing you'll do for me is clean the sluice tracks. Every time the gate fills, they get coated with some unholy sea vermin that gunks up the gears. You'd best get to it. There'll be ships ready to enter by midday."

Taliesin went to pick up the wooden bucket, which could have been used as a small bath. As he gathered the rags a thought occurred to him.

"Uhm, Uncle, what are sluice gates and how do I get to them?"

Seithenyn looked as if Taliesin had asked him if fish swim. He heaved out a forceful sigh through his nostrils and then walked over to the center window. He pointed with his finger at the empty holding space between the two gates.

"When ships need to come in and it's high tide," Seithenyn explained irritably, "we open the sluice gates near the bottom of the doors to let the seawater in. The water rises to the height of the sea. After the incoming ship arrives in the holding bay, we empty the water through the other sluice gates. You have been in the holding bay before, you should understand how it all works."

"But where does the extra water go? It can't flow back out to sea without letting more water inside."

"We drain it into the inner harbor." Seithenyn rolled his eyes. "The water empties on the other side so the harbor and the holding bay are at the same levels when the inner gates open."

"Wouldn't that flood the inner harbor eventually? There's not a drain in the back of the harbor or someplace, is there?" Taliesin was suddenly finding the topic intensely fascinating. "I've never noticed one."

Seithenyn did not share his nephew's enthusiasm. "Of course, there isn't, fool!" he barked. "We drain the extra water back out to sea at low tide through the sluice gates, which you should be hard at work cleaning by now!" He kicked the bucket angrily over to Taliesin, spilling slop water across the floor. "Your endless questions are only aggravating my pounding head. Now get to it!"

***

The sun had dropped low over the sea by the time Seithenyn finally dismissed Taliesin for the day. He had spent hours cleaning out seaweed, barnacles, and every other sort of gunk and slime that could be found on the seafloor. Seithenyn practically chased the young boy out of the holding bay.

"C'mon and be off with you! There are ships bound for the harbor. You want to get drowned in there, do you?" he complained.

"Couldn't I watch you open up the sea gates?" Taliesin asked hopefully. "I'd love to see how the whole thing works."

"No, it would all be too complicated for you. And you'd drive me to distraction with all your questions. Just leave me to my work already, and don't forget to be back before sunrise tomorrow!"

Taking his leave, Taliesin made off down the stairs, intent on jogging past Wyddno tower and maybe catching a performance from Bryn. He was about to dart out of the main door when a smooth melody stopped him mid-step.

The young boy hadn't seen another soul in the sea gates all morning and was surprised to discover he wasn't alone. The enchanting tune came from a rich feminine voice that hummed the ends of the verses. Taliesin had heard Bryn and many other singers from all over the Lowland Hundred but couldn't recognize what the girl was singing. He quietly peeked down the stairs that ran to the left of the door.

Just around the corner, he could make out the shape of a cleaning girl in a ragged maid's outfit. Her hair was tied back from her face but hung low down her back and it swished back and forth as she swept in time with her tune. She began to turn towards him.

Taliesin felt a flash of panic. He turned on his heel and made as if he had been walking by without noticing her. He glided out the door and walked briskly toward Caer Wyddno, terrified of looking back.

As he walked, he wondered what was wrong with him. He had spoken to girls before, and none of them frightened him like that. In truth, he should be overjoyed to have some company other than Seithenyn, so what had driven him to run off?

He tossed the questions around in his head as he cut through the icy air towards the tower. The winter sun reflected off the glittering towers of Caer Wyddno, scattering a thousand beams of sunlight across the harbor and the westward half of the city. Taliesin admired the twilight spectacle as he listened to the church bells from the abbey echo across the harbor. Taliesin smiled and then grimaced at the sound of the bells. They reminded him that he still needed to meet with the abbot.

***

"So, I understand from your mother that you have been having some disturbing sleeps lately, eh?"

The Abbot of Aberystwyth, the village at the eastern edge of Cantre'r Gwaelod, was a portly man. The small bit of hair that still clung to the back of his head was all but completely silver, contrasting starkly to the ruddy complexion of his fat face. Even so,

Abbot Gilgam was a gifted clergyman, well educated in the subtleties of the scriptures, and was even reputed to have studied in Menevia with Bishop David himself. Everyone in the citadel considered him a gentle shepherd of the church, tolerant of the nobility's excessive love of drink and other such revelry.

"There is no sin in enjoying the delights that our Lord has blessed us with, provided we do so with modesty and gratitude," he would tell his congregation. "So, enjoy your ales and mead and roast boar, but don't forget who graced you with such gifts."

Indeed, the only thing that would arouse the righteous ire of Abbot Gilgam was anyone who dared make light of the Holy Scriptures or the church.

Taliesin trailed behind the abbot, helping him place the candles on the altars of the abbey.

"I'm afraid so, Abbot," Taliesin admitted. "My dreams terrorize me almost every night now; some nights are just not as frightening as others."

Taliesin found himself staring tiredly at the stained-glass windows adorning the abbey as the churchman lit the candles. The dim light flickered off the darkened windows, making the images of the saints look waxy and dead.

"Now then, lad," the abbot began, "I know it must seem to you that these visions at night are like some insurmountable enemy, always there to be fought against but never diminishing. Well, don't lose hope, young master. Remember that God rewards those who he tests, so long as they don't lose faith."

"Yes, abbot, I haven't," Taliesin echoed back the correct response.

"Then we shall triumph over these demons yet! Now, tell me, have there been any changes or any other elements that have been entering your head at night?"

"No, abbot. It's just more of the same. First, I just feel cold. Cold and trapped in some dark, dark place. I can't move, I can't breathe. I try to scream and kick and struggle, but it's as if my arms are tied to the back of my neck and my legs are twisted and bound in chains. I feel suffocated, like I'm freezing to death in a great stone tomb."

Abbot Gilgam raised an eyebrow, his round blue eyes darting furtively to the stone walls of his beloved abbey.

"It's wet as well," Taliesin added hastily. "Like I'm in a small barrel of ice-cold pickle brine."

"Gracious!" the abbot replied.

"Then I'll sometimes wake up with a start, sometimes the sheets will be soaked with my own sweat. Other times, there's worse to come. I feel someone with huge hands holding me and I can feel, I don't know, a feeling of disappointment and a great shame come over me, but then it's only madness and panic as something huge and very angry is chasing me. I'm...well, I'm running as fast as I possibly can, but it feels like I'm running through waist-deep water."

"My, my," the abbot said with a shake of his head. "Tell me then, boy. Do you have any idea or glimpse of what's chasing you?"

Taliesin furrowed his brow in concentration.

"Sometimes I feel as if a monster's jaws are following me. But...mostly it's just the sounds of these giant footsteps pounding behind me. Well, they're behind me but sometimes I feel like I'm moving backwards towards them.

"Yes? What do imagine lies there? Back where you and your pursuer began this chase? Can you remember, or even venture a guess?"

Taliesin thought hard. It had never really occurred to retrace his dream steps. He remembered a swift wind all around him, a rushing stream, a field of the tallest grass he had ever seen, and then…

"I…I can't picture it, abbot. It's fuzzy in my mind."

"Hmmm," the abbot rumbled. "This may be a valid question that we could ask ourselves. That's what you should do, lad! Send your prayers to the Lord above. Ask him to reveal to you the source of your distress. What is it you're truly running from? And remember to ask his protection, because, whether your tormentor seems evil or benevolent, it's sure to be the work of some wicked devil. Don't allow his lies to lead you astray!"

"Uh…of course not, abbot. Begging your pardon, but I believe I hear the late evening bells chiming, I wouldn't want to worry my parents staying so late."

"Right you are, sonny! We've had a right good chat here by now," Abbot Gilgam said, as if he were the one bringing their session to a close. "Well, let me know straight away on any developments, but in the meantime don't let these perturbations cause you too much worry."

"Yes, thank you, abbot!" Taliesin had already begun a quick trot out of earshot of the Gilgam.

His advice, though appreciated and sincerely given, rarely amounted to much more than "pray and ask protection," which Taliesin had done nearly every night and morning now since he was seven. That wasn't the part of their conversations that unnerved him. Taliesin could still nearly glimpse the thing that he had run from, and it didn't look "benevolent" at all. Rather, he could almost make out a cackling, lightning-quick creature, with two great powerful legs and snapping jaws full of razor-sharp teeth.

Just behind and beyond the creature though, was something else, something familiar and incredible, though he was sure that he had not encountered it in all his days he could remember. It was more of a feeling than a creature. It was something that churned in his mind, demanding to be let out, to run wild and free. Sometimes, Taliesin could almost feel it, stepping out of his dream world and into the bright light of reality.

But then Taliesin would go rigid with panic and shut his mind and body down in a frozen ball. He had no idea what it was that was trying to escape his head, but he worried that if he ever let it out, it would rival the might of God himself.

***

The following two weeks brought more brutally cold weather and made Taliesin's morning jogs to the sea gate feel like a feat of torture. Some days he'd be lucky enough to catch a ride with Tudno, but more often he would jog down the sea wall clutching his wool cloak around him tightly.

Very little changed during his daily routine at the sea gate. Seithenyn would reprimand him for being late, even if he was early, assign him some menial task to keep him busy, and then complain about how long he was taking before sending him home as early as possible. Except for the maid he had seen on his first day, Taliesin hadn't encountered another living soul inside the gate's towers.

Time felt acutely nebulous for Taliesin as he experienced the weeks drag on monotonously while he slaved away for his uncle. Simultaneously, the time seemed shorter and shorter whenever he reminded himself of Elphin's upcoming departure. At home, his foster parents acted as dramatically as ever with each other. Taliesin would arrive home some nights only to walk straight into a heated argument. Other times he would wake up in the morning to find them passed out together in a bittersweet embrace. At every opportunity, Taliesin found a way to spend as much time with Elphin as he possibly could. Not only did he enjoy his fleeting time with Elphin, but he could also vent his frustrations over Seithenyn.

"It's like he doesn't want me there in the slightest!" Taliesin complained as he accompanied Elphin in the horse stables. "He sends me to clean the sluice tracks again and again and then shoos me off if I ask the slightest question. I thought the point was that I would learn how to open and close the bleeding gates."

"That's your uncle for you," Elphin remarked as he inspected his horse's back leg. "He was never patient enough to explain anything to me or anyone. I've long since given up asking him questions or talking to him if I can avoid it. He's sharp, your uncle is, but he's not willing to share his knowledge."

"Why on earth not? He could leave someone else in charge of

the gates for once and have more time for himself at the alehouse. Seems like he'd prefer to be there than anywhere else."

Elphin shrugged. "I suppose he doesn't want anyone getting the wiser of him. Besides, he doesn't need any more time in the alehouse than he spends already." Elphin indicated the back hoof of his horse to the stable hand. The freckled young boy immediately began heating a thin horseshoe for the animal.

"Do you suppose you'll be long in Gwynedd?" Taliesin asked.

Elphin shrugged for a second time.

"Depends how long Maelgwn's feast lasts. I doubt he'd keep us for more than a few days. The Dragon King likes to impress his guests but doesn't care to spend much of his gold on them."

"That's happy news," Taliesin replied. "Mother and I will miss you terribly, you know."

"Aye, well you'll have to take splendid care of her till I come back," Elphin said, clapping his foster son on the shoulder. "It would be mighty refreshing to come home and see her in a good mood for once."

***

On the second week of December, Taliesin prepared to say goodbye to his guardian. Taliesin walked alongside Elphin's graying horse as they made their way to the northernmost gate, not too far from Elphin's cliffside tower. The horse was burdened down with Elphin's personal sack of possessions as well as a modest-sized box filled with gold and various other token gifts for the rival king.

Elphin also walked alongside the horse, unwilling to ride the animal while Taliesin walked. He pretended to be chipper over his errand, but Taliesin could see the exhaustion on his face and how his shoulders slumped a bit more than usual. Crissiant did not accompany her husband.

Taliesin could think of one positive thing about the morning, namely that he was completely excused from his daily service at the sea gates. He had explained to Seithenyn the previous day that his foster father requested that he wish him farewell. It wasn't completely the truth. Elphin hadn't formally asked Taliesin for his company, but the younger boy knew that his father was counting on his support. Seithenyn only nodded dismissively and waved the youth away without so much as a word.

The King had gathered a healthy attendance of nobles and knights that morning to see Elphin off. The early December sun reflected painfully off the frost-kissed fields that sat on top of the cliffs. Along with the usual contingent of knights, Enid, the captain of the tower guard stood tall at the King's side, her polished armor glinting in the morning sun. Enid had been the daughter of a wealthy landowner in Dyfed, until a Saxon raid had burned her estate to the ground and set her father's head on a pike. Rather than sit uselessly in a convent, Enid pleaded with Gwyddno to allow her to fight against the invaders. Her ferocity, cunning, and sheer strength earned her the rank of captain of Gwyddno's tower, making her one of the few female warriors of Cantre'r Gwaelod.

Elphin greeted his father and immediately began rummaging through his bags, obviously searching for something.

"I know that I packed a damn map. You don't remember seeing it, Tali?" Elphin darted from one pack to another, frantically. "In truth, I don't suppose I'll need it. It's not hard to follow the road to Anglesey Isle. Still, you know me, I like to be prepared."

"For pity's sake!" King Gwyddno said when most of his entourage's backs were turned. "You just leave the guide to worry about which way it is and forget about finding whatever it is you forgot!"

Elphin glanced up at his father's face and reluctantly tied his bag back onto the horse's saddle.

"I'm not sending you off alone, remember," Gwyddno reassured his son. "Bryn will be accompanying you to act as my historian. The two of you will be traveling in caravan with Urien of Rheged and his group of knights. So, you'll be well protected."

Taliesin's head picked up at the mention of Urien.

"The Lord of Rheged is leaving already grandfather?" he asked. Gwyddno threw a glance over his shoulder before responding.

"I'm afraid so, Tali. I've offered him more than a fair tribute for his allegiance, but he's sitting on the fence right now."

"He's worried we're not Christian enough as a kingdom," Enid said in her usual blunt manner. "I guess the monasteries in Urien's territory expect us to donate more than we already do. I don't think he'll side with us."

"We'll just have to stay patient." Gwyddno looked up to see Elphin's brow furrowed in worry. "But look now. All you have to worry about, Elphin, is to behave yourself at the feast. Enjoy yourself of course! You'll be expected to after all, just keep your eyes and ears open. Ah!" The King looked back towards the stone causeway. "Here comes your escort."

Taliesin followed the King's gaze to see an organized line of brightly armored men on horseback. Each of the knights carried the standard of Rheged, three black ravens around a black chevron on a background of silver. The horses were richly adorned in the same colors. At the head of the train rode a tall, bearded man with rich hair as black as the ravens on his breastplate. The line of warriors trotted their horses straight to King Gwyddno and, in stunning unison, brought themselves to a dead halt.

"Well, now," Gwyddno said, making a show of how impressed he was. "Punctual as always. Your presence will be sorely missed in my court, Lord Urien."

"We thank you in turn for your hospitality O King of Cantre'r Gwaelod," Urien spoke in a deep resonant voice. "'Tis a pity, but my men and I would feel more comfortable keeping closer to our own lands as winter sets in."

"Of course, of course!" Gwyddno politely agreed. "Just keep in mind the offer I made. The gates of the Lowland Hundred will never be closed to any man of Rheged who rides in peace to us."

Taliesin watched the powerful man atop his steed nod his

head thoughtfully. His gaze traveled far north over the mountains to his very homeland on the border of Scotland.

"Your offer is generous, King. But you must realize the difficulties my kingdom would face. Like it or not, Maelgwn of Gwynedd is my neighbor. Sometimes, a wise ruler must sacrifice his principles for the sake of his people's survival."

"I only ask that you consider the choice carefully," Gwyddno said, his tone neutral.

Urien cast his gaze down onto Enid, who only stood straight at attention, her powerful jaws set firmly.

"My men and I also find it somewhat…unnatural to see a young woman armored and carrying a sword. This is hardly the code of chivalry championed by our beloved Arthur."

"As you've said," Gwyddno replied.

"Begging his Lordship's pardon," Enid said as she narrowed her eyes at Urien, "but I'd rather be treated as I deemed fit and not by the laws of chivalry."

"The fairer sex deserves to be protected and defended by mankind. There is no creature on God's earth more precious than women. It is only for your own well-being, fair maid. I trust you understand."

Urien made to push his horse forward to the top of the train. As his horse stepped past the King, Enid stepped hurriedly into the center of the muddy path. Urien had to yank back on the reins and brought his horse to a fast and violent stop. Enid only stood calmly in the ankle-deep mud as Urien's horse brayed and protested a foot in front of her.

"Be you mad, lady?!" Urien hollered, visibly agitated. "I nearly trampled you flat!"

"Again, your pardon my Lord," Enid replied. "I always understood that men of chivalry allowed women to pass first. A good journey to you!" Enid turned on her heel and marched smartly to her band of archers on the far side of the field.

Urien turned back to King Gwyddno. "I have all the

admiration in the world for you, O gracious King," Urien began, his furrowed brow tracking the female captain. "But I wish you would see reason a little more often. You would trade my band of elite soldiers to keep one woman warrior. I find it rather incredible."

"More incredible than that, my good friend," Gwyddno said with a smile. "Is that trading my captain for your men would put me at a loss. If you ever saw Enid in battle, you wouldn't be so quick to dismiss her."

Urien nodded curtly and then turned his attention to Elphin.

"Are you prepared to start on the way, Lord Elphin?" He called out. "I'm afraid the winter sun doesn't give us many hours to travel by."

"Uhm….yes!" Elphin sputtered after scanning the road back to his house. "I suppose we'd best be off then." Before he could say another word, Taliesin threw his arms around his foster father one last time.

"Come back safely, and quickly father. We'll be waiting for you."

"Ah, well don't worry, son," Elphin replied. "I won't be longer than if I were at sea."

"That's not much comfort!" Taliesin retorted. "Not when you're always late coming back from sea!"

"Haha! The lad has a point!" Gwyddno laughed. "But don't fret, boyo. Your father's left his ill-luck out in the bay. It can't follow him onto land."

As if in response, Elphin's mare let out a small snort as a jet of steam and liquid splattered onto the mud beneath it. The puddle of piss quickly rolled down the ground and, before he could react to it, all over the hem of Elphin's beautiful sea-green robe. Elphin snatched the garment up instinctually, but only managed to splash more of his clothes with piss-wet mud. Taliesin did his best to hide his nervous laughter behind his hands, while Gwyddno only shaded his eyes and shook his head. The men of Rheged laughed without pity.

"Nothing luckier than horse piss!" Bryn said, riding up on his mule, trying to ease the situation. "That's what the old spinster who raised me used to say. We'd get baths of it growing up. When I was just a boy, I bathed exclusively under an eighteen-hand stallion."

"And do you feel the luckier for it?" Urien asked merrily.

"I live an enviable life. Being the King's chief bard and living in the palace is far better than most. Whereas gold showered me in my youth, so does gold shower me now."

The King only grunted.

"Your pardon, please! Let me pass!" A strong feminine voice pierced the commotion. The crowd opened to reveal Crissiant strutting towards her husband in her finest dress of spotted owl down. All who saw her could hardly keep their eyes off the regal lady. Without regard for the mud or urine staining Elphin's robes, she strode straight to her husband and treated him to a long, passionate kiss. Taliesin looked away in embarrassment.

"Travel well and do your kingdom and wife proud at Maelgwn's feast. Surely you'll be the best man and prince the beastly Dragon will have the honor of hosting!"

Elphin looked positively stunned at his wife's unabashed show of affection.

"My love... I..." Elphin stuttered, completely shocked. Crissiant brought her husband's face to her own, swallowing Elphin's words with her floral breath.

The two embraced one more time, then all departing turned and saluted the King. Gwyddno raised his arm high in response and the riders nudged their mounts forward. Crissiant stepped back and joined Taliesin to wave her husband off.

Their way up north was not a terribly far distance, but enough to stretch conversation thin along the way. As Bryn would relate to Taliesin later though, Elphin spent the entire journey talking, without pause, of his fair, beautiful wife, who he believed to be the most enchanting creature on god's green earth.

CHAPTER 3: The Well Maiden

A wdost beth wyd
Ban vych yn cyscwyd.
Ai corff ai eneid.
Ai angel canneid.

Knowest thou what thou art
when thou art sleeping?
A body, a soul,
or an angel of light?

~Mab Gyfreu Taliessin, Llyfr Taliesin

The days following Elphin's departure were easily some of the most miserable in Taliesin's life thus far. Every morning he would wake up in the frigid dark before dawn and drag himself down miles of stone causeway to the foreboding sea gates. He soon understood that he could rely on his Uncle Seithenyn for one thing only, which was to be completely unpredictable.

Most often, his uncle would keep their interactions sparse and send Taliesin down to clean out the holding bay tracks for the entire day. Taliesin made the most of his drudgery by examining as many kinds of sea creatures as he could identify. It seemed that barnacles were the worst creature for the gate's operation as well as the most obnoxious to clean out. Urchins, jellyfish, seaweed. All demanded a different and precise method of cleaning. Taliesin found it surprising that the King didn't order a whole team of men to constantly clean out the fishy gunk from the gate's bowels.

Every now and again, Seithenyn would surprise Taliesin by actually showing him how the great machines operated and talking to him almost politely.

"Each gate is counterweighted with a large block of bluestone," he explained one day. "You turn this handle here-" he indicated a copper handle attached to a crank practically the size of Taliesin in diameter, "-and interior gates will slowly open. The other crank over there -" he pointed to an even larger metal wheel with a massive handle sticking out, "-opens up the exterior gate. I'm sure I don't have to remind you about what you should never, ever allow... under any circumstances..."

He crossed his arms over his broad chest and waited patiently for Taliesin's response.

"Never allow the two gates to be opened at the same time," Taliesin replied dutifully. "I understand the risk, but even if they were to open up together, shouldn't we be able to shut one quick before the tide enters?"

"Clearly you do *not* understand the risks." The gatekeeper rolled his eyes. "The gates work with complicated machinery that can get snagged, iced over, or broken. If one of the gates gets stuck, we'd have to close the other one in a hurry should the tide be coming in. The faster you close the gate, the more likely it will be to jam. And if the two gates fail, then all is lost, boy. Everything from here to the hills of Aberystwyth."

Taliesin looked out east over the lush plain of the Lowland Hundred, replete with emerald green fields, bustling villages, and the sparkling harbor. He found it difficult to imagine that such a kingdom had once been nothing but an expansive bay, only inhabited by fish and seagulls. He wondered how the sixteen sectors of Cantre'r Gwaelod could possibly survive such a catastrophic failure, should the sea gate ever burst.

"Lad!" Seithenyn called out impatiently. "What did you do with the set of tools I handed you this morning? This wheel is sticking."

Taliesin snapped himself out of his reverie and mentally retraced his steps. "Oh, I must have left them by the sluice gates when you had me change out some of the gears."

The older man let out an impatient sigh. "Well, it looks like you'll have to trudge down and get them, won't you? Maybe as you're climbing up and down the tower stairs, you could think about how not to leave things lying about. Be quick, will you?"

The boy took the hint and started his long descent. Instead of thinking about how to be more responsible with the tools, he found himself ruminating about how quickly his uncle could switch from cordial to surly.

As he descended towards the tower entrance, his ears picked up the distant echo of a female voice softly singing. It had been over a week since he had seen the young maid sweeping the stairs, but the lilting voice brought her image rushing back into Taliesin's mind. He slowed his pace and tried his best to keep his footsteps from making too much noise. Straining his ears, he followed the haunting melody to the banister that looked down into the bottom of the gear well and peered below. From above, he could make out the form of the maid, dutifully brushing her straw broom back and forth across the bare stone floor. Her back was turned towards Taliesin, giving the boy an opportunity to watch her sweep. The maid had light chestnut brown hair tied back neatly and a slightly tattered skirt that swished from side to side in time with her tune. Her arms were bared to the elbow and were gripping the broom with long, slender fingers.

Taliesin was afraid that his heart would begin to pound again and that he would panic and run back up to the tower to face the wrath of Seithenyn. But after a moment of watching the maid at work, he became confident that he could control himself. Whatever had taken hold of him before now seemed nothing more than a passing fit of madness. Taking care not to make any more noise, he continued down to fetch the tool bucket.

The maid's voice echoed off the stone walls and followed Taliesin all the way to the sluice gates. Taliesin found himself unable to picture anything other than the maid's skirt as it swished back and forth rhythmically. He tried to distract himself by repeating Seithenyn's lecture on the gate operations in his head, but the image of the maid would not leave him. The tenacity of it irritated him like a shred of food lodged in his back teeth.

Taliesin found the rusty pile of tools where he left them and started back up the stairs. As he neared closer to the banister, he forced himself not to spare a single glance into the open room below. He nearly succeeded and had made it past the banister when he found himself wondering what color skirt the maid had been wearing. He was pretty sure it had been a light brown, cream-colored skirt, but it also might have been gray or even a very pale blue. His curiosity finally bubbled over, and he quietly slinked back down the stairs to get one final glance.

Looking down, he confirmed that it had been in fact a pale cream-colored skirt, but now he was shocked to see the maid was walking around the freezing stone floor with bare feet. He would have left then, but he stayed a little bit longer, thinking that he could recognize the soft tune the maid was humming. It seemed that every time Taliesin was about to head back up the tower, another detail caught his attention and chained him to the stair aisle. The one detail that Taliesin failed to notice was the girl's sidelong glance back at the young boy who seemed incapable of taking his eyes off her.

"What's taking so long, you scummy brat?!" Seithenyn's voice hollered from above. "I could've gotten my tools from the King's blacksmith by now! You better be up here this very instant!"

The shrill voice sent Taliesin scurrying up the stairs like he was being chased by a wolf. He jumped up the stairs two at a time, thinking about how to explain his dawdling to the gatekeeper. Below the stair aisle, the maid's voice dropped back to a gentle hum as she continued to clean.

**

"I heard from Dad that he was ready to beat you senseless the other day," Tudno said casually. Taliesin was trudging back home in the fading amber light when his cousin jogged up to him with a cnapan ball under his arm. "You don't seem any worse for it."

"He practically shouted his head off at me, but he hasn't yet touched me," Taliesin replied.

"He probably knows that the King will be vexed with him. He doesn't think twice about walloping me and my brothers. When he comes home from the alehouse, we just do what we can to keep out of his way."

Tudno let the cnapan ball drop to the floor and kicked it against the stone parapets of the causeway. The ball was nothing more than a tanned pig's bladder inflated and tied off with a sturdy bit of twine. Tudno's older brothers were known for playing cnapan as savagely as possible, especially when Tudno insisted on participating. Taliesin never had much taste for the brutish game.

"Any news of Uncle Elphin?"

Taliesin shook his head silently. It had been almost two weeks since Elphin had departed. King Gwyddno had assured Taliesin that his foster parent would be back any day now along with the court bard. "Ah, surely they're enjoying themselves a bit more than they should, but they'll be at our gates before you know lad, you'll see," the King explained. Taliesin had lots of practice waiting for his foster father, but the tedious hours at the sea gates did not help in the least.

"Tudno?" Taliesin said after a pause. "Have you ever seen a maid in the sea gates? One who sings when she sweeps the floors?"

"Sure, there are quite a few maids cleaning the gates," he

replied. "It's a big place for just one maid."

"I've only ever seen one doing any cleaning over there. Well, her and myself, I guess, considering how often I'm cleaning the holding bay."

"What's her name then?"

"I don't know."

"Do you like her?"

"I just asked if you knew her, Tud. I haven't said more than a word to her and I'm just wondering who else is sharing my misery over there."

"Aye, alright then." Tudno failed to hide his smug smile on the other side of his freckled face. Suddenly his bushy red eyebrows shot up with recognition. "She wouldn't have particularly long sandy hair, would she? Likes to sing a lot?"

"Yes!" Taliesin said a little too quickly. "That's her."

Tudno kicked the cnapan ball, causing it to bounce wildly off the causeway stone. He skipped ahead a few steps to catch it before the wind could throw it into the sea.

"I remember her from back when she used to fetch water in the abbey," he said. "She was a rotten tease with all of Gilgam's students. She dropped something foul - don't ask me what it was - into all of the ink wells this one time. The whole of the abbey smelt like rotten eggs as we were transcribing the scriptures. It was blasphemous!"

"Why would she do something like that?" Taliesin asked, intrigued.

"Who knows? The abbot said she was unfit to tend to the abbey, so he made a complaint with the King a couple of months back. My dad volunteered to have her sweep up the sea gates, that's about as far away as you can get from Gilgam's abbey inside the Hundred. She's a strange one, you know." Tudno threw a look over his shoulders and leaned in close to Taliesin. "She came to the Hundred with her baby sister from some village out in the woods. Gilgam swears that she's pagan. He says she blasphemes against the church and casts spells and whatnot."

"Bah, Tudno!" Taliesin waved him off. "Half the Lowland Hundred are pagan. It's not against the law. And it's no act of magic to make Gilgam's words stink."

Tudno gave his cousin a mean glare. "Those are the words of the savior, Tal. And who else but a heathen would want to sully them?" Tudno looked back down the wall. Torches were being set along the metal baskets nestled neatly inside small alcoves among the parapets, securely blocking them from the ferocious wind.

"Well, I should be heading to the tavern to check in on dad. Just mind what I said about the maid, I'd keep to myself around her. God save you, cuz!"

Without another word Tudno's wiry frame headed back up the wall's causeway, kicking at the brown cnapan ball. Taliesin hastened along the other direction through the cold, salty wind. He wondered why he should care if the maid was Christian or not. His foster mother insisted that Taliesin attend church weekly, but the boy found the minstrels' stories about the Fae and old gods just as compelling.

Still, Taliesin had never really met a true witch, just like he had never experienced the irresistible pull that he felt while watching the maid sweep and listening to her sing.

Perhaps, Taliesin pondered, *that's what a witch's magic feels like?*

Taliesin shook his head, concluding that it didn't really matter if the maid was a witch or not. All that Taliesin had wanted to get out of Tudno was the maiden's name.

***

"Pay attention carefully now, because I'm only going to go through it once." Seithenyn heaved his powerful torso and rotated an oversized copper crank. "The two big silver cranks control the seaside and harbor side gates. The copper ones control the sluice gates." As he turned the crank, Taliesin heard the chinking of chains and the din of salt-encrusted metal doors shrieking open. He glanced out the window to watch the seawater shooting in from small holes in the outer gate.

For whatever reason, Seithenyn had spared Taliesin from the freezing pit of the holding bay that afternoon and instead offered to teach his nephew how to operate the sea gates. At first, Taliesin suspected Seithenyn of playing a prank on him, but now he soaked up the knowledge eagerly, taken by the monumental machine's simple and effective design. Seithenyn's newfound patience also impressed Taliesin, and the boy could only admire the gatekeeper's skill at reading the tides and keeping the ins and outs of the gate's machinery straight. During his explanations, Seithenyn almost seemed pleasant.

"Turn that silver one over there, will you?" He indicated the crank on the far side of the room.

"But won't that let the water into the harbor?" Taliesin asked, confused.

"I should hope so, that's the point lad!" Seithenyn nearly laughed. "There was a spring tide last night and more water poured out from the harbor than should have, it happens every now and again. We need to slowly let some water back in. See there!"

He pointed to the fortified levy that lined the channel to the harbor. Taliesin followed his uncle's finger and noticed a series of bands painted on the side of the levy.

"See the sixth mark down from the top?" Seithenyn asked. "We need to keep letting water in until it meets that line."

"Won't that take hours?" Taliesin asked. "The water is barely trickling in and the harbor is practically the size of a lake."

"If you can think of a quicker way to do it, please enlighten me." Seithenyn bowed sarcastically. "Trust me, Taliesin, I know what I'm doing. We can't just throw open the two gates or we will flood the whole kingdom. It should only take about three or four hours. And by the time you're done, we'll need to start letting the ships in for the evening."

Taliesin nodded, satisfied with the explanation. He wheeled around suddenly as the gatekeeper's words repeated in his head.

"Wait, when *I'm* done?" he asked incredulously. "Where on earth are you going?"

Seithenyn was already hoisting a small leather satchel over his shoulder and reaching for his cloak.

"I have a business appointment near the alehouse. It won't take long, but I can't leave the sluice gates open unsupervised."

"But what am I supposed to do?" Taliesin asked, trying to hide his trepidation.

"Stay out of trouble, first and foremost," Seithenyn replied. "That's basically it. And if the water should come up to level, turn the crank and shut the sluice gates. Come, now," Seithenyn patronized him. "Everyone is always talking about how clever a boy you are, so act like it."

"So, I'm just supposed to stay here?" Taliesin persisted. "With nothing to do to pass the time except watch a harbor fill?"

Seithenyn heaved out a mighty sigh, obviously agitated. He stomped over to a table and rummaged through a wooden toolbox. He extracted a small bronze hammer and rusty chisel and all but threw them at the boy.

"Here!" He grunted. "There's a pile of gears over in the corner that need to have a mess of barnacles and such scraped off of them. Now is that enough to keep you occupied for a few hours?"

"Yes, Sire," Taliesin answered glumly. He didn't want to push his luck and get stuck with an even more monotonous task.

"Wonderful then," Seithenyn said with a smug grin. He hopped his way over to the stairwell and called back over his shoulder, "And don't get too distracted that you neglect the harbor, boy! If that water rises an inch higher than it should, I'll have the King give you fifty lashes!"

With that, Seithenyn descended the staircase and was gone.

Taliesin gripped the hammer and chisel and made his way to the pile of rusted gears. He brushed through several, searching for one that looked easy to clean. He set to work prying loose the diamond-hard shells that were encrusted onto the heavy wheels.

Every so often he threw a glance towards the pier to check the water level. After what must have been an hour of work, the water hadn't risen more than half of a marking. Fighting restless boredom, Taliesin paced idly around the small tower chamber. He found himself inspecting the copper and silver cranks that controlled the various gates. Several small square windows were cut out from the stone wall just next to the cranks. Peering down through the openings, Taliesin could make out the shapes of the numerous pullies, chains, and gears that connected the elegant cranks with the actual gates. He marveled at the complexity yet effectiveness of the system.

Seithenyn may understand how to open the gates, Taliesin mused to himself, *but there's no way he helped build this wonder.* Now that Seithenyn seemed to be loosening up, Taliesin wondered if his uncle would tell him more about the history of the gates.

Another hour or two passed and Taliesin had just about finished scraping the worst of the crusty gears when he heard it. The lilting voice echoed up the stone stairway and filled the tower chamber so that Taliesin could scarcely ignore it. He shot a glance quickly at the pier, noting that the water only had one more mark to go before he had to shut off the crank. With time to spare, he carefully tip-toed to the chamber's entrance.

The steps gently spiraled their way down to the main doorway, giving Taliesin a bird's eye view of the topmost stairs. He recognized the singer's voice immediately, but his heart still raced to see the young maid diligently scrubbing the stairs about a dozen feet below him. Her song, though soft, had a bounce in its rhythm, making her sound like she was laughing quietly to herself. It made Taliesin's blood rush faster through his veins, although he couldn't completely understand why.

After listening, mesmerized for several minutes, Taliesin began to wonder what he should do next. Should he introduce himself? Say hello? Or should he just greet her as any other servant and maintain his princely status? He looked down at his hands, realizing it might be hard to impress the maid with status when his hands were filthy with rust stains and barnacle sludge. His mind churned furiously even as his feet felt stuck to the cold stone floor. Finally deciding there was nothing to be done about the rusty stains, he prepared to descend the stair aisle and make a simple introduction when he heard the main door crash open, accompanied by careless footsteps.

Peering further down the staircase, Taliesin could make out Seithenyn's shape lurching slowly up the stairs. His steps were erratic and off-balance. His wandering focus suggested that he had spent the better half of the afternoon in the alehouse and had not imbibed modestly. For the past two weeks, Taliesin wasn't sure if he had ever seen Seithenyn sober or just in milder states of inebriation. Even at his worst, Seithenyn seemed to be able to perform all his tasks effectively enough. That dusky evening, however, Taliesin would have bet that the gatekeeper was drunker than he had been all year.

The maid abruptly stopped her singing. The only sound Taliesin's ears could detect was the rhythmic scrubbing and Seithenyn's heavy, wandering footsteps.

"Welll, isn this a fair, fair sight." Seithenyn's voice bounced loudly up the stair aisle. "An whudsa spritely creature like you doin to my stairs?"

"Should it please you, my Lord, I'm only cleaning your precious stairs." The girl answered the drunk prince, keeping her voice even, almost playful, but Taliesin could hear a razor-thin edge under her words. "If your Lordship doesn't take more care, he may slip. There's more grime on these stairs than the rocks have at low tide."

"Hah, there's one with a smart mouth on 'er," Seithenyn replied. He staggered two steps below where the girl was cleaning. Peeking down, Taliesin could see the top of Seithenyn's back twisted around as he leered up at the maid. The girl's brush stopped. After a tense moment of listening to Seithenyn's heavy breaths, the drunk man stomped his foot down and climbed past the cleaning girl, who resumed her scrubbing.

Seithenyn stopped again on the step above the girl. "Mererid."

The name took Taliesin by surprise, not just that he had heard it but that his uncle even knew it.

"My Lord?" the maid responded.

"My boots have tracked the...worse...worse....wwmm...mud." Seithenyn turned unsteadily and lifted his right boot, caked in briny mud. "You should clean em. Doan get mud aall over yer shtairs."

"Your Highness is surely capable of cleaning his own boots," Mererid said, refusing to bring her gaze up.

"C'mon now, you gotta rags. Aren't I master here?"

A crashing thud accompanied by a splash rang out through the tower. Taliesin heard Seithenyn let out a shocked yelp.

"Oh, dear!" Mererid's voice cried out in mock horror. "I was just aiming for the boots, but I guess I gave a right wash all over!" Taliesin looked to see Seithenyn dripping wet from his shoulders down. "A pity the water had to be so cold, but now your boots are cleaned, at least."

Taliesin heard Seithenyn's breath begin to get louder and heavier. Tudno had told him what the gatekeeper was capable of when he lost his temper. He had seen proof of it when Tudno showed him the blistering welts and bruises that covered his body after his father came home from a night of drinking. Judging by Seithenyn's low grumbling, it was clear the gatekeeper was losing control.

Taliesin's heart raced and he frantically wondered what he could do. His eye fell on the heavy bronze hammer he had left on the floor.

"You're an insolent one, you are," Seithenyn's voice rumbled. "You need to be learned some respect, you do."

"Lord, I'm afraid I'm needed at the Matron's. I'll be missed if

I'm late," Mererid replied quietly.

"Oh no! Not this time. I've been to talk with your keeper. You've a new contract now."

"You're too drunk to see, to hell with your poxy contract!"

Taliesin heard the lurching footsteps of the gatekeeper. He heard the smack of skin contacting skin and Mererid's panicked yelp.

"Shut up, you wench! Or I'll grind ya to a pulp inna sluice gears."

"My Lord, STOP!"

"I said be quiet! I could-"

"My Lord, gatekeeper!" Taliesin's lithe frame appeared on the top of the stone stairway. Peering down into the gloom of the stairway below, he could identify the towering shape of Seithenyn standing a step below Mererid's silhouette. She was on her hands and knees with her backside dangerously vulnerable to the drunk gatekeeper. Her face looked up in shock at Taliesin with two wide hazel eyes. Seithenyn, stunned by the interruption, finally recovered himself.

"Get outta my sight you wretch!" the gatekeeper roared, swiping a fist wildly towards Taliesin. "No one's boddering me now, understand?"

"Uh, but of course I do, my lord, but...there's an emergency in the gate tower."

Seithenyn's eyes blazed with fury.

"What type of emergency? Explain yourself, you scum-eating brat! Before I rip your throat out!"

"My Lord, it's the outer sluice gate. I was watching the water level, as you showed me, and went to shut the gates, but something seems caught in the machines. I can't close or even move them now."

"You blundered and allowed some-think-a snag up. Run through the machinery. Fixit fer shit's sake! Now leave me be!"

"I'm sorry Lord, but I've tried that. I simply don't know how the machines work; I don't know what I'm looking for. And the water is rushing in faster now. I know that our King was out sailing today. I wouldn't want him to be delayed getting back into harbor."

Seithenyn's eyes shot daggers at the mention of the King. After a pause he threw his cloak angrily behind him and stomped up the stairs, barely keeping his balance. Taliesin waited until Seithenyn was out of sight before stealing another glance down the stairs, but the cleaning maid had already gathered up her bucket and brush and was fleeing down the dark stairway without looking back.

***

Two hours later, Seithenyn and his nephew finally uncovered the cause of the gate's malfunction. Several yards down the tower shaft, where the ropes and chains of the gate tower wrapped themselves around the giant bronze gears, a small metal hammer had fallen and somehow found itself caught between the two main gears for the outer sluice gate. By this time the harbor had taken on far more water than usual and Taliesin could make out the distant shapes of fishermen and mariners on the docksides. They stomped back and forth, anxious to see the waters pouring out of the gates cease at long last.

Seithenyn did his best to manage the repair quickly, but it proved far more difficult given his heavy state of intoxication. Taliesin tried to speed up the process by helping with the rope that Seithenyn was fumbling, only to find himself dodging a swift backhanded blow.

"Getaway, sea scum brat!" he shrieked. "I wush a fool to leave you in charge. Now get down to the gears and get that bastard hammer out. How'd it wind up down there, anyway?"

"I... I must have knocked it when I heard something coming up the stairs," Taliesin replied sheepishly.

"Yer a clumsy brat, you are! And as unlucky as your father. Only you lot would have the hammer fall exactly into the gear works. Take the rope and lower yourself down there already!"

It took all of Taliesin's patience to avoid snapping back at his uncle for bringing Elphin into the discussion. He grabbed the rope firmly and slowly hoisted himself down the tower interior. They spent the next few hours fixing the gears, closing the sluice gates, and managing the line of impatient boats that had been stuck waiting in the bay.

By the time the last ship had come in and the gates sealed and locked, the sun had long since dipped below the horizon. Seithenyn leaned against the stone frame of a window as a messenger on horseback galloped along the sea wall towards the tower. He stopped outside the gate and hailed Seithenyn with his banner.

"Lord gatekeeper!" he called up to him. "A message from King Gwyddno!"

"Speak!" Seithenyn called back gruffly.

"His Highness wants to talk to you and to Prince Taliesin at once. Parts of the harbor are close to running over with water and his Majesty and other boats were delayed at the sea gates. The King demands an explanation!"

"Go! Tell him we will arrive shortly!"

The messenger took his leave. Seithenyn heaved out a weary sigh and cast a suspicious eye towards his nephew.

"Taliesin," he said softly. The older man had recovered from his earlier libations and appeared tired and hollow. "What did you see earlier when I returned to the gates?"

Taliesin took the briefest moment to consider and then answered as candidly as possible. "I saw the water cresting the mark on the pier. I saw you, uncle, returning from the alehouse hardly able to walk. And I saw you behave most unfitting of your nobility with a cleaning maid."

Seithenyn only nodded absently, his gaze stuck in the far corner of the chamber.

"And is that what you will tell the King, if he asks?" he said without looking up.

"That depends, Sire."

"...on what then?" Seithenyn raised his head towards the boy.

"I could say, if the King asked, that I was careless with the tools and caused the sluice gates to get stuck, and that you did what you could to fix things as soon as possible, and if it weren't for your quick reasoning, the kingdom would certainly have flooded, and nothing more needs to be said," Taliesin explained slowly, making sure Seithenyn followed his meaning.

"You could, then?" Seithenyn replied just as carefully. "And under what condition?"

"When the King asks you what punishment I deserve, you insist mercy," Taliesin said, staring his uncle dead in the eye. "Only that I am to be removed immediately from my apprenticeship with you. I clearly am too thick to be trusted with such an important job like the sea gates. Tell him that. That he should transfer me to a new post starting tomorrow."

Seithenyn furrowed his brow, wondering if Taliesin's offer was more to his own benefit.

"That's all?" he asked.

"Yes," Taliesin confirmed, even as an afterthought struck him. "AND I would suggest you consider your future actions with the cleaning maid, lest I get wind of it and suddenly remember more things I could tell the King. Agreed?"

Seithenyn's nostrils flared, and his forehead began to change to a deep red. The breath crystallized in the icy tower as he spoke through clenched teeth. "Agreed. And may I never see your face in my tower again."

***

Despite a partially flooded dockside and arriving at port late, the King stayed remarkably cool while listening to Seithenyn's account of what had happened. As planned, the gatekeeper placed the blame solely on Taliesin's carelessness. Taliesin confirmed as much when Gwyddno asked him if Seithenyn's story was accurate. Seithenyn kept his side of the bargain and insisted that Taliesin not be punished, but only removed from his service immediately. The

King nodded and ordered Taliesin to report to Enid first thing in the morning for horsemanship lessons and combat training. The King then dismissed them both with a wave of his hand.

Taliesin stopped mid-step on his way out and turned back to the King. A question roiled inside of him.

"Your Highness," Taliesin began, "It has been over two weeks since Prince Elphin departed for the mid-winter feast at Gwynedd. Hasn't there been any news of when he'll be returning?"

The King's face, which had been stoic and hard during the meeting, softened.

"I am awaiting my messengers as we speak, Taliesin," he replied. "But, I am sure your father will be home shortly. Tell your mother that she will have to be patient until he returns. And don't you worry, boyo. I'll be sure to give him proper hell for keeping his family worried. Now be off!"

Taliesin bowed and took his leave. Crissiant had paced around the kitchen night after night for the past few weeks. She had embroidered almost every scrap of fabric in the house pretending not to be anxious over Elphin. Even so, Taliesin hadn't asked the King about news for her sake. Every day that passed, Taliesin missed his foster father's happy laugh and smiling face more and more. The brutal time Taliesin had spent in the gate tower with Seithenyn only magnified his loneliness. At least now he could finally put that particular torture behind him.

Taliesin weaved through the decorated halls that led away from the throne room, passing glittering carvings of sea dragons and heroic sailors. Salmon-colored pearls lined the statues and stonework dazzling all that meandered through Gwyddno's halls. He took note of the line of dignitaries and heralds, each impatiently waiting for their audience with the King. Taliesin felt a secret pang of guilt, knowing it was his hand that delayed the King outside the gate for so long. His grandfather would be up late tonight because of him. Taliesin walked outside onto the stone causeway, grateful for the splash of cool air on his face. Bright stars shone up from the placid surface of the swollen harbor below. In a tumult of conflicting emotions, Taliesin picked up a loose stone from the causeway and hurled it viciously into the water below him.

"Well, what a head of steam we've worked up," a laughing voice echoed. "Whatever has made our dashing prince so upset?"

Taliesin spun on his heel to see a familiar maid leaning on the side of one of the causeway's walls, her large eyes shining in the evening gloom and a delicate hand resting on her crooked hip.

"Uh! I... I was just clearing the path a bit, miss…" Taliesin suddenly felt completely off balance. The maid laughed joyfully.

"Oh my! So now you're taking my job, are you? Should I be grateful or worried over competition?" she teased him while sauntering closer. Taliesin could see that she stood a full head over his lithe twelve-year-old frame. Tudno mentioned that she wasn't older than fifteen or sixteen years, but her young face with her wide grinning lips was set on top of an adult woman's body. Her long patched together skirt dropped nearly down to her cunning feet, but Taliesin could still see the shape of her powerful legs as she walked. "I guess I should feel flattered receiving help from Prince Taliesin himself."

Taliesin blushed to be called 'Prince'.

"E-Excuse me, miss, but how do you know my name?"

"Well, for one, every servant that works in Gwyddno's palace knows who his grandson is. And second, the gatekeeper's been screaming your name several times a day for a fortnight. You really know how to ruffle his feathers, you do!"

"You overheard us?" Taliesin's heart was pounding in his chest. He wondered if he had said anything embarrassing without thinking while he had been stuck in the gate tower.

"Aye." The young lady raised an eyebrow at him. "We maids overhear quite a lot. For instance, I overheard, from a reliable source, that some clumsy apprentice caused the whole sea gate to shut down all because he knocked a hammer into the gearworks. That wouldn't be the truth by any chance, would it?"

Taliesin couldn't suppress himself as he raised an eyebrow. "Where would you have heard that from, milady?"

"The walls hear many things. The servants typically know more about what happens around the kingdom than the King himself. I also hear from the walls -" the spritely young lady took another step closer to Taliesin - "of a very cute, young apprentice, who just started studying with the gatekeeper. There's a rumor on the wind about how this young apprentice really likes looking at the maids as they sweep the tower floors. He seems to especially enjoy one of the young maid's working songs. Do you believe these rumors?"

Taliesin began to panic in silence. How long had she been aware of him?

"Begging your pardon, Mererid, I just-" Taliesin's voice caught in his throat. Mererid chuckled gleefully at the boy.

"Oh! Looks like you have been listening closely to the walls as well! It is hard to keep secrets these days." Mererid smiled and then took a slow breath. "I know you dropped the hammer into the gearworks on purpose, Master Taliesin. I'm glad you did. You have no idea the relief I felt once that pig Seithenyn stormed upstairs. I saw you looking back at me, and I knew you put your neck out for me. I felt like a maiden out of Arthur's court."

"I was...well...horrified to hear him speak to you. I could tell that you wanted none of him. He's my uncle, but we don't care so much for each other. I half thought of bashing his head in with the hammer first."

The maid's laughter rang out like choir bells.

"I wish you were always thinking up your schemes when I go to the gate tower. All of the maids try their best to stay out of his way."

"Why not make a complaint to the King?" Taliesin said. "Taking a woman against her will is against the law of the Lowland Hundred."

The maid snorted softly. "The lords and knights don't get

punished for that bollocks! The code of chivalry burned with Arthur's table, is what us cleaning girls say. Gwyddno would never hold his own son accountable for our sake."

An uncomfortable thought sprang up in Taliesin's mind.

"Do you suppose that Seithenyn will approach you again?" he asked. "Would you feel safe there?"

"I've never felt safe there!" the maid confessed. "We all hear awful stories about the gatekeeper, so I practically flew to the sea when I heard I would be assigned there. It's been complete torture dealing with the drunk sod!"

"Take my word for it, I understand!" Taliesin exclaimed, "The man can barely walk in a straight line most days, let alone operate a massive gate! How has he not destroyed the Hundred yet?"

The maid smiled wider and laughed again. "Nice of you to say so love, but I'm afraid a prince couldn't know what true humiliation is."

"You know…" Taliesin said as an idea hatched in the back of his brain. "My mother is close to the head Matron. I don't see why she wouldn't be able to move your post away from the tower, somewhere you wouldn't have to worry about Seithenyn anymore."

"Oh, yes?" Mererid's eyebrows perked up with interest. "You could do that?"

"Sure!" Taliesin's chest burst out with confidence. "My mam sees the matron every day or so, I'm sure she'd be able to put you to work someplace more cheerful."

The maid looked down at the young boy, his limbs still lanky and awkward, a dark patch of peach fuzz just brushing the top of his lips and wisping across his cheeks. She tilted her head slightly and looked at him through heavy-lidded eyes.

Taliesin felt more than saw her start to lean in, down and closer to his face. He felt her breath warm on his skin in the chilly night air as she planted a kiss lightly on the side of his cheek. Her hair smelt like a flower he knew from years ago.

"So, the code of chivalry lives on," the maid said with a wide grin. "I'd be very grateful. Maybe assisting the cooks in Lord Elphin's tower? I've always wanted to learn how to knead rye bread." She gave Taliesin one more coy smile and then turned and walked gracefully down the causeway, her long skirt swaying and gently sweeping the stone floor as she left. "Just don't forget, my sweet prince!"

Taliesin stood paralyzed to the spot for an entire minute before he began to think again. The icy sea breeze slapped him in the face, but all he could feel was the place where Mererid's lips had pressed against his cheek. He marveled at how warm he felt despite the wintry night air.

A messenger sped past him on horseback, jolting him out of his trance. He turned on his heel and continued on his way home, following the horseman. He thought he would be exhausted after the day's events, but his muscles seemed imbued with a curious new energy. He began jogging down the sparsely lit causeway. The jog sped up until he sprang into a run. A bit farther down the stone path, passers-by were startled to see the usually reserved boy racing and skipping off the slate parapets, laughing at the top of his lungs.

Taliesin made no effort to contain himself, he only prayed that he didn't run into the abbot or anyone that might judge him mad. Whatever had taken hold of Taliesin felt too fiercely joyous to control. It felt as if a young dragon had hatched inside of him and was writhing around trying to escape. It was all the boy could do to keep himself from leaping over the causeway into the harbor below, just to see if he could fly.

Taliesin raced home in no time, arriving at his door with hardly any less energy. He felt he could run circles around the whole kingdom. As he came in sight of his house, he had to dodge quickly to his right as a messenger on horseback trotted past him.

Hadn't he just seen the same messenger pass by him?

His racing mind wouldn't allow him to pay attention. He quieted himself the best he could as he slipped through the tower's heavy oak door.

He had expected that his mother would have said her prayers

and gone to bed. She'd become accustomed to Taliesin's full schedule and usually left some porridge and scraps of meat out for him. Taliesin's energy quickly slithered away when he saw his mother sitting at the table, clutching a handkerchief and mopping away tears that flowed over her swollen face.

"Mother?" Taliesin felt like he had been hit in the face with a bucket of ice water.

"Oh, Taliesin!" Crissiant exclaimed between sobs. "Taliesin, get yourself ready. We must be off to the palace at once!"

"But I just came from the palace mother." He reeled in confusion. "Whatever is the matter?"

"Your grandfather just received word, Tali. Elphin has been taken prisoner by King Maelgwn."

CHAPTER 4: The Midwinter Feast

Medhed Maelgwn Mon ac an llonna.
Ai vedgorn ewyn gwerlyn gwymha.
As cynnull gwenyn ac nys mwynha.

May Maelgwn of Mona be affected with mead, and affect us,
From the foaming mead-horns, with the choicest pure liquor,
Which the bees collect, and do not enjoy.

~ Canu y med, Llyfr Taliesin

A host of grim faces filled Gwyddno's extravagant throne room early that morning. A winter fog had rolled in off the bay during the night and clung to the cliff-like edifices of Caer Wyddno, soaking the air with an unwelcome chill. The fire brazier crackled away in the center of the great hall but did little to comfort the crowd of statesmen, generals, knights, and scribes that milled around the turquoise pillars. Taliesin could see the pale breath of every member of the court. His mother and himself were seated not an arm's length from King Gwyddno, who sat on his throne half-buried in finely embroidered fleece and leather. His face looked weathered and exhausted, but he proudly kept his head raised. Taliesin suspected his grandfather had been up all night dealing with the backlog of dignitaries before having to worry about the crisis of Elphin's imprisonment.

Balancing the seats to the left of the King sat Seithenyn, Father Gilgam wearing his ornate golden brooches, Enid the tower Captain, and a handful of broad-backed generals, their hands fidgeting absently with the hilts of their swords. All the court had their attention turned to the center of the throne room where Bryn the bard sat on a simple wooden stool. His blue eyes were lined and his hair wild and unkempt. He clutched at his cloak of many colors and held his hands out to the fire whenever he could. His harp hung across his back by a thin leather cord.

Gwyddno called for a cup of hot mead.

"Take this and steady yourself, bard. Gather your strength," the King said, holding the goblet of mead. "When you're ready, please tell all here the story of what's come to pass. Tell us what's become of my unfortunate son, Elphin."

Bryn gave a sympathetic glance to Crissiant and Taliesin, drew a long sip from the steaming cup, and then began.

"In all my years singing in the halls of kings and lords, I've never seen such despicable treachery. Poor, kind Elphin. Misfortunate he may be, but even the unluckiest wretch in the world never deserved such punishment…" Bryn muttered into the fire, clutching the mead goblet.

"Please, Bryn," Gwyddno said gently. "Start at the beginning."

Bryn nodded, taking one last swig of mead.

"Aye. So, we had traveled a day and a half up to Maelgwn's black castle on Anglesey Isle. Urien and his men of Rheged kept us well secure. It was as if we were riding amid a school of fish or a flock of sparrows. All his men and horses moved in perfect unison. We arrived in Anglesey without incident.

"We were received courteously and with honors. Elphin

himself was given a kingly robe, and we relayed your Majesty's gifts and greetings to Maelgwn. There were kings and envoys from near every part of Britain, and even some from beyond Hadrian's Wall. For an entire fortnight, Maelgwn graciously entertained, fed, and clothed us. There were fine sports and hunts, dancers, harpists, and singers, and more meat and food than I thought the land of Gwynedd could hold!

"Elphin carried himself properly and per your instructions. His eyes were ever wandering the castle, sizing up the strength of Maelgwn's guards, which was substantial, and keeping close tabs on who Maelgwn was cozying up to."

"Did you see who Maelgwn spent the most time with?" Gwyddno interrupted. "Any inkling as to who he was looking at for potential allies?"

"I'm afraid Elphin observed more of that than I, Sire," Bryn answered, lowering his gaze. "I was often kept away from my countrymen with the other bards, all of whom were distracted preparing for Maelgwn's upcoming tournament of stories. Many of my fellow story collectors did mention that Maelgwn had sent several hunting hounds and horses as gifts to Urien."

"God's wounds…" Taliesin heard his grandfather mutter under his breath. "Did Rheged exchange vows of allegiance with Gwynedd?"

"I cannot say for certain, your Majesty. But I personally witnessed none."

A small murmur bounced through several of the generals as they exchanged knowing looks.

"But what about Elphin?" Crissiant pleaded. "Please, good bard, tell us what's happened to him."

"It was during the last night of feasting on Midwinter's eve," Bryn resumed," I was seated with the rest of the bards and musicians off in the wings of Maelgwn's dining hall. Lord Elphin feasted with the other kings and nobles at the Dragon's table. On that table, I saw heavenly delights of mutton, stag, cheeses, and creams of every sort, and no less than seven roast boars. In truth, I believed there was thrice more food served than guests to eat it.

"As if the mountain of meat and honey wasn't enough for the Dragon's feast, wine and ale flowed from the flasks of the servants in a never-ending river. No one at the table was allowed an empty cup."

"Oh, godfathers," Gwyddno again interjected. "Please tell me that Elphin kept enough modesty while imbibing at the feast."

"He certainly did, your Highness!" Bryn said with confidence. "I can say with pride that I saw him steadfastly refuse second helpings of the wine. He carried himself in a controlled and disciplined manner befitting of his royal status of the Lowland Hundred."

Taliesin caught several lords raising their eyebrows in surprise at this news. He risked a sidelong glance at Seithenyn and noticed that the gatekeeper wore his usual sneer.

"Well…" Bryn continued a little more sheepishly. "He did at first and made a valiant effort, but then I noticed him accept a sampling of the winter season's mead. It's a limited and rare libation, so even the most resolved of lords would see reason in having a small taste. This led to a natural curiosity of the elderberry wine, which in turn whetted his appetite for the aged lagers. He seemed to find those too bitter, so he washed that down with more of the wine and another serving of mead."

Gwyddno pressed his hand against his forehead but failed to hide his grimace. He signaled the bard to continue.

"Not long after, the hall was filled with shouts of merriment and laughter. One of the lords from Pembroke became a bit too bold and began to pester one of the serving girls. Even across the hall, I could see our Lord Elphin reprimanding him for his behavior.

"'What type of man would turn his head twice for these plain waifs, I say!' I heard our Lord yell loudly. 'You rascals would mistake a she-goat for your wife if it weren't in the broad light of day!'

'Hah!' The envoy returned in good humor. 'An' what do you mistake for your wife then, sailor Prince? A sturgeon? No doubt the smell would be sweeter!'

"This roused a chorus of guffaws from Pembroke's side of the table and even a few from our drunken kinsmen. Elphin did not laugh though. His face turned an unsightly shade of crimson and appeared wholly enraged. He jumped to his feet. Several heads around the dining hall turned in his direction.

"'I'll have you know that my wife is by far, the fairest, purest creature in all of Britain, Ireland, or the lands over the seas. Hers is a beauty utterly unmatched by any queen or noble lady in the world!'

"'Ah now!' One of the Rheged men spoke up. 'Lady Elphin is truly a fetching wife, but 'a beauty unmatched in all the world'? Sounds like a Gwaelod fish story to me.'

"'Unmatched in all the world, cur!' Elphin grew agitated. 'From the queens of the Nile to this skinny whore here in Gwynedd, none can match the beauty of my darling Crissiant!'

"Now, nearly all cheer and revelry ceased. Every set of eyes turned towards our emissary prince, including those of King Maelgwn and his royal consort, Queen Bannon.

"' Lord Elphin,' another prince spoke up. 'Surely, you don't really mean to compare your wife to our host's Queen, who has been kind enough to grace us with her hospitality this evening.'

"In my humble opinion, Lord Elphin would have been wise to have conceded this point and thus saved some of his grace. Regrettably, he did not recognize the opportunity.

"' Nonsense!' Elphin bellowed, 'why, my wife is ten times more virtuous than any one of Maelgwn's dried up wenches! Fairer than his skinny Queen by far! I'd stake my honor on it!'

"Those words, those loud and careless boasts, sealed our prince's fate. Maelgwn rose silently from his place at the head of the table. I know not how, the Dragon's face hardly twitched, but it was if a firebolt of rage ignited in the air. Finally, our prince Elphin became aware of his predicament.

"'Nobles! My fellow Cymry!' Maelgwn announced to the silent hall. 'I beseech you, bear witness to these ungracious, crude insults this knave throws at me and mine. Need we repeat them for anyone who hasn't heard?'

"Not a single voice spoke out. Elphin's ruddy complexion drained paled.

"'Good!' Maelgwn continued. 'We would be sorely grieved to have our Queen hear these thoughtless words again, after she has gone through so much to set food on your plates and spirits in your cups. Isn't clear to everyone here the scorn and ingratitude that this prince from Gwyddno's kingdom spits on me.'

"' O King…' Elphin stuttered in response, 'I meant no dishonor to you or your lovely Quee-'

"' Silence.' Maelgwn did not raise his voice the slightest, but his words echoed off the stone walls. 'I ask all gathered here. Who among you, if similarly dishonored by a guest, who would refrain from bringing down the full punishment of the law? Who among you would think twice about delivering death to the ingrate?'

"Again, not a single voice responded. And this was truly an act of cowardice from our fellow lords. Nary one among them would go so far to execute a prince, however drunk he may be!

"Maelgwn nodded to himself, satisfied. Queen Bannon only blushed and hid her face in her hands.

"' Then let all here see the mercy of Gwynedd. We will not dole out death, though the law allows it. But such insults cannot be allowed to go unpunished.'

"Maelgwn may have done nothing more than flared a single nostril, but in the next instant, every guard in the castle came down on poor Elphin. After they subdued our prince, a silver chain was brought to shackle his hands and feet.

"' Lead him off to the north tower,' Maelgwn instructed his guards. 'Keep him well fed and taken care of. He is of royal blood after all and kin to us. We shall send word to Gwyddno regarding the conditions of his release.'

"The last I saw of the prince was his back as they carried him off.

"After the feast, I sought the King out myself in his throne room. I knelt at his feet and begged him to show Elphin mercy.

"' Why, good bard!' the King of Gwynedd said, chuckling. This offended me something awful. 'I will show the greatest hospitality for my royal guest while your master and I come to an understanding. You must understand that I cannot tolerate being insulted in my own hall. Such a thing would show grave weakness. Gwyddno must pay a tithe for this offense.'

"Here, I must confess, I grew a little bolder. 'Begging your pardon, your Majesty, but I would say that it was not you who had been offended, but rather your gracious Queen.' I turned my eyes to the queen's face. Seated on the King's left, she blinked in response to my declaration. 'What tithe would her fairness ask for?'

"Bannon's eyes widened at me. 'Well, I should have your King know that I wouldn't take Elphin's words so personally, but I-'

"'Bannon.' King Maelgwn only raised his fingers an inch. The Queen blushed and looked down into her lap. 'In my hall, during my feast, an insult to my wife is an insult to me and the kingdom of Gwynedd,' Maelgwn said with finality. 'I respect you, bard. My land always welcomes esteemed historians and orators, and your profession grants you certain immunities from punishment.' The King grinned unnervingly. 'But know your place. You are to ride back to Cantre'r Gwaelod at daybreak,' Maelgwn continued. 'Relay all that has happened here and tell Gwyddno that I will return his son safe when my tithe is paid.'

"'And what does his Highness desire for payment?' I asked. The King leaned forward in his throne and all but whispered."

Bryn faltered, pausing during his story to take in one more pull of mead. Gwyddno leaned forward in his throne.

"Go on, Bryn!" Gwyddno commanded impatiently. "What is the Dragon asking?"

"Maelgwn bade me tell you," Bryn said shakily, "that he wants Ceredigion."

Bryn finished his story with another long draught of mead.

All the King's assembly stared at him in shock. He cleared his throat before speaking.

"I was then packed off at dawn and sent to deliver my message, and thus I have done."

Silence hung in the air for several seconds until Enid's voice rang out.

"Maelgwn can't possibly mean the whole of Ceredigion. That's ridiculous! That's practically the size of all of Gwynedd! What fools does he take us for?"

"The Dragon of the isle is ambitious, and it's served him well to be so," a general from the lowland's southern sector called back. "Look how much force he's gathered to himself in just a few years, and the extra territory too. He's not jesting. Maelgwn is truly after our lands to the east."

"He'll not have them of course!" spoke Connwn of Powys. "It will be war first!"

"Don't be rash!" another voice rang out. "Remember the prince's life is at stake!"

"My Lords!" Seithenyn called out to the assembly. "Perhaps we should leave our dear Elphin in Gwynedd for now." His suggestion shocked the raucous court. "After all, with his ever-worsening luck, we could leave him in hopes that his presence makes the fortress of Anglesey collapse on Maelgwn's head. Wouldn't that save us all a large amount of trouble?"

Several nervous chuckles bounced through the court, but most of the assembly shook their heads and looked away awkwardly.

At last, the King rose, and all talk instantly stopped.

"Our gatekeeper chooses an interesting moment to make jests and at the expense of someone not present to appreciate them. We now stand in the face of extortion, ransom, or the possibility of outright war, none of which gives us cause for laughter, Lord Seithenyn." He shot a grave look at his second son.

"My sincere apologies, your Highness," Seithenyn returned.

"I have no use for your apologies," Gwyddno returned. "But

I'm sure that Prince Elphin's wife and child are hardly amused." He glanced knowingly at Crissiant and Taliesin. Crissiant's lips were pressed together so hard they had begun to turn white.

Seithenyn noticed the whole court's attention directed squarely at him and he sheepishly stepped into the center of the hall. He knelt on one knee and addressed Elphin's wife. "My lady, forgive me. My words were ill-considered."

"Indeed, they were, Lord gatekeeper," Crissiant said. "But as you can well imagine, insensitive words are the least of my worries now. I expect that you must be as concerned for your brother's safety as I am."

Crissiant's words were cool and well-measured, but Taliesin recognized the tense look on his mother's face. Underneath her gracious demeanor, Crissiant was livid.

"My King," Taliesin spoke up. "Please, I know Maelgwn's demands are steep and unreasonable, but you, more than any other here, must surely understand our concerns, my mother's and mine. We cannot lose Elphin. He is our world and our joy. We cannot ask you to pay the ransom, but I beg of you, what can be done to ensure his safety?"

"I agree with the boy, your Highness." Taliesin looked over to see Connwn's kind face staring back at him. "We cannot concede to Maelgwn's demands, but neither can we let him lock Prince Elphin away. The Lowland Hundred is a kingdom of loyalty, of unity. An attack on one family is an attack on the whole kingdom. Maelgwn has dealt us the first blow. I say we answer it with the full force of our knights and archers. We must raze Anglesey to the ground to see Elphin back home."

Several voices echoed Connwn's sentiments while several more murmured in disapproval. All of them fell silent as the King's booming laughter filled the hall.

"What clowns do I keep in my court! Do you see this, bard?" Gwyddno jibed at Bryn. "I'd be fretful, if I were you, should one of my generals replace you as a comedian." The King turned his attention back to the crowd. "Elphin is hardly in any danger for the moment, and there's not a chance in hell that we're giving up our rightful territory in Ceredigion. What's more, the King of Gwynedd knows this."

The assembly exchanged looks among themselves. Enid spoke hesitantly. "Are you certain, O King?"

"I'd stake my throne on it," Gwyddno replied. "That weasel of a tyrant is trying to throw us off balance and win big in his negotiations. But let us remember, Maelgwn is also trying to impress his neighbors by presenting himself as a gracious and magnanimous ruler. If he so much as bruises a prince he's invited as a guest, even a guest who comported himself as poorly as Elphin has, he'll lose whatever support he's been counting. Urien is practical, but he won't support cruelty, he's far too pious for that. No, Maelgwn is merely trying to turn a prince's ransom into a kingdom's ransom."

"What does his majesty suggest?" Bryn asked from his stool. "Surely you wouldn't leave your own son at the mercy of the Dragon?"

"For now, I may have to." Gwyddno took on a graver tone. "At least until negotiations are settled. We will send out messengers this very day with a counter-offer of several stallions, a pack of hunting hounds, and ten bushels of smoked salmon."

"Maelgwn won't release Prince Elphin for such a meager amount!" the general of Pembroke objected.

"No, but he'll get the message that we're not about to be pushed around. Don't worry, he'll return the offer with something only modestly outrageous."

"Send me, my Lord!" Bryn jumped down from his stool suddenly. The tall man stumbled, his legs still tired from the hard journey back. "Please! I will deliver the message and barter with Maelgwn in your name!"

"You, Bryn?!" Gwyddno balked. "Come now, you're a bard, not a fool! No, you need your rest and I need my story-keeper back where he belongs. I have enough riders to deliver a simple message."

Bryn only creased his brow before bowing his head in assent.

"Sire!" Connwn's voice called out. The man from Powys stepped forward, his hand on the hilt of his sword. "I must admit that gambling with the life of our prince alarms me and my countrymen. We've put our faith in the Lowland Hundred believing that our allies would respond in times of need. If you cannot show the same fealty to your son, how can we expect you to do the same to our own subjects?"

Across the room, several other lords and warriors tensed as they listened to Connwn. Some started to wonder if the strength of Cantre'r Gwaelod was finally fraying among its allies. Gwyddno felt the tension too as he swept the room with eyes, seeing uncertainty and doubt reflected at him.

"This is the way business is conducted among kingdoms, Lord Connwn. I repeat, Elphin is in no danger."

"And you said as well that you would stake your throne on it," Connwn pressed. "Can the King do right by his word, then? Will he swear to lay siege to the Dragon of the isle, and bring ruination on his lands, at whatever cost, should Maelgwn betray us? For the sake of those that love our prince so dearly?" Connwn cast a meaningful glance over to Taliesin and Crissiant.

Gwyddno took a deep breath in and kept his eyes squarely on the warrior from Powys. "Don't presume to know who cherishes the life of my son the most in this hall. But yes, I, Gwyddno Garanhir, King of Cantre'r Gwaelod, do hereby swear to bring war and ruin to Gwynedd if our kingdom's honor is betrayed. This I swear before all standing here, before God, and before Dylan ail Don of the sea."

Everyone in the throne room fell silent, ruminating on the gravity of Gwyddno's words. The only voice that could be heard was Father Gilgam's indistinct mutterings as he asked for prayers for Elphin's safe delivery and the safety of the kingdom. Taliesin, seated fairly close to Gilgam, could also make out the clergyman asking pardon for the King's invocation of Dylan ail Don, the pagan sea god. Despite Gilgam's sincerest efforts to erase heathen influences, as he referred to them, most of the population of Cantre'r Gwaelod still made offerings to the sea-god.

Satisfied with this response, Connwn sank on one knee and bowed his head low.

"Your Majesty continues to be a bastion of strength in these dark days after Arthur, may God protect and keep the Lowland Hundred!"

With that, Gwyddno dismissed the assembly and gave orders for messengers to relay his offer back to Anglesey. Taliesin and Crissiant gathered themselves to return to their dwelling when Gwyddno strode up to them and addressed them personally.

"Begging your pardon, daughter-in-law," the King said to Crissiant. "I hope you know that should you require anything at all, you need only say so. We all share your grief at these grave tidings."

Crissiant straightened her head like an indignant swan. She kept her garments crossed over her.

"I am grateful, your Highness," she replied. "My only request is that you consider assigning my son, the one family member I have left in my household, a new apprenticeship. His hours in the sea gates are long and I don't like him spending so much time with a brute who thinks it proper to crack jokes at my husband's expense."

Hearing this, Gwyddno's white eyebrows reared up on his forehead and he twisted his fingers into his beard.

"Gracious me! Didn't the lad tell you yet?" he asked. "Too much excitement this morning, I reckon. I've already re-assigned him to Enid, the guardswoman, after he had a little mishap last night. He was to report to her today, but if you feel it best that he stays at home-"

"I can find her first thing tomorrow, grandfather," Taliesin spoke up. "I wouldn't want to sit idle at home, the training would be good to keep my mind off things."

Crissiant now turned a surprised look towards her foster son. "What mishap is this? What discussion have I been left out of, again?"

"I'll explain everything to you at home, mother," Taliesin assured her. The King embraced them and then took his leave. Crissiant took Taliesin by the hand as the two began wandering their way out of the palace.

"Pssst! Taliesin!" A harsh whisper bounced off the stone walls from behind a pillar of bluestone. Taliesin yanked his head around to see Mererid's round face staring back at him with expectant eyes.

"Oh!" Taliesin could hardly believe that he had forgotten last night so quickly. "Uhmm, mother?"

"What is it, Taliesin? I'm not so sure I can take any more surprises right now."

"Uhm...well, I would like to introduce you to someone." He gestured to Mererid, who gingerly stepped out from behind her pillar. "This is Mererid, one of the cleaning maids. She'd like to know if we needed help at home. And I thought with father gone -"

"Oh, yes?" Crissiant turned her gaze at the young lady more than four years older than her foster son and a head taller. She scanned the maid up and down like she was inspecting a gaudy dress. "Honestly Taliesin! I'm in no mood to put up with such nonsense right now! Who knows when or if we'll see Elphin again, the court talks about us behind our backs, and now you think it's appropriate to bring all and sundry over to our house? Leave it until your father returns, would you?"

"But, Mam, it's not like that at all!" Taliesin objected. He tried not to pay attention to the burning sensation flushing through his cheeks. "Mererid has good cause to leave her old duties, I promised her that I would ask."

"Let her ask the King!" Crissiant snapped back.

"Begging your pardon, my lady," Mererid said with a polite curtsey. "But I didn't feel so comfortable talking to the King about it. It was a personal issue, you see."

"I'm not sure that I do see," Crissiant said, folding her arms across her lithe frame. "What were your duties you needed to walk away from anyway?"

"I was the tower maid at the sea gates, Mum," Mererid said, keeping her eyes downcast. "With Lord Seithenyn."

Crissiant's ice blue eyes darted briefly over to Seithenyn, who was lumbering his way through the throng of palace goers with a sour expression on his face. The older woman's face remained stern.

"Ah...I see." Crissiant pursed her lips together. "My head cook has been asking for an assistant for some time," she said finally. "Report to my kitchen at the break of dawn tomorrow and be prepared to work. I will speak to the head matron about your replacement at the sea gates."

Mererid's eyes lit up.

"Oh, thank you so -"

"That will be all...Mererid, was it?" Crissiant said as she grabbed Taliesin by the hand. "See to it that you won't be late."

With that, Taliesin's mother dragged him out towards their escorts before the boy could say a word.

CHAPTER 5: The Dragon of the Isle

Llyffan du gaflaw.
Cant ewin arvawg.
Y neidr vreith gribawg.
Eneid, drwy i phechawd,
A boenir yng hnawd.

A black sprawling toad,
With a hundred claws on it.
A snake speckled, crested.
the soul, through her sin,
Shall be tormented in its flesh

~ Cad Goddeu, Llyfr Taliesin

Maelgwn roared a curse as he dug his rough fingernails into the back of his teeth, searching for any small morsel of venison he could find. His gold rings cut into the soft flesh of his gums, freeing a small trickle of blood that drained, unnoticed, from the side of his mouth. The King of Gwynedd sat at the head of his private dining table, high up the easternmost tower of Anglesey. A winter storm had swept in from the sea and pelted the outer walls of the slate-gray fortress with a sticky layer of ice. Maelgwn typically dined in the eastern tower, the tower furthest from the shores of the ocean. Maelgwn never trusted the sea.

"This leftover dung is getting stringy. Wasn't there any flank of boar left over from the feast, Bannon?"

The Queen of Gwynedd sat by her husband's right side, nibbling on a scrap of cheese. Despite the blazing fire set on the brazier in the middle of the room, Bannon pulled her fur robe closer to her. Queen Bannon seldom ever felt warm enough in Anglesey castle.

"I'm afraid not, my King," she replied. "It seems that your honored guests have impressive appetites."

"Fie on it! That's what I keep telling you, Dad!" Rhun, the King's oldest living son, sat across from his father. He hastily washed down a mouthful of meat with a long pull of wine before continuing. "We go too far trying to impress that lot of jackals, and by the end of the feast, we're left to scrape by on porridge and peasant's stew for the rest of the winter."

"I know our table is barer than we would like…" Truthfully Maelgwn's table was hardly ever without some helping of meat, which was more than many of his subjects could say, "but believe me, it's worth it."

Maelgwn began gnawing on a half-finished thigh bone, scraping off the last bit of cooked flesh with his front teeth.

"Every year we entertain more and more lords from the different kingdoms, and every year we gain more allies. We almost…. almost have the largest army of all the Cymry. If we act wisely, we'll have partridge from all the corners of Britain on our plates very soon."

As Maelgwn talked through his bites of venison, several large hounds that had been piled together on the stone floor began to pace around the perimeter of the room. They kept their eyes riveted to the greasy leg bone, compulsively licking their chops.

"Who do you favor, Rhun?" Maelgwn asked, dangling the

succulent bone over the floor. The dogs whined but obediently stayed put against the walls.

"You mean for the partridge?" Rhun asked, confused.

"The dogs, you dunce!" Maelgwn hollered. "Who's coming away with this?" He shook the bone, letting a drop of gravy splatter to the floor.

"Oh! Barabbas then. Says three gold pieces."

"And you, my love?" Maelgwn turned to Bannon. "Who's your pick?"

"I have no taste for sport at the moment," the queen replied.

"Come, make a pick and place your wager!"

"I'm afraid that wagering is a sin, my King. I couldn't partake in anything that would put the King's piety in doubt."

"Bah! So be it then. As for me, I say Herod." A handsome-looking mastiff picked up its ears after hearing his name. Maelgwn flung the scrap of food into the center of the floor. The dozen hounds stood in rapt attention, but none dared move. The King hesitated, savoring his power over the hungry dogs.

"Hep!" he finally said.

The dogs scrambled braying into the center of the floor, snarling and barking at each other viciously. The black wolfhound, Barabbas, immediately clamped his jaws into the neck of the grey dog next to him, scaring him away. Then he joined the rest of the snarling pack as they watched the two largest dogs, Herod and a Danish hunting dog, furiously square off over the scrap of food.

Maelgwn slammed his hand down on the table and egged on the mastiff. Rhun quietly kept his eye on the black wolfhound while Queen Bannon stared pointedly at the opposite end of the table. The great Dane snarled at Herod and gnashed its yellow teeth. Herod hardly returned the threat before he lunged up and over the Dane, using his incredible weight to knock the other dog off balance and then lashed out with his muscular jaws. A cacophony of feral barking filled the room for a moment before the Dane yipped out in surrender and limped back to the wall, nursing a badly torn ear.

Herod shook himself and caught his breath, his own snout bleeding from the skirmish. He was so pleased with his victory that he never saw Rhun's black wolfhound dart in from the circle and close his powerful teeth over the mastiff's foreleg. Herod's leg made a loud sickening crack as he cried out in agony and scrambled backward on three legs, defeated. The black wolfhound gingerly snapped up the leg of venison and nearly crunched it down in one bite.

Rhun slammed his fist down on the King's table and bellowed in triumph.

"Ha! Barabbas takes the prize! Pay up, Dad!"

Maelgwn sneered as he reached into the folds of his robe and pulled out a trio of sizeable gold coins and flicked them callously towards his son. Rhun snatched it up, looking over the faded Roman letters before tucking it into his pouch.

"Have you talked with the Lord Rheged, yet?" Bannon asked the King. "Have you brought up the offer?"

"Not yet, I was only able to speak to him in passing before that oaf, Elphin, made such a scene."

"Did us a favor, really, didn't he, Dad?"

Maelgwn grunted. "In some regards, yes. But I'll need to secure Urien's support if we expect to put any pressure on Gwyddno. Speaking of such matters, perhaps we should check in on our royal guest." Maelgwn rose from his seat and strode towards the chamber door as Rhun followed.

"Will you be coming, my dear?" the King called back over his shoulder.

"I'm afraid I cannot," Bannon said, glancing up. "I still have prayers to say."

"You spend all day praying, I just hope you're saying enough prayers for my sake."

Maelgwn heaved his way down the stair aisle with Rhun behind him.

"I certainly do, my King." Bannon watched their shadows chase them down across the stone walls lit with orange firelight.

***

Many bards and historical orators claim that Gwynedd's first King, after the Romans, had been Cunedda of the Scottish isles, Maelgwn's distant ancestor. Cunedda fortified the northern coast of Wales and drove out the Saxon and Irish war parties. Since then, the rule of Gwynedd fell to Cunedda's numerous descendants until it eventually came to Cadwallon Lawhir ap Einion, and then finally to Maelgwn himself. Every bard that stepped foot in Maelgwn's halls was required to know this section of history. Those who couldn't did not stay bards for long.

Cunedda himself had laid the foundations of Anglesey tower, leaving each successor to add more as the wealth of Gwynedd steadily grew. The walls, which stretched for several miles in perimeter, stood under the protection of Gwynedd's archers and knights. No one ever entered Anglesey castle without the King's knowledge.

Inside the main gates lay a small village of farmers and peasants, a jousting field, gardens, stables, and pastures. The King's main castle stood atop the crest of a small hill, giving Maelgwn an uncompromised view of his land. In addition, Maelgwn also ordered that a small square of the encroaching forest surrounding the castle be annexed into the castle grounds by surrounding it with towers and parapets. Now, Maelgwn could boast that he needn't leave his own gates to go hunting when the impulse struck him.

Maelgwn and Rhun wound their way through the ever-present crowd of the gentry, landowners, and other sycophants that haunted his halls and made their way to the north tower. Usually, Maelgwn had no reservations about housing prisoners in the spiraling network of catacombs that spread like roots underneath the castle. Few such prisoners ever lived long enough to breathe fresh air above ground again, and many referred to the underground prison cells as Maelgwn's 'tombs for the living'.

This specific prisoner of the King's, despite his reputation as a magnet for misfortune, had the luck to be spared from the dungeons. Due to Elphin's royal heritage, Maelgwn found himself honor-bound to house him in the tallest tower and in relative comfort, with food and water brought to him twice a day. As the King struggled to keep his breath while climbing the steep twisting staircase, he began to consider that a King's honor may have its limits next time.

Finally, the duo arrived at a plain wooden door at the top of the drafty tower. A sturdy iron bar blocked the door from moving so much as an inch. Maelgwn nodded at the burly sentinel standing beside the cell who then heaved the iron bar off its braces and let the door creak open. The King and his son stepped inside.

The tower cell, by anyone's standards, was spartan for guest accommodations, but downright luxurious compared to the King's dungeons. A simple straw mattress supported by a cot lay on one side along with a chamber pot. Elphin ap Gwyddno sat on a simple wooden stool next to the room's only window, facing east. The thick silver chains clamped around his wrists kept him shackled to the far wall. Maelgwn stopped in the center of the room, where he was just out of reach from his bound prisoner.

Elphin brought his gaze away from the window and stood to address his visitors. He had only been in the tower for two nights by now, but it seemed clear by his appearance that he had slept very little during that time. He ran his fingers through his ragged white beard and bowed his head in respect to Maelgwn.

"Isn't it always a nuisance when a guest outstays his welcome?" Maelgwn said as he broadened his shoulders. "Wouldn't you say, Rhun?"

"Especially one who chokes down so much meat and drink," Rhun replied with a sneer.

Elphin lifted his head and rose to his feet, drawing himself up to his full height, just above Maelgwn's head.

"If you're tired of hosting," Elphin said with unbridled

courtesy, "I would be more than happy to take my leave and relay my appreciation back to Cantre'r Gwaelod. I wouldn't want to put your Majesty out."

"Aye, but you already have put us out, Prince Elphin," Maelgwn continued. "You've put us very much out of sorts indeed, what with your carrying on. Surely you must understand that a king, a true king," Maelgwn emphasized, "does not allow himself to appear weak, not in front of so many peers of the realm. It's a pity that your sire did not teach that to you of all people, his own son and heir."

Elphin bristled slightly at Maelgwn's words, but he bit back his churlish retorts. "I can honestly attest that he did. But as any in the Lowland Hundred could tell you, I was always a slow student. It's...illuminating...to have such an effective teacher such as yourself assisting in my continuing education." Elphin's eye flicked over towards the window again.

"May I ask, has my father been informed of my brashness?"

"I should expect so," Maelgwn said casually. "I sent back that lanky bard of yours with the message."

"And a ransom too, I suppose?" Elphin pressed.

"Perhaps," Maelgwn said, "After all, us tutors have steep rates these days."

"What was your price?"

"Gently, friend fisherman, gently," Rhun interjected. He stepped in line with his father and spoke loud enough so that Elphin was sure to hear. "Sire, I'm afraid I have need of this room for some actors I've hired for the tournament soon. It would be most convenient if we could pack off this lout sooner rather than later."

"Aye, but only after he has properly learned his lesson in respect," Maelgwn replied. He turned his crooked smile towards Elphin. "What say you, Prince?" he asked. "Have you learned enough humility yet, or will we need to keep you here until next year's feast?'

Elphin inhaled and then slowly dropped to one knee and bowed his head towards the King of Gwynedd. "My Lord, I humbly apologize for the ruckus I have caused during your feast. I had acted out of lechery and folly and have disgraced my house and yours. Please forgive me and my countrymen for any offence."

Maelgwn raised his eyebrows, looking pleased with Elphin's show. Rhun only scratched his nose. "What about the insults to our queen?"

Elphin nodded curtly. "I am deeply sorry for how I addressed your honorable queen. She is a true woman of virtue and the picture of piety. I have done her a tremendous dishonor with my careless words."

"Hmmm..." Maelgwn rubbed his pudgy chin. "These are very fair words indeed. Perhaps you are deserving of clemency, after all, Prince Elphin." Maelgwn made a great show of deliberating a decision. "But, finally, let us hear one last thing. You claimed that my wife was a skinny whore while yours was the fairest that walked God's blessed earth. That sounds like crude blasphemy to me, and it's well known that you southerners have yet to fully accept the teachings of the savior. Let's hear you take it back then." Maelgwn threw a smirk at Rhun.

"Let us hear you say that your wife is a common sailor's whore rank with rotten cockle stench. Say this for us, Elphin, and we shall grant your freedom."

Elphin stood, still as a statue, without a single twitch betraying a reaction.

"I don't see how my wife has anything to do with my foolishness," he said finally.

"Didn't you begin your whole...performance by bragging about your wife's grace and beauty?" Maelgwn pressed. "If you want to show humility, then take back your claim and tell us she smells of rotten fish, like the rest of your stinking kingdom."

"Before I do," Elphin shifted his weight back, over his heels. "Answer me one thing: what ransom did you ask my father for in exchange for me?"

Maelgwn hesitated before a grin broke out over his face, despite his best efforts to remain collected.

"My boy. I asked him for dominion over Ceredigion. I understand how much you mean to the old man."

"...I see…" Elphin's face betrayed his shock. "Then there's no point in besmirching my wife's honor for your sport. You're not going to release me anytime soon with that ransom at stake. Go have your fun at someone else's expense Maelgwn and leave me be!"

Maelgwn turned a sour expression and addressed his son. "It seems our guest has gotten wise of us, Rhun."

"More's the pity," Rhun said mockingly. "I was hoping to get him to divulge which barnyard animal his poxy wife sounds like when he's putting it to her."

"My wife has more piety in her little finger than you could find in your whole kingdom, you dog!" Elphin snapped

"Such insolence," Maelgwn scolded. "I suppose we should have to discipline our pupil."

Maelgwn did nothing more than stride easily over to where his prisoner's bread sat on a pewter tray against the wall with a jar of water. With one precise movement of the King's foot, Maelgwn pushed the food and water across the floor until it was just out of reach of Elphin's shackled arms. He called for the guard.

"See to it that a hot meal and adequate water are brought to our guest's cell twice a day," he instructed. "But make sure that all of his meals are delivered to this precise spot here -" he pointed to the inaccessible tray with the tip of his toe, "- and inform the errand boy that he is never to offer the prisoner help reaching for his water and food." Maelgwn turned his gaze back to Elphin, who only fumed. "In a few days, I'm sure that our princely visitor will find the fruits of my kingdom desirable enough. That will be all."

Maelgwn turned on his heel and walked back towards the cell door with Rhun in his wake.

"Maelgwn!" Elphin barked after him. Maelgwn stopped but only turned his head slightly back to his prisoner. "You're a fool if you think Gwyddno will concede Ceredigion to the likes of you. You're nothing short of senile for asking."

Maelgwn only snorted. "Don't take me for a fool. I wouldn't expect him to hand over the best of his land for you even if you weren't a worthless fool of a prince. But after the trouble I aim to bring him and his kingdom, he'll wish he had. Until then."

Maelgwn and Rhun walked briskly out of the tower cell, leaving the guard to lock up the heavy oak door. They descended the steep staircase and made their way to the training grounds.

"Do you really think we can challenge the Lowland Hundred?" Rhun asked as they walked. "It would be a grisly battle to take part in. Even if we count in the lords who haven't yet sworn allegiance."

"They'll give us fealty when they see what a shambles becomes of the Lowland Hundred. That's always been Gwyddno's weakness, he listens too closely to all his vassals at once. No one can provide solid leadership like that."

"Still, we cannot hope to lay siege to a kingdom that practically lives on the sea. The ocean would have to run out of fish before they surrendered."

"Who said anything about taking the fight to Gwyddno?" Maelgwn asked coyly. "Honestly boy, use your brain now and again."

"How else then?!" Rhun asked sincerely. "Gwyddno won't be coaxed out of his realm into certain war for nothing."

"That depends on how much he is pushed," Maelgwn replied as the two stepped out in the crisp winter air. They had barely taken three steps when they were approached by the captain of the castle guard who was escorting messengers from Gwyddno.

"Hail Maelgwn! Mighty King of Gwynedd," the head messenger began with a low bow. "My Lord Gwyddno Garanhir of Cantre'r Gwaelod bids you harken to his offer of ransom for the safe return of his eldest son, Prince Elphin. King Gwyddno offers eight of his prize stallions, twelve of his finest hunting hounds, and -"

"Does he concede Ceredigion?" Maelgwn interrupted.

"-and ten bushels of smoked salmon," the messenger finished. "My Lord Gwyddno made no mention of Ceredigion to me, your Highness."

Maelgwn pouted his meaty lips and nodded thoughtfully.

"Tell him that his offer is rejected then," the King said at length. "What's more, tell him to be ready to receive my own son, Prince Rhun, in three days' time, that he may carry on negotiations with him directly in my stead."

"What? I, father?!" Rhun squealed out.

"Go now at once!" Maelgwn addressed the messengers. The two men bowed and wasted no time returning to their mounts.

"You couldn't have sent off one of your knights or generals to carry on this business?" Rhun asked, obviously annoyed. "I have no skill at diplomacy!"

"Certainly not!" Maelgwn agreed. "But I am not sending you in the interests of diplomacy. Gwyddno needs to be pushed, humiliated, to the point that his vassals and soldiers question his authority. That is a task I wouldn't entrust to anyone in Britain except you, my boy."

Maelgwn stood in the thin sunlight, savoring the mask of confusion that twisted his son's face.

"And better still," Maelgwn continued, "I believe that you will genuinely enjoy every minute of it."

CHAPTER 6: Winter Tales

Adwyn med yng hynted I gerdawr
Arall adwyn, am dervyn torv vawr

Pleasant is mead, within the court, to the minstrel
Also pleasant, to be beyond the edge of a great crowd.

~Aduvyneu Taliesin, Llyfr Taliesin

"May your grace save us from the wild beasts and savage men. May your light guide us through the darkest night. May your wisdom--"

Father Gilgam's voice echoed off the stone chapel, droning on as the icy wind whipped through the bell chambers sending an eerie howl through the church hall. Taliesin blinked hard and massaged his face to stifle a yawn. For the third day in a row, Crissiant had woken her son up well before dawn to attend morning prayers.

"It's for the good of your father, Taliesin!" Crissiant insisted.

"We need to keep him in our prayers and entreat the Lord to watch over him."

Taliesin personally didn't see why he couldn't ask the Lord to save Elphin from the comfort of his warm bed, but he knew better than to put up a fuss. Crissiant carried her disquiet remarkably well, but her son could already see the lines in her face etching deeper and the bags under her eyes growing darker. Truthfully, Taliesin prayed for the wellbeing of his mother just as hard as he prayed for Elphin.

The other reason Taliesin didn't mind trudging through the icy weather to listen to Gilgam monologue through the Holy Scriptures was that it provided him with an opportunity to talk with Tudno. His friend had just accepted the role of a page boy for Father Gilgam and executed his duties with zealous fervor. Taliesin had seen less of Tudno since he had been reassigned from the sea gates and he missed having a neutral party to confide in.

"I hear the messengers from Gwynedd are expected back today," Tudno remarked as the two chatted while the congregation began to file out of the abbey. "I pray that they bring good news of your father."

"Perhaps," Taliesin replied. "I don't think Maelgwn will release him anytime soon, not until both kings agree to the ransom."

"I'm so sorry for you, Tali, my whole family is." Taliesin had refrained from telling Tudno the exact reason he had been moved from the sea gates. He knew Tudno understood what the gatekeeper could be like at his worst. He didn't see why he should give Tudno any more reason to be ashamed of his father. In any case, it would violate the agreement he made with Seithenyn to stay quiet.

"Thank you," Taliesin said simply. "You heard that I'm no longer apprenticing at the sea gates, right?"

"No!" Tudno raised his eyebrows in surprise. "Dad hardly ever talks to us about his post. He didn't wallop you, did he?"

"No, not so much."

"What happened then?"

"Uh...I had a small accident. Nearly jammed the gates stuck

and risked flooding the entire harbor."

Tudno only gaped at him with wide eyes.

"And he still didn't wallop you?!" he asked in a whisper. Taliesin began to fear that he may have said too much until Tudno's giddy laughter rang throughout the stone abbey. "Ahaha! Taliesin! God grant me whatever charm you have on your head! I lost a brush once when I was small, and my dad took the skin off my backside for it!"

Despite himself, Taliesin began chuckling along too. It was the first time since Elphin's capture that he allowed himself to smile.

"So, you're off to the training grounds with Enid?" Tudno said as they walked back to the departing crowd.

"Yes, well it will be interesting to see how I find swordplay. I just hope Enid is merciful with her students."

"Right, you'll let me know if you need anything, cuz?" Tudno offered.

"Certainly!" Taliesin responded. He nearly jogged off towards the training grounds when he turned back suddenly. "Actually, you wouldn't happen to be headed towards Caer Wyddno, would you?"

Tudno shot him a quizzical look.

"Well, yes. I have a correspondence to take to the King from Father Gilgam."

"Would you seek out Bryn for me and ask if he could pay my house a visit this evening, after the dinner bell?"

Tudno unsuccessfully attempted to hide his irritation. "I suppose, but what for? Gilgam says the bard spreads lies against the church."

"I'm not asking him for a theology lecture," Taliesin replied. "I just wanted him to tell some stories."

"Stories? What for? You've heard every one of his stories since you were seven."

"I wasn't asking for me."

"Who then?" Tudno asked. Taliesin watched as his friend's puzzled expression melted into exasperation. "Oh godfathers! The sweeping girl? The one that soured the parchment ink?"

"Her name's Mererid," Taliesin answered. "And if you think it's because we're sweethearts you've got the wrong idea completely."

"You've got the wrong idea too if you think that Dad will give her time off to listen to children's tales."

"He won't have to," Taliesin tried his best to keep from snapping at Tudno. "She's been reassigned to our kitchen, and I only thought to help her feel at home. You know, show her some kindness."

"She must have been very kind to get such a cozy place near the warm oven for the winter. See if she's so kind come summer when she fancies tending the royal gardens."

"You really don't understand what you're talking about." Taliesin couldn't stop an edge creeping into his voice. Tudno took the hint and only sniffed. "Will you please summon Bryn for me if you see him?" Taliesin asked more gently.

"Fine, if I see him then," Tudno said at length. "But don't come blubbering to me when you find out what that minx is truly like."

"Appreciate it, Tud." Taliesin watched as the taller boy stalked over to his horse. He suddenly felt very happy to bring the conversation to a close.

***

Mererid had barely spent three days working in Elphin's kitchen but quickly integrated herself into the daily routine of the tower. Crissiant still reserved her suspicion of the crafty young lady, but she couldn't ignore the cook's praise for her new assistant.

"She picks everything up so quick, Mum!" Heida, the portly cook, told Crissiant. "She's particularly fond of baking. I have her making rolls and sweets non-stop all day. And to think that she told me she's never seen a proper kitchen before. She's sharp, that one!"

Crissiant did not object to having extra food on the table but still took care to keep the maiden at work and away from her foster son as much as possible. Aside from distracting her young boy, the maid's entry inevitably began to disrupt the smooth schedule that Crissiant kept in her tower. If she couldn't control her errant husband or her dreamy-eyed son, she could at least maintain control of her own house.

So, it came as a great surprise, and not a particularly welcome one for Crissiant, when Bryn knocked at the tower door that evening asking for Taliesin.

"Taliesin?' Crissiant asked over the wood dining table. "What is the meaning of you calling the royal bard here? This is hardly the time for merriment!"

Taliesin had spent the better part of that day learning how to swing a three-and-a-half-pound broadsword. His arm felt like a dead animal hanging from his shoulder. He speedily crammed another mouthful of bread into his mouth, buying him time to think. Bryn stepped into the room, looking like a wild hare that had wandered into a battlefield.

"Mmmm--I--mmmh--I had just thought to pass the hour before bed with a few stories, mother. Just for a bit of comfort."

"Stories?! What does Bryn know that you haven't heard a hundred times before?"

"But, Mam, it's not for me! It's for the new girl!" Taliesin regretted saying it even as his words left his mouth. "Just to help her feel at home," he added sheepishly.

"But she is *not* in her home, is she? She's in our home."

"Then we should welcome her as a guest, she's done more than her fair share here so far."

"Don't talk back to me!" Crissiant said crossly. "If you wanted to play host you should have discussed it with me first. Bryn will have to come back another night."

"But he's here now!" Taliesin all but whined.

"Begging your pardon, my lady," Bryn spoke up. "But it was a cold and miserable ride over here from the palace. At the least, I would be obliged to you if I could enjoy a hot cup of mead before returning. I'd happily offer you the story for your hospitality."

Crissiant looked back and forth from her foster son to the bard, feeling clearly outnumbered. She sighed in exasperation.

"You won't perform any blasphemous stories, will you Bryn?"

"Only what you and your foster son wish of me."

"Fine," the elegant lady pouted. "Only this once. But I insist on hearing the story as well."

"Oh, that's very thoughtful of you mother, but you don't have to trouble yourself if you have other things you'd rather-"

"I'm sure there is nothing else at all I'd rather be doing. Go and fetch your new friend quickly and have Heida prepare some mead for Bryn."

Taliesin sulked away to find Mererid and the head cook. He had hoped to treat Mererid to a private show and getting Bryn to tell his more exciting stories about the great battles and daring fights of Arthur's time. Now he worried that his gesture would seem childish and naive with his mother hawking over the two of them.

The young boy heaved open the wooden door to the kitchen, basking in the heat that wafted out of the crowded room. The smell of freshly baked bread washed over him. Two servants scurried around Heida as she issued orders for what needed to be prepared for the next day's meals. Unwashed pots and pans sat next to a tub in one corner and a large oven stood on the opposite side of the room over a bed of smoldering coals. Taliesin spotted Mererid hunched over a table sprinkled with white flour, kneading a ball of dough. Her face lit up when she saw the young boy.

"Tali! Look here! I'm kneading rye dough for breakfast tomorrow. See?" She held up the light brown dough. "I've always wanted to do this, isn't the smell just grand?"

"It's heavenly!" Taliesin agreed. "Do you have much left to do? The King's bard happened to stop by, and I convinced him to tell us a story."

"And who is bothering my newest assistant?" a stern voice demanded behind Taliesin. He turned to see Heida, her swarthy frame dwarfing his own. "What's this talk I hear about bards and stories now?"

"Heida! I'm glad I found you!" Taliesin said with faux enthusiasm. "My mam asked for you to bring in some hot mead when you get the chance."

"Don't try to brush me off, sonny! I need all the help I can get if you want to eat more than stale bread for breakfast in the morning!"

"But missus, I've just about finished," Mererid said brightly. "Just give me an hour and I'll do double dish duty after."

"Hmmm." Heida considered the offer. "The dishes and be here early in the morning for prepping and you've got a deal. Don't forget to bring in her lady's precious mead with you." The swarthy woman turned and stalked off. Mererid brushed off her hands and took off the apron from her slender waist.

"I hope your bard is as good as they say he is," she said with a wink to Taliesin.

***

"Croeso! Croeso! Croeso! Welcome one and all!" Bryn said over his cup of mead to his three audience members. Crissiant sat elegantly on her wooden chair while Taliesin and Mererid sat cross-legged on the floor like two eager siblings. Bryn slung his harp over his shoulder and plucked at the strings, checking their pitch.

"What can this humble bard offer his host on this dark winter eve? A song, perhaps? A thrilling story? Or maybe my audience would be content for me to recount the lineage of kings past?"

"Oh heavens, no!" Mererid said while laughing. "Anything but that!"

"I agree, Bryn," Crissiant said, bemused. "There's no need to waste the night talking about Gwyddno's ancestors. You wouldn't happen to know any hymns from St. David?"

"That, I'm afraid, is more the abbot's repertoire than mine, my lady," Bryn answered politely. "I have a few ballads of old if you'd prefer something musical."

"I'm for a story, myself!" Taliesin said, trying to contain his child-like excitement. "What about the one of the lady made from flowers? Or the one with the Lunantisidhe!"

"Oh! What are they?" Mererid asked, intrigued.

"The Lunantisidhe are the Fae folk who wander the woods guarding the sacred trees," Bryn explained. "They can be gracious every so often, but more likely they act beastly and mean with humans. Humans are, after all, the only creature that chop trees down for no better reason than to drive a cart through the forest. Some Lunantisidhe will rip a man's throat out and then take his tongue to the high Lord of Annwn himself, in exchange for-"

"I'll not have another word!" Crissiant said, cutting off the bard. "You promised to keep your stories away from blasphemies like the sidh and fairies. Let's have something more pleasant, or you can get back to the frigid cold!"

"Don't you believe in the sidh folk, milady?" Mererid asked.

"I most certainly do! They are in league with the devil. Mentioning them at all invites bad luck and that's something I can't tolerate right now." Crissiant sniffed suddenly.

"Let's have another story, Bryn," Taliesin suggested tactfully. "Why not tell us a story about Granddad. How did he come to be King of the Hundred? How did he build the great sea wall?"

"Hmmm," Bryn scratched at his chin. "That's another story that can't rightly be told without mentioning the fae folk. Perhaps, instead…" His eyes pushed their way up and back as he thought, as if he were trying to read something inside his own skull.

"Why not this one!" he exclaimed. "This, the story of the Ford of Gwyddno Garanhir, a history. Well, more of an anecdote. I was there myself to see the strange and eerie events that day."

"Oh, yes! Go on then!" Mererid pleaded. "I only have an

hour to myself, and I still haven't heard my story yet!"

Bryn lifted his harp and strummed several chords for effect. He drew himself to his full height, sighed deeply, and then began.

"Only twelve years ago last spring, war had broken out north of Hadrian's Wall. The Saxons had begun to regroup after Arthur's passing and all the kingdoms of Britain were called to help destroy the growing pest while the Saxons were vulnerable. Gwyddno Garanhir, the forces of Rheged, Gwynedd, Dyfed, the warriors of Powys, and the Picts were successful in driving the band back to the eastern shores. Victorious, Gwyddno rode with our warriors back to Cantre'r Gwaelod.

"I rode near the back of the train, doing my best to run through the details of the bloody carnage I had the misfortune of witnessing during the battle. I was still green as an orator and had just newly been appointed the King's bard after my master, the previous bard, had choked to death on his own vomit after a night of heavy debauchery. In my training, I had learned many secrets of memory, music, and rhythm, but nothing had prepared me for witnessing a battle. I had to walk, unarmed, through pits of men gnashing and clawing at each other like dogs, their violence driven by a terrifying determination not to die. I was supposed to be immune to any danger as a bard and historian, but the Saxons don't have the same customs as us. I had to act fast on several occasions to avoid getting an eye gouged out or a pike through my chest."

Bryn jumped and dodged imaginary blows as he acted out the gruesome battle. His audience of three marveled at the tall bard's agility and speed. Bryn mimed being choked by the pole of a spear against his throat. He gagged and lashed out in a panic.

"When suddenly Gywddno Garanhir's sword sliced my assailant's head clean off, leaving me soaked through with the cur's blood!"

"For pity's sake! Spare us the gory details!" Crissiant objected.

"In any case," Bryn continued seamlessly, "we had been

riding four days and were nearly in sight of the first towers of home when we stopped at a curious stream. The water itself flowed swiftly, yet silently. Even as the water rushed over the rocks, not a sound could be heard. Along the banks of the river bloomed every flower of summer, brighter than the morning stars, but it was only early spring.

Gwyddno and his company dismounted. We marveled at the stream and dipped our hands in. The water had what I might describe as a silvery texture. None of us dared to taste the enchanted water.

"'Who knows what stream this is?' the King called out. One of the knights stepped forward.

"' My Lord, I recognize this from my boyhood. It is the stream that runs down from the hills near Llyn Cynwch. In all my years growing up in the hills I have never seen the water behave like this, nor have I seen flowers bloom this early in the season.

"' These waters must be enchanted,' Gwyddno announced. 'Is there a crossing nearby?'

"' There are none that I know of this far up the stream, Sire,' the knight replied. 'It would take a day or two to retrace our steps.'

"Hearing this, many of the men began grumbling and fidgeted restlessly. Beyond the stream, their warm beds and wives lay only a few hours' ride away. I, myself, had a sweetheart back home just aching to run and throw her legs around me.

"Isn't that 'throw her arms around you?" Taliesin asked innocently. Mererid snickered.

"I know what I said, lad!" Bryn answered before continuing. "Anyway, Gwyddno evidently shared the company's impatience.

"'Fie on it!' the King muttered, and, without a word, he led his horse by the reins into the shallows of the stream. At its deepest, the water only came up to the horse's knee, throughout the whole crossing, not a single splash or trickle of water could be heard, just the sound of forest birds and the men's astonishment. Gwyddno passed through the stream unphased and waved us over from the other side. We followed our King's lead and forded the horses steadily across.

"Nearly the last of us had crossed over and Gwyddno and his men were making ready to mount and continue home when one of the horses began lapping at the water. 'Hey now, charger!' one of Gwyddno's men called. 'Don't be taking any of that! It must be bewitched.'

"' Let him!' Gwyddno responded to the knight. 'There aren't any dead animals by the water, only strong healthy plants and fish. It's queer, the water, but I doubt it could be dangerous. Let the horses drink their fill, so that we may ride fiercely up to our gates in celebration!'

"Hearing this, we all allowed the horses to drink and each one gulped down a small tub's worth of water. Finally, we made to continue the ride home, when one of the horses began stamping his feet and shaking his mane. The horse began braying and lifting his head. One by one the other mounts began copying this behavior like something was dancing around the horses driving them wild. The riders tried to soothe and then demand calm from the horses, but they only began kicking and rearing, their shouts making a horrifying din. Any rider who sat on top of his horse was flung off and the King's own horse shook his head savagely from side to side. Many would later say that the horses were overcome with fits of madness and knew not what they were doing. But I saw something different that day. As I tried to settle my own horse down, I glanced into the beast's wide eye, and I saw...an awareness...perhaps. A glint of intelligence that sages and small children possess when they look at the world. I am certain that the stream imbued the horses with the knowledge of men that day and they seemed aware for the first time of the bridle in their mouths and the saddle on their backs. I believe that the poor horses understood, for the first time, their place in the world and understood the world of men better than I did. I allowed the reins to slip past my fingers as the horse yanked himself free, my entire being filled with a dark shame.

"Gwyddno and his men shouted and wrestled desperately with their mounts, but it was no use. In a massive cloud of dust, the horses broke free and raced off in every direction. We searched the bogs and fields around the stream the best we could but found no trace of the horses. We were left with no choice but to return home on foot. Our company arrived at the Aberstywllch gates a day late, our victory in the north tainted by the loss of our horses."

Bryn finished his tale with a long pull of mead. Crissiant grumbled something to herself while Mererid stared raptly at the bard.

"I remember hearing that story twelve years ago!" Crissiant said haughtily. "I didn't believe it then, and I don't believe it now. Really, how could a rushing stream of water not make a single splash?"

"Were that I was a sorcerer myself, mistress, that I would know," Bryn said with a shrug.

"I think you all made a ruckus at an alehouse on the road and had the horses stolen from under you while you slept," Crissiant insisted.

"Did father ride to battle as well with Grandad?" Taliesin inquired.

"No, he was out tending the fishing weirs," Bryn reported. "He offered to ride with us, but many in Gwyddno's company thought it would bring ill-luck. A strange thing too, because shortly after we lost the horses, Elphin had a great stroke of luck indeed -" Bryn suddenly shut his mouth and an expression of shock crossed his face for an instant. He seemed to exchange a panicked look with Crissiant before adding, "-but as for the horses, we found only a few a week or two afterwards wandering the fields of Ceredigion, worn thin by the weather but otherwise healthy. The madness of the horses remains a mystery to this day."

"What was that about Elphin's stroke of luck?" Taliesin pressed.

"Right then!" Crissiant announced loudly. "You've had your stories, and you've had your mead, Bryn. I'll give the highest reviews to the King for you, now you may be off!" Taliesin's mother rose from her chair and waved her arms at the bard like an angry goose. Bryn took his cue and bowed low to Taliesin and Mererid before heading off.

"God save you then!" he called back.

"Mererid, dear. I believe it's time you return to Heida for your evening chores," Crissiant told the younger girl. Her tone made it clear that it was not a suggestion.

"Right away, mum!" Mererid replied. She looked back at the chair that Crissiant had sat in. A spool of yarn and a sewing kit lay haphazardly on the small blue cushion "Oh, my lady! Beg pardon, but you'd best take care that you don't lose your embroidery! It's awfully easy to misplace needles in this dim light."

Crissiant murmured a thank you and turned to gather up the delicate sewing. As quick as a fox, Mererid turned and silently pressed a kiss on Taliesin's cheek as she made her way to the doorway. She pushed her lips to his ear. Taliesin could feel her hot breath on the side of his face.

"Thanks for the story, love," she whispered quickly. "Come to the North Gardens at daybreak."

Crissiant looked up from the chair only to see Mererid's back as she drifted out of the room and her twelve-year-old son beaming from ear to ear.

***

Due to Cantre'r Gwaelod's unique location, on the floor of what was formerly Cardigan Bay, the whole kingdom resembled a gigantic bowl, with the center of the kingdom sunken in lower than the perimeter walls. By nature, some parts of the kingdom received more sunlight than others, particularly during the dim winter days. The interior side of the southern edge of the bowl had its view of the sun blocked by the bordering mountainside almost year-round. The northern portion of the walled kingdom, by contrast, enjoyed uncompromised sunlight even in winter. Here, along the landside border, gardeners made the most of the strong sun and grew fresh crops, exotic fruit, and tracks of the most stunning flowers in all of Britain.

The North Gardens were one of the brightest jewels of Cantre'r Gwaelod.

Taliesin had none of his usual difficulty rising out of bed the next morning. Before the sun illuminated the horizon over Ceredigion's hills, the boy was already jogging over the causeway that led north from Elphin's tower. He had visited the North Gardens several times before but never felt as much enthusiasm for them as he did that morning.

He arrived just as the sun poked up over the eastern hills. Mererid was already waiting for him and waved him over to where she stood, admiring a patch of geraniums.

"I hope I haven't gotten you into more trouble than I should," she explained. "I know that Enid expects you to be punctual for training."

"I can make up some excuse. That I had to escort mother to church this morning, maybe."

"It's your skin, then," Mererid replied with a smirk. "Anyway, I can't linger very long myself. Heida will be looking for me soon to knead the rye again."

"How did you enjoy Bryn's story last night?"

"Oh! It was a treat! I haven't had anyone tell me stories like that since my mother would tell bedtime stories to my sister and me."

"Does your mother also work as a maid?" Taliesin asked impulsively.

"No, love. She died back before we came to the Lowland Hundred. She would tell us all kinds of fairy tales and songs. She may have been a minstrel herself when she was younger. She knew all sorts of rhymes."

"Really?" Taliesin asked, enchanted. "Did she sing, like you?"

Mererid laughed and waved her hand dismissively. "No, but I imagine that I sing like her."

"Do you remember any of her songs? I love to hear new

verses from other places. Bryn is talented, but there's only so many rhymes one head can hold."

"I try to repeat them to myself while I'm hard at work. It helps me pass the time and it gives me something to remember her by."

"Would you tell me one?"

Mererid looked at the boy with a hint of suspicion, like he was a child asking to play with a precious glass bottle. She swept her gaze across the sparkling flowers and let her eyes finally wander out west to the small thin line of the sea over the distant gray wall. She chanted softly.

"Whence is the dew pleasant?
Whence is wheat a blessing?
What attracts bees from shelter and storm?
What lies hidden beyond the sea?"

Mererid wove the flowing words together with her musical voice and Taliesin thought that the morning breeze itself held still to listen.

"Don't go repeating that around carelessly. I wouldn't want to hear my mother's songs bawled out from the sots in the alehouse."

"I don't think anyone in Wales could sing your songs better than you, not even a talented singer like Bryn."

Mererid only smiled coyly.

"Truth be told," she said, "I would have much rather have heard of the Lunantisidhe from your bard last night."

"Me too, but I didn't want to upset Mother. She acts brave and all, but I know that she's worried for Elphin. I am too, I suppose."

"I should expect you are! It seems to me you've barely had any sleep."

"Well, that's nothing out of the ordinary," Taliesin admitted. "I usually get rather frightening dreams at night."

Mererid only favored Taliesin with a smile as bright as the crisp winter morning, her eyes eagerly searching his.

"I hardly ever remember much of my dreams. I'm so tired by the time I lay myself down," she said. "I should love to hear what some of yours are all about."

"Oh, no. I'm afraid they'd scare you."

"Nonsense!" Mererid braced her arm against her hip. "Come now! I shared a line of song with you, you can give us a dream in return."

Taliesin hesitated. Even when he talked about his dreams with his mother, or reported them to Father Gilgam, he would always leave out details he wasn't prepared to share. He nearly backpedaled from the topic, but, before Taliesin knew it, a soft cool hand entwined its way into his own. He looked up to see Mererid's pleading expression and began to pour everything out.

"Well, I'm not always sure how they begin, sometimes I feel like I'm tending a great hearth, or working in a hot dark room. I always get the feeling that there's something out in the shadows of the room that's watching me, but I can never see it. Then, something happens, but what it is I can never tell. I always feel a huge rush go through my body, but it all happens in my head. It's hard to explain like my body turns into the very air it touches, and my thoughts come by so fast I can hardly tell what they were. It feels like I could do anything, anything I wanted to, but I also hold all the heartache in the world."

Taliesin glanced over, wondering if Mererid was frightened by what he was saying. He only saw her eyes riveted to him in quiet anticipation.

"What happens then?" she asked.

"Then....then I feel like I have to run, like I have to run fast away from there as soon as I can and never come back. As soon as I start running, I can hear something chasing me. The faster I try to run, the closer I hear it. I can never tell what it is. Sometimes it's a huge vicious hound, sometimes it's a giant hawk or a bear. And I always feel like I'm so small and helpless, like a frightened rabbit or a mouse."

"Oh, I've had dreams like that!" said Mererid. "My sister too. I think everyone has nightmares like that when they're young."

"You said you don't remember your dreams," he countered.

"Yes, well, I imagine I must have dreams like that then."

"And what else do you imagine you dream of at night?" Taliesin asked, happily shifting the topic away from himself.

"Ha! Not of sweeping floors or scrubbing dishes, that I can say!" Mererid laughed.

"You don't fancy life as a chambermaid?" Taliesin felt a little ashamed of his princely status suddenly.

"Hard to believe but, no, not particularly. I suppose at night, I dream about what I think of during the day. You do know why I requested a post in a kitchen, yes?"

"To be away from the gatekeeper."

"Oh, well, yes, but besides all that. No, Tali, remember my mother died when I was still young, and I never learned how to properly cook or bake. Now, what type of man would bother with someone who couldn't cook?"

Taliesin tried to hide his displeasure at Mererid mentioning other men. Judging by the maid's fit of laughter, he didn't succeed.

"Steady now, young sir, I don't have anyone in mind for the job yet. But it has always been my dream to marry a handsome fellow and keep my own house for a change. And when I have daughters of my own, I'll teach them at once to bake delicious bread."

Suddenly, a cloud blotted out the bright morning sun, and in the distance, a faint claxon of horns sounded over the hills. The boy and young lady turned towards the east to see a strange sight emerge from the forest line on the other side of the wall. A small escort of horsemen was riding south towards the gates of Cantre'r Gwaelod, their flags specks on the distant hillside.

"Look!" Mererid shouted. "Isn't that Gwynedd's flag? Riders have come with news of Lord Elphin perhaps!"

Taliesin squinted into the eastern sunlight. The riders flew banners of red and gold crossed and embroidered with what looked like the lion of Gwynedd. The group of riders galloped swiftly down the sloping hillside until they passed directly in front of the rising sun, making Taliesin wince. As they passed farther down the hill, away from the sun, a strange and disturbing sight caught Taliesin's eye: in the center of the group of horsemen, charging forward at the same pace, was not a rider, but rather a monstrous, feral wolf. The closer Taliesin peered into the glaring light, the more he could make out the thick coal-black coat, raised menacingly on the creature's back. He could see the beast's powerful claws rip the countryside beneath him as he ran and glinting in the sunlight were razor-sharp fangs dripping with thick drool. The nightmare of a wolf was just as big as the horses surrounding him.

"Mererid!" Taliesin said, beside himself with fear. "In the middle of the pack. What do you see? Can you make it out?"

Mererid shielded her eyes from the sun and raised her head higher. "I see, maybe the head messenger, or a knight perhaps. He's rather tall and has a dark cape flying out behind him. He's riding a dark gray stallion."

Taliesin snapped his head back to the riders who had already passed by and were making their way to the city's main gate. In the center, he could only see the tall knight that Mererid had described, his cape flying out wildly behind him. There was no sign of any ferocious wolf.

"I think I'd better report to Enid," Taliesin said at last. "Something tells me she'll be with the King."

"Aren't you excited that we might have news of Lord Elphin?" Mererid asked, her eyebrows knitted.

"Maybe, but I'm worried what kind of news we'll hear today. Fare you well, see you this evening!" Taliesin replied before darting off down the causeway.

CHAPTER 7: A Prince's Ransom

Aduwyn gaer yssyd ar ton nawuet.
aduwyn eu gwerin yn ymwaret.
ny wnant eu dwynuyt trwy veuylhaet.
nyt ef eu defawt bot yn galet.

There is a fair fort upon the ninth wave;
Fair its folk in resting themselves.
They do not make their pleasant life through shame;
'Tis not their custom to be stingy.

~Etmic Dybych, Llyfr Taliesin

The arrival of Gwynedd's riders ignited Caer Wyddno into motion like a dry hay bale catching fire. Usually sleepy and quiet during the first few hours of the morning, the fortress now clanged with activity and motion. Knights rushed to and fro in their brilliant armor. Standard bearers and heralds swarmed the turrets of the castle walls while foot servants scurried about in a mad state of confusion. Archers and pikemen were ordered to the eastern gate that opened to Ceredigion's countryside. For the arrival of only five riders, Cantre'r

Gwaelod might as well have prepared for war.

As Taliesin ran down the stone pathway towards the castle, he could see the soldiers surrounding the group of foreign horsemen as they trotted down the main causeway towards the King's castle. Up close, Taliesin could see that the Gwynedd envoys were men and horses only. There was no sign that the group had anything close to a wolf with them.

Four warriors with plumed helmets marched in a diamond formation around a richly adorned man, riding a dressed stallion. He wore no helmet and let his black hair fly back over his shoulders. A dark charcoal grey cape whipped behind him. His expression, while smug, gave him away as a first-time visitor to Gwyddno's realm. The crash of the ocean waves on the sea wall tended to bounce off the whole curved border of Cantre'r Gwaelod and echo loudest in the center of the kingdom. As a result, Caer Wyddno seemed to roar with the sea's voice from time to time, making it feel like the ocean was right below the castle and crashing waves could spring up at any moment. The caped rider, more amused than frightened, would dart his face one way then another, instinctually looking for the phantom sea.

Taliesin ran the rest of the way down the stone bridge towards the castle and rounded a wide corner to place him on the same causeway the visitors were riding on. A crowd of onlookers had already begun to gather behind the Lowland Hundred soldiers. Taliesin squirmed his way to the front of the crowd and immediately regretted it.

Saddled on horseback, her armor blinding in the bright sunlight, sat Enid, captain of the palace guard. Her silver and coal-black hair was swept neatly to the side of her scalp and her face looked chiseled from stone as she watched the men from Gwynedd ride up to meet her. Her horse stood at the point of a small phalanx of knights that blocked the entrance to the King's tower. For a moment, Taliesin wondered if he should stay still or try to slither back into the crowd and avoid Enid's attention altogether. While

Taliesin deliberated, his legs decided for him, and he instinctually staggered backwards. The motion was all it took to attract the astute captain's attention and she shot Taliesin a lightning-quick look before turning her head back to the visitors. The brief glance was all it took to broadcast Enid's displeasure with her tardy student.

At last, the five horsemen arrived in front of the knights of Cantre'r Gwaelod and brought their steeds to a perfect stop. For a moment, the two groups of mounted, armored fighters stood still while the center rider from Gwynedd shot Enid a warm, toothy smile like the two were old friends.

"Hail! You must be King Gwyddno's woman captain. We of the northern kingdom have heard many tales of you."

Enid stared back at the Gwynedd man, hardly twitching a single muscle.

"We bring tidings from King Maelgwn of Gwynedd. I'd like to deliver my message to King Gwyddno with all speed-"

"Have you brought Prince Elphin back?" Enid asked bluntly.

The man from Gwynedd shrugged off the question. "That is what we have come to discuss. Can you show us to the King, or should we start shouting for him?"

Enid made a curt nod to her attending knights as they wheeled their mounts around. "Follow this way. Your horses will be taken to the stables for you."

"Thank you," the rider said with a grin. "And make sure you announce to your King that Prince Rhun of Gwyn--"

"I know who you are," Enid barked out. She nudged her horse forward, leaving the prince to follow in her wake.

It took Taliesin a second to recognize the man's name. Rhun, Prince Rhun, the eldest son of Maelgwn of Anglesey, renowned for his sharp cunning. He could feel the crowd around him slowly react to Rhun's name. Whispers and murmurs snaked through the ears of all standing outside Gwyddno's castle. Those whispers would soon get carried down to the harbor on the morning breeze and then would make their way over the water passages to every home in the

Lowland Hundred. The Dragon of the Isle had sent his crown prince to negotiate for Elphin's freedom. The buzz kicked up by the news and rumors would ensure that all eyes were on King Gwyddno in whatever discourse ensued.

Taliesin let the flow of the crowd carry him down the causeway behind Rhun's escort and into the tower. Stable hands met the riders in the castle courtyard to relieve them of their horses before proceeding on foot. Taliesin side-stepped around the bulk of the crowd and began darting through the pillars that led to Gwyddno's throne room.

Maybe he had only imagined that Enid had spotted him. Maybe he'd be lucky, and the commotion of the morning would distract Enid enough so that she wouldn't think about punishing Taliesin for missing his sunrise training session. Taliesin knew he had taken a risk by agreeing to see Mererid in the gardens that morning, but the rational part of his mind that understood the risk had been strangely silent.

Until now at least.

Taliesin did his best to stay as inconspicuous as possible, only daring to move over to the next pillar when he was sure that Enid was looking the other way. Even while trying to keep out of sight from Enid and her knights, he made sure to keep one eye on Rhun's sweeping fur cape as he strode through palace halls.

Taliesin succeeded in getting as far as the throne room door, pleased to see one of the great, turquoise-plated doors slightly ajar. Checking again to see that Enid was distracted, Taliesin prepared to quickly slip through the opening and act the picture of innocence once on the other side. That plan fell short as Tudno's lanky frame stumbled out of the throne room carrying a spent pot of oil.

"Taliesin!" Tudno called out far louder than necessary. "God keep you cousin! Shouldn't you have been with Enid this mor--"

Taliesin's hand clamped firmly over Tudno's mouth as he pulled him into a narrow alcove set in the wall. Tudno's eyes screamed questions at Taliesin, but he kept silent as the guards approached the doors just a few feet away. The lead guard lifted a massive bronze ring attached to the door and rapped four and then three times, signaling a matter of extreme urgency. The doors were immediately pulled open from the inside and the waiting crowd of knights and curious lords of the court were pulled in as if a great whale were engulfing a school of fish.

Taliesin took advantage of the scuffling crowd and hurried Tudno inside the throne room, managing to squeeze them into a small corner near the back.

"What's all the commotion?" Tudno finally asked under the din of the crowd.

"That tall man with the fur cape is Maelgwn's son, Rhun. He just arrived to negotiate over my father's release," Taliesin summarized. Tudno blinked rapidly, coming to terms with the surprise.

"Let's go for a closer look, then!" Tudno tried to push his way through the forest of onlookers, but Taliesin caught his robe and held him.

"We can see plenty from here. I'm trying to avoid Enid, see? I was a little late to archery practice today."

Tudno made a face that obnoxiously mirrored Father Gilgam's expression of moral disapproval.

"You'll get lashes for that," he chided.

"Which is exactly why I don't care to move up front!" Taliesin said crossly. Tudno took the hint and backed off. Taliesin surveyed the incoming faces and noticed several knights who usually didn't attend regular court. Connwn and his men from Powys filed in along with Lord Elby from Dyfed. In his usual place, off to the left of the throne, sat Bryn. He absently tuned his harp but stopped and reared himself up high as he caught sight of Rhun, fixing him with a glare. Rhun barely noticed.

"Do you think this might be promising?" Tudno whispered. "Maelgwn wouldn't send his own son unless he was keen on making a deal, wouldn't you say?"

"That could be," Taliesin admitted, wondering why all his nerves were burning. "Something feels wrong though. He arrived too suddenly out of nowhere. Maelgwn may just be trying to push us off balance." A thought occurred as he spoke. "What were you doing in the throne room anyway, Tud?" he asked his cousin.

"I came to fill the candles with the church's oil. The King only uses oil that was blessed by Gilgam. Here's Granda' now!"

"All Hail! King Gwyddno Garanhir!" Enid shouted out to the court. The King strode easily to his marble throne, turned to regard the visitors, and then sat down, narrowing his gaze at Maelgwn's prince.

"Well, Rhun, go and introduce yourself," he said finally.

Rhun stepped forward and dropped to his knee. "Hail, O' Neighbor King Gwyddno!" he said simply, "It's rather impressive you still remember me, after so many years since we last fought together."

"That, and I was told by five different people this morning that you had arrived at my tower. So, indulge us then! To what do I owe this surprise?"

Rhun stood up and threw his cape back over one shoulder. "My father, Maelgwn, King of Gwynedd, would like to express his thanks on your counteroffer in the matter of Lord Elphin's ransom-"

"That would be Prince Elphin, go on," the King interjected.

"Nevertheless," Rhun continued seamlessly, "a handful of livestock hardly seems appropriate for the ransom of a prince. King Maelgwn has demanded the countryside of Ceredigion in exchange for Elphin's safe return. Truly, that is a more fitting price for a father's firstborn."

The court audibly balked at this while heads turned in different directions, wondering if battle was imminent. Gwyddno's face hardly twitched.

"It may be," he agreed, "but it's bad policy for my subjects whom I swore to protect. As King, I have more than just family obligations to consider, as any king or queen should understand."

"Isn't that a bit harsh of Grandad?" Tudno whispered to Taliesin. "I thought the King missed Elphin."

"Of course, he does, Tud!" Taliesin whispered back, irritated. Gwyddno continued.

"At present, I'm curious about another option." He tilted his head back as if he were considering a mathematics puzzle. "Wouldn't it be fairest to trade for something of mine with the same of Maelgwn's? Wouldn't the most fitting ransom for a first-born prince be another prince? Please, Rhun, give me a reason why I shouldn't shackle you this instant and keep you held here, in Caer Wyddno, until my own son is returned?"

The four of Rhun's escorts let their arms drop down to the hilt of their swords. Taliesin felt the tension in the room begin to simmer. The only calm face was Rhun's as the prince smiled good-naturedly.

"Now then, dear cousin…" Rhun said, lifting his open arms.

"That would be 'dear Uncle' to you actually, am I mistaken bard?" the King threw a glance at Bryn.

"Distant uncle," Bryn confirmed with little humor.

"Very well, uncle," Rhun said with a drop of agitation. "Please, hear me out. My father is very aware of the sensitive nature of our negotiations and it's for that very reason he sent me personally. If we cannot agree on a reasonable price for Elphin's return, you are welcome to hold me prisoner until we do."

Gwyddno squeezed his face together, perplexed. "And what would Maelgwn consider reasonable this time?" he asked cautiously.

"King Maelgwn would ask that you consider thirty head of cattle, no less than twelve chests of gold, and grant Gwynedd three ships of my choosing from the great harbor of Caer Wyddno. Grant us this, and Elphin will be returned in no less than a week's time."

"…I see," Gwyddno said after a pause. "And while we wait for Elphin's return, I take it you would remain here as…collateral?"

"I shall happily subject myself to your darkest dungeon until our kingdoms reach a deal that honors us both," Rhun said, his face a painting of angelic innocence.

Gwyddno's snowy eyebrows plucked up at this offer, and he brought his steepled fingers over his lips. The price was steep but fitting for a prince's ransom. Taliesin could only suspect that his grandfather would want a graceful solution to such a political quagmire. But could the Prince of Gwynedd be trusted?

Gwyddno turned his eyes out towards the lords of his court. For the briefest moment, his gaze seemed to linger on Taliesin, huddled more than fifteen yards away in the crowded room.

"This is a most interesting offer, Prince Rhun," the King said after some consideration. "But I should take time to hear the opinions of my court first. In the meantime, I will send for food and drink for you and your men and musicians to entertain you. We shall resume negotiations by nightfall, should it please you."

"That it would, your Majesty!" Rhun bowed so low it looked to Taliesin that he was presenting his hindquarters to the guards behind him. He watched as servants came to lead the men of Gwynedd away to their rooms. Taliesin noticed Rhun's bemused look as the prince admired the stone arches decorated with pearls and opals of the sea. He found himself wanting to spit out a bad taste in his mouth as he watched Rhun saunter down the halls as if he rightfully owned them himself.

King Gwyddno returned his attention to the crowd of spectators that filled his throne room. "I would see all my men at arms in the war chamber immediately, you as well, bard." He nodded towards Bryn. "As for everyone else, the court is dismissed. Go and occupy yourselves until I've reached a decision over this new offer. Leave us!"

With a wave of his hand, the throne room dissolved into a sea of movement as each person scurried to their next task or otherwise found the nearest friend to gossip with.

"Quick Tudno, out through the side entrance!" Taliesin prompted his cousin.

"Do you think Grandad will pay up? That was a hefty price

the prince asked."

"It's nothing Grandad can't afford, but I'm sure he'll try to bargain his way down as much as he can." Taliesin scanned the crowd in front of him trying to pinpoint Enid before she caught him by surprise.

"That must be such a relief for you, Tal!" Tudno yelled a little more loudly than Taliesin cared for. "Elphin will come home at last!"

"I wouldn't celebrate anything yet, I'm not sure about Prince Rhun's motives." Taliesin was privately excited about the two kingdoms potentially reaching a deal, but he vowed not to let his hopes up in case anything went sour. Neither did he enjoy the idea of his mother celebrating too early. He might be able to deal with disappointment right now, but the tear stains that dotted the kitchen tablecloth in his house betrayed his mother's fragility. He couldn't bear to see her suffer any more pain than she was already.

"I'll be off to the abbey, Father Gilgam will surely be thrilled," Tudno said, beaming.

"Right, but don't go blabbing about this to the whole church just yet, we still don't know wha-"

"Ah, there's my errant pupil!" A rich voice boomed over the din of the shuffling crowd. Taliesin whirled to see Enid's grinning face shining at him over her polished breastplate. "I was getting concerned when I found myself all alone for archery lessons this bright and early dawn."

"Oh, Captain Enid!" Taliesin yelped, feigning surprise. "I had been looking all over for you this whole morning. I spied Prince Rhun's band early from Elphin's tower as they rode over the hills to the east. I thought it my duty to rouse as many people as I could, including yourself, even though it meant sacrificing archery. I feared the Gwynedd men meant to stage an attack! Pity that I couldn't find you in time, but all's well in the end, eh?"

"Brilliant work, boyo! Brilliant, I must say!" Enid laughed cheerily as she let her gauntleted hand clap down heavily on Taliesin's shoulder. Taliesin had only made it to a handful of his training sessions with the flinty warrior, but he knew enough to hold his posture high when addressing the captain. Her unexpected exuberance did not put Taliesin at ease.

"uhm...Thank you, milady! As you so often advised, I thought to put my kingdom's needs before my own."

"Yes, by doing the job of the lookout instead of training with the rest of the company at dawn. Such selfless bravado from such a tender age." Taliesin did not like how the conversation was turning out.

"Well, anything for King and country. Speaking of which, I would be loath to keep you from the urgent meeting King Gwyddno has called so I'll just make my way -"

"-straight down to the tower kitchen, then? I like this ambition of yours, Tali!" Enid absently tightened the leather straps keeping her heavy scabbard tied to her hip. She waited for Taliesin to respond.

"Uhm...the tower kitchen you say? Yes, at once." Taliesin had played the game out as far as he could now. "And, if you could, please remind me what duty I should be performing at the tower kitchen, milady?"

"Why, to work off the ten demerits you've earned by running a fool's errand instead of showing up to your post on time, that's what!" Enid said with a broad smile. "Rhun didn't come within sight of Cantre'r Gwaelod's gates until well past sunrise, making you hours late in any case. Off you go then!"

Tudno couldn't help letting out a snicker at his cousin's slip. Enid's head snapped over to the page boy.

"And you'd do well to have some company with you, such as a loitering altar boy who just earned himself five demerits of his own by sneaking into the royal court without proper permission. What a bustling morning it's been indeed. I'll be down to talk with Cam later this evening, so don't be tempted to put off reporting to him another minute. So, until tomorrow, Taliesin!"

Enid snapped on her heel and sauntered off to the King's war room, humming pleasantly to herself. The two cousins could only exchange glares as they made their way down to find Cam, the tower kitchen master.

***

"Didn't I say that maid would be trouble? Didn't I say it?!" Tudno grumbled as he plunged a horsehair brush into the oily water pooling at the bottom of the porridge pot he was scrubbing. "I've been proven right in no time at all, and who's to suffer from it? How unfair that I should be paying the price for what I warned you not to do!?"

Taliesin couldn't say that he was enjoying picking off the burnt trimmings plastered to the sides of his own pot, but he would gladly wash twofold his share if he could do so without his cousin's constant griping.

"Pox on it! She's only been cozying up in the kitchen for less than a week before she's driven you to distraction. Here I am telling you not to give her a story, not to let her worm her way into the house while Uncle Elphin is gone, and already you've got your head screwed on backwards."

"You didn't need to stay in the throne room with me," Taliesin bit back. "You could have been off and away back to the abbot to listen to him drone on about Mary and Joseph."

"See if I don't next time! At least I wouldn't have to do the abbot's dishes!"

Taliesin couldn't help feeling a twinge of guilt for his cousin's predicament. Truthfully, he knew that Tudno was only being supportive and had ended up down here because of him. Even so, a week's worth of washing dishes seemed inconsequential compared to the morning's developments. As he attacked each cauldron in turn with his worn-out brush and handful of pig's tallow, he kept an eye up near the top window of the tower kitchen, the only source of natural light. He watched the sunbeam that spilled in slowly inch its way across the floor and then the wall. The blue slice of sky in the window had now turned a pale pink.

"Do you think Rhun and the King are still negotiating?" Taliesin asked, trying to change the topic.

"I suspect so, I saw the castle guard change over when I went up for more dishes. I haven't heard any horns or commotion, so I suspect the King's still in his conference room."

"I hope they settle on a fair trade," Taliesin muttered.

"Seems like they will, isn't Prince Rhun's life at stake? You heard Granda'. If things go sour, he can always chain Rhun up and offer him to Maelgwn for uncle. Eye for an eye."

"Seems like a very foolish mistake for the Dragon King to make," Taliesin pointed out. "There has to be something else going on here. Maelgwn is a butcher and a monster to be sure, but he's no idiot. Why put his own son in harm's way like that? What has he got to gain?"

Tudno shrugged, keeping his nose next to the slimy pot he was cleaning. "Who knows, Tal? Maybe he thinks Rhun is the best player to win him a pretty ransom."

"So why not meet in the countryside, on neutral ground? Why is Rhun so bloody sure of himself if he knows he's in danger? There's a rat here and it stinks to heaven."

"No, that's the rotten mackerel you're avoiding on that pile there." Tudno jabbed his brush at a stack of dishes buzzing loudly with black flies. "I tell you, it's as the abbot says. Trust in the Lord. Allow him to find the best path forward and resist the hubris of man. He who tries to lift a river will only drown."

"I don't need Sunday school lessons," Taliesin said irritably.

"Clearly you do!" Tudno barked. "If you had learned your lesson the first time around, we wouldn't be in this mess. I told you to leave your mop maid alone when she was scrubbing the sea towers. You wouldn't have been rushing about like a fool and she would be just as well off."

"Just as well off with the gatekeeper grabbing under her dress."

Tudno stopped scrubbing.

"What the devil are you talking about?"

Taliesin regretted it as soon as he said it. Not only because he had promised to keep quiet and let the matter stay in the past, but also for his cousin's sake. It was no secret that Seithenyn beat his children more than befit a nobleman, but of all his seven children, Tudno, the youngest, was the one that would always have new welts on his face to hide every week. Despite this, Taliesin always heard his cousin defend his father citing verses from the Bible and the Ten commandments. "He's mean and he can be cruel, but it's not God's will that the child should question the father. I've read it," Tudno would tirelessly insist. Taliesin knew that bringing up Seithenyn's vile nature would not just upset Tudno but would also risk bringing down Seithenyn's severe punishment on the boy if he found out he knew.

"Uhm...nothing Tud, it's nothing truly."

"That's not what it sounded like," Tudno pressed, his face turning darker. "Do you have some evil to accuse my dad of? I'm all ears!"

Taliesin made a quick glance back at the open chamber door, confirming that they were alone.

"During my apprenticeship," Taliesin did his best to sound casual, "I was up cleaning gears and he came back from the tavern nearly dead drunk. Mererid was scrubbing the tower stairs and when he passed by, he...well, he grabbed her Tudno." Taliesin could see Tudno's jaw constricting as he bit down on his cheek. "She told him to bugger off, he yelled something about a contract, and then she got him with the freezing cold wash water. I didn't see much of what happened next, but when I-"

"I'm not so sure how you could have seen any of what happened at all," Tudno interjected tersely. "Weren't you up scrubbing gears, or what have you? Isn't that what you said?"

"All I had to do was peek down the stairs, it was easy enough-"

"And how would you know your pretty maid wasn't teasing with dad? Did you think about that?"

"She told me herself what happened," Taliesin huffed.

"And you believed the wicked thing? I told you she runs against the church. I wouldn't trust her any more than I would a snake."

"He had her pinned down underneath him, Tudno!" Taliesin all but yelled. "Do you really feel that's something Uncle Seithenyn isn't capable of? When he's drunk and loses his temper?"

Tudno's face turned scarlet. His eyes were open wide, projecting his knee-jerk wrath. Inside that anger though, Taliesin could sense a cutting pain and anguish as part of him was forced to acknowledge Taliesin's point. Tudno stood still for a moment, a statue of rage, before chucking the metal pot he had across the room, letting it clatter loudly on the stone floor.

"What's with that nonsense down there?!" Cam, the kitchen chief, hollered. "I'll give you lashes myself if one of those pans gets dinged!"

Tudno only huffed out a sigh. "I'm pretty sure I've met my five demerits, I'll leave you to it, cousin," he said icily before barging out of the washroom.

"Gracious!" Cam's ruddy face poked in from the doorway on top of the small stair aisle. "Did Seithenyn's brat just head out? He did finish his washing, din'n he?"

Taliesin glanced over to the two-foot-high stack of iron pans and cauldrons heaped together with wooden spoons. He watched the small cloud of flies buzz around it as he considered how much more work he would end up doing tonight.

"Yes, he finished them," he lied.

CHAPTER 8: The Eaves Dropper

Beth gwadal Jdas?
Dovn aig, iawn adas

What should the lot of Judas be?
The sea would be a fit retribution

~Cadeir Taliessin, Llyfr Taliesin

The next morning, news that the ransom negotiations had ended bled out of Caer Wyddno with the rising sun. It flowed down to the harbor and ferry ports and drifted out along the great stone causeways. Every household opened its doors to the sound of neighbors and passers-by chattering among each other. Rumors abounded over what had taken place at the negotiation table. Some reported that Rhun's offer was an invitation to peace and accepting it could help forge a solid alliance between the two kingdoms. Others said that Rhun had followed up one impossible offer with another. In any case, each version of the news made the same promise; that Prince Elphin was coming home.

Taliesin might have been the last person in the whole kingdom to receive the news. He had left the castle kitchen late the night before and forced himself to return before dawn so he could meet Enid on the archery fields and avoid another week's worth of washing dishes. Part of the reason he had retired so late from the kitchen, aside from having to do Tudno's share of the washing, was restless curiosity. Every time he thought he could hear the conversations above, he would stop scrubbing and hoped they would divulge some news about the King's talks. When he left around midnight, he still had not heard a single word of it.

As Taliesin stood in the muddy archery pit, trying to string a bow that was as large as him, a rider sounded a trumpet and barreled down the causeway above them. Enid glanced up, her chain mail ringlets jingling musically with the movement.

"Well, come along then!" she barked out at Taliesin before turning on her heel and marching away across the sandy mud. Taliesin blinked through his fugue and trotted along after the captain.

"Are we not finishing training?" he asked, doing his best to stifle a yawn.

"A true soldier is never finished training," Enid replied. "But our King is about to make a proclamation. I have a duty to attend, and I would think you, of all people, should be very interested in what the King has to say."

"Well, of course!" Taliesin said, snapping wide alert. He trailed behind the powerful lady as the two made their way up the stone staircase that led to the outdoor court of Caer Wyddno. The steps were slick, and Taliesin had to concentrate to keep his footing.

"Weren't you at the negotiations? Do you know how they might have turned out?"

"I have an idea, but I have no leave to divulge what I heard," the captain said dutifully. "You can hear directly from his Majesty in a minute, lad."

Another call sprang out from the silver trumpets. The milling crowd began to gather around the base of Gwyddno's tower, on the public court. Overshadowed by a stone balcony, the court opened to the west and over the harbor. Gwyddno usually reserved public proclamations for times of celebration and typically made them as the last afternoon sun bathed the tower in shimmering reflections of the grand harbor. In the morning, the sun tended to glance off the side of the tower from the east, casting the balcony in dark shadows.

Enid and Taliesin rounded the castle wall onto the court of polished bluestone. The stunning public square was lined by exquisitely carved statues of beasts and saints of the ocean. In the center of the square, a glorious white marble fountain erupted, somehow drawing pure water from the brackish tide that filled the great harbor. Enid grabbed at Taliesin's arm and pulled him over to an archer's parapet built into the corner of the square.

"Stay here and harken to the King," Enid explained. "I'm needed in the tower, but we will continue training once this is over. Understood?"

Taliesin knew the proper response by now.

"Yes, Captain!" He saluted.

"Well spoken." Enid disappeared into the gathering crowd.

Taliesin spent the next few minutes shifting back and forth on his feet restlessly while listening to the crowd chattering to each other.

"I heard that he offered up half of Ceredigion!" said a hulking blacksmith nearby.

"Bah! The King has more sense than that!" answered his companion.

"I personally wouldn't give up a lame goat for that fool Elphin." A woman's sharp voice rang out. She was feeding a small child under her gown. "The stories I hear about how he leaves his wife alone for weeks on end. It's shameful!"

"Take that Prince Rhun, though," replied a lady that could have been her sister. "He's a looker, eh? Maybe Gwyddno could offer him a bride? I'd volunteer."

"He'd give you the chop by the end of the month!"

Taliesin listened to nearly a dozen separate such comments

from every side of him. Finally, the crowd tensed and fell silent. There, on top of the wide palace balcony, entered a group of four guards bearing the banners of Cantre'r Gwaelod. Heralds again sounded their horns as King Gwyddno entered, clad in his customary ocean blue robe, his sword resting in its jeweled scabbard. On his right side stood Enid, Connwn, Elby, and Bryn, the latter dressed in his formal half-cloak of feathers. On Gwyddno's left stood Rhun, wearing a dazzling red tunic, and flanked by two members of his honor guard, a thin-faced man with blond hair, and another swarthy dark-haired man with a crooked scar disfiguring part of his face.

The King held up his hand.

"Blessed be this morning!" Gwyddno announced in a strong voice. "For we have defeated two threats in one night. Firstly, we have secured the life of our prince, my first-born Elphin!"

Cheers and applause rang out on all sides of Taliesin, and he felt ten times lighter suddenly just hearing those words. Gwyddno raised his arms benevolently, calling for peace.

"We shall part with forty sacks of gold and one ship from the royal armada, for Elphin's safe return."

Hearing this the crowd let out a wave of murmurs. Forty sacks of gold was a sizeable amount, to say nothing of a fully rigged ship.

"If there are those among you who feel I am paying too hefty a price, I would not disagree with you!" The King paused for effect. "But for the arrangement that we have now reached with our esteemed emissary from Gwynedd." Rhun nodded and waved at the crowd.

"Bryn! Recite the royal word!"

The bard stepped to the forefront of the balcony and spread his arms out wide.

"To strengthen the prosperity of each nation and to ensure their security from outside invaders, King Maelgwn and King Gwyddno shall unite their forces together as Britons. In the spirit of Arthur's past reign, the two kingdoms shall aide any Cymry in need and subjugate none. In consequence of this alliance, Gwynedd shall grant free access to the northern hunting grounds and an annual share of fine game caught. Cantre'r Gwaelod will grant ships from Gwynedd free access to the grand harbor as well as a yearly tribute of mussels and salmon. Any village or vessel attacked by the invaders shall be avenged by both kingdoms as their own. In this way will the Cymry's lands and ships be safe from the Saxons, while prosperity is shared for no less than seven generations."

Bryn finished with a curt nod of his head as his strong voice rested. Taliesin knew the bard well enough to see the bitterness in his motions. He knew Bryn did not approve of his own words.

King Gwyddno stepped forward.

"May this day mark a new age of peace in Wales and Britain!"

Cheers erupted as people threw their hands up in the air in joy. Taliesin hardly dared to breathe. He feared that the announcement was all a hopeful dream and that he would wake up in bed the next instant, hours late for training again. Finally, he could contain his excitement no longer. Elphin was being released. He put one hand to his mouth and another to his chest as his heart began to pound with joy.

Up from the balcony, Gwyddno continued.

"To prove his good faith, the Prince of Gwynedd will remain with us until our own Prince Elphin comes within sight of Cantre'r Gwaelod's gates. The forty sacks of gold will be secured in his ship until the time comes for him to depart. He shall be treated as our honored guest while word is sent, and Elphin makes his journey back home. At his request, the prince would like to say a few words."

Rhun grinned from ear to ear and nodded graciously to the King. He stepped past his honor guard and hailed the crowd with a powerful-looking sword arm. The crowd stared back at him, wary of the renowned warrior.

"It does me great honor," he announced in a clear voice, "that it should be I, of my family, to speak today with your great King of legend, here in the land that is Britain's greatest marvel. Tales of the wonders of Cantre'r Gwaelod and Gwyddno's tower do them no justice. And I take great pride that my place in history shall begin at such an extraordinary place!"

Rhun scanned the faces of the people below him. Many looked puzzled and cautious, others seemed fascinated.

"I know that our countries have oft disagreed and that many of you are afraid to believe what has happened here today. But you must understand what revelations my father has had since turning to the church for wisdom. He has seen what common enemies threaten us. The Saxon hoards that lurk in the east, the Irish from the west, and now for the last few years, the cursed plague that has seeped to our shores from the ruins of Rome. Whatever our differences may be, we are called upon by the rulers of the past to stand firm together to protect the country we love. I tell you now, that nothing would please me and my father, King Maelgwn of Gwynedd, more than to see the work of Arthur, our common royal predecessor, completed here today, with a Britain united in peace. May this be the day that we stop fearing each other as rivals and start sharing as brothers!"

The gathering stood silent for one heavy second, too stunned by the prince's eloquent words to react. Then from the rear of the crowd, a single voice stirred up a cry.

"Hurrah! Long live Gwynedd! Long Live the Hundred! Long live Britain!"

At once the crowd all hollered and echoed the call.

"Long live Arthur's Britain! Hurrah!" The people below applauded and cheered. Several of the younger ladies whistled shrilly at the dapper prince. Rhun beamed and saluted the people before graciously stepping back.

Gwyddno again stepped up and raised his arms for quiet. "May Arthur's spirit and vision live on by the grace of God above, his son, and by the blessing of Dylan ail Dunn! May his soul rest in the hallowed crystal towers west of the sea."

"Right then!" Gwyddno said cheerily, "Enough with stuffy formalities. Tomorrow we shall bestow the ransom unto the

Gwynedd's prince, but today is a time for celebration. By royal decree, all ale and mead shall flow freely this night, and feasts will be held in all sectors of the Lowland Hundred. Let's give our northern allies a true taste of merriment here in the sunken kingdom!"

This last decree brought the loudest cheer yet, enough to rattle the walls of Gwyddno's stone towers. Men threw their fists up in the air and leaped for joy. Women clapped their hands and laughed gaily. By the top of the balcony, Gwyddno and Rhun shook hands, while both countries' guards saluted each other. Connwn and Elby embraced and cheered in joy. Taliesin would have cried out himself, but for the look of one individual on the balcony. Perched on a stool in the corner of the balcony, sat Bryn like some pet bird. He didn't caper around or offer any triumphant ballad on his harp. He merely sat there with a sour glare on his face, casting sidelong looks at Rhun and his entourage. His lips were squeezed down to a thin white line.

Taliesin could hardly allow one person's bitter face to ruin this moment. Hope had finally, solidly arrived and his foster father would be safely returning at last.

***

Despite the shaky ground that Taliesin stood on with Enid, the young boy was able to plead with the captain to release him earlier that day to share the news with his mother.

"She'll be desperate to hear the news, Captain!" Taliesin said, doing his best to keep his back ramrod straight. "It should only be right that I make sure that she's heard it properly!"

"Very well." Enid may have been firm, but she was hardly cruel. "Take an hour off and sing praise with her. It is a day of celebration, after all. Just be back at the kitchen by dusk, Cam will need help getting fresh pots, what with there being a royal feast and all."

Taliesin placed his wooden bow down on the rough bench along with the quiver of arrows. He reached around his waist to

127

unfasten the leather strap that kept the heavy broadsword on his hip, grateful to be rid of the weight.

"Keep the sword," Enid said cheerily.

"Beg pardon?" Taliesin asked.

"Think of it as an extension of the training," Enid explained. "Many lords and grand knights might get to ride to battle on a strong horse, but most foot soldiers have to march miles with sword, shield, and arrows. It takes a fine deal of stamina to manage that, Tali. You should be able to take responsibility for a simple trainer sword for a few days."

"But my house is several miles from here!" Taliesin protested. "I'll have to run to make it back to the kitchen on time, and with more weight…Anyway, when would I ever see battle? And couldn't I count on my own horse by then?"

"Not with your riding skills," Enid said with a scoff. "And it's a poor warrior indeed who doesn't appreciate the burden he puts on his horse or his men. Return the sword to me in a few days and see if you can't find the time to practice some footwork with it in the meanwhile."

So it was that Taliesin found himself half jogging, half stumbling up to his door, short of breath and with several large bruises on the side of his leg where the sword had bumped and bashed against him. He reached up for the iron ring fastened to the sturdy oak door when it suddenly swung open.

Mererid's large blue eyes peered out at him from behind the door frame.

"Well! If our little soldier-man isn't back early from training?" She teased him as an older sister would. "I hope the captain hasn't been giving you any more dish duty for sneaking out."

"Mererid! Is mum here? There's news!" Taliesin explained excitedly.

"Of the negotiations!?" The young maid's face lit up. "What news? Did they settle on a price?"

"That and more! We've struck an alliance with Gwynedd, and

Elphin is to be released and transported home by the end of the week!"

"So I've heard." Crissiant strode like a ghost into the room, her soft leather slippers hardly making a noise on the chilly stone floor. She had an embroidery circle and needle in her hand. "The King sent messengers early this morning."

Crissiant's eyes were crystal clear and her face clean and washed. There were no more swollen red lumps under her eyes or dried tears staining her face as Taliesin had seen so often since Elphin's departure. Still, Crissiant carried a remarkable coolness to her that felt unnatural, like an icicle that refuses to melt in the springtime sun.

"Oh, my lady! You must be so thrilled!" Mererid exclaimed.

"I suppose I must." Crissiant only turned her eyes down, following the golden lines of thread she was weaving into the linen cloth.

"Mother," said Taliesin, "tell me you must be happy. The whole kingdom is celebrating today. Our Lord Elphin is on his way back to us and we have nothing more to fear from Anglesey."

"Thanks in part to Elphin himself!" Mererid concurred. "If it wasn't for his pride in you, milady, this day wouldn't have ever come about. Prince Elphin is the unlikely hero of the Lowland Hundred!"

Crissiant looked down at the two young people before her. She placed the embroidery down on a shelf and drifted over to Taliesin, her white gowns flowing gently behind her. She placed her delicate hands on Taliesin's shoulders, studying his face, searching for the bright child she had placed to her breast almost thirteen years ago. She drew Taliesin into a tender embrace and then turned slightly to address Mererid.

"This is fine news, fine pretty news," she explained calmly, not to Taliesin, but to Mererid. "It's a wonderful opportunity for King Gwyddno to show off his wine collection before our guest chooses and counts out his prize. But a celebration is sweeter at the journey's end, not halfway through. This is a fine promise from the

King and Prince Rhun. A fine and pretty promise.

"My Elphin has made me many fine promises over time. Promises about wealth and families and love. That man, with his big heart and gracious soul, would promise me the north star itself to wear on my brow and all the stars in the milky way to sew into my gown. And the sweet fool truly means it, thinking that one day the stars would surrender themselves to him as a favor. But in the end, my child," Crissiant kept her eyes fixed squarely on Mererid as he held Taliesin close, "that's all they ever are. Fine and pretty promises."

Crissiant drew back from Taliesin and looked him again in the face.

"I am overjoyed and relieved that Elphin will return home and Gwynedd will threaten us no more. I truly am, Tali," Crissiant told her foster son. "But until I see my husband back on our doorstep, I will continue to ask God for his deliverance."

"And I'll ask that God delivers him from your blows, the ones you always give him when he returns late," Taliesin said with a good-natured grin.

Crissiant smiled wistfully as she gazed back at her only child. "Be that as it may, I hope that one day you grow to have a heart as big as his but mind you with none of his ill-luck."

She turned back to the serving girl who stood attentively in the corner. "Mererid, please tell Heida that I will be attending church this evening and will be back late. Have the kitchen serve Taliesin something in the meantime."

"Oh, don't bother with that, mum!" Taliesin said somewhat bitterly. "I only stopped by to share the news with you, I'm to report back to the kitchen. I'd best start off now before I'm too late."

Crissiant heaved out an annoyed sigh before nodding her head absently. "See to it you stay away from all that debauchery going on tonight. I don't want to hear stories about another feast ruined by one of my own."

"I'm sure I'll be busy enough scrubbing out the pots, figures that I would miss all the fun." Taliesin kissed his mother farewell and hiked up his cloak against the bitter wind that was beginning to rush in from the sea.

"And mind you don't forget that sword of yours!" Mererid called to him, throwing him a quick wink. "Lest you need to slay any dragons on your way to the kitchen!"

***

That night, as if responding to the King's will, the ocean wind and waves that crashed against the city walls fell silent. For several miraculous hours in the gloom of evening, the only sound that could be heard was laughter and music and the harsh slam of pewter cups against oak wood tables. Heavenly smells of villagers cooking roast geese and braised mutton seeped into the air, wafting up to every room in the highest tower of Caer Wyddno. Minstrels played and leaped about while jug after jug of wine and mead were rushed to the nearest tables. A mood of victory and celebration infected the whole countryside.

Inside the King's feasting hall, knights and soldiers cheered and goaded each other. Gwyddno and Rhun sat together trading anecdotes about the higher profile kings while Rhun's honor guards slapped the table raucously. Connwn and Elby challenged each other to feats of strength. Seithenyn called out for more wine practically as soon as it was brought out. Bryn sat in the corner, plucking at his harp absently, but even he took heart enough to sing a festive tune in between his libations.

It was no small irony that the two people who had the most reason to celebrate the turn of events were the two not feasting in the least. Crissiant, as per routine, was off visiting the chapel, invoking the heavenly father for Elphin's safe return. Taliesin, by contrast, saw firsthand the extent of the nobility's indulgence since he was the one that had to clean every dish and cooking pot that came back from Gwyddno's feast.

Deep down, Taliesin didn't mind missing out on the festivities. His mind felt a whirl with strange thoughts and conflicting desires. He pondered about whether Rhun and his father could be trusted to keep their alliance. He wondered when Elphin would make it back to his doorstep and what kind of shape would he be in by the end of it. He also wondered whether Elphin would approve of Mererid working in his kitchen.

A wet dish rag smacked Taliesin heavily on his shoulder, interrupting his musings. He wheeled around to see Tudno standing in the doorway gnawing on a dripping apple.

"Y'know you're missing all the fun, cousin!" he said cheerily.

Taliesin smirked and whipped the soggy rag back.

"I would have been finished with all my demerits, except I had to stay late last night to finish up someone's extra work!" he teased.

"I heard, sorry about it Tali." Tudno shrugged. "I didn't mean to stick you with extra dishes, I was upset, is all."

"I gathered that," Taliesin said. He turned his back on his cousin and continued scraping out the large cauldron.

"Ah now, don't be bitter about it. I should've taken my punishment like a man. I'm sorry, truly I am. I'm supposed to be helping out dad with the horse and everything," Tudno explained. "He was enjoying himself but then snuck off. I thought I'd sneak you down an apple while I looked for him." Tudno handed Taliesin a plump red apple. Taliesin raised an eyebrow at it, but finally gave in and began biting off crisp chunks.

"Did you talk to your dad about what I said last night?" Taliesin pried cautiously.

"Uh...well...no. Dad didn't seem like he was in the mood to talk last night. I just said my prayers and went to bed."

"Well, maybe it's for the better. I wasn't really supposed to go around mentioning it. It's hard though. I always feel better when I can let you in on things, cousin."

"Same here, Tali. You're more a brother to me than any of

that unruly lot waiting back home."

"Could I ask you a brotherly favor before you head off then?" Tudno nodded eagerly. "I need to empty the porridge cauldron out on the back ledge. Think you could help me heave it up the stairs to the pigs?"

"Ah, that'd be cake, that!" Tudno said. The two boys heaved the giant iron pot up one small stone step at a time until they arrived at the back door to the washroom. Taliesin undid the metal latch and let the wooden door creak open.

The back door to Caer Wyddno's washroom opened out to a small ledge set in the side of the mighty fortress. To avoid attracting rats into the kitchen area, all food refuse was dumped from this ledge about fifteen yards down into a swine pit. Across the drop-off, a narrow stone path circled the back of the tower, and then beyond that was the great harbor, its calm waters reflecting the waxing moonlight.

Taliesin braced himself as an icy breeze whipped up from the harbor. Amid the rush of wind, Taliesin suddenly caught the sound of heavy clanging footsteps making their way across the raised stone path. He poked his head around the door and spied the shape of a single knight draped in a black cowl making his way down the deserted walkway. Taliesin had never once seen a single pedestrian walking along that particular stretch of the walkway. He had assumed that the entrance was blocked off and the path only kept for bringing in hauls of fish to the tower. The cowl rode up and over the man's head, completely obscuring his face.

"Isn't that strange?" Tudno remarked from the other side of the door. "Who do you suppose that is?" He pointed down the other end of the walkway.

Taliesin turned his head to see another figure, walking down the stone path towards the first man. Even with his hood up, the knight's large face still gleamed out in the moonlight. Taliesin could make out a neatly trimmed beard and a deep scar that ran down the side of the man's face. The same scar that one of Rhun's men had when he arrived.

"Tudno, quick!" Taliesin kept his voice low. "Duck down behind the cauldron!"

The two boys crouched low. The stone path stood maybe ten yards away across nothing but salty air. As far as Taliesin could tell, neither of the men took notice of the washroom ledge, let alone the two boys gawking at them from behind an oversized pot. Hopefully, it stayed that way. Taliesin wanted to hear what these two figures had to say to each other alone in the dark, while everyone else was feasting.

The larger man with the scar approached the cowled man and then made to smoothly step past him.

"God save ye!" the man called out politely as he passed.

"Heaven protect thee," the cowled man replied. The two began walking away from each other down their respective paths. Taliesin wondered if he had only just witnessed two men innocently strolling the castle grounds. But after three paces or so, both men stopped, glanced down the path, and then turned back to each other.

The larger man spoke first, his gruff voice barely audible over the laughter from the tower.

"Sút dah! chi?"

"In dá yawn tw i dioh! ha tithai?" the cowled man replied.

"Sút ma', sút mai?"

Taliesin nudged Tudno with his elbow.

"Can you make out what they're saying?"

"No," Tudno whispered back. "It sounds foreign, like Cornish or Cumbric if you ask me."

"Can you understand any of it?"

"No, I only speak Welsh and a bit of Latin I learned from the Abbot. I don't know a soul in the Lowland Hundred that can speak Cumbric. Except maybe Bryn or Grandad."

The two men carried on their conversation in the rough-sounding language. Rhun's guard spoke with an air of fluency while the cowled man halted and stuttered several times, obviously not used to such a strange language in his mouth. They whispered excitedly to each other, frequently checking behind them down the path.

"What do you suppose they're talking about?" Tudno whispered.

"I don't get the feeling they're here for language tutoring," Taliesin said wryly. He steadied himself against the door by holding onto the frame with his right hand. "Whatever they're talking about, it's something they really don't want anybody else to overhear."

At that very moment, a small but forceful breeze picked up from over the harbor. It gusted up the side of Caer Wyddno and spread out down the path, making the men wince from the cold. The burst of air slapped into the side of the tower until it butted straight into the open door of the washroom where Tudno and Taliesin were crouching. The door creaked slightly and then swung inward hard, pinching Taliesin's right thumb between the hinges in the process.

Taliesin wanted to yelp out in pain, but instead, he shook his hand hard and then instinctually shot his thumb into his mouth to quell the pain. He bit down gently to keep from groaning.

"I'm sure you understand I'm running a big risk with this."

"Nobody ever gained anything worthwhile without risk."

Taliesin's eyes opened wide. He still heard the strange foreign language, the same rough and guttural sounds wound into words and phrases. But suddenly, he understood them! The meaning of each sentence shone clear in his mind like a crystal bell.

He took his thumb out of his mouth. The cowled man spoke, but all Taliesin could make out were indecipherable sounds.

He again placed his thumb between his teeth.

"You're sure that your master won't be caught?" The cowled man was speaking.

"That's more your responsibility than mine," the scarred man from Gwynedd responded. *"My team is loaded up with King Gwyddno's gold. We switched them with bags of hay while the guards were distracted. Our horses are swift and strong. We should arrive back in Anglesey before noon tomorrow if we*

ride through the night. But you need to ensure you hold up your part of the bargain."

"That won't be a problem, I can ensure that the northernmost gate remains deserted for precisely a half-hour tomorrow after the midnight bell. Make sure that your prince is done with his business and ready to fly at once. I can't stall the tower guard longer without raising suspicions."

"Will anyone sound the alarm if they see the prince out of the King's tower?"

"The citizens of Cantre'r Gwaelod are free to travel as they please. If he goes without his entourage, nobody should stop him."

"They're talking about sneaking Rhun out before the deal's gone through!" Taliesin whispered, aghast. Tudno snapped his head over to his cousin, his draw dropping to the floor.

"You can understand them?!"

"I...I think so. Let me concentrate!" Taliesin kept his thumb pressed against his teeth and strained to hear the men's whispers over the wind.

"It's strange, asking for the prince to visit her. What does he plan to do to her exactly?" the cowled man asked.

"The prince didn't say. I've seen him slice women open like pigs before. But never a noblewoman like her. I suspect he'll just take her maidenhead and be done with it."

"I can attest that she is a lovely bird to look at. Elphin was right to brag about her."

"Aye, well I can't say the same for Bannon, too much of a waif for me. Maelgwn keeps her since she has the support of the peasants. She was a commoner from some backwoods village before marrying the King."

"I've heard as much." The cowled man darted his head up and down the pathway. Taliesin gripped Tudno's shoulder, praying that nothing gave the two eavesdroppers away. The man turned back to his scarred companion.

"We shouldn't tarry so long. Did you bring my pay?"

The scarred man let out a quick scoff and then reached under his tunic. He tossed over what might have been a small sack of flour if not for the audible jingle of metal coins inside.

"*It's a handsome price,*" the cloaked figure said appreciatively. "*And all for sparking a merry war. Your King really believes that he can win against Gwyddno?*"

"*Of course, we can!*" the scarred man replied indignantly. "*We gather allies like shit gathers flies. As long as Gwyddno comes to us, and out of his shell of a fortress, we shall dominate the battlefield. My King is generous, but I wouldn't call him merciful.*"

"*Aye, well I'll see to it he arrives at the trap. Mind you a little more motivation wouldn't hurt.*" He lifted the sack of gold once more for emphasis.

"*This next message doesn't come from the prince, it comes from the Father. Arthur's true heir can grant gold in heaps for those loyal to him, and he can bring brutal vengeance to those who betray him.*" The man tapped his fingers against the hilt of his sword. "*Nice bit of poetry, isn't it? I think it's an old family motto.*"

"*I'll keep my word, but Maelgwn better do the same.*" The man turned his hooded head out towards the harbor. Lights from the fishing boats and the alehouses across the city glimmered in the water. "*Cantre'r Gwaelod and its fleet of ships go to me and my own. Take Ceredigion, take the southern kingdoms and all their grain for your bleeding empire, but I get the Lowland Hundred!*"

"*That's up to my master,*" the scarred man said with a contentious shrug. "*But take my word for it, I've never seen him fail to reward his subjects, either for loyalty.*" The bulky man reached up and traced the line of his scar up across his cheek. He continued and pulled back a portion of his hair and chain mail to reveal a swollen purple stump of flesh where an ear should have been.

"*-or for treachery.*"

The scarred man dropped his hand and turned on his heel. He began walking back down the path as if nothing had ever happened. The cowled man hefted the sack of coins up in his hands giddily. He called out in his foreign tongue. "*The lady will be back at home by sundown tomorrow. Tell the prince to give Elphin's wench a good stabbing for me as well!"*

The two men parted and headed down their respective paths, making their way back to the festivities. Taliesin kept a death grip on Tudno's arms to keep him from standing up too early. He waited until the sound of their footsteps was covered up by the wind and the two conspirators were out of sight. He had to force himself to open his fingers. His whole body felt like it had turned to ice. His heart beat furiously in his chest and he heaved, hardly able to catch his breath. He finally was able to turn his head towards Tudno. His cousin was staring at him with a mixture of concern and confusion.

"Were you able to get any of that?" he asked innocently. "Did that one with the hood mention something about Elphin at the end?"

CHAPTER 9: Deaf Ears and Playing Dress-up

Bann gwir pan discleir-
Bannach pan levier

Clear is the truth when it shines-
still more clear when it speaks

~ Cadeir Teyrnon, Llyfr Taliesin

By the time Taliesin made it home that night, the only person awake was Heida, the kitchen matron. He asked her if his mother had gone to bed.

"I reckon so, boyo! And a wonder you haven't done so either! I've only just risen myself. Do you know how much time it takes to make a proper breakfast?"

"It's urgent that I see her!" Taliesin explained. "I'll be needed back at the castle later, and I have news."

"I can give her the news then," Heida offered.

Taliesin didn't quite know what to say. How was he supposed to explain to the old kitchen spinster what he had overheard? A plot to betray Gwyddno and harm his mother amid the kingdom's celebrations? Heida would demand proof or else she'd try to tan him for making up nonsense.

"No, thank you, Heida. I'll find mother myself in the morning," he told the kitchen matron.

"It is the morning!" Heida chided. She waved the boy off and went back to organizing the kitchen.

If Tudno hadn't been there to witness the whole thing, Taliesin doubted that even his cousin would have believed him. After the treasonous men left, the boy hastily explained everything that he had understood to his cousin. That Gwynedd was plotting to dishonor the negotiations and make off with the King's gold. That Maelgwn, presumably, meant to topple the Lowland Hundred and annex the entirety of Wales. And that Rhun, the prince of Gwynedd, was aiming to violate and possibly kill his foster mother. Tudno himself could hardly believe it and kept asking him again and again how he could be so sure.

"I don't know either!" Taliesin finally said, exasperated. "I heard all of their words in a language I can't speak, I know I did. But...I understood them! It's like part of my head just knew what they were talking about! You saw them pass a bag of gold to each other, you saw how they kept their voices low and met far away from the King and the court. What else could they have been doing? Paying for a basket of fish?!"

"We need to tell someone then!" Tudno exclaimed.

Taliesin let out a long sigh and felt his body sink to the floor against the rough stone of the wall. He had come to the same conclusion about halfway through the overheard conversation, but another thought stopped him in his tracks.

"Tud, who do we tell? What do we even tell them? That I suddenly learned Cumbric well enough to uncover a treasonous plot, and right in the middle of us celebrating our day of peace?"

"We can't just let it go, Tal. This sounds serious!"

At any rate, they both agreed that not much could be done

that night since every able-bodied man appeared passed out drunk over the feasting tables. The next day they would bring it to Enid's attention and see if she had anything to say on the matter.

At the break of dawn, the two boys found themselves standing in front of Enid on the training grounds.

"So, you and your cousin wish me to believe that a member of the court is conspiring with one of Rhun's guards to undermine the peace agreements?" Enid said slowly after the two recounted last night's events.

"Yes, they mentioned that they would arrange to leave the north gate untended so that-"

"Impossible." Enid cut Tudno off brusquely.

"But, why? It would make sense that-"

"The only people capable of commanding the gate patrol is me, our King, and his most trusted lords. Who among us has cause to betray our King and country? Gwyddno provides everything for his own. This is nonsense."

"Do any of the lords speak Cumbric?" Taliesin inquired as innocently as he could.

"Cumbric!? God's wounds, Taliesin! We don't harbor any Scots or Picts here! Not at Gwyddno's table. You should know that!"

"It's just that Taliesin heard them speaking in Cumbric so that no one would overhear their treason!" Tudno stated.

"Oh, really?" Enid said with her usual bemused tone. "And how many words of Cumbric do you speak, lad?"

"Erh, well, none of course," Taliesin admitted. "But it seems that I understand it incredibly well."

"Yes! Incredible it is!" Enid's voice boomed. "So don't be surprised that I don't believe a word of it."

"But you don't understand!" Tudno insisted. "Lady Elphin could be in serious dang-"

"Give me one more word of it and I'll dock you both with another twenty demerits, a piece! I don't want to hear any more of this bleeding minstrel's tale you two put together to get out of your training!"

Enid turned to give Tudno a stern glance.

"You, boyo, should best be off to the abbey already and report to Father Gilgam. You, Taliesin, have yet to start your drills and I already see the sun coming up over the hillside. Go to it now, this instant!" With that, she turned on her heel and stalked off through the training grounds. Tudno and Taliesin exchanged worried looks.

"Go!" Taliesin said. "I'll try to reach the King this afternoon. I'll find you at the abbey before supper bell."

Enid only kept Taliesin until about midday since the royal guard was needed to oversee Rhun's tour of the shipyards.

"How's your swordplay going, then?" Enid asked as they packed away the training equipment.

"Decently, I suppose," Taliesin replied. "I hardly notice it on my hip by now."

"What about your technique, did you get a chance to practice the drills I showed you?"

"Well, as best as I could," Taliesin replied cautiously.

"Hmmm, well, keep it for another few days, it's never too soon to develop technique."

Taliesin nodded, strapped the sword to his side with his belt, and scrambled up the tower stairwell. He had been told time and again not to interrupt his Grandad under any circumstance. However, Taliesin could hardly think of a more pressing emergency to bring to the King's attention. Even if Gwyddno didn't take him seriously, he was sure he'd be forgiven for his brashness. Taliesin swept through the palace courtyard, throwing a quick salute to the sentinels by the doorway. He raced through the main halls and up the stairs that led to the King's war chamber that was serving as the headquarters for the peace talks. The great silver-plated doors stood at the top of the wide staircase. Taliesin had skipped up all but three steps when the door suddenly opened with a loud creak.

The hulking figure of Seithenyn, clad in his usual dark tunic and leather vest, skulked out of the room. Taliesin had to stop short to avoid crashing headfirst into the gatekeeper's chest.

"What are you doing here?!" Seithenyn hissed at the boy.

"Uncle! Uh, God save thee!" Taliesin said, trying to hide his exasperation. "I was charged to bring a message to the King! Is he within?"

"Yes, and quite indisposed at the moment. He doesn't need to be bothered by the likes of you!"

"I...I was told the message is urgent."

"Then you can relay it to me. I'll deliver it to the King."

"I was also told that the message is private, for the King's ears only."

Seithenyn's eyes squinted into slits and peered hotly at the youth.

"Really? And who entrusted you to deliver a message that none but the King should hear? How private could it be that a piece of jetsam like you knows it?"

"Sorry, but that's not for me to tell. I'm sure King Gwyddno can fill you in once I tell him-"

"Who sent the message, boy?!" Seithenyn planted his foot next to the door, warning Taliesin not to push by him.

"Well, it's ...just a message from my mother, of course. Is there a problem?"

Taliesin had hoped that his lie would sound plausible enough to let him by the malicious gatekeeper. Apparently, that was not the case.

"Oh, is it?" Seithenyn said. His eyes looked like they were about to pop out of his head. "Maybe she should take the time to come to court and seek the King out herself if she has something to say about someone."

"I never mentioned it was about anyone particularly," Taliesin responded, somewhat confused.

"Be off!" Seithenyn rasped. "The King is not free to listen to idle gossip right now! It was foolish enough of her to trust you of all people with a private message. A wonder that the whole kingdom hasn't heard it yet."

A thought had been gnawing at the back of Taliesin's brain since the other night. Who was the man in the cloak that so callously sold his country for a bag of gold? There were only a few people in the whole kingdom that Taliesin could imagine may be tempted to do so. Even though he would never admit it to Tudno, the gatekeeper was one of them.

Taliesin could see that Seithenyn would probably strike him if he insisted any longer, so instead, Taliesin thought to test his uncle on something.

"The thing is, Uncle, my mother gave me the message a bit oddly. She made me memorize the message in a language I can't understand. Cumbric, I believe it was. I can recite the message, but I haven't a clue what it means. You don't, perchance, know any Cumbric, Uncle? I could give you the message then and be off."

Taliesin studied his uncle's face as he mentioned the conspirator's language. Seithenyn's only reaction was a deeply furrowed brow that might have been a sign of consternation or mere irritation. In any case, Seithenyn snapped back at the boy quickly enough.

"I am out of patience with these pranks, sea-brat! How in damnation would I know Cumbric? There's hardly a soul in Cantre'r Gwaelod that speaks the northern tongue, least of all Elphin's goose of a wife! Now begone at once before I call the guard to tell them you've been eavesdropping on the King! Go!"

Taliesin only nodded curtly and briskly walked down the stair aisle and out of the palace.

***

"This is madness, this is!" Tudno exclaimed as the two jogged their way up to Elphin's tower. "I've talked to nearly everyone I could find that would lend an ear, and they all called me daft and a traitor! Do they think that I'm happy to see the peace talks upended?! I'm only trying to do what's right for the kingdom!"

"Who did you talk to?" Taliesin asked, empathizing with his cousin's frustration.

"Just about every soldier I could find, and Father Gilgam, naturally."

"And how did the abbot react?"

"Well, he at least seemed sympathetic. He thought that we may have been deceived by the devil and made me recite the Lord's prayer. He did promise to pray that the Lord deliver us and protect us should evil truly be at work. It's something isn't it?"

Taliesin had to bite the top of his lip to stop him from snapping at his cousin.

"I would have preferred that the abbot used his words to tell the King instead of the heavenly father. Gwyddno is the only one who can ensure that Rhun doesn't escape, and I haven't been able to see him all day long!"

The two arrived at Taliesin's doorstep and barreled through the heavy oak gate. Taliesin had no better luck than his cousin sounding the alarm. Every ear in Caer Wyddno had turned deaf to their warnings. Taliesin had met Tudno as promised by the abbey and decided that their only course of action was to warn Crissiant herself. At least she could be spared whatever humiliation Rhun supposedly had in store for her.

"LADY ELPHIN!" Tudno called out as he entered the house. "LADY ELPHIN! PLEASE HEAR US!"

"The whole tower can hear you!" Mererid's voice shot out from the kitchen. "But the lady isn't at home." The maid's slender figure sauntered out of the kitchen wearing an apron dusted with flour. "What is all this? I was enjoying myself splendidly while I kneaded the rye, and then I hear you howling like a dog! Are you drunk, altar boy?" She fixed Tudno with a condescending glare.

"I wasn't asking for you, you urchin!" Tudno spat back. "We need to talk to the Lady Crissiant, not her servant!"

"Hmmph! That's the kind of chivalry I should expect from one of the gatekeeper's brats. Is this the kind of company you keep, Taliesin?" Mererid retorted.

"You mean the God-fearing kind?" Tudno replied.

"Stop this! Both of you!" Taliesin demanded suddenly. "I don't care what either of you thinks of the other. We have a crisis on our hands right now, and you two are maybe the only souls in the Lowland Hundred I can trust right now. So please save your petty bickering for another day!"

Mererid, obviously taken aback by Taliesin's outburst, peeked her head back into the kitchen, checking to see if they were alone, and then softened her tone.

"Whatever is the matter, Tali?" she asked.

"Mererid, where is my mother? We need to speak with her."

"She's just gone off to the abbey, not a half-hour ago. She said she wouldn't be back until evening."

"Ah! Well, that's in our favor, eh, cuz?" Tudno said chipperly. "Rhun won't be able to do us any harm if she's not even here."

"Rhun? Gwynedd's Prince?" Mererid asked, dumbfounded. "What's the meaning of this? Please, answer me already!"

For the first time that day, the two boys found themselves recounting their tale of conspiracy and betrayal to a willing audience. More remarkably, despite the questionable details and the miracle of Taliesin suddenly understanding a foreign tongue, the girl only opened her blue eyes wide, listening to every word they said.

"Oh, Godfathers!" Mererid said when they finally finished. "Does Rhun actually mean to start a war?"

"I suppose he does, and he's aiming to use Mother to start one," Taliesin concurred.

"But wouldn't that be as bad for Maelgwn's kingdom as it would for the Lowland Hundred? What if King Gwyddno presses on to victory and ends up claiming Gwynedd?"

"That's not likely," Tudno said glumly. "I hear my dad go on about it when he comes home from the alehouse. Cantre'r Gwaelod is nearly impenetrable for an invading army, but Gwyddno and our allies are outnumbered outside of the kingdom's walls. If we march north to Maelgwn, we will go marching to our own destruction."

"But, if Rhun manages to sneak off with his forty sacks of gold and insults us all by…well…by doing whatever he's planning to do, Grandad may not have a choice," Taliesin continued. "He would lose half of his allies for appearing weak, and then no castle stronghold would save us."

"Hmmm…" Mererid brought her hand to her chin and furrowed her brow. "So even if he passes over Elphin's house, without seeing your mother, he'll still bring us to ruin. Oh my…"

"Unless…" Taliesin could feel an idea uncoiling itself in his brain. "What if he didn't pass us by and didn't escape. What if we could get word out to the King about what was happening before Rhun left? We could capture the brute and hold him in ransom against Elphin like Grandad wanted to do at first!"

"Would that really stop a war?" Tudno asked, skeptically.

"It would allow us to stay safe inside Cantre'r Gwaelod, and it wouldn't cost us allies."

"What about the traitor you heard Rhun's man talking to? Couldn't he still bring us harm?" Mererid asked.

"I suppose, but that would be true in any case. And if the King knows about the traitor, he might be able to smoke him out before he could fly off."

Mererid's eyes glowed with excitement hearing the boy concoct his plan. Tudno only knitted his eyebrows together and kneaded his face with one hand.

"Well…well how are we supposed to capture him anyway?" Tudno asked. "There aren't any guards around. Are you saying we need to whack him one when he's not looking?"

Taliesin shook his head stiffly.

"No, if we catch him without proof of what he was doing and why he would just lie his way out of it. We need to expose him and his lies to the kingdom."

"But if your mother isn't even home, how would we do that?" Mererid asked.

"Shall I run and fetch her?" Tudno asked sincerely. "I could get back maybe no more than a half-hour after Rhun is due to arrive."

"...that leaves too much to chance." Taliesin pondered. "Rhun might sense something was amiss. And honestly, I don't like the idea of offering my mam up as bait."

"Let me then!" Mererid suddenly exclaimed. Both boys snapped their heads over to the taller girl, stunned.

"Let you what?" Taliesin asked dumbfounded.

"Let me be the lady of the house, just for this one night, and just to get Rhun to reveal his awful intentions. The rest of the house can see the prince make an ass of himself and we can send for the tower guard to nab him!"

"You!?" Tudno gawked. "Do you actually believe the Prince of Gwynedd will take you as the lady of a household?"

"Why not?" Mererid replied. "He's never met the actual Lady Elphin, has he? Face to face? I'm tall enough to pass for the part, aren't I? Just give me a few of your mum's dresses to wear for the evening and I'll act finer than the King's own minstrels."

"That's madness! You're just looking for an excuse to get your fingers through Lady Elphin's dress pockets!"

Before Taliesin could object, Mererid narrowed her eyes into lethal slits and spat back at the page boy.

"It's a lucky thing I'm more concerned for Taliesin and his mother now, or I'd give you a darker bruise on your face than your drunkard father leaves!"

"What Tudno meant to say," Taliesin butted in hastily, "was that how can you be sure that Prince Rhun won't bring you any harm? He's skinned people alive before just for getting on his bad side."

Mererid turned her blue eyes towards Taliesin, her eyebrows raised in surprise. "Well, I just thought you would be there to protect me if things got out of hand."

Taliesin balked.

"I mean, you do have that sharp sword on your hip the captain gave you. Hasn't she trained you, yet?" she asked innocently.

"Oh, well...yes, she has. She... she seems to think I take to it very naturally, actually."

"Tali, Prince Rhun is a master swordsman!" Tudno objected.

Taliesin weighed the sword in his hand as he lifted the hilt slightly. It already seemed lighter and more familiar in his grip. He could imagine it flashing dangerously in Rhun's face should he step out of line. He had to admit he found the image enticing.

"Tudno," he said finally. "Go at once to the abbey and find my mother. Tell her everything that's happened and take her directly to Grandad. He'll listen if mother is the one speaking. Tell him to send Enid and as many guards as can be spared to Elphin's tower at once. We will keep him occupied until then."

"You must be jesting!" Tudno said exasperated. "You think you can stand up to Rhun Hir of Gwynedd? You're inviting a wolf into your very dining room!"

"I'll have him hang his sword outside the dining hall before he goes in. He'll be unarmed. I can handle a mad dog especially if it doesn't have any teeth!"

Tudno looked like he was watching the world fall apart. He looked over from Taliesin to Mererid and finally threw his hands in the air.

"Oh, fine then! I better make haste. I get the feeling you'll be needing help from the guard as soon as possible."

Tudno turned on his heel and began jogging down the path towards the abbey. Taliesin glanced out the window, noting with concern that the sun was already beginning to sink below the sea wall to the west of the tower. If the conspirators could be trusted, Rhun should already be on his way, giving them about twenty minutes to prepare.

"We better hurry and prepare," Taliesin muttered, feeling his nerves begin to chafe in his stomach.

"Let's hurry, then!" Mererid replied. "You'd better find me something fine to wear if I'm going to play lady of the house tonight."

***

"You know, I certainly wouldn't mind entertaining princes and knights more often," Mererid called over her shoulder to Taliesin, who was standing at the door of his mother's boudoir, watching that no one barged in on the kitchen maid while she rummaged through his mother's clothes. "This is a great deal of fun!"

Mererid stood in front of Crissiant's looking glass. Full length, it let her see her entire figure as she compared it to the shape Lady Elphin's dress was accustomed to holding. She was taller than Mererid for sure, but Mererid nearly matched the older woman for all other proportions and womanly measurements. By cinching up the skirt a little higher up on her waist, the sixteen-year-old girl fit naturally in the bodice of the woman approaching her thirtieth spring. It was one of the only times in her life Mererid could recall looking into a mirror.

"Your cousin better get here with the King's guard quick. I have no intention of entertaining this lout for long."

"You won't have to, just keep pouring out the wine and serving him extra portions of mutton. He'll take his time with a good meal and if he gets the opportunity to brag about himself, so much the better."

"And just what happens when he decides he's had enough mutton and wants dessert?" Mererid asked, still turning herself in front of the mirror.

"If it comes down to it, I'll fly out from behind the curtains and intervene. He won't have more than a dagger on him. If I act quickly enough, I should be able to keep him at bay until help arrives. And then we've caught the scoundrel in the act. Gwyddno will have to imprison him after that."

"You just better know what you're doing with that sword is all," Mererid replied curtly.

"I do! Enough to keep a drunkard in his place at least!" Taliesin said hastily.

Mererid smiled a bit slyly. She examined a quaint shawl draped over his mother's dresser.

"You haven't been around too many drunkards, have you, my dear princeling?" she chided him. "They seem like they can't piss without falling into it but believe me they can get out of hand in the blink of an eye. When you're so far in the drink, you begin to behave like someone who hasn't anything to lose."

"I'd make the beast kill me before he lays a hand on you!" Taliesin said, his blood suddenly boiling. The older girl turned her head and favored the younger boy with a bemused look.

"Well, I suppose I haven't anything to fear then," she said coyly. Mererid gingerly picked up another of Taliesin's mother's gowns and held it in front of her, gauging how well it would fit her. "And what about this traitor you overheard last night?" she asked. "Don't you have any idea who he might be?"

"No," Taliesin answered. "Only suspicions."

"Suspicions like who?" Mererid pressed.

"Many, and yet very few. There are so many knights and captains at Gwyddno's command, but I can't think of any aside from Enid and maybe some of the generals who could command so much of the causeway guard. I didn't want to mention it to Tudno, but I thought for a moment it might be Seithenyn."

"Couldn't it be him?" Mererid asked flatly. "If anyone is willing to sell out their honor, I would name him first."

"That's what I imagined," Taliesin concurred, "but the man I heard the other night was speaking Cumbric. I've never heard uncle speak anything besides Welsh in all the years I've known him."

"I speak some Cumbric, didn't you know?" Mererid said cheerily. "My mum was from the Northern Isles." She placed the white gown she was holding carefully back in the woven hamper she found it in. She returned to smoothing over the soft velvet gown over herself.

"Hmmm," she said thoughtfully. "It's fetching enough. But I'm not sure the prince will believe me to be Lady Elphin. I don't think I look elegant enough."

"I think you look stunning," Taliesin said before he could stop himself.

"Appreciate it, dear," Mererid said with a smirk, "but I need something else to show I'm nobility, don't I?"

Taliesin's eyes darted to his mother's night shelf and the ornamental salmon carving on the left side. He stepped over and ran his finger under the fish's upper lip. He lifted as the backside of the fish swung open on hinges hidden in the joints of the fish's tail. A small pile of pearl necklaces, gems, and rings glimmered from the fish's open belly. Taliesin hastily plucked out a sizeable necklace and the largest ring he could find.

"This might fool the scoundrel," he said, presenting Mererid with the jewelry. Mererid's eyes lit up as she surveyed the fine string of pearls and draped them around her shoulders. She held the ring up to examine the engraved crest.

"Is this Elphin's sigil?" she asked.

"Yes, Rhun won't have any cause to doubt you once he spies that."

"It's so small, Tali!" Mererid exclaimed. "How does your mother put this on?"

"Actually, Mother almost made my dad take it back to the jewel smith because it was so large for her. She has very delicate hands, my mother. It may go on if we twist it gently."

Without thinking, Taliesin took Mererid's hand and began slowly working the pale gold ring over her smooth skin. Hoping to find a better angle in the flickering torchlight, Taliesin brought Mererid's hand lower and knelt to get a better grip on the ring. Taliesin carefully pulled the metal loop over the bump of Mererid's second knuckle. He looked up to see Mererid staring back at him with a fiendishly amused smile.

"Well, at least I can say that one member of royalty put a ring on my finger," she said. Taliesin suddenly realized how suggestive it was to be kneeling in front of the young lady. He hopped to his feet, his face warm.

"Ah, ha ha, well...you...you certainly deserve a fair prize for, uhm...helping me, us like this," he stammered.

"Maybe we could find more ways to help you, love," Mererid whispered with a sparkle in her eyes. Taliesin hoped that Mererid couldn't see his heart jumping in his chest.

"Master Taliesin!" Heida's voice rang out from down the hallway. Mererid and Taliesin jumped in surprise. The young boy quickly shooed Mererid behind the wardrobe just as the kitchen matron arrived at the door.

"Master Taliesin!" Heida said, obviously perplexed to see the boy in his mother's bedchamber. "Is the lady back from the chapel, yet?"

"Why...why yes, she is, Heida," Taliesin replied. "She's gone to compose herself. She was frightfully emotional when she arrived back no more than an hour ago."

"Oh!" Heida said. She turned to look over her shoulder, her eyebrows knitted together.

"What's wrong, Heida?"

"Oh, young master. I swear I jest not, but the Prince of Gwynedd himself is on our doorstep right now! He insists that he would dine with Lady Elphin tonight to comfort her over her Lord's imprisonment. I wasn't told about this master! Lady Elphin never said she expected company tonight."

"Yes, it was a last-minute arrangement, as I was told," Taliesin said smoothly. "Don't you worry over it. Just show the prince to the antechamber. I will receive him there myself. And lay out supper on the table. The prince can have my meal. My mother will be down shortly."

Heida looked at the lad with a mask of bafflement. She wrung her hands nervously.

"Don't fret so, Heida. I know this is a change of plans but trust me, everything is fine. Just set the table if you please, and then leave me to wait on the guests tonight. My mother had hoped to make an impression on the prince for granting Elphin his freedom."

"But master, it is very strange that-"

"I will handle everything, Heida. So please do not disturb us as we dine."

Heida seemed to raise her eyebrows to the heavens and breathed out a long, exasperated sigh.

"Very well then. I can only pray no evil is at work here tonight." She turned to move back to the kitchen and then called back over her shoulder. "But I'm sorry to say that the lady will be without her bread tonight. That little wench from the gate tower scampered off, leaving the dough in the oven. It's a miracle the kitchen didn't catch fire." Heida stalked down the stairs muttering to herself as she went.

Mererid finally poked her head out from the wardrobe.

"I told the other girls in the kitchen to take out the poxy bread!" she protested. "Just let her call me a wench once more. I'll roll her into a good loaf of rye."

"Don't take any heed of her," Taliesin said. "Just wait until the food is set and then sneak in through the wine cellar entrance so no one sees you. I'll lead the prince in after you."

Mererid took one final look at herself in the mirror.

"Oh, this will be a story to tell for sure!" she said giddily. "I'm off then. Just keep a good watch over me while I'm playing my role."

Mererid picked up the hem of Crissiant's gown and began to stride down to the dining room. She stopped next to Taliesin and with casual grace, planted a warm kiss on his lips. With one last coy look, she disappeared down the stair aisle.

Taliesin took a moment to steady his breath, which suddenly seemed out of control before he moved again. He turned and viewed himself in the mirror. He ran his hand over the hilt of the training sword hanging from his belt. Since Elphin had been sent off to Gwynedd, Taliesin had been tossed from one apprenticeship to another, he had been ignored, demeaned, and brushed off by almost everyone he knew in the Lowland Hundred as he watched his life slowly unravel over the course of a fortnight.

Tonight though, he was the one with the upper hand. He was the one that understood the danger the whole kingdom was in, and it was his house that the wolf had decided to poke his nose into.

And tonight, he would be the one holding the sword.

CHAPTER 10: The Wolf's Dinner

Ev yd an'rhevna
ni diwg a wna

When he works confusion
he will not repair what he does.

~Canu y Gwynt, Llyfr Taliesin

Rhun's footsteps echoed loudly as he padded around the tower antechamber. Next to the wooden doorway, a nervous-looking squire stood at attention, watching his master closely. Taliesin peered at the prince from behind the hallway curtain, trying to read his mood. The boy scowled to see the two-faced brute appear so at ease with himself. The prince strode casually from one wall to the other, inspecting the various decorations and heirlooms that lined the walls. The cretin even had the audacity to remove one of the helms and inspect the metalwork as if it were a trinket at market.

Taliesin took a deep, quiet breath, and then stepped purposefully into the antechamber.

"Good evening, my Lord!" Taliesin greeted the prince. Rhun half jumped and turned to face him. "We received word that you would be coming. You honor us with your presence this supper time."

"Ah, gracious then!" Rhun sputtered, taken slightly off guard. He looked up and down over Taliesin's short frame and then glanced past him, looking for any other unexpected hosts. He brought his attention back to the young boy standing before him and smeared on his oil-slick smile.

"Would you be Elphin's fosterling, then? I've heard many fine things about you from your foster father."

"Yes, Taliesin is my given name, and I, along with my mother, have waited many long nights to hear news of our lord. We owe you much, honored prince, for bringing us tidings of Elphin's release. Be welcome here tonight!"

"Well, well, aren't you a most well-spoken lad. Elphin told me as much, but I shall have to confess that you are far brighter than I ever believed." Rhun looked around the open hallway, his gaze trying to penetrate the very stones of the walls. "Tell me then, where is the lady of the house? I would reassure her that her husband is safe and well."

"She's waiting for you within, good prince," Taliesin replied, his every gesture and movement oozing congeniality. "She will receive you after you've left your arms outside the dining hall."

"Is this a new custom of the Lowland Hundred?" Rhun asked. His hand twitched unconsciously at the sword resting on his belt. "No one from King Gwyddno's court has yet asked me to hand over my sword."

"The knights of King Gwyddno's court are plenty able to defend themselves. As you well know, my mother and I haven't had our protector home for weeks and he made us promise not to admit any guests, however amiable, to our halls who carried any sort of weapon."

Rhun then barked out a laugh that was a little too loud.

"And I trust that Elphin's foster son has no weapon on his person either? It would hardly be gracious of you, as a host, to take unfair advantage."

In response, Taliesin simply patted at the sides of his tunic and turned a full circle in front of Rhun, showing to him clearly that he was indeed unarmed. Rhun scowled for the briefest moment before putting his greasy smile back on his face. He carefully unhooked his sword and scabbard from his belt and handed it to his squire and instructed him to keep watch over it outside with the horses. The squire nodded and left, clutching the ornate sword closely.

This left Rhun and Taliesin alone in the antechamber. The two held each other's gaze for a moment, their faces serene and smiling, but their eyes glinting with unspoken challenges. Each one knew the other had a hidden motive. Taliesin had known this about Rhun from the start of course, but now it was obvious that Rhun suspected the young boy was up to something. He couldn't be sure exactly what and that gave Taliesin the advantage.

"Right this way, my Lord. The Lady Elphin awaits."

"Welcome Prince of Gwynedd! Heaven and the saints bless us this evening!" Mererid rose out of her chair as soon as she heard Taliesin lead the prince into the dining hall. She curtsied to him in a fashion completely unfitting of Taliesin's mother. Taliesin tried not to wince.

"Mother, here is the man responsible for sending Elphin back to us, safe and whole. With your leave, he would dine with us this evening," Taliesin announced, hoping to keep some semblance of formality.

"God send health and good fortune to your household, fair Lady Elphin," Rhun said, taking Mererid's hand and kissing her on the ring that Taliesin had placed there not half an hour ago. "Though Prince Elphin has angered the King of Gwynedd to say so, I would confess he had great reason to declare you the fairest lady in all of Britain."

Taliesin couldn't help but notice Mererid blushing.

"Taliesin, dear," Mererid addressed him. "Be a good lad and allow the Prince and I to dine in private tonight. I'll have you brought a nice slice of lamb and bowl of porridge later."

"But, mother, why can't I just-"

"Hurry along then," Mererid finished curtly. Taliesin shot Rhun a sour look. Rhun for his part maintained his gentlemanly composure, but the hint of a smile curling on the corner of his mouth didn't go unnoticed by Taliesin as he briskly walked out of the dining hall. He walked about fifteen paces before breaking into a quiet jog to the wine cellar.

Taliesin's objection to being sent away had been purely for Rhun's sake. He figured that by keeping Rhun overconfident, he would have the best chance of stalling him before the tower guard arrived. In addition, it allowed the young lad to sneak up through the stair aisle of the wine cellar that climbed up to the back wall of the dining chamber. Elphin had the shortcut installed for when he was entertaining "thirsty company" as he tended to put it, but now the hidden passage would serve an entirely different purpose.

Taliesin darted as quickly as he could through the gloomy cellar. He stopped next to a hefty barrel of ale and groped blindly behind it until he pulled out Enid's sword that he had stashed before going to meet Rhun. Sword in hand, Taliesin willed himself to keep as quiet as possible and slowly ascended the stone staircase.

Heavy velvet curtains lined the back wall of the dining chamber, embroidered with ornate gold thread. After reaching the top of the stairs, Taliesin had no difficulty passing unnoticed behind the back of the curtains until he was able to position himself right next to Rhun, who sat at the head of the table as if he were the master of the house. Taliesin could also make out the snowy white side of Mererid's face. He practically held his breath, trying his best to listen in on the conversation.

"-can't tell you enough how much this all means to me, and my son, of course, my son and I." Mererid was saying as she poured wine into Rhun's drinking horn.

"Of course, the pleasure is all mine," Rhun replied after a long swig. "If I had known how charming Elphin's wife was, I would have happily made more diplomatic visits to Gwyddno's country years ago."

"Oh, well…you wouldn't have found me so charming back then," Mererid said, sipping her own drink modestly. "I have grown much more… ehm… tame in the household since."

"Surely all your ladyship needs is a bit of excitement in her life to regain her youthful vigor," Rhun replied. "Tell me, doesn't Elphin take you hunting or on great rides through the countryside?"

Mererid let out a forced laugh. Taliesin wondered what Rhun was making of this performance. So far, he did not seem to notice anything amiss.

"My lord rarely spends time in the country," Mererid admonished him. "His pastime of choice is sailing over the sea to weirs and coasts and…uhm…islands far from the walls of Cantre'r Gwaelod."

"And he hasn't taken you to see these far shores either then?"

Taliesin bit his lip. He hoped that Mererid knew Cantre'r Gwaelod's customs. There was hardly a sailor in all of Ceredigion that would take a woman on board a ship.

"Why of course not sir!" Mererid replied indignantly. "We women anger the gods of the ocean, so they say. Something about our wiles and beauty keeping the sailors' eyes from their knotwork."

She crooked an eyebrow up at Rhun. Taliesin was in no position to see the prince's reaction, but his posture suggested a growing intrigue.

"You are quite the trusting woman to allow your husband to stray, if I may say so. Do you ever wonder what might keep him at sea for so long? What might keep him warm during the cold nights in some foreign port?"

"Well, my dear Prince," Mererid replied, "let's not forget why my husband has been locked away, to begin with. Tell me, did you see my Elphin keeping unfit company in your father's halls during his Christmas feast?"

Taliesin gave a silent thank you to the maid for subtly defending his father's honor.

"Ah, well, there you have me, my lady. I do recall Elphin was only kept company by his drinking chalice. Lustful for the drink, but faithful all the sssame."

Rhun had already downed his second horn of wine, at least by Taliesin's count, and was beginning to run his words together. Mererid's hand was already reaching for the flagon when Rhun's own snaked out to grab hold of her.

"A woman of your obvious beauty and vitality would do well to experience the thrill of the hunt, the beauty of the woods." His face pressed in closer to Mererid's. So close that Taliesin could see Mererid's nose crinkle at Rhun's offensive breath. "If you would ever desire to see a truly outstanding hunting skill, I could show you many things indeed. I hate to boast, but many do praise me for my skill with a knife and the carvings I fashion. I may even have a wee man of wood hidden under the table."

Taliesin tightened his grip on his sword, wondering if this was the moment he'd have to intervene.

"Ah, but I have seen many little wooden men in my maiden years-"

*Steady, Mererid…*Taliesin thought to himself. *Just take care about how you're portraying my mother, please.*

"-and I know that, though some wooden men claim to be made of the sturdiest oak, they all too soon get soft and flimsy in unfamiliar waters. Your wooden man would surely show more fortitude than that."

"Surely," Rhun agreed, his sweaty hand now grasping onto the satin sleeve of Taliesin's mother's evening gown worn by the young maid. "With size comes strength as I've heard the bards and wise men tell it. Therefore, I doubt my wooden man lacks fortitude."

"True, but cleverness and agility have undone many, however

large and strong," Mererid replied with a flirtatious grin. She took up Rhun's empty cup with her free hand and brought it under the flagon as she poured more wine. "Perhaps another toast to the health…and luck of this mysterious wooden man of yours?"

Taliesin strained his ears for approaching horses, the clangs of armor, anything to imply the arrival of Tudno and the tower guard. They must be on their way soon. A second too early and it would be Taliesin's word against Rhun's. If they showed up a second too late, well, all Taliesin would have to do then is keep Rhun, unarmed and drunk, at bay long enough. He tried to keep himself from breathing too loud and wiped the sweat of his palms off on his tunic.

"Ha! An excellent idea!" Rhun rose dramatically to his feet, lifting his horn high over his head. "To full horns of mead, full bodices, and very fortunate wooden men!" He drained his horn in almost one gulp and then threw it back down to the table. He stayed standing, looking down at the woman in the sheer evening gown before him.

"Now my lady, I have one last parting gift for your hospitality," he said, taking a staggering step forward.

"Is it one of your wood carvings?" Mererid teased, beginning to drop the pretension of status. Thankfully Rhun seemed too full of himself to care. "Perhaps the bedroom would be a better place to view such trinkets. But first, I must insist you try some pudding for dessert."

"Aye, but sadly time is fleeting, my dear woman." His arms landed down on her wrist, pinning her in place. "And yours is a beauty that tries a man's patience."

Without warning, Rhun's hands darted to the neckline of Mererid's gown and tore the fabric down to the girl's navel in one sharp motion. Mererid gasped and swiped at Rhun's hand with the table knife. The blow didn't cut, but it was enough to make Rhun lose his grip on the dress while Mererid recoiled, covering herself with the shreds of fabric.

"My, your husband makes you parade about in cheap clothes. Look how easily your dress has ripped. I clad all the ladies of my court in fine linen and silk from over the sea."

"Then they must hate it when you tear at them so! Such a terrible shame! I'd rather have shepherd's wool touching me than your greasy hands!"

NOW, TUDNO! Taliesin pleaded mentally. *Burst through the door with Enid and the foot soldiers. This is the perfect moment!*

Rhun heaved an annoyed sigh and gulped down one final horn of wine in a single swallow.

"I guess I'm out a bet with my captains. They wagered you wouldn't bed me willingly. Well, I guess even charm has its limits. But, in any case, they won't argue about it back at Anglesey. Willing or not, your honor won't be worth shit there, and that's really all that mattered."

Rhun took a menacing step forward, his eyes locked onto Mererid's body like a snake's. He took another step and then froze as a steel blade slid out of the chamber's curtains and pointed itself straight at Rhun's throat.

Rhun didn't twitch a muscle, hardly daring a sudden movement with the blade so close to his neck. He looked down to see Taliesin holding the handle. His knuckles were white as he gripped the sword. His eyes bore into Rhun's face with a triumphant rage although his breath came fast. The inside of the young boy's leg trembled ever so slightly.

"Well, I had heard that swords were forbidden in the dining hall," said Rhun.

"Only for wild animals like you, you dog," Taliesin spat. "How dare you even think to approach my mother while you have her husband in the tower to rot?"

"Ha! Your father was practically asking for his lady's honor to be put to the test. An empty boast too, judging from how your mother has been flirting and carrying on, and then only to tease me at the end. Elphin must be one hen-pecked old sot."

"You'll have plenty of time to eat your own fool words in the dungeon of Caer Wyddno. We'll see how generous a negotiator you are when it's your own neck you're bargaining with. I'm sure your Dragon King Maelgwn would-"

Taliesin's words fell short as Rhun, lightening quick for his apparent level of inebriation, knocked the point of Taliesin's sword away from his neck and, with his other gauntleted hand, delivered a whipping blow to Taliesin's windpipe. Taliesin reeled back, his free hand clutching at his throat just as Rhun drove a powerful fist into his stomach.

Mererid shrieked and then, with expert aim, kicked Rhun squarely between the legs, drawing a moan of pain from the large man. Taliesin staggered back against the wall, losing his footing. He felt like his throat was closed shut and all the breath had been knocked clean out of him by Rhun's attack. A wave of vertigo overtook him as he lost his grip on the sword. He looked over to see Mererid throw herself at Rhun's doubled-over form only to be pushed back against the table by the man's powerful arms. Fading and dark as his vision was, Taliesin made one last effort to grab his sword and swing it wildly at Rhun. The man, although hobbled in pain, dodged the sword easily and then elbowed Taliesin square in the side of his head.

Taliesin spun around himself to the floor and then lay still.

"You damned wench!" Rhun hissed. "Did you think to stab me in the back with your brat assassin? Lead me on only to slit my throat!?"

"I just thought it would be wise to have a bit of protection in case our 'guest' turned out to be a pig-poking drunkard. Not so eager to show me any wooden men now, are you? Or do you need another kick to shove him back into your arse?"

Rhun stood up, finally managing to let go of his crotch.

"Oh, we may not have time for the romantic courtship I had planned for the two of us, but don't worry-" Rhun reached into the breast pocket of his tunic and pulled out a glittering dagger. "I'll make sure Elphin gets a veritable sign of his wife's character."

***

"More fuel for the fire, I say!" King Gwyddno called out from his throne. "The wind blows in the ice from the northlands tonight! And the cold is distracting me from draughts, I swear it! You there, lad!" Gwyddno singled out a young foot servant as he collected pewter trays off the floor of the throne room. "Go and fetch more wood for the brazier, would you? My court will freeze otherwise!"

The diminutive boy immediately set his trays down and walked briskly over to the door. He had to sidestep his way around several lords who pounded on the table too hard when they won their game of backgammon. Several skins of wine lay spilled on the usually tidy floors. For the second night in a row, Gwyddno had followed an evening of feasting with a night of revelry in the company of his closest members of the court. Connwn and Elby mentally sparred over their game pieces while Seithenyn pestered the servants for another helping of ale. Bryn dutifully plucked a soft song on his harp in the background. The King allowed himself to gaze contented into the wavering flames dancing in the brazier.

Three days ago, he had the prospect of total war on his hands, but now he was celebrating the beginning of an age of peace and prosperity. The awesome responsibility that came with the throne pressed down on Gwyddno night and day ever since he watched his fortress get built from the depths of the sea. Such a weight would be enough to drive lesser men mad, but there was a reason that Gwyddno stayed king for so many years. Despite the countless threats and warnings of doom that arrived every morning on his doorstep, Gwyddno Garanhir never appeared to lose his calm or lose control of a situation. His secret was childishly simple. He merely always took the time to appreciate his victories as much as his defeats. And tonight marked a welcome victory.

As the serving boy approached the throne room door, he

suddenly found himself jumping backwards in surprise as the doors swung wildly open. The sudden interruption and crash of the doors reverberated from the tapestried walls. Some of the more jittery knights even leaped to their feet with their hands grasping at their swords.

Crissiant sailed in through the open doorway, her stride fast and her face livid. She strode straight to the middle of the throne room and stopped directly in front of the King's chair. She bent no knee and made no customary bow like most of his subjects were expected to. Trailing sheepishly in her wake was Tudno, looking like he was doing his best to remain unseen. He only bowed his head humbly at the gathered lords and murmured, "God save you," to several of those he passed.

"Why Lady Elphin!" Gwyddno exclaimed, cheerily. "To what do I owe this oddly timed and evidently urgent visit?"

"You wench!" Seithenyn slurred out from the side of his ale horn. "How does she have such...disrespect, forra King."

"My apologies to the court," Crissiant said, notably without bowing, "But this is a family issue, and so I'm not here to speak with my King, but instead with my father-in-law."

"So be it, daughter," Gwyddno said evenly, "Then let's hear it. What's given you cause to barge in on our merriment this evening?"

"Where is Prince Rhun?" Crissiant asked without ceremony.

"Away with his countrymen, I'd suspect," Gwyddno answered.

"That's not what I asked," Crissiant said purposefully. "Where IS he? Right now, this very instant?"

Gwyddno looked a little less sure of himself just then. "Away in his own chambers. Or perhaps down by the tower alehouse if he fancies."

"Can you produce him for me?"

This request took the King completely by surprise.

"Well...well yes I certainly can. But first I need to ask why you are so distraught, daughter-in-law? Has someone wronged you?"

"Fetch me the prince and you shall have your answer," Crissiant replied.

The King's eyebrows knitted together, but he nodded towards the same servant boy, who was watching the exchange in dumb confoundment.

"Go and find the Prince of Gwynedd," he commanded. "Bid him show himself at the court at once, or at least bring me tidings of his location. Be off!" The boy darted down the open hallway. Crissiant rested her weight on one hip with an air of impatience. Tudno shifted nervously on his feet while the men in the room exchanged confused glances

"What game is this?" Elby said, breaking the tense silence. "Does her ladyship have a grievance with our King? If so, let her speak instead of waiting all night for Prince Rhun."

"Whether Prince Rhun shows or not will determine the nature of my grievance," Crissiant replied smoothly to the lord from Dyfed. "I wish to confirm whether my nephew, young Tudno, has told me the truth. I certainly hope, for all our sakes, that he has not."

"Boy!?" Seithenyn hollered at Tudno. "Have you been making up mischief? I should have known after your fosterling cousin pestered me about speaking to the King. What lies have you been peddling?"

"Well...uh...I would say, father, but...I... Auntie made me swear not to say a word until we had heard from Rhun."

"Tell me at once or I'll flay your arm with skewers when I get-"

"What is this!?" Gwyddno interrupted Seithenyn with a roar. "Are you saying, gatekeeper, that Taliesin asked to see me with a message? Why was I not informed?"

"Sire," Seithenyn said meekly. "You were steeped in meetings and court sessions that I thought-"

"I am always steeped in meetings and court business! That's my duty! Did anyone else receive a message from Taliesin that should have reached me?"

The hall fell silent except for the crackling of the dying fire in the center brazier. After inhaling deeply and removing her helm, Enid stepped forward keeping her eyes downcast.

"I talked with the lad earlier today," she said grimly. "I thought he was talking nonsense about conspiracies and plots, but I didn't believe they made any sense, your Highness. I thought the boy was looking to skip his day's training."

"I will judge such importance for myself. From here forth, not a single word or deed of any significance will be kept from me while Cantre'r Gwaelod remains mine to defend. Is that perfectly clear to everyone?"

The King took his time and swept the room with a furious gaze making sure each and every soul understood the gravity of his command. No one dared turn away from the King nor raise any voice against him.

Gwyddno sat back in his chair, satisfied his command had been received. He turned his attention back to Crissiant, who may have been the only person in the room that was left unimpressed by the King's wrath.

"Daughter-in-law," Gwyddno tried to sound understanding. "From what I hear, there may be a great deal of urgency to this news. Would you not kindly impart what you know so I may move to remedy what I can?"

"No, I would not," the elegant lady replied haughtily. "There's been urgency this whole bleeding day, but none of you were willing to lend an ear. And why not? Because the messengers were only small boys who couldn't have been up to anything but no good?" Crissiant's eyes shone like fire, but she hardly raised her voice above a whisper. Even so, every person in Gwyddno's court felt her words lash at them like a whip. "No one here was so dismissive of my adopted son when he was brought here thirteen years ago. You all saw the boy's nature then, and yet you brush him aside as some trouble-making brat during the time you should be paying extra attention to him. Isn't that what the King decreed?" she asked Gwyddno.

"Weren't we to wait thirteen years to see how the boy's true nature would reveal itself? You were there, gatekeeper. Did you forget?" she asked Seithenyn almost good-naturedly. Seithenyn's face turned a shade darker, but he made no response.

"It's plain to see that you all could have saved yourselves a great deal of pain and embarrassment if you had thought to listen to my foster son at all. Now, we will have to see how it plays out."

Almost as if on cue, the errand boy raced back from the hallway, puffing and gasping for breath.

"Your Majesty!" he said between breaths. "I called on every servant in the palace to see if anyone could locate the Prince of Gwynedd. None could, Sire. What's more, I raced to the stables myself. Not only is Prince Rhun's steed missing, but so is the whole of his escort. Have mercy, King, but I'm afraid there's no telling where the prince could be."

"Well, then!" Crissiant said, obviously satisfied with herself but far from joyful. "Allow me to answer the young lad's inquiry. The Prince of Gwynedd is at my home this very instant, plotting some evil against me before he flies back to the Dragon's Isle with all the gold he can carry. This boy and my son heard Gwynedd's man pay off a traitor to grant them passage just last night. So, pox on your grand peace treaty, pox on your merriment, and to hell with any hope of seeing my husband alive again. Peace be with you, O King!"

Crissiant turned on her heel and stormed out of the King's chamber with hardly a sidelong glance at the stunned lords, her dress cascading behind her. Tudno for his part remained sheepishly waiting by the door frame, looking timidly at his father and the King as they both took a moment to process the bleak news. Gwyddno's brow furrowed as he stared aghast into the floor in front of him. As Crissiant exited the chamber, he snapped his head up and turned immediately towards Enid.

"Captain! Take all the riders you can muster and charge to

Elphin's tower with all speed. And send word to all patrolling the gates not to let any rider from Gwynedd in or out of Cantre'r Gwaelod. Apprehend Prince Rhun and bring him here bound and gagged. Go at once!"

"Yes, Sire!" Enid barked as she flung her armor on and ran out of the chamber. All around the King, the various lords flew into action, calling for their arms and armor and yelling for their mounts. Gwyddno merely sat in his throne, pressing his face into the support of his knuckles, his illusion of peace and security thoroughly demolished.

***

The frigid stone floor made Taliesin wake with a start. He kicked his legs spastically as he struggled to breathe through a bruised windpipe. His head felt like it might crumble to pieces if he held it the wrong way. The young boy tried to pull himself up on his feet but sank back down as a wave of nausea hit him. His vision rocked in and out of focus, making him sick.

Soft sobbing from across the room jolted the boy to his senses. He steadied himself against the wall and peered through the flickering torchlight. Mererid sat huddled over herself on the floor, her bronze hair covering her face. Her shoulders heaved up and down and shook with every breath. Taliesin whirled around, suddenly remembering Rhun. The wolf was nowhere in sight. The overturned table and the scattered, spilled wine horns were the only sign that he had been there at all.

Taliesin staggered over to Mererid's form and knelt by her side.

"Mererid? What's happened? Did he hurt you?"

Mererid only recoiled from him, as if he were the one that had attacked her.

"Mererid? Please...let me help you," Taliesin pleaded.

"Help me?" Mererid asked, her swollen eyes peering out

through a curtain of hair. "How could you help me?" she asked
bitterly.

"Well...well tell me what happened first," Taliesin replied.
"What has the brute done? Did...did he force himself on you?"

"And if he did?" Mererid's face was a swollen mask of scorn.
Her voice, usually so sweet and musical, now sounded harsh and
torn. The young lady kept her arms crossed in front of her while she
bent herself over from the waist. "How could you help me then?
Could you replace what he took?"

Mererid's face contorted into a terrible visage of pain.

"You had your chance to help me, Taliesin!"

Taliesin felt every word from Mererid's lips tear through him
like hot knives. He *had* Rhun on the point of a sword. Why couldn't
he have kept him there? How could he have allowed himself to
founder so catastrophically? He felt a pit of shame grow in his
stomach and climb its way up to his throat.

"I'm...so sorry, Mererid. I didn't expect Rhun to be so quick,
I just-"

"You fool," Mererid said quietly, bowing her head back down
over her arm. "You stupid, weak fool."

"Please! I can help! Let me help! I'll find a healer, we can
mend you!" Taliesin begged as he collapsed to his knees. He felt tears
begin to drip down his face and he swiped at them furiously.

Mererid wheeled around to him, her face livid. Quick as a
dart she threw her left hand practically into the boy's face. Several
drops of blood splashed onto Taliesin's cheek as he reeled
backwards.

"Mend it, then! Can you mend this?!" she shrieked.

Taliesin looked at the delicate hand in front of him lined with
streams of blood flowing over smooth porcelain skin. The thick
rivulets trickled down from the space between Mererid's middle and
pinky finger. Where the fourth finger should have been was a single
mutilated stump dyed dark red.

CHAPTER 11: The Bud of War

erglyt a molet.
gworwyd a gworgret.
aercol ar gerdet.

Battles arose.
A woeful spreading flame,
There raises up a great fire.

~Trawsganu Cynan Garwyn, Llyfr Taliesin

The soldiers of Cantre'r Gwaelod pounded their way into Prince Elphin's dining hall. They found no sign of their fugitive, but only two poor souls sitting on the floor, completely lost in remorse and shock.

Enid ordered her men to tend to the wounded girl, who was clutching her hand into a cloth napkin. A healer was sent for, and the young serving girl was ushered away to have her wound treated with herbs and leeches. The captain of the guard then turned her attention to the small boy, hardly thirteen years old, who sat on the floor staring off into space. Enid knelt in front of him, paying no heed to the dark pools of spilled wine or streaks of blood. She slowly reached out and gently unclasped Taliesin's fingers still clenched tight around the metal broadsword. She patiently untangled the hilt from the boy's fist, like she was freeing a bird from a trap.

Enid then turned Taliesin's head so that the boy's eyes met hers.

"I am sorry, lad," she said. "It was you who tried to warn me of this, and I didn't listen. I feel like I haven't known shame until today."

Taliesin blinked several times and then focused his eyes on the captain at last.

"Enid?" the boy asked softly. "Enid? What of Rhun? Did you catch him? Did Tudno reach you in time?"

Enid only sighed. Her face looked like she was under a great weight.

"Nay!" she spat. "I've gotten reports from my men at the north gate. By the time our riders reached them, they had found the gate barricaded from the outside. Rhun and his lot are gone and are sure to be halfway back to Anglesey by now. The liar prince has well and truly stabbed a knife in our backs."

Taliesin sunk further into himself, completely at a loss for words. Enid reached up and removed her crested helm. She sat beside the boy and looked up and down his side.

"Are you hurt?" she asked.

Taliesin only shook his head, but the boy could have had an arm ripped off and he would have been too numb to even realize it.

"Enid…I tried," Taliesin said, his voice quivering. "I tried to defend her. I didn't know how…"

Enid bit her lip and looked up trying to pierce the stone ceiling of the tower to the very heavens above.

"Nobody is a warrior at birth, lad," she said at length. "Nobody that I ever trained ever won their first fight. Probably because the first person they fight tends to be me," she said without humor. "But I have to be honest, lad. I know when a young boy has the promise of a champion inside of him. I know the difference between the young pup that can be trained into a glorious warrior and the small child that is pushed onto the range by ambitious parents. I've seen too many boys trying their best to be men never live to enjoy their fifteenth summer."

She paused and looked meaningfully at Taliesin.

"I don't want that to be you, laddie," she said. "Not when you have the promise of such a charmed life." She rose to her feet, her armor clanging against itself as she did.

"Do not come to the training arena anymore," she told the boy flatly. "There is nothing there that I will teach you."

Enid left the boy sitting there on the stone floor and walked out of the dining hall with the broadsword in her gauntleted hand.

Taliesin finally pulled himself to his feet and began walking aimlessly, not so sure what to do with himself. Some of the royal soldiers were sweeping the tower's rooms, checking to see if anything had gone missing. Some were trying desperately to console Heida, who had just about exploded into conniptions to hear that the Prince of Gwynedd had attacked the lady of the house who in fact was not the Lady Elphin.

"Oh, of all the devilry I must contend with!?" she wailed. "I'm only concerned with putting food on the table! How was I to know the devil would visit tonight?! Oh, Lord forgive me! Oh, Heaven save us!" She moaned pitifully as the flustered knight in front of her tried to calm her.

Taliesin walked past all these people, hardly focusing his eyes on them. For their part, most of the guards ignored Taliesin, a few favoring him with a pained expression or an awkward clap on the shoulder. Taliesin wandered the tower in shock until he found himself opening the door to his mother's bedchamber, where, maybe two hours ago, maybe twenty years ago, he had draped his mother's best gown over Mererid. The oversized sword in his hand convinced him he could shield the girl from all the harm in the world.

The gown was now stained with blood and torn down the

front.

With hardly any strength left in his frame, Taliesin crumpled and fell face-first into his parent's goose feather pillow. He may have passed out and smothered himself there had it not been for the touch of two gentle hands on the back of his head.

Taliesin jerked his head to the side to see the placid face of his mother, gazing at him with a combination of relief and kind sympathy.

"Taliesin, my love." She whispered. "What on earth happened?"

The boy's words rushed forward out of his mouth along with his tears and cries and anguish. He relayed everything that had happened since overhearing Rhun's plot and how he wanted more than anything to stop the villain and save Elphin and give his mother something to truly be proud of. He confessed how he had snuck into her chamber and gave away her best dress and jewelry, about how sure he was he could defend himself and Mererid with the borrowed sword.

Through the whole thing, Crissiant only shushed his whimpers and ran her fingers over his back, holding him to her like a newborn.

"I fear it's all lost now, Mam," Taliesin said, finally finding his composure. "Grandad will be forced to go to war, won't he? The other lords will demand it." He found himself staring into the torch flames on the chamber wall. "Will we ever see Father again?" he asked numbly.

"We can only be patient and pray," Crissiant said. "No one is ever gone for good until they pass on to the heavenly father. And Elphin is not dead. Neither is your friend Mererid from the kitchen. She'll need some time to heal, but she'll be right as rain with only a missing finger to show for it."

"I'm sure she'll despise me now," Taliesin said glumly. "I thought I could save her from the brute. I just wanted to save you."

"But you have, love!" Crissiant said proudly. "You were the

only man or child that suspected Rhun's mischief. You were the one to see it all and spoil the coward's fun. If Rhun hadn't been fooled by you into staying here, who's to say he wouldn't have attacked me on my return? Rhun left here empty-handed. No doubt he wanted to harm or rob me to humiliate Elphin. But, at the very least, he won't be able to do that now."

Taliesin considered this perspective with fresh thoughts, not realizing the benefits his actions certainly had brought. In an instant, a detail came rushing back to him, dashing his comfort.

"He didn't leave empty-handed," Taliesin said as he stared into space. "He took Dad's ring. The one he gave you two years back with his sigil on it."

Crissiant took a moment to catch up with her foster son before brushing off the ring as a keepsake she hardly used. Inside her mouth, Crissiant gnawed on her lip with worry.

***

The next morning the people of Lowland Hundred found themselves preparing for war, only a night after celebrating their peace with Gwynedd. Riders and heralds were sent to every district of the sunken kingdom to announce Rhun's treachery and the ransom scorned. They called for all able-bodied men to report to Caer Wyddno's training grounds with any weapons they could wield. The declaration had not been officially made yet, but everyone in Cantre'r Gwaelod understood. The long-anticipated confrontation with Gwynedd had finally arrived at their door.

Representatives and dignitaries from all the southern kingdoms were summoned at once to the King's war chamber to report how many soldiers each could offer and how soon they could be produced. Some took objection to the King's plan.

"Every day we see more and more of the Norsemen's ships sneaking past our shores," one of the lords from Towy complained. "Gwynedd is a far less pressing threat to us. We would rather keep our warriors and men in their own land where they can protect their villages."

"And who would protect you from Maelgwn when he's gutted the Hundred and looks for his next meal?" Connwn demanded. "We must deliver him a strong answer, or we risk falling apart in front of this adversary."

"I concur," said Elby of Dyfed, "My lords have always been appreciative of Lord Elphin's generosity to us southerners. We wish to see his honor defended and our lands protected from the Dragon of the Isle! If Towy wants protection, let them do their part for us all!" he argued.

The King was far more patient with many of the hesitant clans.

"Towy, and any other people along the sea, may only pledge every other fighting man to us so they may keep the other half to guard their own. Mind you, Towy would then only be entitled to a half share of the spoils when we achieve victory."

The offer pleased most and even enticed some of the vulnerable kingdoms to pledge beyond half, in hopes of winning more wealth than their neighbors.

"My liege," Enid called to the King during a pause in the discussion. "This brings up a very pressing point of our own vulnerability." The captain kept her voice low, but every ear in the room paused to listen. "My vows demand I remain here and safeguard the citadel no matter what. Yet, you must understand how I long to run my sword through that cur Rhun's gut as soon as I can. Along with that, my men are the fiercest fighting force in all your domain. Our chances for victory would increase dramatically if we were to accompany you to Gwynedd."

"You and the guards' presence would be a comfort, certainly." The King nodded thoughtfully. "But we would be left defenseless here ourselves. Hardly ideal when we have this slippery snake to deal with."

"Hellfire take it!" Seithenyn moaned from opposite the table.

"How much time do we waste quibbling over problems with such obvious solutions? Have Enid take her lot with us to battle and take someone else's men to mind the Hundred."

"Mind your place, sonny!" Gwyddno shot Seithenyn a warning look. "Is there any lord here that could volunteer a contingent of troops to remain in Caer Wyddno?"

The war table fell silent, each man shooting looks to his neighbor. Finally, Connwn of Powys spoke up.

"I suppose I could spare a band of archers and the like. Mind you they won't enjoy missing out on the glory of battle."

"More the fool are they," the King replied curtly. "So be it, Powys will supply a substitute guard here, while Enid and her company will ride with us. How many fighters does that make all told, Bryn?"

The tall man sitting by the King's side began to stare off into space and flicked unseen beads around with his fingers until he arrived at his conclusion.

"That would be three thousand swordsmen, six hundred archers, and just under four hundred war steeds, your Majesty. That includes forces from Ceredigion, Powys, Dyfed, and Towy," the bard reported.

Gwyddno scratched the underside of his chin, wincing as he did. He followed by rubbing his hand, bejeweled with various gems and pearls, over his forehead. He finally asked quietly, "Are there no northern kingdoms that will aide us? Any word from Urien?"

"No messages have yet been returned, Sire," Bryn replied with a creased brow. "But riders were only sent out last night. It's doubtful that word has reached him yet."

"It's doubtful he would answer, too," Seithenyn added for spite.

"We shall seek him out anyway, and any other warrior in Britain willing to bear arms. Send out more messengers, promise a ewe and a lamb for any villager who would join us."

Bryn nodded to a foot servant who rushed to carry out the

order. Seithenyn again flashed a sour expression.

"We could have a legion of villagers, what good would it do us? With the northern kingdoms in his pocket, Maelgwn will pick them all off from the safety of his fortress."

"That's enough, Gatekeeper," Enid warned the King's second son.

"This will be the ruin of all our lands!" Seithenyn yelled carelessly.

King Gwyddno's fist nearly broke through the oak table set in front of him. The powerful blow shocked the armor of the gathered generals leaving the room with a fading metallic ring. Gwyddno turned his head to Seithenyn, his eyes blazing fury.

"I am waiting to hear a better alternative!" the King scolded. "Should we allow Gwynedd to run off unchecked, until every one of our allies deserts us? In the meantime, we're to let Prince Elphin, MY Prince Elphin, rot away after paying forty sacks of gold for it?! We have no option here, boy! There is no other course of action other than bringing the fight to Maelgwn and making him hurt so much for it that he shits himself into a cesspit, and I am willing to die to make that happen!"

The King turned his attention to the rest of the generals. Without meaning to, he had risen to his feet.

"Make all of your men and fighters ready!" he commanded. "Marshal all of our forces in the tower. In a week's time, we will bring destruction and fury to Gwynedd!"

***

Urien of Rheged flung himself out of the white linen tent pitched on a hill in Maelgwn's spacious field grounds. A squire approached him immediately and helped him into his polished armor padded with leather. A messenger from King Maelgwn had arrived early to summon Urien to the throne room as soon as he was able. Typically, most visiting lords and generals would accept guest chambers within a host's castle and enjoy fine treatment and warm fires at night while their soldiers were left to pitch tents and endure the elements. Urien always detested such practices and made himself an oddity among the British nobility by insisting on making camp with his own troops.

"Arthur's table was round to grant each an equal place at it," Urien would explain to anyone who questioned him. "Like so, by my honor, I will sleep on the same ground as my soldiers. On the battlefield, death will care not for my noble title."

Urien rounded up two or three of his honor guard and the group began hiking to Anglesey tower at a brisk pace. Maelgwn had practically insisted on Urien staying within the castle, but the Lord of Rheged would have none of it. Urien was no fool. He knew that the Lord of Anglesey was trying to win him over with gifts and flattering treatment. He understood how valuable his support would be to the vainglorious king, and that made him doubly wary.

However, Urien had to deal with the reality of the situation. All over the north of the country and beyond Hadrian's Wall, kings and landowners were throwing their lot in with Maelgwn, convinced that unifying under Gwynedd's flag was their only recourse to stopping the encroaching Saxons. Urien, by contrast, feared the Saxons less than he feared his own neighbors. He could see that Maelgwn was more interested in expanding his rule than repelling any invaders. He and any other lords that pledged fealty to Maelgwn would end up finding themselves used to destroy Maelgwn's only rival, Gwyddno Garanhir. But not siding with Maelgwn now would mean total destruction later. For his refusal, Urien was sure that Maelgwn would turn the full force of his might against Rheged, and then all the neighboring lords and Picts would fall on him like an avalanche.

The choice was a simple calculation for Urien: take the side of a Dragon to avoid getting scorched.

Urien and his men entered Angelesy's main tower, passed through the spacious feasting hall, and ascended the twisting stone stairs until they arrived before Maelgwn's throne room doors. The Lord of Rheged silently wondered what gift or bribery Maelgwn would offer this morning. What he beheld inside genuinely surprised him.

Sitting in the middle of the throne room on a small wooden bench sat the King's son, Prince Rhun, looking as if he had spent all night out in the savage cold. His face was pale and his tunic was soaked in sweat. A gash had been opened above his right eye. Maelgwn hovered anxiously over his son while the Queen of Anglesey sat on her throne, observing all with her lip nervously pressed into her mouth. As Urien entered, Maelgwn turned to address him.

"You see, good cousin?" Maelgwn implored, taking a step towards Urien. "Do you see what honor the men in the southern kingdom carry? What honor is it to abuse a king's dignitary like this?"

"Father, please. There's hardly reason to carry on so," Rhun pleaded.

"What has happened here?" Urien asked, taken off guard. "Did the prince encounter the Lowland men while hunting?"

"Bless us, no!" Maelgwn replied. "You should know, I sent my only son, Prince Rhun, to the Lowland Hundred to try and negotiate an honorable ransom for Gwyddno's son. There was no malice. If a son comports himself badly, I would only ask that the father compensate me fairly for the loss of face, isn't that lawful? Instead, my own son is returned to me with barely more than his life. Isn't that so, Rhun?"

"My life, and I was lucky to keep only that. Listen well, Lord of Rheged. The King of the Lowland Hundred is spiteful under his smiling mask. I arrived, was taken in, behaved myself like a monk, but was still betrayed. After a day of back and forth, we settled on the price of seven sacks of gold for Elphin's return. I should have known there was evil at work because I could tell that the price did not sit well with the King of Cantre'r Gwaelod. But he agreed, and we exchanged oaths of brotherhood and unity. More's the shame, because as we were celebrating our agreement late last night, I caught the King sending a signal to his castle guard, and then before I knew it, my men and I were surrounded by Gwyddno's soldiers. My comrades acted quickly, and we were able to fight our way out and down to the stables before the alarm could be properly sounded. We rode back for Anglesey all night, wasting not a single moment for rest. On our way through the main gate, we were accosted by the Lowland Hundred guard. I narrowly escaped having my head chopped off. Thankfully this wound was all the abuse I received."

Rhun took a long pull from the goblet of mead he was drinking and then braced his body on his knee.

"Peace, son! Peace," Maelgwn chided. "You need to recover your strength."

"I don't understand," Urien said, perplexed. "You say you reached an agreement with King Gwyddno for Elphin's ransom and then he tried to attack you?"

"Yes!" Rhun said, holding his side in pain. "He hollered something about 'trading a prince for a prince'. I guess the King wondered why he should pay full price when he could figure me into the bargain. But this isn't any way to treat an honorable messenger who's shown his host nothing but grace and respect. Can he say the same for his own son when he was at our table?"

Urien could only gape at the wounded prince. Three times he tried to find the words to answer Rhun, but none came.

"Do you not see the urgency here, Lord Urien?" Maelgwn asked. "Those of the Lowland Hundred are just that, low indeed. They do not adhere to the bonds of honor that we observe here in the north. It is a ghastly betrayal on Gwyddno's part."

"And very out of character for Gwyddno," Urien added. He turned to Rhun. "Do you swear that all you told me is true? Can you think of no other reason the King of Cantre'r Gwaelod attacked you other than to take the advantage in the negotiations?"

"I speak the truth!" Rhun insisted. "And what's more, in the hours leading up to our attack and most certainly afterward, we noticed that the men of Cantre'r Gwaelod were mustering their strength, calling for any forces their allies could spare. It seems obvious to me. Gwyddno means to bring war to Anglesey!"

"What!?" Maelgwn asked in alarm. "Are you certain, son?"

"We saw the guards hard at work sharpening their swords and filling their quivers. No less than a dozen territories from the south are sending their fighters to Gwyddno's gate. Why else would he leave his vassals so unprotected unless he thought to overwhelm us and lay siege to Anglesey Island?"

Rhun brought his hand up to his gash in pain. Maelgwn wrung his pudgy hands together and anxiously paced back and forth.

"You see!" Maelgwn implored Urien. "Do you see the aggression that we of Gwynedd have to endure from our southern neighbors? After the armies of Cantre'r Gwaelod sack us, do you think Gwyddno will stop there? Oh, no, my cousin! He will not stop until he conquers every northern kingdom to claim for his own." Maelgwn cast one last pitiful look at his son who looked like he was a breath away from collapsing completely.

"Lord Urien," Maelgwn said seriously. "My allies are prepared to help me defend the North's sovereignty, but they will take time to send reinforcements. You and your company of fine warriors are camped here by happy chance. I must ask you, Urien, even though you have not pledged fealty to Gwynedd just yet. Will you stay here in Anglesey for the time being and help defend us against this invading force?"

Urien cast his glance to the King, his son, and his wife Bannon in turn. The King's eyes shone hopefully while Rhun looked up expectantly from under his arm. Bannon on the other hand only steepled her fingers and pressed them urgently against her lips as she turned her eyes away from Urien. Her eyebrows knitted and her delicate lips murmured something that may have been a prayer or incantation.

Urien turned slightly to his trusted lieutenant.

"Send out one of our scouts immediately to the Lowland

Hundred. Have him confirm that Gwyddno is mustering his forces together and return with haste." The man at arms bowed his head and then marched off to affect the order. Urien turned back to Maelgwn. "In the meantime, O King of Gwynedd, I give you my word that should the Lowland Hundred move to attack Anglesey while my men and I are your guests, we shall rise to your aid and help you push back this threat."

Maelgwn reared himself up to his full height, looking like Urien had just offered him his firstborn child.

"That, gentle cousin, is a great comfort to this burdened King. The people of Gwynedd will surely remember your aid and heroism in song and story for generations."

"I have no interest in glory," Urien said, unimpressed. "I only wish to see peace and unity return to this realm and if I need to fight a fire before it becomes an inferno, then so be it. Please keep me informed of the situation then. Good morning, your Highness."

Urien bowed low and then made to leave the throne room with his honor guard. Maelgwn called out after him.

"Please recall, good Lord, that my annual tournament of bards is still scheduled to start in three days' time. It is a jolly event full of songs, stories, and merriment. My four and twenty bards put on quite a spectacle."

"You speak of minstrels and bard's tales while war marches towards you?" Urien said, raising a perplexed eyebrow.

"Oh, but you must understand." Maelgwn waved off the chastisement. "The tournament of bards is a rich tradition started by the great Cunedda himself. We must not stifle art and culture at every little threat. But rest assured, my dear Lord of Rheged, I will ensure that my archers and champions remain on high alert during the festivities."

Urien's face seemed to make it clear that, given the same situation, he would choose a far different course of action for his own keep. But the dark-haired man only nodded politely.

"As you wish then, your Majesty," he replied neutrally, and

then paced out of the throne room with his honor guard trailing in his wake.

Rhun waited until he could no longer hear Urien's footsteps clanging down the stairs before he sat up straight in his bench, downed the horn of mead in one great gulp, and then callously tossed the empty horn at the feet of a nearby attendant.

"Oy! You there! Fetch us another horn of mead!" he demanded without the slightest hint of pain or discomfort. The young boy ran off like a dog was chasing him.

"'A prince for a prince?'" Maelgwn echoed mockingly at his son. "You couldn't have come up with a better reason for Gwyddno to attack you?"

"That's the best part, dad!" Rhun said with glee. "Gwyddno actually said that to me when I first arrived and hadn't yet shown him the bait. The best lies are always wrapped in bits of truth."

"Well, I can only be grateful that Urien is more gullible than I. I would have seen straight through that amateur performance you just gave."

"If you say so, dad," Rhun replied.

"I still object to this deception," Bannon said from her place on the throne. "We are guilty of bearing false witness. Oh! The prayers I will have to say for the Lord's forgiveness."

"A King acts with the authority that the supreme has vested in him," Maelgwn snapped at his wife. "If I see fit to bend the truth to protect my kingdom, then so be it. As King, I am the will of God!"

"But such pride and vanity always precede the fall of the wick-"

Maelgwn slammed his fat palm down on the table he was leaning over with a loud smack. The Queen cringed slightly at the sound and left her sentence unfinished.

"Your place is not to deliver scriptures to me, wife," Maelgwn said softly and crisply. "Neither is it to criticize how I rule."

Bannon only turned her face away and towards the floor. Her

breath wavered as she tried to keep her lithe frame from trembling.

Amid the sudden tension in the room, Rhun jumped to his feet and clapped his hands together.

"All of this talk and I haven't even had an opportunity to show our guest the souvenir I snatched before slipping past Gwyddno's walls. Shall we send for him, Father? You know how impatient I can be."

Maelgwn glanced at his son and wife before nodding his head in agreement.

"Aye," he said, "that would bring us a good cheer after all. Go fetch Prince Elphin from the tower." He turned to address one of the servants standing by the doorway. "Bring him here, but do not loosen his chains. Have the tower guards assist you."

The servant bowed and made off at once.

"With your permission, I shall retire to the abbey for prayers," Bannon said as she made to get up.

"You shall sit where a Queen should sit," Maelgwn commanded. "I want you to see Elphin's humiliation and understand what fate awaits any man that dares question your honor. It is what any loving husband would want for his wife."

"As you command, Sire," Bannon said softly as she sat back in her throne reluctantly.

A few minutes later, the heavy clanging of chains announced Elphin's arrival. The throne room door opened, and two pikemen led the ragged prisoner in. Elphin had gone the last four nights without any food and only the water he could cup in his hands from the window during the rain. The food that had been dutifully brought up to Elphin twice each day and left just out of reach, had been devoured by rats while Elphin was left to watch and envy the vermin. The ordeal had left Elphin hollow-eyed and pale. Despite his exhaustion, Elphin drew himself up to his full height as he stood in front of the King of Anglesey.

The errand boy brought Rhun his extra horn of mead, and the cocksure Prince sauntered his way over to Elphin, making a show of enjoying the hot drink in front of the starving man's face.

"How now, Prince Elphin?" Rhun asked overly casual. "It hasn't been too drafty for you in that tower of yours, has it?"

Elphin sucked in on his lip and inhaled deeply through his nose as if he were trying to inhale the moisture out of the very air.

"I think your castle may be coming down with a flea infestation," he replied, his voice raspy. "I hear that happens when too many rats run amok." He glanced meaningfully at Maelgwn and Rhun.

"What's this all about then?" Elphin asked, letting his exhaustion seep into his words. "Has dad conceded Ceredigion to you yet? Or maybe you just brought me here for a hearty breakfast?"

"You might say that," Rhun said with a grin. "I'm sure you're pining for a substantial meal, so I thought that I might serve you up your own words to choke on."

Rhun then turned his back on Elphin and reached inside the folds of his tunic. He produced a small cylindrical parcel no larger than the palm of his hand wrapped in a neat linen cloth. He held up the wrapped object and presented it to Maelgwn and Bannon.

"O Sire," he said, addressing Maelgwn, "surely I don't have to remind you of the dishonor this guest of ours delivered at our grand feast some time ago and the insults he shouted at you, dear mother." Bannon turned her glance away modestly. "What's more, when offered his freedom for the price of an apology, this ungrateful guest threw more insults at us. And what was the claim he made? Do you recall your own words, cretin?"

Rhun turned back to Elphin, who only looked back at him confounded and tired.

"Let me remind you then," Rhun said, his smirk still plastered onto his face. "Our guest, Prince Elphin, claimed that there was more piety in his wife's little finger than in our whole kingdom of Gwynedd. Well, here I have proof to the contrary!" Rhun handed the cloth package to the King who began to untie the woven string that held the cloth. Rhun continued.

"During my stay in Cantre'r Gwaelod, I made pains to meet with the Lady Elphin face to face. She is many things, but pious she most certainly is not." Elphin's face suddenly changed from deathly pale to a dark, furious red. "With her husband imprisoned and her home empty, she eagerly invited me to sup with her, wearing gowns and jewels most scandalous for a lady in her situation. She offered me food and wine and shamelessly flirted with me as she drank herself into a drunken stupor."

"You lie!" Elphin sputtered. "My Crissiant would never-"

"You hold your tongue!" Maelgwn barked. One of the sentinels holding Elphin's chains pulled tightly as if Elphin were no more than a dog on a leash.

"Oh, but I speak the truth!" Rhun retorted. "She carried herself more like a fresh harlot than the pious wife you spoke of. As she sat passed out from the goblets of wine, I could have taken her right there and sampled the meat that Elphin prizes so dearly, but unlike Elphin, I have standards. So instead, I decided to take a small keepsake to show our guest the merit of his wife's honor."

Maelgwn opened the linen parcel. Rhun had told him bluntly what he had brought back for Cantre'r Gwaelod, but Maelgwn wanted the satisfaction of looking at his son's gift in front of Elphin's face. The sight inside the parcel did not disappoint Maelgwn in the least.

"Oh, ho!" Maelgwn chuckled as he plucked the object from the linen cloth. "Oh, this is a rich sight indeed. Behold, prince of fishermen! You say there's more piety in your wife's little finger?"

Bannon, sitting next to the King, glanced over her shoulder at the contents of the linen wrappings and then turned her face away in disgust.

"Well, behold! Here's her finger right before you. Take a good look and draw out all the piety you need from it!" Maelgwn flung the severed digit at Elphin's feet as the chained man stared at it with horror.

"Cut from her own hand after she passed out from

intoxication, and after flirting so outrageously with me," Rhun boasted. "I only did the good Lord's work, friend prince! After all, such shameless behavior shouldn't go unpunished."

Rhun and his father broke out into riotous laughter at this. Bannon turned her face downward, looking like she was trying to drop flat through the floor. Elphin, with trembling hands, picked up the small dead finger, holding it as gingerly as he would an injured bird.

"See you the ring near the base?" Rhun further chided. "That is your sigil, is it not? At least you needn't worry about some other fishmonger slipping his ring on your wife while away!"

Elphin turned the finger over to view the ring, and then suddenly frowned and brought the severed finger up close to his face, studying it like a jeweler.

"Right," Elphin said at length in an unsettling calm tone. "And you're sure that you cut this finger from my wife, then?"

"I just told you I did, you fool!" Rhun replied, somewhat agitated. "She could barely keep her hands off me, so I decided to keep a bit of one to remember her by!"

"Truly, now?" Elphin's voice remained completely neutral and his posture upright. He was still examining the finger fastidiously, turning it over in his hands and inspecting each and every angle.

"Do you doubt my own son's word, Prince Elphin?" Maelgwn all but boomed. "That is your sigil on the ring, is it not?"

"Oh, absolutely, in truth, there is no mistaking that this is my ring that I gave to my wife on our tenth wedding anniversary if I remember correctly. But, with your grace's leave, there are three things that give me cause to doubt your son's tale."

The royal father, son, and mother all stared at Elphin expectantly.

"For one, I remember this ring - which I recognize from the small pearl set just above my sigil as you can see here - was a size too big for my wife's hand and would barely sit around her thumb without falling off. Somehow, the owner of this finger was able to pull the ring over the second knuckle of her fourth finger, but it certainly isn't coming off in a hurry now. Secondly, if you examine the nail of this finger..."

Elphin held the tip of the still bleeding finger up to his face for emphasis.

"You'll see that the nail hasn't been pared for a series of weeks if not a month. I can assure you faithfully though, that my wife has pared her nails almost obsessively every third night for the last ten years at least. And finally, if you'll look closely under this nail...this UN-PARED NAIL, mind you!" Elphin erupted. "You'll discover that this finger has been kneading..." Elphin put the end of the finger up to his nose and sniffed hard twice, "...rye dough...somewhat recently and definitely routinely. My wife however has not kneaded rye dough or any dough for that matter since my wife she has been."

Elphin paused to see the King and Prince before him exchanging incredulous glances. Bannon, although Elphin could barely make out the Queen's face, hid the barest hint of a smile behind her royal cowl. Elphin then held the cut finger in his right hand and shook it accusingly at his captors, as if he were pointing his own finger at them.

"My only question to you, Prince Rhun, is what poor, wretched maiden did you so nobly mutilate for this charade?"

"Away with him!" Maelgwn commanded the guards. The chain-mailed men began dragging Elphin's weak frame up the tower stairs.

"I still say!" Elphin called back over his shoulder. "More piety in her little finger! That's the one on the end of the hand, not in the middle! Mind yourself next time!"

CHAPTER 12: The Choice

Ae vn hynt gwynt ae vn dwfyr mor.
Ae vn vfel tan twrwf diachor.

Is one the course of the wind, is one the water of the sea?
Is one the spark of the fire, of unrestrainable tumult?

~Preiddeu Annwn, Llyfr Taliesin

As Elphin was enjoying the only laugh he'd had since the infamous feast, Taliesin was making the most of the morning in an entirely different way. Sleep had not found Taliesin that night, but occasionally he found himself staring through the stone walls of his room, hallucinating the angry waves outside the castle or the craggy mountains away north. The visions brought no rest, but they did calm Taliesin's mind for a few moments. Then the spell would break, and all his raw emotion would flood back to the boy, stabbing him in the gut and up his spine. Guilt, shame, and existential terror were his only companions that night until Taliesin finally saw the first beam of sunlight skip over the hills and paint the walls of his room blood red.

Taliesin roused himself to his feet, wincing at the pain in his head and torso from where Rhun had battered him. He peered out the window to see Cantre'r Gwaelod come alive with people loading ferry boats and rushing messages down the causeways. He wondered how the legendary kingdom would look in a week's time, with every able-bodied soldier gone to do battle against Gwynedd. He wondered what his home would look like a week after, when the Lowland Hundred inevitably failed against Maelgwn's' superior forces, and the Dragon brought every sword in Anglesey to Cantre'r Gwaelod's gates. Taliesin found himself wondering numbly if Maelgwn would even spare the women and children, or simply sell them off as slaves to the Irish.

During this dark rumination, ideas began to dance through the boy's head uninvited, sparked by the first rays of the sun. The Lowland Hundred's doom was all but ensured, so what difference did his own actions make? He could rip out his heart in front of Mererid and bleed to death for her sake, and nothing would change. He could throw himself into the sea and be done with it all before he had to see Gwynedd's flag raised in Caer Wyddno. He could even squeeze his way through the walls of the city and escape into the hills and forests and wander alone for the rest of his life. He may even be able to wander his way to Anglesey and maybe, just maybe, he could even see the only father he had ever known from his cell window.

The morbid train of thought suddenly began to churn in Taliesin's mind, driving his body. Still reeling from shock and a nearly sleepless night, Taliesin pulled on his clothes, packed a small bundle of warm cloaks and a small bit of cheese, and walked out of Elphin's tower. His only second thought hit him as he glanced back at his mother, fallen asleep on one of the couches near the fire brazier, a melancholy expression draped on her sleeping face. He knelt and gave her a tender kiss on the forehead and then left.

***

The sun was low over the ocean as Taliesin made his way to the royal stables. All the King's family kept spare mounts in the lavish holding pens in case the King needed a horse for guests or messengers. Taliesin would have gone to Elphin's stables beside his tower, but the boy needed to be discreet.

As he approached the wooden gate, an armored guard lowered his pike to block the boy's way.

"Halt! State your business here, master!" the guard announced.

"Careful with that thing, Goedd," Taliesin said in a friendly manner. "You're sure to slice my neck open next time. I've been sent to fetch a training mount for Enid at the jousting ring."

Goedd, the rotund guard, screwed up his face with confusion. "Wasn't the captain preparing for war with the King this evening?"

"She was. And now she wants to tally all the cavalry units before the sun sets. Shall I pass then?" Taliesin purposefully let a hint of impatience creep into his voice. The guard only stretched out his face thoughtfully and lifted his pike. Taliesin nodded graciously and made his way into the reeking stables.

With all the commotion of fighters and horses coming and going, Taliesin suspected that nobody would notice a missing horse until he had put a decent bit of distance between him and the stables. More troubling was how he was going to manage to ride a horse without looking conspicuous. He'd held the reins of a horse only twice in his twelve years.

Near the back corner stood Seithenyn's dozen horses. The gatekeeper favored hunting on land more than fishing out at sea and kept the best horses for himself and his older sons. For his youngest, Tudno, Seithenyn only kept a gray pony. Taliesin had seen his cousin training on some of the healthier mounts and he imagined Tudno wouldn't miss the poor animal.

He came to the last stall and pushed open the gate.

"Tudno?!" Taliesin asked in surprise. Seithenyn's youngest boy was busy shoveling manure. He glanced over his shoulder and then turned his attention hurriedly back to the shit pile.

"Hi Tali," Tudno said without facing him. "I heard what

happened last night. Are you alright?"

"In body, yes, but my mind is another matter. What happened to you last night?"

Tudno stood up and went to empty the old horse's water bucket. He turned awkwardly around the horse, taking care to keep from showing his face.

"I did as you asked. I found your mother in the chapel, I told her Rhun was at her house right then. She turned as pale as a sheet and dragged me off to find Grandad."

"And what happened after?" Taliesin asked, trying to peer around the back of Tudno's head.

"Well...my father sent me home, he did," Tudno said, his hands a flurry of nervous activity. "Said he wanted me to stay out of harm's way until he got back. He was in a bit of a state, of course. Still is, really. I came down here to check on the family's horses, give myself something to do while father calms down a--"

Tudno didn't have a chance to finish his sentence. A quick, violent shove from Taliesin sent the boy off balance and forced him to wheel around before he tripped over into the freezing water trough. Taliesin looked at his cousin's face and immediately understood.

Tudno's cheeks and lips were swollen and bruised to discoloration. A dark black ring surrounded Tudno's left eye which could hardly open. His nose looked like it had been smashed with a hurley bat and had a rivulet of dried blood curling down from his nostrils. His bottom lip was almost split in two.

"Oh gracious, Tudno…" Taliesin gaped. He felt a wave of guilt rush over him. "Did...did Seithenyn…?"

"Father said I embarrassed him," Tudno said quietly. "He said I should have told him myself about any treachery and not to have sent you to talk with him."

"But you didn't send me, I was the one who tried to reason with Seithenyn," Taliesin pointed out.

"He says he would have listened if I talked to him first."

"Do you believe that?" Taliesin asked gently.

Tudno only sniffed, painfully wiping away blood and snot from his face. "It doesn't much matter. Maybe if I make myself useful, father will forgive me and leave me alone tonight. He should have other things on his mind anyway."

"And say that he does forgive you," Taliesin said, attempting to steer the conversation somewhere else. "What will you and your brothers do? Surely you're not about to ride off to war with everyone else?"

"Do I look old enough to carry a sword?" Tudno asked bitterly. "Let's face facts Taliesin. Neither of us is worth much for fighting."

"No." Taliesin inhaled sharply. Tudno's comment stung worse than his cousin could realize, but Taliesin had to accept reality.

"No, we're not. So, what are we to do, Tudno? If we can't help anybody on the battlefield, what good will we be when Maelgwn's armies arrive here? We'll be devoured like a school of fish along with the rest of the kingdom. You can see that, can't you?"

Tudno heaved a heavy sigh, gingerly setting himself down on the frigid ground of the horse stall. He braced his body against his folded knees and tucked his head down.

"Of course," he admitted. "Everyone can see it. I don't know how the fighting men can act so brave. All we can do, I suppose, is pray to God for deliverance."

"And what if we could do more?"

Taliesin's question made Tudno whip his head up suddenly despite his injuries.

"What in heaven's name are you talking about?" he demanded.

"You just said it right now. If we stay put, we'll be destroyed along with the whole kingdom. If we ride off to war, we'd be skewered in seconds. So, what if we leave before the battle? What if we leave now, this very hour?"

Tudno opened his eyes so wide, his left even managed to peer out through the surrounding purple bruise.

"Where on earth to?" he squealed. "That's abandonment! We'd be branded as traitors and disowned, surely!"

"No, we're not abandoning anybody Tudno, you're not understanding me. We have no future here. So, if we're doomed anyway, let's take a chance and try something that may just fix this whole mess and save Elphin and the kingdom both."

Tudno only wore a mask of exasperation and shook his head at the grimy floor.

"I certainly don't understand you, cousin. Are you trying to tell me you've gone mad?"

"I'm telling you that one way or another, I am leaving tonight for Anglesey's fortress. I'll get there however I can and pull Elphin out of the dungeons even if I have to sell my soul!" Taliesin could feel his heart begin to race. He had tried to keep his emotions in check, but visions of Mererid sobbing over her own blood tormented him raw. He felt like he had spent the whole day teetering on the edge of desperation.

Tudno spat out a mocking laugh. "Oh, yes? And how are you going to do that? Can you bend iron and break chains? You'll just get caught and thrown in the dungeon with Elphin and left to rot."

"As long as I can hold him again, I don't care if worms eat out my eyes!" Taliesin's voice had echoed off the stone and wood of the stables. Taliesin took a steady breath, willing himself to stay calm and collected before the guards took too much notice. He focused his gaze squarely on Tudno.

"All I want to know before I go, cousin, is will you come with me?"

Tudno kept still at last and only looked at his cousin and the small, packed satchel hanging from his shoulder. He gulped in a mouthful of air.

"You could be killed," he whispered. "In a hundred different ways, you could perish."

"We've been over that," Taliesin replied calmly. "We'll die

here anyway if we stay. At least this way...we can have a chance."

The two boys stood face to face, the setting sun outside coloring the drab stable a brilliant crimson. After giving Tudno a moment or two to think it over, Taliesin finally took the initiative.

"Very well. God keep you, cousin. I mean that sincerely." Taliesin turned and began walking, silently ruminating about the best way to pass through the kingdom gates without being identified.

"Taliesin!" Tudno's voice called out. He turned back to see the boy fixing a set of leather reins to a stout pony and leading it up to him. "We can take Stomper, here. I'd get a proper horse, but they're all mounted with war gear now."

"He'll do fine. We're not out to win any races. Thank you, Tudno," Taliesin said, giving the pony a gentle pat. Tudno raised his eyes at the satchel of clothes.

"Would you happen to have an extra cloak in there?" he asked.

***

The two boys waited an hour after dark and then mounted up the stout pony and made their way to the kingdom's main gates. Taliesin did not have more than a single cloak for himself, so he gave Tudno an extra-large shirt he had grabbed instead. The boys adjusted the shirt under the collar of Tudno's tunic so that the fabric draped over his head like a hood. Taliesin only prayed that the dark would keep anyone from questioning the bizarre outfit.

Moving within the kingdom by pony carried no risk to the boys but trying to pass through the gates would be risky. Even during peacetime, the sentinels were supposed to question anyone leaving after nightfall. If Taliesin was recognized leaving the kingdom without permission, he was sure to be brought before the King, and although he could usually trust Gwyddno to be lenient, he was sure that he wouldn't be given another opportunity to leave the kingdom.

As the cob horse trotted down the main causeway that led

from the stables to the gate, several trains of horses and men passed them in the other direction. The horses were draped with the colors of Powys and the men wore battle armor and carried bushels of arrows and weaponry.

"These must be the fighters from Powys that my dad mentioned," Tudno said under his breath to Taliesin. "Gwyddno's calling in all the allies he can gather."

"It probably means that they've assigned more security around the gate," Taliesin mused grimly. The boys plodded along, doing their best to hide from the passing knights. As they neared the main gate, Taliesin noticed something ahead of them.

"Tudno!" he exclaimed, "Up ahead! That train of ten or so horses making to leave, go and get behind the last one." A small line of horses was weighed down with hay, flour, and, by the smell of it, bushels of freshly caught fish. The men and horses were waiting patiently to be permitted to leave. Many of Cantre'r Gwaelod's fishermen resided just outside the walls of the kingdom in Ceredigion and used the harbor to haul in fish for their markets. With luck, the two boys might be able to pass for being part of the train and sneak out of the kingdom unnoticed.

Tudno steered the pony so they were in step with the final horse loaded down with burlap sacks. As the lead horse approached the gate, a brightly armored sentinel lowered his pike bringing the line of horses to a stop. The merchant leading the train began talking with the guard. The two boys did their best to sink into their cloaks and avoid getting seen. It looked as if the merchant had handed over his tribute and was about to lead the train through the gate when a tall man riding a mule trotted past them.

"HOLD, I say!" Bryn's recognizable voice rang out to the guard. "Word from the King! No man, horse, or ship is to leave the Lowland Hundred's wall by night! The gates are closed to outgoing travelers until sun up!" he announced.

Both the guards and the stalwart merchant visibly balked.

"What!?" the merchant whined. "And how am I to keep this

haul of mackerel from spoiling, eh? The King will ruin my livelihood!"

"Apologies, but I'm just the humble messenger for my Lord," Bryn returned good-naturedly, staring into the torchlight to make out the vexed man. "You can take your complaint to the King tomorrow if you would."

"But then I'll lose even more of my fish!" the merchant said, turning a shade of irritation. "Where am I supposed to stay the night, at any rate?"

At this point, the guard holding the pike by his side spoke up.

"Ah now, Bryn," he said in a friendly tone. "It's only old Gabber here. He comes in an' out of the Hundred every week. He's no spy. Besides, he's already paid up his tribute."

Bryn heaved out a sigh and then waved his hand dismissively from his mule.

"Aye, go on then!" he said. "But I never saw this happen. Have him pass through and then close the gates."

Gabber the merchant nodded respectfully at Bryn and began leading his horses and carts through the towering gate. Taliesin gently nudged Tudno, who urged the pony forward. They had made it as far as where Bryn was seated on his mule when the bard suddenly spoke up.

"What ho, now!" he said with a puzzled look at the two cloaked shapes seated on the pony. "What happened to your lot of fish to carry?" he asked.

"Uhm...we're the master's fishing pages..." Tudno said in a ridiculously deep voice.

"His what?!" Bryn asked, immediately suspicious. Taliesin considered grabbing the reins from Tudno and barreling the pony through the open gate but thought better of it when he realized he would have nowhere to go before the King's horses overtook the slower pony. "Who's there, by Arawn?"

"We are sailors from Cered...ahh...from Powys!" Tudno tried

to explain, unsuccessfully.

"Oh, yes?" Bryn said sarcastically. "And isn't it just the latest fashion in Powys to wear one's overshirt on their head?" Bryn's hand darted out quick as lightning to fling Tudno's impromptu cloak away from his face. The boy's bruised face stared back at Bryn in the torchlight.

"Ah, so it's Tudno, Seithenyn's son up to mischief tonight, is it? And which of your brothers is taking you for a ride this evening?"

Bryn yanked the cloak off Taliesin's head and fell silent when he saw the young boy's face staring into him, his eyes pleading with his friend to look the other way and let them pass.

"Oy!" Gabber the merchant called back. "Those two are not part of my team!" he announced, noticing the stand-off between the boys and Bryn.

Bryn glanced back over his shoulder at the merchant and the guards and then back at Taliesin.

"Of course not!" he called back. "It's only a pair of young fools looking to make trouble. I will escort them to the King this very moment." He saluted the gate patrol and wheeled his mule around, beckoning with a jerk of his head. "Come along then!"

Tudno exchanged an anxious glance with Taliesin, who only sighed and nodded. Tudno led his pony to follow Bryn and the trio clopped their way down the causeway back towards the palace. Bryn waited until he could barely make out the palace gate ahead of him before turning to face the two boys directly.

"Alright, out with it," he said quietly but sternly. "What business do the two of you have outside the walls? I want answers right now if you don't want your hides tanned black tonight!"

"Bryn," Taliesin pleaded. "Please, you need to let us pass tonight."

"I don't *need* to do anything, except sing and dance when the King commands. So why don't you tell me, young master, why I should even consider letting you and your cousin out of my sight, now that I can see you're bent on treason."

"WE'RE NOT TRAITORS!" Tudno exclaimed loud enough for several knights riding down the causeway to turn their heads. Bryn waited patiently until they were out of earshot.

"Then explain yourselves!" he resumed. "We're on the brink of war and I catch two royal princelings attempting to sneak out in the black of night. What do you expect me to make of it?"

"Bryn," Taliesin said calmly. "Tell us now, in all honesty. Do you think that Gwyddno can win against Maelgwn's forces? Truly, now?"

This question clearly struck the bard, who exhaled heavily and turned his face out towards the misty harbor.

"Aside from Prince Elphin, I am the only soul from Cantre'r Gwaelod that has visited Anglesey since the summer. I saw the fields of tents and horses from half of Wales there. The rest of the men and the generals only fear the worst. I know it in my bones. We haven't a hope."

"Exactly right!" Taliesin said. "We're not going to be able to fight our way out of this. So, we need something drastic to turn the tables around."

Taliesin gulped deep and stole one last glance around him, checking for listening passers-by.

"We're going to see if we can free Elphin ourselves," he said softly.

Bryn sat back on his mule, staring at the boys in mute shock. He sucked in the top of his lip and ran it underneath his teeth. For a moment, the bard had nothing to say and just sat there chewing his lip while his eyes darted back and forth from the boys to the gate and then off towards the dark horizon. Taliesin waited close to a minute before speaking again.

"Bryn, will you please let us go?"

The bard snapped his attention back to the boys, his blue eyes flashing in the gloom. His face had turned deathly stern, an expression that Taliesin never would have thought the congenial man was capable of.

"You two follow me and don't say a single word to anyone. Keep your cloaks over yourselves, or your shirts in any case." He raised an eyebrow at Tudno. "If you two take one step in the wrong direction or say one word to anyone, I'll sound the alarm and see to it you two spend the night in the dungeon for treason. Am I clear?"

The two boys nodded. Bryn held their gaze for a few more seconds to emphasize how serious his ultimatum was, and then yanked his mule back towards Caer Wyddno. He began trotting along as casually as if he were out to observe the stars. Tudno risked a quick backward glance at Taliesin before following.

The trio plodded along until they arrived at the entrance to the palace. Bryn pulled his mule over to the right next to the stone banister that kept careless pedestrians from tumbling into the harbor's cold waters below. He gestured for the boys to join him with a flick of his fingers. As Tudno steered the pony over to the shadowy portion of the causeway, Bryn swung his leg over the side of his mount and gracefully leaped to the ground.

"You two stay here and keep out of sight. Don't forget my warning. I'll be no more than ten minutes."

Taliesin was about to ask what the bard was headed into the palace for, but the older man had already gone with a spry turn of his heel. They watched him all but caper into the palace, joking with anyone who crossed his path.

"Do you think he'll bring Enid?" Tudno asked nervously. "Are they going to lock us up?"

"If that's what he was after, he could just bring us before Granddad," Taliesin observed.

"Then what is the demon up to?" Tudno replied.

The boys hardly had to wait a minute before they got their answer. Bryn returned from the palace's warm interior with his harp and a small leather bag. He flung his effects over his shoulder and clambered up on top of the mule.

"Follow me now," he whispered and pulled his mule down the southern leading causeway. Taliesin and Tudno followed obediently. After a minute with hardly another living soul passing them on the deserted causeway, Taliesin mustered up his courage to speak.

"Bryn?"

Bryn only brought his finger to his lips, insisting on silence. Taliesin paid him no heed.

"Bryn, where are you taking us?" Taliesin asked in a muted voice. "We'll make a run for it anyway, whether you sound the alarm or not. So don't think you can just lead us off to a dungeon someplace."

"Of course not!" Bryn said, obviously no longer concerned with secrecy. "I can't let you two live out the rest of your short lives in a dungeon, and I can't allow you to foolishly run headfirst into Maelgwn's prison. So, it looks like I'll just have to go with you."

Tudno couldn't help but let out a surprised squawk.

"What?!" he nearly shrieked. "Why not just let us go out when we had the chance!? What game is this?"

"It'd be a bit suspicious, wouldn't it?" Bryn replied. "Two boys on a pony trailing a fish merchant? You would have been tracked and caught by sun-up. Up here's the better way to leave the kingdom."

As he spoke, the group rounded a gentle corner in the stone causeway. Bryn leaned his mount over to his right and surprised the boys by descending a narrow ramp set into the side of the stone wall that supported the causeway. Taliesin must have passed down this causeway at least a dozen times in his life, and he could never once remember seeing such a ramp. Tudno led the pony down the incline as it twisted and curved, sometimes cutting through the stone walls and pillars through concealed tunnels. Taliesin looked up to see more and more of the night sky get overtaken by the dark stone walls of the castle. The deeper the group went, the less sky he could see. The rampway began making sharp angular turns down a square-shaped pit. The vertical hallway was barely wide enough for the horses to walk five or six paces before having to turn against the next wall.

The ramp made one more sharp turn and then ended at the bottom of a moss-covered courtyard, guarded by several statues clad in overgrown vines. Bryn soundlessly jumped off his mule and began inspecting the far wall covered by creeping vines and thick brambles.

"By the saints! Where are we?" Tudno asked impatiently.

Bryn brought his first two fingers to his lips, hissing for quiet, and then answered in a soft voice.

"Your grandfather had this passageway installed when the Lowland Hundred was being built. The only people who know about it are me, the King, his sons, and now their sons. The guards are instructed to never come down here. Everyone believes it's an unused vegetable cellar. Ah, here it is!"

Bryn's fingers tore out small bits of stem and leaves until he uncovered a small gold ring set into the stone of the wall. Prying it loose with his fingernail, he looped his finger through the middle of the ring and pulled, releasing a strange groaning creak from the stones of the wall. With an extra twist, Taliesin could hear the click of a latch being undone and suddenly a gate-sized portion of the wall swung open, tearing at the overgrown vines and creating a rumble of sound. The other side of the stone doorway was inky dark. A cold salty draft wafted out from the darkness and a rhythmic rush of noise filled the tunnel.

"Here we'll be able to leave the city without anyone spotting us," Bryn explained proudly.

"Are you sure you want to come with us?" Taliesin asked.

"I'm not staying here while everyone marches off to war. I've seen battles before Tali, and if anything can be done to avoid it, even if it means risking our skins, it's well worth it."

"But the King will see you've run off," Tudno objected. "If he catches you, he'll banish you or execute you."

"So be it," Bryn replied grimly. "It would only be one more death on top of thousands. And maybe before then we can do some good and foil the battle before it happens."

"But Bryn," Taliesin said, trying to be gentle. "Wouldn't you be a bit of liability? Everyone in Maelgwn's court knows who you are. You would give us away as spies."

"That's the best part, sonny!" Bryn said exuberantly. "In a few days is Maelgwn's tournament of bards. He has it every year, feast or famine. Any bard, musician, or minstrel is welcome at Anglesey as long as they bring nothing other than the tools of their trade." Bryn patted the harp on his back for emphasis. "You two are officially my new assistants and together, we three can march straight into Maelgwn's keep and get to Elphin as soon as the opportunity presents itself."

Tudno scoffed, obviously unimpressed. "That's sheep's feathers, that is!"

Bryn scowled and took on a biting tone. "Well, if it doesn't suit your fancy, then please allow me to let you go back to sneaking past the guards with your shirt pulled over your head."

"How are we even supposed to get through this?" Taliesin asked, indicating the tunnel. "There's barely any light down with us, how are we supposed to lead a pony through a path we can't even see?"

In response, Bryn ran his hand over the edge of the tunnel, until he curled his fingers around a thin wire set into the side of the stone walls. He stepped a pace into the dark tower and then reached back for the reins of his mule.

"Hand me my satchel, Tali," Bryn asked. Taliesin handed over the leather sack to the bard who then fished out a small carrot glazed with honeycomb. He held it out to his mule who took one sniff and then obediently followed his rider into the tunnel.

"Here!" Bryn passed back an extra honeyed carrot to the boys. "Grab hold of the wire and don't let go. Keep a hand with your pony and shut the door behind you. C'mon now!"

Taliesin sucked in a deep breath and fastened his hand tight around the wire. As he was about to head in, his cousin's hand clamped solidly on his arm.

"Tal, do you think this is a good idea? What if he gets us

killed?" Tudno asked under the echo of the tunnel.

"Like he said, there'd be a lot more deaths if we do nothing. I can't think of an easier way to sneak out of the kingdom right now. You?"

Tudno reluctantly shook his head.

"So, let's get the pony through here and worry about how things will turn out afterward. I'm willing to accept any help we can get right now."

Tudno sucked in his lip and waved the carrot in front of his stout pony's hairy face. The creature crinkled its nose and took a few timid steps forwards into the clammy air of the tunnel. Taliesin placed Tudno's hand along the wire and reached back to close the door, submerging them in blackness.

Taliesin felt a little claustrophobic in the pitch-black tunnel, like he was free-falling in the disorienting passage. He kept a death grip on the wire and tried his best to gauge Tudno's distance ahead of him by the heavy breathing of the pony. He winced, thinking about the pain he'd receive should the pony get spooked and kick back at him. Slowly, the boys felt their way down the damp passage listening to the rush of noise get louder and more forceful with every step. As Taliesin listened, he suddenly realized where he had heard such a noise before. The same crash would ring out throughout the whole sea gate fortress whenever the tide began to turn violent, and waves pounded down on the walls.

"Bryn?" Taliesin called out.

No answer.

"Bryn!" he said again.

"Over here!" Bryn called back. "We're just about out. I just need to find that bastard latch."

"Bryn, are we about to walk into the sea?" Taliesin insisted. "I can hear the waves crashing through the very walls!"

"That's why our timing has to be just right. Here we are!" he said triumphantly. Taliesin heard the loud metal click. He and Tudno arrived just behind the tall man.

"Our timing has to be right for what?" Tudno demanded.

In response, Bryn made a hissing shush and listened as the roar began to die down. Then in one swift motion, he threw his weight against the end of the tunnel, shoving an unseen door wide open and flooding the tunnel with moonlight. The boys winced as their eyes adjusted. Taliesin looked out of the passage to see what must have been the bottom of a small cliffside, its base half-submerged with quick receding water. Leading from the tunnel door across the water to a narrow footpath in the cliff was a small levy of slick rocks, half-covered with barnacles and seaweed.

"What in heaven's name is this?" Tudno asked.

"This is the King's secret passage that was built into the city walls when Cantre'r Gwaelod was first constructed. The original shoreline had a few places where the jagged cliffs didn't agree with the stonemasons and parts of the wall had to be built back a little from the cliff. This is one such spot, but we're so close to where the cliff meets the open sea that the tide continuously sweeps the ground with oncoming water. Here, see?"

Taliesin heard it before he could see it. The crescendo of sound that built up like a storm near the seaside end of the crevice rang out even as the water below them began to quickly swell.

"One side now!" Bryn announced as he violently shut the door. In an instant, the door practically shook as a wall of water smashed through the cliffside. Taliesin stooped down briefly to feel the dark floor.

"How can this be?" he asked. "There must be a good two feet of water at least on the other side of the door, but not a single drop passes through?"

"This is witchcraft!" Tudno moaned, beside himself.

"Pah! Witchcraft, eh?" Bryn chided. "It's only the same sorcery that keeps Cantre'r Gwaelod's walls strong against the ocean or how the harbor stays tamed."

"And how is that, then?" Taliesin pressed.

"I haven't a clue lad!" the bard answered with a chuckle. "I'm just a storyteller, I'm no visionary architect or stonemason. Ask the King next you see him."

"How are we supposed to get my pony here across that grimy bridge before the water smashes us against the castle walls?" Tudno asked.

"Keep her focused on the carrot I gave you and have a steady hand on her. There's plenty of time if you listen and go across as soon as the water recedes. Watch, I'll go first."

Bryn placed a hand on the side of his mule's back and kept his ear crooked at the door. As the three of them heard the rushing water outside begin to slip back towards the open bay, Bryn threw the door wide open and briskly led his mule over the slimy rocks. The two boys only watched him from the door's threshold, listening for the sound of the returning water. Bryn had crossed the narrow trench of seawater and had led his mule up a step or two on the opposite cliffside trail when a thunderous roar announced another incoming wave.

"STAND BACK FROM THE DOOR!" Bryn called out to them. "And keep in mind where the latch is!"

Taliesin barely stepped back in time before the oncoming water slammed the door shut like a raging bull. They waited patiently until they heard the water recede and then opened the door again.

"You see?!" Bryn called out with a wide grin. "I told you there's nothing to it. Hurry now, before you waste time!"

With a jolt, Taliesin grabbed the pony's thick mane and tried to drag her out onto the rocks. The animal brayed in protest.

"Tudno, quick the carrot!" Taliesin hissed.

Tudno dangled the sweet carrot in front of Stomper, but the pony had no appetite.

"Lead him with the reins! Hurry!" Bryn insisted.

Tudno grabbed the reins and placed a hand gently on the pony's muzzle.

"C'mon then, Stomper!" he pleaded with the pony. Taliesin did what he could to push from behind the pony, while Tudno tried to drag the frightened animal from the front. Between the two of them, they were nearly able to struggle their way across the level rocks and had begun climbing up the cliffside path when the ocean water shot down the bottom of the trench with unexpected ire.

The crashing water would have doused Taliesin, condemning him to a night of hypothermia, if it wasn't for Bryn's hand shooting down from the cliffside and grabbing Taliesin by the scruff of the neck. With surprising strength, the bard yanked the young boy out of the path of the charging water at the last second.

"There!" Bryn said as he picked himself off the ground. "That wasn't all so difficult, was it? Are you intact, lad?" He addressed Taliesin.

"I…I think so." Taliesin said, "Just a bruise on my knee, I'll manage."

Bryn lifted Taliesin up by the hand and led him over to his mule. "Sit up here now, I'll walk alongside for tonight. All the better the disguise after all! Everyone around these parts knows of Bryn the towering bard of King Gwyddno, nobody knows about the bard Taliesin who wanders the countryside on his mule with his two attendants." Bryn threw a wink to Tudno, who only scowled and rolled his eyes.

"Let's hurry then, this path will take us up to Ceredigion's fields. If we can make it to the forests up north by sun-up we should be out of reach for now."

"Aren't there any patrols along here?" Tudno asked nervously. "Why doesn't anybody just come back down and bash their way through the door there?"

"What door, lad?" Bryn asked innocently.

Taliesin and Tudno both turned their gaze back to the side of the city wall. Taliesin could see the cliff path, he could see the rocks they trekked over, but all he could see in the stone wall were just patches of barnacles and sea kelp tossed up by the churning tide. The wall looked as solid as a mountain without the barest hint of a door visible. Taliesin and his cousin shared a confounded look.

"You really should see if King Gwyddno will ever tell you the complete history of how Cantre'r Gwaelod was built," Bryn said as he led his mule up the path and Taliesin with it. "He'll tell you that there are a lot more secrets in his kingdom than just hidden passages."

The three men and two beasts began their hike up the cliffside, the world around them only illuminated by the stars and the sinking light of the moon. Taliesin stared at the back of Bryn's head, his chestnut hair tied back neatly into a braid. He wondered what the bard had meant and what his grandfather wasn't telling him. But he also wondered why a bard, of all the lords, knights, and officiants in Gwyddno's court, would be privy to the same secrets as a King. It made him look at his older friend in a new light as he pondered what other secrets the bard was concealing.

***

As the first rays of light began to brighten the eastern skies, Mererid awoke in the infirmary hall of Caer Wyddno. She had the strangest sensation that as she slept a shadow passed over her face and down her body. She threw the thin quilt off herself and sat up, still as a deer. Rhun's sneering face floated through her mind. She could still smell the reek of his breath and the feel of his weight on top of her. Her hand recalled the cold metal of the dagger as Rhun drove it down through flesh, muscle, and bone.

Mererid gripped the fabric of the quilt tightly to her. Her eyes focused on the white linen bandage wrapped around her hand, splotched with patches of brown-red dried blood. Coming back to her wits, she relaxed her hand, wincing as the pain came rushing back. She took one more glance around the small room. There was nothing there with her except the shadows cast on the walls from the brightening sky.

When she was brought in the healer had ordered her to drink a horn of distilled rye liquor. The spirit plunged the girl into sleep while the stout healer put leeches to the wound and bandaged her hand. The next day and a half were one long fever dream for Mererid as she contended with the loss of blood and chills from battling infection. Now, the young girl sighed in relief to be able to at least think and feel clearly again.

She threw herself back down onto the straw mattress, savoring the peace of the early morning. She turned herself onto her side and let her gaze wander to the faint light of the window. As her eyes focused, she noticed a small bundle balanced precariously over the stone ledge. She sat up and saw a dozen different flowers that had been collected and tied together with a white ribbon. Mererid was certain she hadn't received flowers before going to sleep that night. She swung her bare feet out of the bed and walked across the clammy stone floor to examine them. Some were plants and herbs that she knew well from cooking such as sage, thyme, and rosemary. There was one plant that she did not recognize. A few twigs tufted with pairs of small, round, leathery leaves and dotted with sticky white berries. Mererid screwed up her face trying to recall where she had seen such berries before. She didn't remember them from any of the gardens in Cantre'r Gwaelod, nor could she recall seeing them on any of the flowers laid out in the chapel when she helped clean the floors for Father Gilgam.

Mererid's mind began clearing with the growing morning light, and she tightened her right hand around the bundle of stems, hearing a faint crack from the drying wood.

"Daila!" she called for the healing matron. "Daila! Are you there?"

"Yes? Yes. What is it, dear?" Daila shuffled her buttery frame into the small infirmary room. Her eyelids looked like they were stuck together with honey as she wiped the sleep off her face. "Are you warm enough?"

"Uhm, Dalia?" Mererid held up the dried bouquet of plants. "Did anybody pay me a visit during the night?"

"A visitor?" Dalia said bringing her hand up to her fat cheek.

"Oh gracious, no," she muttered. "No, I haven't seen anyone come in."

"You're sure?" Mererid pressed. "You didn't maybe see a sad, sickly little boy come around? Carrying a bunch of weedy flowers? Maybe came by only a few moments before I woke up?"

"Oh no, darling--" Dalia had to bring her hand over her mouth to stifle a massive yawn, "I---I would've seen him, I've been up like an owl all night."

"Is that the truth?" Mererid asked rhetorically. Dalia finished her extended yawn and only smiled a sleepy grin.

"I swear by it," she replied. "Why do you ask?"

"I was just wondering who left these here while I was asleep." Mererid held up the thin bouquet to Dalia's matronly face. The healing lady opened her eyes wide with shock.

"Mary and Joseph!" she exclaimed. "The little scamp must've come in while I had my back turned! Crafty little devils those boys can be, especially when they're trying to court a pretty thing like you, dear!"

"He's not my sweetheart! W-whoever he is!" Mererid added quickly.

"Well, he knows his medicine." Dalia studied the handful of flowers closely. "Lots of healing plants here in this bunch. And not just whatever you can find at the apothecary's, either." Dalia suddenly grabbed a twig from the parcel and yanked it free.

"Saints above! It's mistletoe! As I live and breathe, is it really mistletoe?!"

"What?" Mererid asked, clutching her woolen blanket closet around her.

"These white berries here." Dalia held them up for the girl to see. "This is mistletoe! Powerful healing magic, you can't find any of this growing here in Cantre'r Gwaelod. The abbot had it outlawed."

"What's it for then?" Mererid asked perplexed.

"Oh, my mammy taught me how to make a right powerful balm out of this. It will clean your wound and stop the pain in a flash, it will. Give me a few hours and I'll have some for you by midday, you'll be right as rain by evening, love!"

"Really?" Mererid asked, surprised. All the other healers who had tended to her said she would need to stay in the healing house for another two weeks while leeches sucked pus and extra blood from the wound.

"You'll see, love! It's like a miracle! But don't go telling everyone what it is now. Abbot Gilgam could see me in trouble for all of this. We'll keep it our little secret, hmm?"

Mererid nodded, confident that she could refrain from talking to Gilgam about her surprise medicine. Actually, she'd be absolutely fine not talking to Gilgam about anything at all.

Dalia spun around and glided easily out of the bedchamber. Mererid called out from her bed.

"Dalia?" The older woman stopped and turned back. "Are you positive that you didn't see anybody who came in? It wasn't the princeling Taliesin, was it?"

Dalia's face screwed up in concentration as she tried to process the questions. Suddenly a flash of comprehension crossed her face.

"Oh, Taliesin, was it? Elphin's skinny foster son?"

"Yes, him," Mererid confirmed. "Did he come in?"

"Oh, no, love, no!" Dalia shook her head half to herself. She seemed to be trying to make the pieces of a puzzle fit inside her head. "No, it couldn't have been him. He's gone by now!"

"What?" Mererid's head snapped up.

"Yes, I heard some of the night watch guards talking about it. Two of the princelings, one of Elphin's, one of Seithenyn's, they've gone missing! So has Bryn the King's bard. Some of the guards say they saw three people fleeing the city in secret in the middle of the night. They'd be miles away by now"

"Oh…" Mererid found the news unexpected. She half-expected that Taliesin would try some clumsy gesture as if it would replace her missing finger. She had planned to show stern dismissal of any display that he could make. She did not expect to hear that he had fled the kingdom hardly a day after she had been mutilated in his name. Mererid could hardly say she was disappointed by the news, but she found herself wondering why the boy would leave in secret.

Dalia had already skipped down the hall bent on turning the sticky berries into a paste. Mererid allowed herself to sink back into the goose feather pillow. She looked out of the window and watched the amber rays of the sun reflect off the inner harbor throwing golden veined reflections on the towers and alleyways of the fishing village. She brought her hand up to her face only to get scratched by the rough bandage embracing her hand tight over her missing finger. She could feel the skin and blood under the bandage, drying and crystallizing into a hard and protective scab, unyielding and strong. She mouthed the words quietly to herself.

"I don't care if you ever come back."

CHAPTER 13: The Ford of Gwyddno's Horses

Mawrhydig sywyd!
Pan dy gyv rensid?
Pan och awel gryd?

Majestic is knowledge!
Whence has it been imparted?
Whence the moan of the wind that stirs?

~ Gwyndawd, Llyfr Taliesin

The sun shone clear as crystal over the jagged hillside of Ceredigion as the two stout boys on a pony and the towering bard on his mule loped haltingly down the mountain pass. Taliesin was pleased to discover that they had made it out of sight of Cantre'r Gwaelod's towers before the first light of morning. It had been several hours and no horsemen from the kingdom had overtaken them yet, so Taliesin assumed they weren't being followed.

Earlier in the morning, the group had been surprised by a war party from Powys marching towards Caer Wyddno, but none of the warriors had any reason to look twice at the three strange travelers.

Otherwise, no other soul passed them along the rocky hillside that morning, which would have suited Taliesin perfectly if it didn't mean he had to listen to Tudno and Bryn argue.

"Just how is it that you know every crack in the 'Hundred?'" Tudno pressed the bard. A night of hard travel with no sleep had left the boy ornery and unpleasant. "Who showed you all these secret passageways? Father Gilgam says the sea walls were built by pagans and slaves and they left holes in the walls for the devil to come destroy us. Out with it already, Bryn! Are you in league with the devil?"

"By Annwn! So many words and only one trivial point among 'em!" Bryn called back from his mule.

"What do you mean?" Taliesin asked, somewhat bemused.

"The sea walls were indeed built by slaves."

"Really?!" Taliesin balked. "But Grandad doesn't keep servants without compensation."

"I never said they were our slaves. All the same, Gwyddno was content enough to let them build the Sarn Badrig, the sea wall, in his name. Most of them you could consider pagan, I suppose, if 'pagan' is what we're calling anyone who can't stomach Gilgam's sermons."

"Hah!" Tudno crowed, "So they did leave openings for the devil! It's sacrilege!"

"Oh, come off it!" Bryn snapped back. "I didn't hear these complaints when I was smuggling you and your pony out last night!"

"But it proves you knew of the pagan tunnels! You're a devil-worshiper, you are!"

"And you're as ignorant and stubborn as Gilgam and your father combined!" Tudno's face turned livid white. "And as for my own religious proclivities, you should know damn well that I hold to the old religion. It has the best stories, after all!" Bryn let out a sharp laugh. "Now have either of you fine gentles ever, in your lives, heard your King's royal bard praise Lucifer, or Herod, or Pontius Pilate, or any of the other villains the clergymen care to invoke at their convenience? Well?"

He turned his chiseled face back at the following boys seated on their pony. Taliesin looked back at him wide-eyed while Tudno stared sourly at the dirt path.

"No, you haven't," Bryn answered for them. "So, we can put to rest that the bard of King Gwyddno Garanhir is a devil-worshipper. Pagan? Yes, and what of it? Every third house in Cantre'r Gwaelod is a pagan family."

"More's the pity!" Tudno spat. "To think they're passing up all the wisdom the abbot has to offer. He's studied at the abbey of the Llanwenarth Priory you know. He can teach reading and writing. Whoever heard of a pagan who could write?"

"Hah! We're not foolish enough for that!" Bryn replied.

Taliesin gave the bard a puzzled look.

"Don't you consider language and scriptures a blessing?" he asked sincerely. "How much knowledge has been kept safe over the years by writing?"

"Oh, writing is all well and good for monks and scribes telling their dead tales of dead men. But I don't write my stories down, I tell them. I live them!"

"You're a foul-mouth liar, Bryn!" Tudno said, practically squirming in his saddle. "What did your druids leave us with? If they were smarter than the scriptures, maybe they could have written it down for us living folk to enjoy."

Bryn whipped his mule around so hard that he careened the animal's head into Tudno's pony. He stood up proudly and waited until the boys had adjusted to the sudden movement before speaking.

"This is exactly what is wrong with your abbeys and scribes," he said with a quiet ferocity. "You think that just because you can piece together a few sounds from some letters on a page that you have the right to every piece of knowledge in the Library of Alexandria, is it?

"Well, this is wishful thinking, boys! If you want knowledge, no, not just knowledge, but wisdom? Inspiration? Enlightenment?

You cannot ever read that. You must live it, speak it, breathe your knowledge into every part of you, not just your eyes and your head! Do that, lads, and you won't just know the truth, but you'll understand it!"

Bryn's sharp and sudden reproach sufficiently shocked Tudno into keeping his peace for a minute. Taliesin took advantage of the pause to change the subject.

"Hmmrpph!" He cleared his throat. "So, shall we go over how we're getting into Anglesey when we arrive? It seems like it might be a more productive conversation."

"Agreed!" Bryn said, keeping a stern eye on Tudno. "Well, it shouldn't be so difficult. Maelgwn's tournament of bards begins the day after next. We should make it to Anglesey tomorrow morning and when we arrive, I am none other than Bryn, the bard of Caer Wyddno."

"Won't they hang you then?" Tudno asked, his tone markedly less severe. "Aren't you the bard from an enemy nation about to launch a war?"

"That won't matter!" Bryn announced grandly. "I am a minstrel of the realm, participating in the cultural event of our time. It is tradition that any singer or orator be permitted to participate whether his King is at war with Gwynedd or not."

"And how should we present ourselves?" Taliesin asked.

"You won't!" Bryn said as he surveyed the mountains ahead. "As far as anyone will know, you two are my assistants. Filthy little farm brats is what I'll say."

"That's a far cry from the truth!" Tudno objected.

"Well, that's the point, isn't it?" Bryn chided. "But if you prefer to go and announce your royal status, then be my guest! Mind you, you won't be welcomed. I have leave to enter the kingdom as a bard, but two princelings from an enemy nation? You'd be locked up tighter than Prince Elphin the second they figured that!"

Theoretically, the plan was simple and effective. With such a great deal of commotion from the tournament, Taliesin and Tudno would be able to snoop around the castle until they found a way to free Elphin. He wondered what kind of cell the Dragon, Maelgwn, had fashioned for his foster father. Was he chained high up in a tower, or buried down in some catacomb beneath Anglesey castle? In any case, Taliesin was not expecting to find his foster father in decent health. The only first-hand report he heard on the matter had come from Rhun, and it was painfully clear now how little Maelgwn's prince could be trusted.

A gust of icy wind slapped Taliesin in the chest as their pony crested another peak. In a flash, he realized he had never traveled this far north from Cantre'r Gwaelod. Gwyddno had taken him and Elphin on several outings, but usually only to the hamlets and villages south near Dyfed and Neath, where life tended to be calm and peaceful. The countryside this far north was riddled with warfare and shifting borders. Taliesin heard from Enid that Saxon war parties were beginning to regroup not far from these hills. She said it would only be a matter of time before they became bold enough to make another bid for the land that Arthur had defended.

Taliesin could understand the attraction. The rolling hillside swelled with veins of tin and copper, luring invaders from across the sea since the time of the Romans. Taliesin could smell flowers and plants putting down their roots, fresh buds waiting patiently for winter to end. For the first time that he could remember, the boy didn't have to tolerate the sharp odor of low tide that lingered in the water alleys of the Lowland Hundred. The countryside was nothing short of pristine and gorgeously peaceful. Taliesin could almost forget that he had come from a kingdom gone mad for war or that he was headed straight into a hostile nation, into the jaws of the Dragon himself.

Out on the exposed hillside, battered by sunshine and blistering wind, Taliesin felt untouched by either world. He could almost imagine himself slipping away from his companions and living free in the country, away from every trouble in his life. Away from the painful memory of Mererid's hand and her missing finger. He dismissed the idea as quickly as it came. No amount of liberty could take away his desire to see Elphin or the weight in his heart at the thought of his foster father being imprisoned. He gazed wistfully one last time at the distant snow-topped peaks and then turned his head purposefully towards Anglesey.

The rest of the day's travel passed calmly. Tudno's pony made up for his lack of speed in stamina and trotted steadfastly up the steepest parts of the road. Bryn led the way up the hills merrily, obviously familiar with the well-worn path. He would occasionally tune his small harp and hum several melodies on the mundane portions of the trail. Tudno eventually stopped sulking and reluctantly enjoyed the music.

As the sun began to drop in the western half of the sky, the trio came to a small rushing stream that cut its way across the path. Bryn eyed the white-crested rapids warily and then peered deeply into the center of the stream.

"Well, we should be alright," he muttered to himself. The boys both shot him the same anxious expression to which Bryn responded, "The water has become faster since I passed through here last, must have come from the snowmelt. But the stream is hardly any deeper. We should be able to ride the mounts straight through without incident."

Tudno eyed the choppy water suspiciously and then looked at Bryn's mule, which stood several hands higher than the stout pony.

"Oy! Who's to say that Taliesin and I don't get soaked as we go through? We'd freeze to death by nightfall!"

"Well, that's more reason to be careful. If you're worried about getting wet, just pick up your feet so you don't get your shoes soaked. You'll be fine!"

With that, Bryn spurred his mule onward. The creature brayed in protest but eventually marched across the swift water. As Bryn passed through the center of the river, Taliesin saw that the water only came up to the knees of his mule. Bryn drove the animal to the other side and then jumped off.

"You see? It's perfectly safe. Come on now! We'll need to start looking for a place to sleep before the sun goes down," Bryn called.

Tudno grimaced, but he had no reason to refuse. He brushed Stomper's mane back out of his eyes and picked his feet up and rested them on top of the pony's back. He instructed Taliesin to do the same.

"Keep an eye on our pack, will you?" Tudno asked. "I didn't get a chance to grab much food and we'll need some before we get to Anglesey."

Taliesin nodded and picked up his feet, imitating his cousin. Tudno let out a sharp "Hup!" and Stomper shook his head and reluctantly began to trot through the cold water. As they crossed into the deep of the river, Taliesin was relieved to see that the water stopped at the belly of the pony. He wondered how the pony would manage being soaked with cold water in the winter air. Taliesin let his hand dip into the water to check the temperature.

As his hand dropped into the painfully cold water, Taliesin felt a wave of vertigo wash over him. He looked up to see if Stomper was drifting in the quick current, but Tudno was driving the strong animal straight towards the other side. He reached down to the water one more time.

"Rapid…rapidly…brightly, brightly…"

Taliesin looked up, certain that he had heard whispering voices from…somewhere? He scanned the banks of the river but only could see the rocks and grass lining the water. One last time he reached his hand into the water.

"Bright…brightly…radiant…radiant…radiant one…radiant…bright brow…radiant BROW…TALIESIN!"

Taliesin withdrew his hand from the water with a jolt. Someone, or something, had whispered his name. Nobody should have recognized him outside of Caer Wyddno. In his haste, he felt his elbow knock against something soft.

"Oh, Saints above us, Taliesin!" Tudno suddenly cried out in alarm. "Our pack!"

Taliesin turned his head to see the brown leather satchel filled with food and supplies getting carried down the river by the rushing waters. The two boys watched in dismay until the leather pack foundered and disappeared under a rock.

"Oh, by Mary, Taliesin!" Tudno chided, "I told you to take care of the pack!"

"I'm sorry, cuz!" Taliesin said, bewildered. "I...I thought I heard somebody."

Bryn called out from the far bank of the river. "Just get the pony out of the water already! He won't last forever in there!"

Grumbling furiously to himself, Tudno steered the pony directly to the dry ground and then whipped his leg over the creature's back to jump to the ground. He shook his hands violently and paced restlessly up and down the river's edge.

"Tudno, I'm sorry!" Taliesin repeated, trying to calm his cousin down. "I thought I had heard something in the water. I'm sure there's nothing in there that we can't find on the road."

"Your cousin's right, lad!" Bryn assured him. "It's getting late in the day anyway. I know of a small village around here that should have an open barn we could sleep in. Let's get going while we still have light."

"We can't just go up to any town while we're still in Ceredigion!" Tudno protested. "What if somebody spots us and recognizes us?"

"Don't be daft, boy! Which of Gwyddno's knights are going to be moping around here, especially while there's a call to arms at Caer Wyddno?"

"Enid did say that she sends her patrols out regularly to Ceredigion to watch for spies and new recruits. Maybe we should be cautious," Taliesin interjected.

"And in any case, I'm not leaving until we've fished my pack out of the river. I stashed a few gold pieces in there just in case. I'm not going to just leave it here without a fight!"

"Oh, hell's fire! Fine, gatekeeper's brat! You two stay and catch the ague while I scout out the town ahead for patrols. I'll be back in twenty minutes, no less. And then we're gone from here whether you have your poxy bag or not!"

Bryn pulled the reins of his mule and brought the animal around to the path ahead. He cantered no more than five paces before suddenly stopping. He turned his head back, looking at the two boys with concern.

"Is there something wrong, Bryn?" Taliesin called out. Tudno was already scrambling down to the shores of the water, peering anxiously into the rushing depths.

Bryn shot his gaze at Taliesin and then again at the river.

"No. No, it's nothing." Bryn said and then added, "Taliesin, lad?"

"Yes?"

"...Just don't let your pony drink from the stream," Bryn said cryptically, and then made off down the path.

Taliesin watched him disappear over the curve of the nearby hills. He scratched his head, trying to piece the bard's words together.

"What do you suppose he meant by that?" Taliesin asked his cousin.

"Meant by what?" Tudno asked, distracted. He had snapped off a long switch of a birch branch and was attempting to fish out the drowned satchel from the stream.

"He said not to let Stomper drink from the river. Do you think it's poisoned or something?"

"Oh, that heathen is just trying to scare us with fairy tales!" Tudno said irritably. "He didn't have any problem when we were soaking her up to her haunches."

"I just find it strange," Taliesin said, furrowing his brow. "What stream is this anyway?"

"Who cares? But it looks like there's a fair number of villages alongside it. I haven't heard any stories from these hills about a poisoned stream.”

The two boys continued trying to rescue the satchel, but Taliesin kept finding himself distracted. The bare trees and the low winter light gave the landscape an eerie, surreal feeling, like Taliesin was inside of one of Bryn's stories, but he couldn't say what would happen next. A breeze gently swayed the thin branches of the trees as Tudno finally managed to pull his pack out of the water. He let out a triumphant shout and began inspecting the contents of the bag.

“Well, the coins are still good, but the food I packed away has all gone soggy. It will freeze by morning,” he said grimly.

“Let's hope that Bryn can find us somewhere cozy to sleep. Oh Tudno-!” Taliesin pointed his finger at the riverbank where Stomper was busy gulping down mouthful after mouthful of river water.

“Oh, come off it!” Tudno was beginning to lose his temper all over again. “I'll let my pony drink wherever he wants. I'm sure the water's fine. Here!”

Tudno knelt by the frigid river water and scooped up a handful. He slurped it down without hesitation.

“See? It's rather refreshing. Try some, why don't you?”

The pony lapped at the water happily as he flicked his tail back and forth and shook himself, trying to keep dry. He didn't seem in the least bit of distress. Neither did Tudno, who had returned to moaning over his ruined satchel. Curiosity got the better of Taliesin and he knelt down near the flowing water.

He could see his face staring back at him in the gentle ripples. For a minute, it looked as if his own reflection could jump up through the fragile water's surface, and step into a world unimagined outside of the water. How distorted and limited would the reflection's view have been under the river? How many revelations would rush over it as it glimpsed the vast new land that stretched away from its former dwelling? How much knowledge of the world could be gained by such a simple change of perspective?

During his musings, Taliesin's hands reached into the cold

water on their own accord and curved themselves into a small bowl. They lifted a small pool of water to his face and he suddenly found himself sipping down gulp after refreshing gulp.

Taliesin inhaled quickly and then held his breath. His heart was still beating, he could feel his blood rushing around his body like normal. He looked up to see a small bird fly up to perch on the top of a birch tree. Taliesin exhaled in relief.

"The water's actually quite clean," Taliesin called back to Tudno.

"Of course, it is!" Tudno replied. "I told you your bard over there doesn't know his ass from his arse. Remember that next time he's mouthing off about Gilgam and the church, won't you? I remember one Mayday that sod went and got so drunk that he…"

Taliesin mentally tuned out his cousin's rantings. He bent down to drink once more from the stream while he thought about what to do when they reached Anglesey fortress. The problem gnawed at him. It was like predicting a chess game ten moves ahead when he wasn't even sure if his opponent would play by the rules.

While unraveling the tactical puzzle, Taliesin unconsciously allowed his thumb to drift up towards his mouth. Distracted, he fit his thumb between his incisor and molar teeth and bit down gently.

Taliesin couldn't understand it, but suddenly he felt the ground below him shift. Turning back to his cousin, he noticed a small wavering in the air just above Tudno's shoulders, like his cousin was boiling and releasing a cloud of steam. Tudno continued criticizing Bryn, working himself into a near fit, but all Taliesin could see was the young boy begin to shine and start to exude…colors.

That was the only way that Taliesin could describe it. It was as if his cousin had become so enraged that he was bleeding out thick plumes of red, but not red smoke or blood. It was more like Tudno was being consumed by invisible flames and the fumes were no more than red light wafting away from him. Taliesin gaped.

"-with a pig no less! Who could ever-" Tudno cut his speech off as he caught sight of his cousin's face. "Taliesin? What's the matter?"

Taliesin blinked rapidly. He peered at Tudno again and could see the same plumes of light, but they had suddenly cooled to a dull blue-grey color.

"Uh...nothing. Do you…? Are you doing that, Tudno?" Taliesin stammered in confusion. Tudno frowned and went to grab his cousin by the arm. Taliesin staggered backward and spun around uneasily. He gazed out over the same riverbank he drank from just two minutes prior.

He could hardly recognize a single thing.

The water looked like it was standing still yet raging all at the same time. He could see young saplings, flowering adult trees, and decaying logs all springing from the same roots. A screeching whistle made Taliesin look above at the sparrow sitting on the birch tree. The sparrow looked as large as an eagle now. With another screech, the bird flew off in several impossible directions at once. Taliesin watched as the bird flew down to the ground on the other side of the river. The sparrow placed his feet on the ground and suddenly turned white and withered before dropping to the ground. In a second, the body decomposed, and tender seedlings began to sprout over it. Taliesin dropped to his knees reeling from nausea and vertigo. He let his eyes gaze down once again at his reflection in the shallows. Taliesin could see his own bewildered face and the towering birch tree hanging its branches above him. Against all laws of reality, Taliesin watched his reflection look behind itself back at the reflected birch tree in the water. The reflection's face contorted into a mask of awe and terror as if it were beholding the very soul of God.

It was the last vision Taliesin could remember before collapsing directly into the river.

***

It took Bryn close to thirty minutes to finally return. When he did, he returned to find Tudno frantically yelling and slapping an unresponsive and soaked Taliesin.

"By Annwn's hounds! What on earth happened?" Bryn shouted as he leaped off his mule.

"He started babbling nonsense and then just collapsed over into the river!" Tudno yelled back. He had taken off every extra piece of clothing he could spare to put on Taliesin and was now running around bare-chested in the frigid weather. Bryn instantly reached into his pack and took out a thin blanket.

"For pity's sake boy, cover yourself!" Bryn ordered. "I can't have you freezing to death too! Now, quick! Take off his wet clothes, all of them!"

Tudno, for once, did as he was told without complaint. After they had stripped Taliesin down to the skin, Bryn wrapped the boy in his own bard's coat of colors and propped him sitting up against a rock. Bryn lay his head close to the unconscious boy's chest, his ear hovering over Taliesin's mouth. He then grabbed Taliesin's hands and began to rub them between his own. When he could feel warmth return to the boy's stiff fingers, he folded Taliesin's hands into his armpits. Almost immediately, Taliesin began to shake violently.

"Is he dying?" Tudno asked in concern.

"No. The trembling is a good sign," Bryn replied. "Now tell me what mischief happened here that got him in the river? He wasn't after your wretched bag, was he?"

"It was your fault!" Tudno accused. "He took a drink out of this vile stream you led us to, that's what! And then he began rambling about colors and time...none of it made any sense...and then he kept yelling out some demon's name, Beddu, or something like that. All from drinking this devil's water!"

"Well, I did warn you not to drink the water, didn't I?" Bryn returned.

"You told us not to give water to the pony! How were we supposed to know better?"

"Here's some advice! Next time somebody tells you not to give water to a mangy, worn-down pony, don't drink the water yourself either!"

"Fie on it! I'm half-convinced this was all a plot of yours to steal our souls for the devil!"

Bryn only scoffed and spat on the ground. He kept his attention on Taliesin, who continued to shake and tremble uncontrollably in the bard's cloak. Bryn had to rub the boy's arms through his light tunic to keep him warm. He looked up at the white birch they had placed Taliesin under.

"What was the name your cousin kept repeating?" Bryn asked.

"What? Before he nearly drowned? It sounded like Bedu or Bethu…?"

"Beith?" Bryn asked.

"Uh, yes! That was it!" Tudno squinted suspiciously. "What's the meaning behind that?"

Bryn thought to himself for a moment.

"I'm not sure," he said at length. "But there's certainly meaning behind it."

"What in blazes does that mean? Give me some explanation bard!" Tudno demanded.

"I've ceased explaining things to people who have no interest or capacity to understand them. Let me tell you it's saved me a wealth of my own breath over the years!"

At that moment, Taliesin began murmuring, shaking his head back and forth before finally opening his eyes.

"Taliesin? Are you steady?" Tudno rushed forward.

"Give him some room first!" Bryn held him back. Taliesin was breathing heavily, and his gaze darted this way and that like his eyes couldn't decide on what to focus. They finally rested on Bryn.

"Wha…what's h-happened to me?" Taliesin asked meekly.

"Steady, cuz!" Tudno urged.

"You collapsed into the river and now your body is chilled to the core," Bryn explained. "What do you remember?"

"Bryn…the water…I drank!" Taliesin confessed haltingly.

"I know...Did you have visions?"

"I...I am still having visions!" Taliesin cried as he pressed his hands solidly into his eyes as if he were trying to block out something hideous. "Something's happened to me! The world looks completely different and new! I can see a halo around you, clear as my hand in front of my face!"

Taliesin couldn't say for certain if it was in fact a 'halo' or not. But he could plainly see a wash of green flowing out of Bryn's head and shoulders and flowing around him like a cape when he moved. He could see the same, but in blue, from Tudno and in the fine movements of every bird and insect. He could hear his cousin talking like he was far away underwater.

"I knew you were leading us to disaster!" he cried at Bryn. "You knew the stream was tainted! What game are you playing?"

"The villagers and peasants around here all drink out of this stream every day and nobody has gone mad from it!" Bryn barked back.

"Then why did you tell us not to give water to the pony?"

Bryn glanced again at Taliesin, who only looked on wide-eyed.

"Because this is the stream that Gwyddno crossed with his horses, the day when all of his company's mounts went mad and disappeared. It hasn't caused anybody or their horse any harm since, but, well, I just didn't want to take chances."

"What's happened to Taliesin then?" Tudno pressed.

"I'm not sure." Bryn knelt in front of the half-frozen boy. Taliesin stared back at him. In the boy's eyes, Bryn's face constantly changed from young to old to young to a ghostly skull set inside a bag of skin. Taliesin's thoughts raced in his head. He had seen his uncle and countless knights drunk before, although he had never been inebriated himself. He did not feel like he was drunk, but rather the complete opposite. Taliesin felt as if his every sense was crisp and clear and sharp enough to slice down his body. The world was focused to such a high degree that Taliesin found himself completely disoriented. His thoughts flew through his head so fast that he dared not open his mouth for fear of ranting non-stop like a madman. But Taliesin didn't feel mad either, he could still think and reason, but at a pace far too fast to keep up. A memory bobbled into Taliesin's head as he turned to Bryn again.

"Bryn! Before I drank...the river...knew. It knew my name. It called me...Radiant Brow!"

Bryn's face seemed cast in stone and his eyes slid from Taliesin to the river and back. Taliesin could practically see Bryn's thoughts move out and away from his head like ripples in a pool of water.

At last, the bard spoke.

"Who am I to understand this enchantment?" he said, picking himself up. "I have no idea if Taliesin has second sight or is possessed or even both. But that's not what we should be worried about right now." The winter sun had begun to drop below the tree line, bathing the countryside with brilliant stripes of shadow and color. "We have a warm barn house waiting for us in the village along the road. We need to get you to a fire tonight and get the chill off you. If you fall sick, there won't be much point in continuing to Anglesey."

Working together, Tudno and Bryn were able to hoist Taliesin up on the bard's mule while Tudno carried what supplies they had on his pony. Tudno shivered and reluctantly clutched Bryn's blanket tighter to himself.

As they traveled, Taliesin watched in astonishment as every tree and blade of grass they passed told him their own story. He was further amazed to see that he remembered them all. Taliesin's head was a mix of bafflement, elation, and deep fear. He had dreamed terrible, tremendous things before and woken up frozen in terror countless times, but this felt different somehow. Reality itself seemed to be breaking at the seams for the young twelve-year-old. The boy would be terrified that he had gone completely mad except for the beauty and queer peace that he found waiting behind the world he thought he knew.

The group eventually made it to a small farmhouse with ample amounts of room and hay in the back. The peasant family brought them an honest meal of turnip soup and a small brazier of fire for Taliesin. After expressing their gratitude, the weary travelers curled up in their tufts of hay and finally fell asleep.

CHAPTER 14: The Fortress of Anglesey

Dogyn dwfyn diwerin.
Dillygein elphin.

A task deep and pure
To liberate Elphin.

~Cadeir Teyrnon, Llyfr Taliesin

The next day's dawn marked the third since Rhun's flight from Cantre'r Gwaelod. It was also the limit of the infirmary's hospitality towards Mererid. With her wound sufficiently dressed and halfway healed, thanks in part to the mistletoe balm Dalia had made, the head cleaning matron saw it fit to summon the young lady back to her maid duties. Knights and soldiers from all of Britain were pouring into Caer Wyddno and the head matron needed help keeping the guest wing presentable.

The work detail suited Mererid fine despite the obnoxious amount of pain in her wounded hand. Her younger sister, Awena, had worked as a chambermaid in the tower since their arrival to Cantre'r Gwaelod. After her tumultuous experience working for Lord Seithenyn and then Lady Elphin, Mererid was happy to keep her sister company. The bright girl's innocent humming and singing gave Mererid more solace than any herb or medicine from the infirmary. She watched Awena happily go to collect the chamber pots and bring them carefully to the manure pit on the far side of the castle.

"I try to walk around on the east side of the castle!" Awena explained to her older sister as she proudly guided her through the routine. "That way the breeze blows from behind me and blows the smell away from me. And sometimes, when the wind is strong and blowing the wrong way, I walk backwards with the pot behind me!"

The nine-year-old girl turned and shuffled backwards on her feet to demonstrate.

"See? Aren't I clever?" she asked Mererid.

"You're sharp as an arrow, you are!" Mererid humored the girl. She beamed back at her brightly.

"Well, I'm glad the matron let you work in the castle with me!" Awena went on. "I never got to see you too much when you were off cleaning the church, and then the sea gates...and then...where did the matron send you last?"

"To Prince Elphin's tower to work in the kitchen. And it wasn't the matron. Lady Elphin requested me personally."

"To work in the kitchen?!" Awena's face opened wide with shock and jealousy. "But what can you cook besides old stew?!"

"I didn't say I was the cook! I worked to help clean the kitchen!" Mererid explained. Just to further annoy her sister she added, "And, maybe sometimes, I got to bake bread for the house."

"They let you bake bread?!" Awena whined in agony. "Why didn't you get any for me, sis!?"

"They don't let servants just take whatever food they want! And I wasn't there for so long, was I?" Mererid responded a little harsher than she wanted. The truth was that Mererid had tried to find the opportunity to tuck away a roll of bread or so for her sister but hadn't been confident it wouldn't have gotten her kicked out of the warm kitchen duty. Now she had to contend with her guilt.

"If I was working in the kitchen." Awena dragged out her

own pronoun, "I would have saved a loaf of bread for you every night so that you and me could stuff our mouths before bed."

"Well, I'll send you next time I get a kitchen job," Mererid said as they approached the covered chute that led down to the foul cesspits. Awena put the chamber pot she was carrying down, took a deep breath and held it dramatically, and then slid back the thick wood cover. Mererid turned her face away from the open pit to keep from getting sick. Only after Awena had dutifully emptied the pot and replaced the cover did both girls allow themselves to breathe again.

"Well, it's a pity that you're not smelling bread and porridge all day," Awena remarked wryly. "Is that how you hurt yourself, sis?"

Awena pointed to Mererid's bandaged hand.

"Did you cut yourself with a knife or something?" she asked.

"Something like that," Mererid replied. "It's not something I want to talk about right now. Which room is next?"

"We have to do the generals' quarters now," Awena said. "But I'm not allowed to go down that hall myself."

"What?! According to who?"

"The head matron," the young girl answered. "She says that one of the grown-up maids has to do that hall. She says that she doesn't want me to see something I shouldn't."

"Oh? Ah...I see," Mererid said, suspicious about how much her younger sister really understood of the world. "Well, I think I count as a grown-up. Why don't you start on the steps here and I'll go to get the chamber pots? There's plenty I don't want to see in there."

Awena thanked her sister and went to get the mop from the lower floor. She stopped in her tracks and called out over her shoulder.

"And sis! Don't forget to knock before you open the door. Matron says that you'll disrupt the dancing lessons the generals give in their rooms!"

Mererid rolled her eyes.

"I'm sure the lesson will be very boring and far too short, now go start on the stairs!" Mererid called back before heading to the first chamber.

***

"Put some 'oomph' in that step, you puddle of misery, you bunch!" the burly guardsman of Anglesey barked out. A veteran member of Maelgwn's army, he had controlled the South Gate of the fortress for six years and had developed a substantial girth from his privileged position. When he first took up the helm of gatekeeper, many of the peasants who crossed back and forth every day over the gate's threshold were deathly afraid of him and his blustering threats. "One step out of line and I swear I'll throw you out to deal with the wolves and bandits, see if I don't!" he would holler every sunrise and sunset. After six years of hearing the same insults and shouts, the peasants' fear had faded into mild annoyance.

"You sniveling lot make me retch, by Christ!" Secretly, the guardsman was the star of his private fantasy. Every morning, he imagined himself as a grim specter allowing the dead to wander out into the fields of purgatory, and every evening, he would imagine himself ushering in the souls of the damned. Their long shadows stretched out to the east and would fall and disappear as each weary body stepped over the drawbridge as if the cavernous gate was devouring their souls one by one.

The pikeman's daydream was rudely interrupted as he noticed a small party of travelers that were not of his usual horde of commuters. One tall man on a mule rode forward leading two skinny boys behind him. One boy walked with the reins of a saddle-back pony while the other rode on top. The tall man was dressed modestly enough but held himself much higher than the guardsman liked. The boy walking the pony was dressed simply, but the boy riding made him look twice. He was clad in a patchwork cloak of dazzling colors decorated sparsely with Osprey feathers.

"Halt! You three filthy bastards!" the guardsman yelled. With the barest of nods, he signaled his team to block the newcomers' way with their long pike handles. He took a moment to gather his heft and lifted it up so that it pushed out his tarnished armor and then sauntered over the group of riders.

"What's your business here? State your name and patron."

Bryn swung his long leg over the mule and leaped gracefully to the ground. He bowed low to the guard.

"In faith, I should have hoped you remembered me from my last visit. I am Bryn, bard of King Gwyddno of Cantre'r Gwaelod. I have come to participate in Maelgwn's tournament of bards!"

The guardsman looked Bryn over like he was bargain livestock.

"Well...sure that I do! I have a memory sticky as pitch, of course. But you're a brave one, you are, coming to Anglesey at a time like this."

Bryn tilted his head, looking like the picture of innocence.

"Has the tournament been canceled? Doesn't Maelgwn accept singers from both his friends and foes?"

"There's been some alarming news about what Gwyddno's up to in his fish kingdom. The King has every reason to be suspicious of spies."

"Bah! I am free to perform where I will, with or without my master's leave. If Maelgwn doubts my honor as an orator and historian, then he may speak with me directly."

"You should watch how directly you speak yourself," the guard growled. His eyes darted to the two boys leading the pony. He cleared out the phlegm from the back of his throat loudly, his breath steaming out his broad nostrils in the bitter dusk air.

"Who're these?" the guard asked. The skinnier boy leading the pony looked sufficiently terrified of him, which greatly pleased the guard. The other boy on top of the pony seemed unfocused and yet alert like he was watching an invisible bird dart around.

"Those are my wards, my apprentices that shall learn much by watching Maelgwn's own bards. They are invaluable assistants!"

"This boy here doesn't look so fit," the guard said reproachfully, indicating Taliesin. "The kingdom is nervous these days about the yellow plague sweeping these parts, we won't have to burn your ward before you leave here, will we?"

"The boy has a touch of the ague, nothing more, I assure you. His cousin next to him had the same thing only a fortnight before and he recovered within a day or two. Travel in this cold weather can be very demanding on one so small."

"He won't be very useful to you during the festival if he's puking his guts up. I would have left the dead weight back in your hovel if I were you."

"Yes, but your job is not to train apprentice bards. Now will you be so kind as to let us pass in the name of King Maelgwn?"

The fat guardsman sneered and gave one more suspicious look to the two foreign boys. He jerked his thumb and called out to his men.

"Search them for weapons!" he yipped. Like a pack of trained dogs, the armored guardsmen immediately grabbed what they could and started recklessly pawing through the trio's effects. Bryn's prized harp and Tudno's damp satchel of clothes were all that they could produce.

"There!" Bryn said, "Now may we pass and prepare for tomorrow's festivities?"

"Aye, then, follow the path down the center of the courtyard and you'll find where the foreign bards are camped for the tournament, now keep moving!"

Bryn's smile had all the sincerity of a fox grinning at a rabbit. He made no other reply and urged his mule forward, with his two 'apprentices' and the pony in tow.

An iron hammer pounded against a great bell from one of the high towers of Anglesey.

"Last bunch of them in, then close the poxy gates!" the guard chief hollered. A commotion ensued as several travelers rushed to get their carts and wagons over the narrow bridge at once. "Steady, you whoresons!"

At long last, the paunchy guard hollered to drop the grate and close the doors. He always looked forward to this part of the nightly lock-up procedure. It reminded him of a fearsome Dragon's mouth snapping shut, locking tight the kingdom of perdition until the next dawn. The guard marveled at these passing fantasies of his, finding them an endless source of job satisfaction.

He went back to watching the heavy doors creak closer, foot by foot, until they slammed shut with a reverberating *clang*! The gates of hell had shut for the night.

***

As the bard and his companions trotted down the muddy path to the minstrel encampment, two riders charged past them kicking up dirt and muck onto Tudno and the pony.

"By the Saints!" Tudno moaned, "You'd think Gwynedd's riders would know how to carry themselves down their own roads."

"Those weren't riders from Gwynedd," Taliesin said. It had practically been the first time he spoke all day.

"Wha--why do you say so?" Tudno asked back.

"The standards they bore, the three black ravens, that's Urien's of Rheged's flag."

"Urien's still in Anglesey?" Tudno asked himself. He stared into the mud in front of him as he pondered what Urien's presence implied. Bryn, meanwhile, allowed his mule to slow down enough so that it dropped back to the pony's side as it trudged forward. He bowed his head low to try and see under Taliesin's hood.

"How fare you, Tali?" Bryn asked gently. The boy had spent most of the day sitting on top of Tudno's pony silently gazing into every stone and mountain with a razor-sharp focus. He hadn't touched a single scrap of food the entire day.

"I…I am well, thanks," Taliesin said quietly. The visions that had overwhelmed him near the riverside had mostly subsided. The world had returned to the laws of time and logic it possessed before he drank from the stream, but the line between the everyday world and the chaotic sea of colors and spirits he had seen felt thin and fragile. His mind still reeled with a thousand thoughts and sensations he could hardly grasp.

"Bryn, I feel like there is more in my head than usual. Like a storm came and every window in my head flew open and now my brain is flooded. What is this curse?"

"Curse?" Bryn said puzzled. "Curses don't flood the mind, Taliesin. They lay a mind to waste. They dull the senses and turn men blind and deaf towards each other until the wretched victim is so numb and unthinking that their enemies can lead them around like cattle."

The group passed half a dozen soldiers huddled around a campfire. The armored men laughed loudly as they clanged pewter cups together. One of the larger men belched and teetered uneasily on his seat. Another paused to vomit while the others jeered.

"That's what a 'curse' looks like," Bryn said after they had passed out of earshot. "Find a man who loves the drink too well and he will be plagued by all sorts of trouble."

"What? You drink mead!" Tudno objected.

"Yes, but not to the point of inebriation. There's a difference, child!"

"Well, I certainly don't feel drunk," said Taliesin. "It's more like I know that there are hidden secrets for every creature and tree that I pass. I can feel them in my gut, and when I do this..."

Taliesin took his right thumb and gently placed it in his mouth. He gently bit down on his thumb and watched anxiously as the world began to bleed into a dizzying array of ethereal colors and ghostly sounds. He kept biting down on his thumb as long as he could bear, until he thought he could see gruesome faces pop out from every shadow, fixing him with fearful stares. He opened his mouth quickly and popped his thumb out of his mouth.

"...I can see such strange spirits dancing from every corner. What is it, Bryn?"

Tudno, who had pretended not to hear the blasphemous conversation, suddenly knit his eyebrows together.

"Isn't that the same thumb you pinched in the door when we overheard those scoundrels plotting? That time when you suddenly understood Cumbric?"

"What's this now? Since when do you southerlings speak Cumbric?" Bryn asked, surprised.

"We don't, of course!" Tudno explained. "But Tal can understand it when he wants. He watched that spy and traitor talking and only had to put his thumb between his teeth to understand what they were saying."

"Is that right?" Bryn asked, scratching his chin. He turned to address Taliesin "Then I wonder if your visions have less to do with the stream and more to do with your thumb."

"But...but I've always had a habit of biting my thumb when I get nervous. It used to drive my mother mad when I was a child. I never had any visions then."

"Well, what do I know lad?" Bryn shrugged noncommittally. "You're nearing your thirteenth year after all. Maybe manhood has more in store for you than just putting some hair on your chest."

The trio finally neared the small block of tents that marked the minstrels' camp. Bryn wasted no time hitching his mule and mingling with the odd assortment of musicians and orators. Per the bard's instructions, Tudno and Taliesin waited with the animals while Bryn tried to arrange food and accommodations for them.

"He certainly doesn't have any trouble making friends," Tudno observed as he watched Bryn seamlessly move from one group of artists to another. "I think he's talking to some Frank vagabonds now. I didn't even know he spoke the Franks' language."

"Well, words and songs are his trade. And he has traveled further than almost anyone in the Lowland Hundred."

"What about Cumbric then?" Tudno asked under his breath.

Taliesin understood his cousin's implication at once. Could Bryn have been the traitor that sold out his mother to Rhun? It was a thought that made Taliesin's stomach turn.

"I wouldn't be surprised if he could speak it," Taliesin said. "But I don't think he was the traitor. Bryn's taller than almost anyone in Cantre'r Gwaelod. The man we saw was at least a head shorter than Gwynedd's man."

"I'm sure he knows how to stoop well enough," Tudno said wryly. "If anybody is capable of skulking around in disguise, I wouldn't put it past our royal performer."

As much as he hated to admit it, Taliesin couldn't deny that his cousin had a point. Nobody was beyond suspicion and Bryn was well versed in language and assuming characters other than his own. Taliesin threw the thought out of his mind like rancid cheese. Bryn had absolutely nothing to gain by betraying Elphin and then helping to rescue him. Still, Taliesin couldn't shake the feeling that the bard had ulterior motives for seeing them to Anglesey.

At last, Bryn turned to the boys and waved them over.

"Here now! One of the minstrel troupes has a spare tent to lend us for the night, and there's some hot soup still left. Let's get a good night's sleep in. We all have a busy day ahead of us tomorrow."

Taliesin nearly forgot the tournament would begin in the morning. After slurping down the surprisingly filling soup, he laid out what spare clothes and blankets they had and curled up inside them, trying to avoid the rocks pointing into his back through the tent. Tudno began snoring no less than five minutes after lying down, but Taliesin lay still for over an hour gazing at the dancing light of the campfires skipping over the tent fabric. His mind raced with thoughts of how the tournament would progress, when the easiest moment would be to sneak around the castle, and where Elphin was most probably being held.

He absently nibbled on his thumb, wondering if any inspiration might present itself. But he only managed to make different colors and sounds fill the tent, offering no answers for his tired mind. Exasperated, he let his thumb fall from his jaw and lost himself in sleep.

***

Mererid might have been standing still for either seconds or years. Her mind was inundated with wonder and shock that roiled over her. She had come into Lord Connwn's room that evening to clean out the chamber pot as promised. She had pulled off the goose-down blankets to fish out the putrid-smelling vessel when she first noticed it. She hardly thought anything of it until she went to return the emptied pot. Something had begun to pick at her mind, something about the small stuffed satchel laying so innocently under the mattress.

It was the tiniest of things sitting there, catching the flickering light of the chamber candles. A round coin that gleamed gold. Curious, Mererid used her nail to pry the coin off the floor. She wondered to herself if anybody would notice one small coin gone missing.

That was when she saw it; the small detail that had frozen time. Every kingdom in the south of Britain had mostly kept the old roman coinage as simple currency but some of the ambitious Kings and warlords had thought to mint their coins, as a testament to their wealth and power. Instead of the old Roman emperors, the kings engraved each coin with their own standard or coat of arms. Gwyddno was guilty of this as well, issuing a line of silver pieces engraved with the sea dragon of Cantre'r Gwaelod.

The coin that Mererid held in her hand however had no sea dragon and no pompous emperor staring back at her. On the face of the golden coin that had been hastily stashed away out of sight, was the fierce lion of Gwynedd.

CHAPTER 15: The Dragon's Court

i wlad, tudwed er'grynig,
nim gwel, nis gwnav o'r newig
An'hawd wnollwng ad'loned

His country, a state perturbed,
will not see me; I cannot revive it.
It is a hard task to restore cheerfulness

~Rhun ap Owein Gwyned, Llyfr Taliesin

Mererid barely heard the footsteps that echoed down the hall or the creak of the door as Lord Connwn returned to his chambers. The clang of the metal latch made the young maid jump in surprise and she instinctively hid her hands behind the back of her skirt, assuming the picture of innocence. Connwn, for his part, balked to see a stranger in his quarters and his hand immediately grasped for the hilt of his sword.

"Oh! Forgive me, lord!" Mererid squeaked out. "I was just emptying the chamber pots for the night. I didn't mean to frighten you!"

Connwn visibly relaxed, but not without throwing a suspicious glance to the corners of the room.

"Ah, you should be careful next time child," the older man said with a condescending grin. "These are tense days and everyone's on edge. A hastier man might have hurt you by mistake."

And some on purpose, Mererid thought to herself.

"Well, forgive me then, my lord. I was just finishing up!" Mererid pushed the chamber pot back under the bed discreetly with her foot and gathered her brush and bucket up to leave. As she bent down, she could feel Connwn's eyes raking over her body. It brought back unpleasant memories of the sea gate tower.

"You're a new girl working the southern wing," Connwn remarked. "I usually ask the wee young girls to stay out of the halls after dark. Some of the other lords can fall victim to lechery, you see."

Oh, how gracious of you! Mererid thought sarcastically. "That's rather thoughtful," she replied with all courtesy. "My sister was saying as much to me. I'm thankful that an honorable lord such as yourself is looking out for her."

I'll scratch your damn eyes out of your head if you take one glance at her!

"How well spoken!" Connwn said, resting his weight on one hip. "Where did the kingdom find such a comely thing like you?"

"Uhm...my sister and I came to Caer Wyddno from Northumbria, our home was burned by the Saxons." It wasn't a complete lie. Mererid had merely tweaked the location.

"Oh, what tragedy!" Connwn said in a voice that contained no remorse. "How brave of you to travel such a far distance. You should have sought shelter in my kingdom. Powys is always generous to our fellow Cymry."

You could always use another slave for your poxy castles!

"So it is, my lord," Mererid returned politely. "But we've heard so much about the miraculous land of King Gwyddno, and I had to see it for myself, so my sister and I traveled here."

"Well, I should be thankful that you did." Mererid heard it in

Connwn's voice and she could see how he began circling her, leading ever so slightly from the pelvis. It was the same slow, careful pace that Seithenyn would so often use. "I've rarely seen such a fetching chamber maid, and an exotic maid from the north lands at that!"

Mererid tried her best to keep her stomach from turning. She kept a neutral smile in place as she felt her muscles begin to freeze. Connwn kept his face benevolent, but Mererid recognized the predator behind his smile. It was the same smile that Seithenyn had, that Rhun had.

"You seem a little overworked, my dear," Connwn said with a smirk. He reached out and grabbed hold of the girl's right hand and stroked the back of it with his thumb.

"I'm sure nobody would complain if you took a moment to rest. My bed could use a sweet creature like you to warm up the sheets." He brought his face close and pressed his lips against the skin of her hand. Mererid would have almost found the gesture chivalrous if not for the telling glint in the older man's eye.

Mererid flashed him her warmest smile.

"Oh, my Lord! To rest in a fine bed with such a strong warrior as yourself watching over me. How grand!" Mererid brought her left hand up and clasped it over Connwn's, making sure that the bandaged stub of her fourth finger rested right in front of his oversized nose.

"Oh! Heavens!" Connwn exclaimed, recoiling slightly. "Child, whatever happened to your finger?"

"Oh?" Mererid feigned surprise. "There was a horrid accident in the kitchen while the cook was chopping the meat. I was careless of my hand when he brought down the knife."

"How gruesome!" Connwn said, taking a step backward and dropping her hands like they were covered with rats. "I must say, shouldn't you have the healers tend to your wound?"

"Oh, they have, lord. But the matron told us, 'No one needs ten fingers to pick up a chamber pot.' I still have my duties after all."

"I see," Connwn murmured, his face skewed in mild disgust.

Mererid herself could pick up the faint odor of healing flesh through the bandage, and she was certain that Connwn received a stronger whiff when she brought up her hand. "Well, we certainly wouldn't want you dripping any blood in the other lords' chambers. You'd best head back to the matron and explain that you need your rest. If she gives you any trouble over it, just say that it was on my orders."

"Oh, that's rather kind of you, sire! Are you sure the other lords won't mind?"

"All of them are too busy with the war party preparations, I'm sure a dirty sheet or two won't bother them," Connwn replied.

"If you say so then, Sire!" Mererid hoisted up her bucket and made to leave the chamber. She was genuinely grateful to be sent away, but less over escaping another bout of cleaning and more over not having to spend another second with the lustful general. As she made her way to the threshold, she suddenly remembered the bag stashed under Connwn's bed. A thought suddenly overtook her.

Mererid stopped at the threshold, shifted her weight on one hip, and flashed Connwn a smoldering side-long glance.

"I certainly hope that once my little finger has healed, I can repay you with some very warm sheets indeed."

Connwn smirked and again leaned his pelvis forward ever so slightly. "Once you've recovered your strength, then." He leered.

Mererid reached deep into her memory, searching for the right words. She remembered her mother saying them just before she would go to bed every night. They were memories from another lifetime.

"Well then, *nos dda*, my lord," she said, doing her best to pronounce the Cumbric phrase for 'good night' while keeping her tone flirtatious.

Connwn raised an eyebrow and his smile broadened.

"*Eth weal voch*, my dear," he replied.

Mererid smiled, pretending she understood, and backed away slowly, shutting the door as she did. She turned and walked three steps before she broke into a run. She knew she had to tell somebody, anybody that would listen. She looked back, making sure Connwn wasn't following her and then continued running. Panic seized her and she came close to retching everything inside her out onto the floor. She knew that Lord Connwn, the King's own second in command, was the traitor who sold his kingdom out to the enemy. Now she only had to find someone who would believe her.

***

The next morning, the sun rose over the fields of Anglesey illuminating an explosion of color and bustling activity. Any other day of the year, it would have been Gwynedd's soldiers preparing for their war games and hunting parties. This day, however, all of Maelgwn's troops kept to their tight patrol schedules and stationed themselves stoically around the King's fortress. The commotion overrunning the field on this morning belonged to the minstrels.

Shouts and laughter rang up through the vibrant tent village while banners and coats of all colors rose and sank, like bubbles in a roiling tub of paint. Minstrel troupes took stock of their instruments and costumes. Jugglers and acrobats cartwheeled about, throwing their ornate knives and wooden rings into the air. Storytellers could be seen pacing up and down on the frosty ground, muttering madly to themselves, trying to cement every word in their memory.

From the back of a discarded log, Taliesin and Tudno observed the madness unfolding before them. Taliesin looked on, fascinated by the variety of instruments and artists that paraded about, yelling at each other in every tongue in Britain. He wondered at how chaotic the scene looked and yet there was a natural level of organization to the throng's movements. Unlike soldiers who were dependent on a hierarchy of command, it was as if the wind itself was directing each bard and singer to their proper place in the crowd.

Tudno, for his part, watched the frenzied crowd and tried to discern who might have left some food scraps lying out.

"I knew I should have gone to grab some dried meat before

we left," Tudno moaned. "That cold soup last night hardly did the trick. I don't think I've had a proper meal for over two days now."

He grimaced as he clutched at his empty stomach.

"Do you think one of the groups might have left a sausage out?" he asked, scanning the different campfires.

"All I've seen anyone eat so far has been bread and some old cheese," Taliesin replied.

"Here's something hot for you to put down your neck, boyo!" Bryn crowed as he leaped over to the boys with two steaming bowls of porridge. Bryn had spent most of the morning, and the evening prior, skipping from one camp to another swapping stories and gossip about the royal family. Sadly, nobody he had talked to had any inkling about where Elphin was being held or his current condition.

"Sorry to say so, Tali," Bryn said as the young boys reluctantly choked down yesterday night's porridge. "But it looks like we'll need to sniff out Elphin ourselves."

"And how would you suggest we pull that off?" Tudno asked.

"The best time to do it would be today, during the tournament's opening performances." Bryn gestured widely at the commotion being caused by his fellow minstrels. "Most of the crowd here only have today to perform for Gwynedd's court. Maelgwn gives out a small prize for general revelry, one for best musical performance, and one last prize for best bardic recitation." He crinkled his nose as he mentioned the last prize. "That last one is a sham, by Annwn. It almost always goes to one of the four and twenty bards of Anglesey, just so Maelgwn can continue to boast."

"Will you compete with them?" Taliesin asked him. Bryn stared off into the distance and shrugged noncommittally.

"If it serves us to do so, I suppose I will, but I'm not fond of that lot. For now, I'll just be happy to perform with the openers and give you two a chance to sneak around the castle to find Elphin's cell."

"I suppose we're just going to turn ourselves invisible then?"

Tudno asked. "Or maybe Taliesin can see through stone for us."

"You could lower your voice, for starts," Taliesin retorted. He wasn't interested in the whole camp of strangers knowing his name.

"You'll have to do your own work at being inconspicuous, for once," Bryn said as he reached behind himself to grab two slightly worn crimson tunics. He tossed them to each boy. "Of course, a good disguise never hurt."

The tunics were the same style worn by the page boys of Gwynedd. The cousins wasted no time trading them for their drab traveling clothes.

"It's always fortunate to know theater types wherever you go!" Bryn said with a laugh.

A trumpet from Anglesey fortress brought every head in the camp to attention. After the call, everybody appeared to move at double speed. Taliesin could feel a rushing tide of urgency sweep through his own feet.

"We're being summoned," Bryn announced, rising to his feet and hoisting his harp over his shoulder. "Well gentlemen, may our performance bring all the shit in Britain down upon us!" he said before marching in step with the rest of the minstrels. Taliesin turned and smirked to see his cousin's outraged face.

"That rascal!" he sputtered. "Did you hear what he just said?! Whose side is he on?"

"Calm down Tudno! It was a joke!" Taliesin said, surprised to find himself chuckling for once. "That's what all performers say before they go on stage!"

"Oh, that's terrible! What a blasphemous, arrogant way to begin anything! I don't recall hearing the savior start the last supper with -"

Taliesin allowed his cousin to continue ranting as the two of them fell into step with the swelling army of musicians, bards, and performers. The energy of the march was contagious. At Caer Wyddno, Taliesin had seen Enid lead her troops around the castle grounds in perfect unity that radiated undefeatable strength. The minstrels and bards on Maelgwn's fields marched with a wholly different strength. There was no uniformity, no commands shouted. Every musician and artist was their own entity, clad in every color of the earth and sky. Each one played to their own beat and sounded their own horns and drums to a different tune. The cacophony of these chords, colors, and personalities intertwined and rose above, carried by an irresistible force of nature that welled up from the ground itself. It was a vibrant and expansive force that swept them along in one fluid wave.

By the time that wave had crashed on the gates of Anglesey fortress, Taliesin watched as the performers spread out, each to their own hallways and courtyards, while he and Tudno stood gaping at the doors of Maelgwn, the Dragon's court.

Bryn moved out across the expansive castle with the rest of the performers. Jugglers and fire handlers took up the entire breadth of some of the hallways as finely robed nobles gathered around them to gawk. It occurred to Taliesin that, as supposed page boys, their inaction was drawing curious glances from some of the nobility and even the guards.

"Quick Tud!" Taliesin hissed. "Head down that hallway there. If anyone stops you, say you're delivering a message to the dungeon keeper."

"Right, good luck, cuz!" Tudno whispered back before pacing off. Taliesin turned in the opposite direction and stalked away, trying to look like he was walking with a purpose.

Taliesin found it strange to move almost casually through another castle, particularly an enemy's keep. He noted several differences between the people of Maelgwn's court and Gwyddno's. Back in his home, he could hardly hear more than a yard in front of him because of the deafening shouts of laughter that crashed through the halls. The tight faces that roamed around Maelgwn's castle looked muted. Hardly anybody spoke above a murmur. Wondering why nobody had thought to question or glance at him, Taliesin realized that most of the nobility were grouped together in clumps, their backs turned outward as they talked to each other.

Most of the hushed whispers seemed to flow across the stony halls and gather around one striking woman wearing a regal dress. The woman paced across the room with a team of foot servants flanking her, hardly bothering to look anybody in the eye. Her thick, dark hair was covered by a Christian's white veil. Taliesin strained to listen to the crowd as they whispered the same name as she passed by.

Bannon.

Taliesin then understood that he was right in front of the Queen of Anglesey herself. His eyes darted around, wondering if Maelgwn would be close behind or, worse yet, his son Rhun. Seeing nobody who drew more attention, Taliesin took the risk and began discreetly following the Queen's entourage.

Taliesin tried to focus on mapping out Anglesey castle in his mind. They took a wide circle through the main courtyard and then through a narrow passage that looked like it led towards the throne room. A dense crowd congealed around a harpist singing an energetic satire. Taliesin had to squeeze around the outside of the crowd to make his way past. He paused in his tracks when he saw the harpist was in fact Bryn, singing songs the boy had never heard in Gwyddno's kingdom.

The Queen and her servants paused as well.

Bryn sang and capered as he recited a biting satire against some ancient Pict chieftain or something close. He played his voice and body as skillfully as he played the harp, pausing every odd moment to allow the crowd to laugh or hiss in turn.

"And if a word from these lips shall prove untrue--" As Bryn sang, a paunchy, balding man, dressed in a crimson coat, pushed his way through the crowds, practically charging at Bryn.

"BRYN!" he called out. "BRYN from Cantre'r Gwaelod?" The man walked straight up to the tall bard, hardly caring that he was interrupting the performance. Bryn only twirled gracefully and addressed his final line at the incensed man.

"*-Then may this humble bard turn as ugly as...you!*" Bryn fixed his gaze directly at the man. The crowd chuckled and laughed as Bryn bowed low. He turned on his heel back to face the bulky man who rested his fists on his waist, making him look like an angry hen.

"Why, Heinin Vardd!" Bryn said enthusiastically. "I was wondering where you've been all morning!"

"What in heaven's name do you think you're doing, you prick!? Do you have a death wish!?" Heinin, Maelgwn's head bard, bristled.

"I am only here to compete in the tournament, as per King Maelgwn's invitation, 'to all bards and musicians from allies or no,'" Bryn said, repeating the traditional lines.

"Allies or no, but certainly not from invading tyrants! Your King is set to march against Gwynedd by tomorrow! The news has spread! You'll be thrown into the dungeon as a spy, harken to me!" Heinin moved to call one of the armored guards over.

"Heinin!" Bannon's voice called out. Sharp as a bell, it froze the King's master bard in his tracks.

"My Queen!" Heinin bowed low. "I beseech thee! I have uncovered an enemy spy and I-"

"A spy?" the Queen asked incredulously. "This lanky bard who was feasting with us no more than a fortnight earlier?"

"Much has since changed, your Highness," Heinin said, keeping himself bent slightly at the waist.

"But tradition still stands, and the kingdom will not turn away any bard or musician, ally or no. He is an orator, bard! Like yourself. His place isn't war. Am I clear?" The Queen spoke directly but hardly raised her voice above the soft volume of the room.

Heinin's plump lips quivered, but he bowed his head at the Queen's order and scampered off, throwing Bryn a sour look behind him.

"I apologize, friend musician." The Queen turned to address Bryn. "It appears our head bard doesn't like competition."

"Truth be told, O gracious Queen," Bryn said bowing respectfully, "I had no intention of contending with a bard as highly regarded as Heinin."

"Is that so?" The Queen's voice seemed eerily neutral to Taliesin. "Well, Bryn of Cantre'r Gwaelod, I must ask you-" Here the Queen leaned in close and almost hissed the words out of her mouth through clenched teeth.

"What in God's name are you doing here?"

Her eyes pierced into Bryn as she turned and continued her way down the hall, not waiting for his response. The last thing Taliesin could see before the crowd swept him away was a faint smile crossing Bryn's lips.

Taliesin noticed that most of the nobles were shuffling to the wide ornate throne room, whose entrance stood maybe a dozen yards away. Peering in, Taliesin could see the towering hood of the King's throne, but several taller guardsmen blocked his view of the man sitting in it. He weighed the idea of sneaking in to see Maelgwn from afar as he watched the rotating acts of his tournament. He decided against it, thinking instead that the hour would better be spent exploring the passageways of the castle, while most of the royal family and nobility were distracted. He turned to walk away from the throne room.

-WHAP!-

Without warning, Taliesin felt his head slam into the leather breastplate of a solidly built man's chest. The collision sent the boy reeling backwards a step or two.

"Mind where you're going, you wretched whore's son!" an irritated voice snapped at him.

"A thousand apologies, Master!" Taliesin said, recovering himself. "Pardon my haste, but I have a message for the dungeon keeper to --!"

Taliesin's voice died in his throat. His feet were completely frozen to the ground as he lifted his head up to see the oily face of Prince Rhun staring back at him. Taliesin knew he shouldn't have hesitated. He should have merely excused himself and hurried off someplace, anyplace that wasn't where he was just then.

Rhun's eyes swept over Taliesin. His irritation softened as he studied the boy's face, frozen in terror. Taliesin held his breath and wondered if Rhun would walk past him, oblivious to his identity. Those hopes quickly faded as Rhun's expression changed from irritation, to puzzlement, and finally shocked recognition. His mouth flapped noiselessly before finally muttering to himself.

"...Elphin's brat?..." he whispered in astonishment.

Taliesin didn't reply but only turned on his heel to try and sprint away as fast as possible through the shuffling crowd. Rhun proved quicker however and shot his hand out before Taliesin could get away. It clamped down solidly on Taliesin's arm, like a wolf snatching up a hare.

CHAPTER 16: The Prophecy

Sywedydyn yt uo.
Haelon am nacco.
Nys deubi arotho.
Trwy ieith taliessin.

An astrologer then he may be.
The generous ones refuse me.
There will not be one that will give.
Through the language of Taliessin,

~Angar Kyfyndawt, Llyfr Taliesin

  A storm of music, laughter, and bravado filled the majestic throne room of the King of Gwynedd for the first hour of the morning. Dancers capered to the tune of harps, pipes, and drums while jugglers and acrobats climbed on top of each other, competing for the audience's attention. Knights and noblemen and women shuffled around the edges of the room, taking in the rare spectacle. Urien of Rheged stood off to one side of the throne, looking on bemused but never ceasing to scan the great hall for anything amiss. Bryn was discreetly strumming along to the various tunes on his harp as he meandered on the far side of the room.

On the other side lay a heavy slate podium supporting a golden throne shimmering in the red torchlight. Seated high, draped in robes of red velvet lined with a mosaic of game furs, reigned Maelgwn flanked on his left by Queen Bannon. The corpulent monarch lifted his chin and regarded his prize annual festival like a dragon marveling at his hoard. During his darkest hours, little else gave the King more comfort than proving that he enjoyed the best of everything in Britain, even its songs and stories.

In an instant, that comfort evaporated as a mighty shout rang out from the back of the hall. Several hapless bystanders were shoved this way or another as Rhun came charging through the crowd.

"LET ME PASS! MAKE WAY, DAMN IT ALL!" Rhun was bellowing. He shoved an unfortunate juggler hard enough to send the young boy flying off the ground, breaking his glass prop as he landed. The commotion caused the music to die, and the audience shrank back leaving the center of the throne room clear.

The prince of Gwynedd stepped forward as Maelgwn rose to his feet, incensed.

"What is this, Rhun?" growled his father, "You arrive late, and now this disrespectful show? I should lash you myself!"

"Maybe I can send you someone else to lash!" Rhun barked with his chest thrust forward. He swung his arm, sending the scrawny boy he had been holding by the neck tumbling to the foot of Maelgwn's throne.

"Behold!" Rhun announced to the crowd and the King. "I've seen this 'page boy' before, and I profess that he's none of Gwynedd. This is the fosterling of Prince Elphin and the adopted prince of Gwyddno Garanhir's kingdom!" Taliesin could feel all eyes pierce straight through him, none the least the burning gaze of Maelgwn. "What's more, I found him skulking about our halls, disguised as one of our own. His aim is clear enough. Surely, he means to sabotage us, Sire! Even as we prepare for the onslaught of his barbaric kingdom!"

Maelgwn studied Taliesin like a specimen under glass. He

could feel the King's eyes raking over every inch of his body, sizing up the boy who was hardly thirteen years old.

"This is Gwyddno's own foster grandchild, is it?" he grumbled to himself. "This is a mighty strange and suspicious thing to find such a boy lurking in my halls unannounced. I cannot abide such mischief during my tournament and certainly not on the edge of an attack." Maelgwn raised his hand, summoning four burly men at arms to the throne in an instant.

"Seize the lowland brat and hold him in the dungeon until we can make better sense of this," he commanded.

The guards moved toward Taliesin with hands outstretched. Taliesin could only silently pray that maybe this would allow him to get closer to Elphin's cell, but he knew the King wouldn't be foolish enough to imprison father and son so close to each other. The guards were nearly upon him when a voice rang out from the crowd.

"Ay me! What did I tell you, lad!?" Bryn suddenly staggered forward into the center of the throne room, drawing everybody's attention with his cries. "You're in for it now! And don't expect me to stick my neck out to help you!"

Bryn's sudden appearance was enough to make Maelgwn jump to his feet again, halting the guards mid-step.

"God's wounds!" Maelgwn erupted, "Why do I see two knaves of Gwyddno's festering kingdom sullying my halls?!" The King's pudgy face flushed a deep red. "Why are you returned to my castle, slave of Gwyddno?" Maelgwn demanded from Bryn.

"Hail! O' Maelgwn, King of Gwynedd!" Bryn said, bowing courteously. "Begging your Majesty's pardon, but I thought it would be well obvious what I am doing here, on this late winter's morning." Bryn held up his harp innocently. "I have come to compete with the finest bards and musicians in all of Britain, as per your Highness's invitation."

"You are a brave bard if you think that you'd find my halls welcoming to your lot. Reports have been pouring in about your King's intention to bring war to Anglesey."

"My trade has nothing to do with war, your Highness," Bryn replied coolly. "In the past, you've been gracious enough to allow minstrels from rival Kings to compete in good faith. It is only with the same good faith that I show myself here today."

"Good faith?" Maelgwn sneered. "You only showed your face after one of your own was caught. What good faith is there in that?"

"Well, I would have presented myself to your Majesty sooner, but it appears that your kingship is just too popular with your guests. I had the hardest time elbowing my way past the crowds around you."

Bryn turned slightly, delivering the line to the audience as well as the King. Several of the minstrels tried to hide their sniggering.

"And as for this one-" Bryn pointed his harp at Taliesin. "I told the lad time and again that this was no place for him to make his debut as a bard, but you know how young boys can be. He must have followed me here by night, crafty as he is."

"This welp, a bard?" Rhun scoffed. "That's rich. When I was last in his poxy kingdom, this scrawny rat tried to stick me with a sword. He is no bard in training!"

"And what were you up to that caused a boy to brandish a sword at you?" Bryn replied. Rhun opened his mouth and then seemed to think better. From the corner of the throne room, Taliesin noticed Lord Urien squint pensively at Maelgwn's prince.

"I swear to you, O King! I swear it before God and all the saints in heaven! There are things you do not understand about this boy, things that only me, and his foster family know. The boy can perform miracles!"

"Pah!" Maelgwn spat. "That is a flimsy excuse if I ever heard one. You two are foreigners in enemy territory before the eve of war. To the dungeon with them both!"

At this point Urien stepped forward and, before saying the slightest word, bowed low before Maelgwn.

"With all due respect to your Highness, but I believe that

Gwyddno's bard has a point. You've invited every performer to your keep whether they be hostile or not. The boy may or may not be up to some evil, but the bard has only a musical instrument with him and has every right, under our great people's laws, to freely observe any happenings that go on in public. He should not be treated as a criminal."

Anybody in Anglesey knew full well how futile it was to try and change the King's mind about anything once he had given his official decree. It was plain for everyone in the throne room that Maelgwn was hardly interested in stepping back his words. The King, however, was very mindful of the small army of skilled fighters camped on his fields commanded by Urien. They were fighters he would need when Gwyddno's forces arrived at his doorstep.

"My liege -" Queen Bannon spoke up softly next to her husband. "I pray thee, consider what-"

The King's arm raised up suddenly, silencing his queen without favoring her with anything other than a backwards glance. He turned back to Urien of Rheged.

"You speak with much wisdom, my colleague of the realm," Maelgwn said with a thin smile and turned to Bryn. "You may freely perform your bardic duties, Bryn of Cantre'r Gwaelod, but only those duties."

Maelgwn turned back to Taliesin, who kept himself bent on one knee before the tyrant.

"As for this one, I see no harp nor pipe with him, nor anything that a bard would carry. Why shouldn't we lock this princeling up for deception and espionage?"

"He has no instrument because he is no musician!" Bryn protested, turning to the crowd. "Nor is he a juggler, nor story-teller!"

Rhun scowled, wearing his frustration on his chest. "Then, by hell's fire! What kind of 'bard' is he, fool?"

Bryn capered and struck a pose, capturing the attention of every pair of eyes in the throne room.

"This boy...is a prophet!" he announced.

Heads in every direction turned in confusion. Some of the gentry even began asking each other whether they were the unwitting audience to a clever piece of theater, while others marveled at Taliesin, wondering what miracles the boy could perform.

Taliesin only sat dumb and baffled.

For Lord's sake, Bryn, what are you trying to do?

His mind raced desperately. He felt so out of his element that he would have preferred to be led away to the dungeon just then, if only to have some time to try and think his way through his predicament.

Maelgwn leaned back on his heels while pushing out his bulging gut.

"Oh, a prophet now, is he?" he said, bemused. "Well, we don't usually entertain soothsayers during our tournament, but, as we've already interrupted our schedule, we should very much like to hear a prophecy then."

The crowd murmured excitedly to each other, throwing piercing glances at Taliesin. Taliesin lifted his head cautiously, barely daring to meet the dragon King face to face.

"Let's have it then, boy!" the King commanded.

"Forgive me, your Highness," Taliesin said. "But I'm afraid I don't understand you."

"Your countryman over here says that you are a prophet. So, let's hear your prophecies, or are you too guilt-ridden to even speak?" Several of Maelgwn's sycophants laughed heartlessly.

Taliesin looked wide-eyed at the King and then brought his gaze over to Bryn's face. Bryn had his eyes opened wide and bobbed his head discreetly as Taliesin looked to him for help. Bryn raised his eyebrows, silently urging Taliesin to attempt some form of divination.

Taliesin sucked in a mouthful of fresh air and began to drag his fingers over his head in exasperation. As he brought his right hand down across his temple, he allowed it to continue down his cheek until finally, his thumb was resting right in front of his mouth.

Careful that nobody was watching, Taliesin allowed the thumb of his right hand to enter his mouth, and then bit down.

No words could ever describe the sensation that overtook Taliesin when the feeling came. The closest description he could think of was feeling like a flood of water welled up from the floor and submerged him completely. Only the cold thick water was a sea of thought and visions that saturated not just his mind, but his body and soul. It was a thousand doors opening in his mind all at once, revealing parts of him that he never had conceived of before.

Taliesin rose to his feet. All the court appeared like they were moving in slow motion. Taliesin could see plumes of color radiating from every person in the crowded hall, writhing and weaving together, until the room filled with opaque tension.

Then there was Maelgwn.

Taliesin finally looked at the aging man in the face. Even then, he was still nearly pushed backwards from the King's powerful displays of crimson dancing with feverish orange as white hot sparks sizzled out of his skin. The sheer volume of color nearly made Taliesin look away in pain, until he noticed something out of place.

Whereas most of the King's aura shone brighter than fire, there was a small patch of a sickly yellow color, flowing out of what must have been the King's liver. It wasn't the brilliant, effervescent glow the rest of his body made. Instead, it was a dull, washed-out pale yellow, like some ethereal lapdog had pissed itself on Maelgwn and left a stain. As Taliesin observed further, he could see a fine network of veins that branched out from the dull area, carrying the pale-yellow color to every corner of the King's body, like a fungus that slowly festers in a field of barley.

Taliesin reined in his focus back to the sounds and faces of the court room. The thick fog of color rolled back and away, even as Taliesin could feel each person's emotions and obsessions broadcasting into the ether. He looked up at Maelgwn, no longer blinded by his fiery aura.

"O, King of Gwynedd," Taliesin began. "I shall make you a

prophecy, but I should warn you that the nature of a prophecy is not for the prophet to decide."

Maelgwn flared a single nostril.

"Make your prophecy first, and then we will consider what judgment awaits you," he said, coldly.

Taliesin inhaled loudly, trying to steady himself.

"As you wish, your Highness," the boy replied. Something strange had begun to churn inside his gut. "But remember that I only divulge this foretelling on your command."

Heinin, Maelgwn's bard, now stepped forward. Taliesin didn't need his extra vision to see the disdain on the bard's oval face.

"By your leave, your Highness," Heinin said. "It is folly to take the word of this boy as prophetic truth, just as it is foolish to trust the word of your rival's own bard." Heinin threw a dirty look at Bryn. "But I would say that these two schemers before us have won their own glory. Truly we should bestow them the award for the most convincing work of comedy for this year's tournament."

Several loud guffaws echoed from the walls of the throne room, most of them coming from Heinin's contingent of orators that made up Maelgwn's four and twenty bards. Their laughter rang with derisiveness and scorn. Taliesin felt whatever was roiling inside of him surge at the bards' ridicule. He felt like he was about to throw up and, despite himself, he opened his mouth and felt something rush out of his throat.

"Be silent, then, ye unlucky rhyming bards!
For you cannot judge between truth and falsehood.
If you be primary bards formed by heaven,
Tell your King what his fate will be.
It is I who am a diviner and a leading bard,
And know every passage in the country of your King;
I shall liberate Elphin from the belly of the stony tower;
And will tell your King what will befall him.
A most strange creature will come from the sea marsh of Rhianedd

As a punishment of iniquity on Maelgwn Gwynedd;
His hair, his teeth, and his eyes being as gold,
And this will bring destruction upon Maelgwn Gwynedd!"

"Discover what it is
The strong creature from before the flood,
Without flesh, without bone,
Without vein, without blood,
Without head, without feet,
It will neither be older nor younger
Than at the beginning
It is also so wide
As the surface of the earth;
And it was not born
Nor was it seen.
I will cause consternation
Wherever God willeth.
On sea, and on land,
It neither sees, nor is seen.
Its course is devious,
And will not come when desired:
One Being has prepared it,
Out of all creatures
By a tremendous blast
To wreak vengeance
On Maelgwn Gwynedd."

The words poured out of Taliesin's mouth like an escaping gale storm. Taliesin barely had time to think of the sounds his tongue was shaping before they flew through the room. He could only feel their raw weight and meaning surge up from the depth of his gut.

As he sung, the once clear sunlit morning began to turn darker and a howling wind picked up in the fortress of Anglesey. The winter starlings and ravens began cawing and crying out. The icy wind whipped through the throne room sending sparks flying from the burnt down torches. Everyone gathered huddled closer, some fearing that the whole castle might drop down on their heads. Taliesin's voice reached its pinnacle.

I am Taliesin, Chief of Bards!
And I've come to free Elphin from his golden fetters.

The raging storm inside Taliesin's throat finally subsided, as did the wind and clouds that had suddenly appeared over the fortress. Despite the commotion and mortal peril he surely faced, Taliesin could only feel relief pouring through him. He had been half afraid the words that had been festering in his gut would tear him apart as they flew out.

For the rest of the throne room, any reaction was overshadowed by sheer astonishment. How could one so young recite poetry so powerful that it could shake a castle? Several of the higher lords of Gwynedd began to whisper. What was the mysterious, unseen beast that would bring vengeance down on Maelgwn? The King himself had flinched at the violent wind brought by Taliesin's words, but was now standing tall on his dais, demanding respect. Rhun seemed completely terrified of the ceiling as he looked up at the large wrought iron chandelier that was now swinging precariously above him, its erratic motion caused by the strong gale. Queen Bannon, by contrast, looked down into her hands, her eyes as wide as saucers.

The King spoke first.

"Hmphh! Well, that was indeed an impressive performance," he said slowly. "This young lad may be far more a bard than I've given him credit for. But I am hardly convinced of the title of prophet."

"Your Majesty!" Bryn spoke up, doing his best to keep his tone in check. "Begging your royal pardon, but what further proof do you need? The boy sang flawlessly and the heavens themselves were moved enough to bring such a wind to shake your castle!"

"My castle has been shocked before, bard!" Maelgwn snapped back. "Even as my ancestor Vortigen built this fortress, it toppled five times until he could exorcise the demon dragons lurking below. I will not cower over some ill-timed storm."

"And what of the words themselves, Sire?" Bryn insisted.

"Hah!.." Maelgwn scoffed. "Some vague poetic lines hardly make a prophecy. Any wretch can ramble off threats about beasts unseen yet with golden eyes and hair. Come off it! What does any of it mean to us?"

"Oh Saints!" The Queen suddenly drew the focus of the crowd as she called out wailing. She fell from her throne to her knees and began grasping at a wooden cross she wore concealed around her neck, calling out invocations to the heavenly father and all the saints of Christendom. "Oh MERCY! O Heaven forgive us! Save US!"

Rhun and several men-at-arms rushed to the Queen's side and helped her to compose herself. Maelgwn only looked on, quietly enraged that his royal consort should shamelessly call so much attention to herself.

"Bannon! Calm yourself, for pity's sake!" he reprimanded. "What has caused you to cry to the almighty so?"

"Can't you tell?!" Bannon cried back. "A beast unseen, from before the flood, with hair, eyes, and teeth of gold? It's just as my dreams have warned me! The yellow plague has arrived at our door!"

The whispers among the crowd grew more frenzied now. It was obvious to Taliesin that panic lurked just below the nobles' hushed voices, simmering like a pot primed to boil over.

Maelgwn could sense the rising terror too and did what he could to keep control of the crowd.

"That's enough! Hold your tongue before I have it cut out!" Maelgwn hollered.

"It won't do you any good!" the Queen screamed back. "It's the yellow plague that ravaged the northern shores! It doesn't care for titles or power, it cuts all men down the same! Oh, God has punished us for our sins! We will all find ourselves in the jaws of the beast!"

"Take the Queen to her chambers!" Maelgwn ordered his knights. "She is having a fit of madness. Take a physician to tend to her. Have her brought back to her senses as soon as possible!"

"You'll be the one in need of a physician before I, O King!" Bannon retorted as the King's men held the younger lady by the arms, shuffling her off and out of the throne room even as she pleaded and prayed for mercy all along the way.

It was only after the Queen had left the throne room that Maelgwn allowed himself to process her words. For a tense moment, the throne room watched the King begin to turn over the idea in his head, his face muscles twitching noticeably.

"Is this the hidden meaning behind your poems, boy?" Maelgwn asked Taliesin at length. "Are you saying that I have the yellow death upon me?"

"Verily it is, your Highness," Taliesin confirmed. He might not have known that before the Queen had said it, but he suddenly understood what his unbidden words meant. "It may be invisible to most, but I see it as plain as day. The yellow plague has made its way into your Highness' liver. I foresee that in two years' time, the plague will spread to the heart and bring about your termination, King Maelgwn of Gwynedd."

Taliesin tried to sound as clinical as possible. He knew that if he gave away any hint of venom or if he seemed at all pleased at his prediction, the King would use it as an excuse to lock Taliesin up for the rest of time. Maelgwn's face betrayed a mixture of shock, fear, and outrage. Rhun, seated next to the King, only leaned back in his chair, watching thoughtfully as the events played themselves out.

Maelgwn's beady eyes darted in several directions before he finally opened his mouth to speak again.

"This is a plot," he muttered, almost to himself. "This is a plot to intimidate me, and my keep, on the eve of war! Why should I trust these forecasts of doom from any of Gwyddno's kingdom?"

"I speak truthfully, Sire!" Taliesin objected.

"He's right, your Majesty!" Bryn said, stepping forward. "The boy is a highly celebrated orator in the Lowland Hundred. Gwyddno and his sons have good reason to believe he has the gift of second sight!"

"And what reason would that be?" Maelgwn challenged.

Bryn hesitated, glancing quickly to Taliesin who looked back at Bryn confused.

"I am afraid I am not at liberty to say, your Majesty," Bryn replied apologetically. "I have taken an oath of secrecy on the subject. But you yourself and all here have seen with your own eyes. Who else can sing such verse that it causes the heavens themselves to tremble?"

"It's true! The boy speaks with the voice of God!" a voice shouted from the crowd.

"He is possessed by the devil! He'll bring ruin to us!" shouted another. Soon the throne room boiled over into a cauldron of cries and protests. Half of the court seemed to side with Maelgwn's inclination to have Taliesin imprisoned, why just as many urged the King to take the boy's words seriously, for the sake of his health. Bryn led the chorus defending Taliesin, while Heinin and some of the other bards from Gwynedd urged Maelgwn to lock him away. The only voice that did not join the cacophonous discord was Urien's. The powerful lord only gazed at the commotion with knitted brows, contemplating which direction the raging tide of opinion would turn.

At length, Maelgwn raised his hands above his head, demanding order. The crowd settled, bit by bit. Finally, the King spoke, directing his words at Taliesin.

"You've brought much discord to my halls, Lowland bard! And for that, I am much inclined to have you do penance for it, and I mean that in the most physical sense."

The King's face distorted into an impossibly fierce snarl, leaving Taliesin little doubt over what horror he could inflict. Maelgwn then turned out to the crowd, effecting a posture that screamed magnanimity.

"But no respected ruler should ever leave his subjects divided, or in doubt. So, it seems appropriate to us that we should test this 'gift' of our young bard."

Maelgwn looked down his nose at Taliesin who, having finished with formalities, stood tall. A test meant that he had a chance. Any chance of seeing Elphin again with their lives was a chance worth taking. He stared back at the King all but glaring in determination.

"I am at your Majesty's mercy," he said.

Maelgwn only snorted and continued.

"You claim that you are 'Chief of Bards' and can see when a man shall meet his ultimate fate. This sounds like blasphemy to me. A heresy against our heavenly father and savior, who is the sole keeper of all knowledge. So, let's have this test then.

"Tomorrow each of my four and twenty bards will openly compete with any who think they can compare with their knowledge and grace. Enter the tournament, 'Chieftain of Bards' and prove beyond a doubt that you are more well versed than my famed singers."

"Who judges the winner?" Taliesin asked, afraid that he already knew the answer.

"Why, I do, you dense fishman." The throne room chuckled knowingly. "As well as a panel of the royal family and my closest vassals. We tend to see eye to eye with each other."

"That sounds like a rather subjective test, your Highness," Taliesin said cautiously. "Do you swear to judge me fairly, as you would any of your own bards? And what will my prize be exactly, should I win?"

"As King, I shouldn't need to swear anything, so there you have it. As for your prize, I will happily allow you to take your precious foster father home to Gwyddno with my blessings, but not until you prove yourself for what you are."

Taliesin had enough experience with Maelgwn's own son to

know empty words when he heard them. More than that, Taliesin could almost see dishonesty oozing out from the King's mouth like a foul plume of smoke.

"And should I fail?" Taliesin pressed.

"Well, then we shall all see you for the fraud and conspirator you are," Maelgwn said with a crooked grin. "At that moment, I shall take my liberty as ruler of this isle to punish you for your heresies in manners that I deem fit. And trust me, my young orator, I take little pity on those who dare blaspheme against the crown and God."

At the implication of torture, Prince Rhun interjected.

"Those who use their tongue against the will of God will see it ripped from their mouths. Isn't that what the law requires under your rule, Sire?" Rhun asked cheerfully.

"That, as well as many other parts of the body that can be removed," the King replied with a horrible smile.

"And what's to become of me until tomorrow?" Taliesin asked. He kept his face unimpressed, but under the surface, Taliesin shuddered at the thought of what punishments Maelgwn had in store.

"I certainly can't allow you to roam free or receive unfair help from your second-rate bard. You shall be sequestered in the west wing of the tower and receive all the comforts of my royal guests. Enjoy the hospitality of Gwynedd while it lasts boy, I do not foresee you keeping that privilege for very long."

Taliesin couldn't imagine defeating every single one of the King's favorite bards and he knew that Maelgwn had no intention of holding up his side of the wager, but there didn't seem to be any choice now. He would have to play the King's game, not in the earnest hope of winning, but maybe he could distract and stall Maelgwn long enough that Tudno or Bryn could find Elphin and smuggle him away. At least some good would come from his peril then. He swept his eyes through the crowd and found Bryn's face staring back at him, grim yet determined. Tudno was nowhere to be seen, a fact that gave Taliesin a bit of hope. Maybe his cousin had found a way to sneak into the dungeons. Maybe he was talking with

Elphin this very moment and only needed another day to lift the keys off some careless guard. Taliesin held this slim hope in front of him, warding off the crushing tide of fear that threatened to overtake him.

"If this be your royal will, then I accept," Taliesin announced. "I trust that you and your judges will come to understand the wonder that is Elphin's bard." He rather liked that title. While everyone in the throne room saw him as the foster prince of Gwyddno Garanhir, it was for his father's sake he was standing there, about to enter an impossible contest under the risk of torture. It felt right to name Elphin as his patron.

"Very well," Maelgwn announced with finality. "It shall be at midday tomorrow. Prove that you can recite more of my lineage and sing fairer than any of my own bards, and you shall have your prize."

The King looked out once more, taking stock of the impressions of each nobleman and knight. When he was satisfied that his proclamation had been heard by every pair of ears, he rose to his feet and collected his royal entourage.

"The court is retired!"

***

Tudno swam through the jostling crowd exiting the throne room. The small boy did not expect to be recognized in Maelgwn's castle, but he kept his head down all the same. This, in turn, made navigating through the crowd far more difficult and Tudno found himself accidentally colliding headfirst with the rear of several different noblemen, soldiers, and most painfully, a stone wall. In truth, Tudno probably drew more attention to himself by keeping his head down than if he had simply looked where he was going.

He rounded a corner and was moving towards the open inner courtyard when a large hand clamped around his far shoulder and yanked him into a dark alcove set in the castle wall.

"What the devil?! Let me go! Mercy! HELP-!"

The hand quickly moved from his shoulder to his mouth,

stifling him. A thick red curtain was drawn over the alcove's entrance. Tudno screamed and bit into the hand. As his eyes adjusted to the low light, he made out Bryn's face grimacing in pain. Tudno stared back and then relaxed his jaw.

"Fie on it!" Bryn hissed out in a whisper as he clutched at his hand. "You're a savage bleeding whelp of the gatemaster's, Tudno! Were you going to chomp off my whole thumb, then?!"

"It serves you right for scaring me so!" Tudno hissed back. "Why didn't you just tap me on the shoulder or something?!"

"I don't want anybody to see us talking, so I had to get us both in here quickly. It was for your own sake, you ungrateful brat!"

Tudno took a minute to look around at the small stone cavity they were huddled in. The thick red scarlet curtain walled them off from the passersby and a small wooden board with a hole cut out sat on top of a wooden bench on the opposite wall.

"What's that god-awful stench?"

"We're in a commode," Bryn explained. "It's the shit of all of Anglesey, and it's the one place where we can count on a moment of privacy. Now tell me quick. Did you see where your cousin was swept off to?"

"I followed him as well as I could. They didn't take him to the dungeon. It looks like they placed him in a guest chamber for now."

Bryn nodded. "That would follow, he's not condemned just yet."

"What was all that rubbish you were spewing just now?" Tudno demanded. "What was all that about Taliesin being a prophet and performing miracles? What game are you playing?"

"For pity's sake, not so loud!" Bryn demanded. "I'm not playing at anything! You saw what your cousin can do. He may not understand it himself, but there's far more power in that child than anyone here in Anglesey realizes."

Bryn quickly peeped out of the curtain one last time, checking for eavesdroppers.

"Quick, tear off a piece of your sleeve, just a square of linen."

"What on earth for?" Tudno protested.

"Never mind why, just give it to me!"

Tudno rolled his eyes, but obeyed, nonetheless. Bryn snatched up the cloth and squeezed his knuckle on the hand that Tudno bit. A small droplet of blood oozed out.

"Do you recall when Taliesin fell into the river as we came here?" Bryn asked as he purposefully smeared a line of blood on the cloth. "Do you remember how he fell beneath the birch tree? Do you remember what he called it?"

"Uhhm… Be- Beith, I think?" Tudno ventured.

"That is an ancient name for that tree." Bryn continued smearing lines of blood over the cloth. "It is a name that hasn't been taught in any hall since the time before the Romans. Yet Taliesin knew it still."

Bryn finished whatever he was making and blew several times to dry the blood.

"Take this to Taliesin, however you can!" Bryn placed the bloodied cloth in Tudno's hand. "See what he makes of it; if it means anything to him. And whatever you can do to aid him, don't fret or ask questions, just do it!"

The bard shook excess blood off his hand and made to leave the toilet.

"What the blazes is this about, Bryn?" Tudno whispered. "Why don't you just find Taliesin and explain all this yourself?"

"Because I am a hair's breadth away from getting thrown into the dungeon myself and if I do anything that looks like conspiracy, I'll be locked up until the castle crumbles. If I'm to be of any use whatsoever I need to lie low for now, and I suggest you do the same."

"But can't you just tell us plainly what you mean for once?"

Bryn turned back and regarded the young boy with sympathy, maybe for the first time since leaving Cantre'r Gwaelod.

"I almost wish I could, lad," he explained. "But try to

understand this: your cousin has awakened something that goes beyond plain language. He will either have to learn how to command it himself, or he will go mad trying. I couldn't teach him anything even if I had the chance."

The tall graying man clapped Tudno warmly on the shoulder.

"Show him the cloth, see what he makes of it."

Tudno looked down, only then seeing the strange symbol scrawled out in blood on the clean linen. He scowled in confusion.

"Do you really believe Taliesin is a prophet?" Tudno looked up, but the bard had already slipped through the curtain and had disappeared into the crowd.

CHAPTER 17: The Discourse of Kings

A vollei honnyn, nis myn pwyllad.
Yssyd bechadur am'nivereid,
Collawd wlad nevwy, plwyv offereid.

He who has accepted assertions, cares not for reasoning.
He who sins times without number will forfeit
the heavenly country, the home of devotion.

~Bardd gybreu Taliessin, Llfyr Taliesin

    Lord Connwn of Powys counted the rhythm of his steps as his boots echoed down the polished stone hallway. As far as nobility went, Connwn was an oddity. He never had parents of high birth and thus never expected to find himself the ruler of a small kingdom. Yet after countless skirmishes with the invading Saxons and Vikings, Connwn built such a reputation that he was awarded control of Powys from the former, heirless king by virtue of his fighting prowess. Connwn took great pride in this and made sure to show off his military precision and discipline wherever he went.

The halls of Caer Wyddno had been a flurry of chaos the last few days. Soldiers from all over Gwyddno's realm crowded the courtyards and passageways reinforcing their shields, sharpening their swords, and counting their arrows. Connwn passed through a hallway that looked out over the harbor. The evening light was beginning to fade and dozens of campfires sparkled from across the water where most of the incoming armies were camped. They had tonight and then one more day before they were set to depart for battle against Maelgwn. The mood was more than frantic. Nobody knew whether the Lowland Hundred would emerge victorious or fall before Anglesey's gates, but the battle would certainly cost both sides dearly. Amid all the activity, there was a distinct feeling of doom that haunted the castle walls.

It also put the lord of Powys ill at ease to be summoned immediately by the King.

Connwn came to a crisp halt and saluted the two guards standing in front of Gwyddno's throne room. The guards nodded and pushed open the heavy ornate doors.

Gwyddno stood with his back to the throne as he gazed out at the harbor shimmering with the purple violet light of the evening. If he noticed Connwn's entrance, he didn't show it until Connwn knelt at the foot of the throne. The King turned his body first followed by his head.

"Powys is at your service, my liege!" Connwn announced himself. The King only turned and slowly paced back to the throne framed on either side by the finely embroidered tapestries that adorned the stone walls. He stood over the powerful general in stony silence. The moment stretched long enough that a small ball of nerves began to gnaw at Connwn's stomach as he feared the King might have found reason to punish him.

"What news from Gwynedd then?" the King asked plainly. "Have our scouts seen anything?"

"All my men north report what we already expected. King

Maelgwn is pulling all his allies into Anglesey. He's trying to be quiet, but it's obvious that he is preparing for a siege. We should expect to be away for some time."

The King nodded his snowy head, his gaze set beyond the walls of the castle.

"We thought as much, didn't we?" he remarked. "And what else have our scouts observed?" The King's tone was filled with hidden meaning.

"I'm sorry, your Highness. None of my men have seen any sign of your grandchildren or Bryn. Has your Highness discovered why they ran off in the first place?"

The King grimaced, shaking his head. "No, the boys I'm sure probably wandered off on a fool's adventure. That's nothing so evil at their age, but by Dylan, what a horrible time for it! Bryn concerns me. In his twenty-odd years as my bard, he's been the very picture of loyalty and honor. His disappearance could mean there is something more sinister working against us. Some sorcery or conspiracy maybe."

"I can't imagine anybody so close to your King's grace should be guilty of conspiracy, Sire!" Connwn quickly suggested. "But minstrels and clowns are an unruly lot. I've never much cared for them myself, Sire."

Gwyddno shrugged his hefty shoulders. "In any case, there isn't much we can do for my grandchildren or Bryn right now. We have enough work ahead of us." The King returned to looking out the window at the firelight dancing on the harbor. "How goes your contingent of archers that you are planning to leave in Caer Wyddno?"

"They are ready, Sire! I have given them stern instructions about how to best defend the citadel."

"Are your men loyal? With all this talk of mutiny, I should be careful that your soldiers don't betray us for a scrap of gold."

"The captain of my warriors has been my right-hand man since he was in training. I assure you, your Highness, the forces of

Powys will not betray you."

"All the same," Gwyddno mused. "I would feel better if command of the city was left to somebody known by the people. Morale across the Lowland Hundred is sinking like a wrecked ship. The peasants would be suspicious if a foreigner were left in charge, even if it's an ally."

"I suppose I could stay, if you command," Connwn said, "But I would be ashamed to leave you and my comrades before battle."

"And I would be at a disadvantage not to have you!" Gwyddno replied. "No, Lord Connwn, I would have you where you are needed most, striking fear into the hearts of Maelgwn's men."

The King pressed his knuckle to his lip in thought before continuing.

"Is there anybody here in Caer Wyddno that you trust to command your men?"

Connwn inhaled deeply through his nose while pacing a few steps back and forth, mentally going through a list of names. Finally, he stopped and faced the King.

"I suppose Prince Seithenyn would be the best choice," Connwn said with a shrug. "Your Majesty won't be able to take the gate master away from his post anyway and he is well known to the kingdom. He could take responsibility for the defenses."

Even as Connwn finished his sentence a noise, no more than a small gasp or cough, fluttered through the chilly air. On the wall to the right of the throne room, one of the thick curtains lining the stone walls shuffled ever so slightly.

"What's that?!" Connwn started, his hand flying to the hilt of his sword. "There is a spy behind the curtains!"

"What?" Gwyddno asked, following Connwn's gaze. The King raised his finger to his lips and drew a silver dagger from his robes. He motioned for Connwn to follow him as he crept up to the blue and silver draperies with hardly a sound. The King held Connwn's gaze, urging him to be ready for anything, and then swept the curtain away with a broad stroke of his arm.

Connwn and the King saw only a bare slate wall on the other side.

"Ah! It's that damn western breeze again. It's been driving me mad all day!" Gwyddno signaled for Connwn to put his sword away. "You see? Even the ocean wind conspires against me in this tense hour."

Gwyddno paced back to the open windows. Connwn gave the curtains one last quizzical glance before trailing behind the King.

"So, Prince Seithenyn shall oversee the defense of Cantre'r Gwaelod with your merry band of men. That seems a fine solution. Can I trust you to relay the message to the prince and your men?"

"I am at your service, my liege," Connwn affirmed, bowing at the waist.

"Good. Then see to it. We depart at first light the morning after the next. Ensure that you and your men are ready."

"Will that be all, Sire?" Connwn asked as he straightened himself up to go.

"Yes, but I have one last trouble that makes me uneasy about leaving the fortress." Gwyddno said, staring out into the sky and then continued.

"It's these rumors of treachery in my court. How can I be assured that I won't leave my kingdom open to some rat hiding under my nose?"

Connwn brushed his hand up dismissively and almost seemed to laugh off the King's concerns.

"These rumors abound in the halls of every king on earth, Sire," Connwn said. "Even in my own keep in Powys, there are always whispers about some dagger in the night aimed at my throat. It is a wise king that can discern truth from rumor."

"Aye," Gwyddno concurred. "Have you seen any evidence of this treachery? It's been said that the traitor was given a sack of gold from Maelgwn. Have you seen anybody using coin from Gwynedd?"

"I have not, Sire!" Connwn replied immediately. "If I had

found any coin with Gwynedd's lion on it, I would have brought it straight to your Majesty along with the rogue who used it."

The King raised his head high and stared at his lieutenant for a moment too long. "Well, keep your eye sharp in case you see anything suspicious. That will be all, Lord Connwn. Dismissed!"

Connwn bowed low and took his leave, his boot steps echoing down the long corridor that led away from the throne room. King Gwyddno listened until the footsteps had faded away, drowned out by the distant crash of the waves on the sea wall. He walked silently to the thick curtain on the sidewall and gently drew it back.

Mererid's head poked out of the folds of the fabric, her wide eyes sweeping back and forth across the room.

"You nearly gave the game away, my dear," Gwyddno said gently to the girl. "We would have had to come up with a jolly good story indeed if the lord of Powys had actually found you back here."

"I know, your Highness. Forgive me," Mererid pleaded. "I'm not at all used to staying still for such a long time!" Mererid threw a glance towards the door of the throne room, half-expecting the chief of Powys to return. "Did your Majesty find proof of Lord Connwn's treachery?"

A heavy sigh escaped Gwyddno's bulky frame, and the King puffed out his lips as he exhaled. The end of his snow-white beard trembled in the gusty breeze that swept through the throne room.

"Proof? Hardly," he answered. "But there is plenty to be suspicious of. In all the years I've known Lord Connwn, I've never seen him voluntarily shrink back from battle, and yet here he is practically jumping at the chance to stay behind and play housekeeper! What's more…" the King sat down on his throne and stared into the ground. "…is his knowledge of Gwynedd's currency. Nobody in my kingdom or farther south uses coins from Maelgwn. Still, Powys does border Gwynedd, so maybe Lord Connwn's seen the money from passing hunters or peasants. Who's to say? But he was very quick to deny ever seeing them."

"Well, shouldn't that count as proof, my Lord?" Mererid

asked. She had been extremely lucky to be able to get a hold of Gwyddno's ear, bribing a young page boy with the promise of a kiss so she could get into the throne room unbothered. "I've said that I found a heaping sack of gold coins with lions all over them in the lord's chamber. If he says that's he's never seen them, then he's lying. What else do you need?"

Gwyddno nodded, exhibiting well-practiced patience. "I believe that everything that you have told me is true, child. But you need to understand the tenuous position I find myself in. If I search a member of my own court, I will be asked why. And when I explain that I only had suspicions and the word of a young chambermaid, there will be yet more questions. No, we will catch Connwn in his own net, but now is not the time to reel him in."

Mererid could feel her irritation begin to boil over. "When do you feel would be the wisest time, O' King? In two days, you'll be riding side by side with the man who might well stab you in the back!"

"Mind your tone, my lady," Gwyddno said without ire. "The reason I insisted that he accompany me is so that I can keep an eye on him, so that he'll be away from his little band of men that may usurp the throne. There is no safer place to keep him."

"And what of who will be commanding the men?" Mererid asked quietly. "It was Connwn himself who suggested Prince Seithenyn. Do you feel he can be trusted?"

"My own son? I'm hardly concerned about his loyalty. All the better should Connwn try to buy him off. That would give us the proof that we need!"

Mererid could hardly contain herself. "Is his word better than mine, then!? Do you honestly think a cur like him has more honor than I do!?"

"He is the second prince of Cantre'r Gwaelod!" Gwyddno returned, all but shouting. "He may have his faults, but he fulfills his post as gatekeeper faithfully. Every high tide we trust him with the fate of the whole kingdom."

"Then every day we put the fate of the kingdom in the hands of a drunken lout!" Mererid's head finally caught up with her mouth and she brought both of her hands over her lips. The King only looked back at her, his eyes wide and brimming with sympathy, like he was beholding somebody gone mad beyond hope. His sympathy only enraged Mererid further. At that moment, she would rather be lashed publicly if it meant that the King would take her words seriously. His kind and gentle dismissal felt more offensive than if he had brutally screamed at her.

"Forgive me, your Highness. I spoke in haste. Lead us as you will, Sire. Good evening!" Mererid turned, without waiting for the King's dismissal, and stormed out of the throne room. She managed to make it past the doorway before tears of anger began streaming down her face.

***

Maelgwn trudged up the same flight of stairs that he had ascended less than two weeks ago. Before, he had bounded up the steep staircase in the bright morning sunlight, his mood almost jovial. Now, he navigated the hallways and steps through flickering torchlight that cast his disfigured shadow across the bare walls and floor. The shadow would grow and dance across the cell doors of Maelgwn's condemned prisoners, like a ravenous monster, hungering for the very souls of the wretches wasting away behind the walls. Every now and then, Maelgwn would find himself in front of his shadow as it loomed forward menacingly, ready to devour anything in its path.

Maelgwn quietly hurried forward, arriving at last at the undecorated oak door at the end of the hall. The stout, dark-haired guard picked his head up.

"Open it," Maelgwn commanded softly. The guard rose without ceremony and lifted the heavy iron latch off the door's handle. Maelgwn ducked his head as he stepped through the threshold, trailed by the guard who brought over a torch.

On the other side of the room, Elphin sat on the floor, his head buried in his arms as he rested huddled against the wall. A plate of stale bread and jug of water lay just out of reach of Elphin's hand. He stirred weakly in the torchlight before finally prying his eyes open and catching sight of Maelgwn.

"Ah, it's the King of Gwynedd again," he said weakly. "The King must have a lax schedule indeed if he keeps finding so much time to visit with me." Elphin had passed almost half a month in the cold bare dungeon cell, much of that without food nor hardly any water. The man looked shrunken, starved, and weak as a kitten. However, despite Maelgwn's efforts to the contrary, the prince retained his churlish, defiant tone. That irritated Maelgwn to no end.

"Your foster child appeared in my halls today," Maelgwn said casually. "He caused quite the ruckus too, during my annual tournament of bards."

The King looked for any trace of deception or cunning in his prisoner. Anything that might suggest a clever conspiracy on the Lowland Hundred's part. He only found shock and bafflement from his hapless captive.

"Taliesin? That's…that can't be…how could…" Elphin grimaced suspiciously at Maelgwn. "Oh, very clever, very sly of you indeed. What's your game, Maelgwn? I'm not fool enough to believe your lies!"

Maelgwn only nodded to the swarthy guard. Immediately the guard grabbed Elphin's thinning hand and jabbed his fingers in the seam where the wood slat that served as Elphin's bed hinged to the wall. The guard used his foot to apply pressure to the board crushing Elphin's fingers against the rough stone. Elphin snarled in agony.

"A king does NOT lie!" Maelgwn said. "And any worthwhile prince should know that. Your fosterling. Thin brat, sharp features, sandy hair and speaks like a man twice his age. Why is he here?!"

"I had no idea he was here!" Elphin said through the pain of his crushed fingers. "The boy is headstrong enough and very clever.

If he made it here, I'm sure the only person who sent him was himself and no other!"

"Your court bard is here as well," Maelgwn added.

"Him I cannot speak for!"

"He had interesting things to say about your foster son. He mentioned the boy was found in a most rare manner, though he wouldn't reveal how. He claimed the boy was a prophet right before the brat named my death date! What scheme is this Elphin?!"

Elphin only clenched his teeth tighter as the guard pressed the edge of the wood board harder into Elphin's knuckles. Maelgwn basked in the sight for a moment before signaling the guard to let up. Elphin grabbed his hand back and held it protectively into his chest.

"I don't have any idea what my bard or foster child are doing here," Elphin replied finally. "If I had any say in it, Taliesin wouldn't have come within a hundred leagues of your rotten throne!"

"What of the boy's talents as a prophet? Your bard made it sound like Gwyddno and the whole kingdom regarded him as some mystic seer."

"He made you right nervous, didn't he?" Elphin said, daring a grin. "What should it matter to you anyway, Maelgwn? What are Taliesin's gifts to you? He won't lead you to victory or help you rule over the other kingdoms. Just turn the poor boy away to trot back home."

Maelgwn shook his head. "It's too late for that. The whole fortress heard his blaspheming lies and now I must discredit him before I can do away with him honorably."

"'Honorably?!'" Elphin all but spat. "How do you even know that word?! Just turn him away. Kill me already so he won't come back but cast him out! What harm could a slip of a boy like that cause you?"

"That's just the point!" Maelgwn nearly roared as he grabbed a blazing torch from the iron basket attached to the wall. He jabbed it within an inch of Elphin's face. The dancing flames singed Elphin's stray hairs from his beard, filling the room with an acrid smell. "Is he a harmless brat that wandered into the wrong castle, or can he see what he claims? Should I care to announce when I am to die? What other secrets can this whelp uncover to bring about my ruin? All rulers have their share of secrets Elphin-"

Maelgwn grabbed Elphin by the beard and pulled his face down into the rising heat of the torch. He looked the terrified man in the eye to make sure his meaning was not lost.

"-*All* kings have their secrets."

Elphin squirmed in the heat but refused to cry out. Maelgwn watched until sweat started pouring out of Elphin's leathery face before he withdrew the flame. The man shook his face hard, breathing heavily.

"What do you want of me, Maelgwn?" Elphin asked.

"I want to know. Your bard said that Gwyddno celebrates the lad as a prophet. Is that what he is, Elphin?"

Elphin sat back against the stone wall. The silver chain around his ankles clinked as it dragged on the floor. He pressed his fingers into his forehead before sighing in resignation.

"Only a few in the Lowland Hundred know it, but yes. We knew it when he was only a babe, but we were unsure how much the boy knew of his own gifts. We decided to watch him for thirteen years to see what the babe would turn into. And now at the last of it, the boy's gift is stirring once more."

Maelgwn stared at his captive in disbelief. He would have much rather been told that the boy was an abject fraud sent to sew mischief.

"And what exactly made you believe the boy was a prophet? Answer me!"

Elphin winced and shook his head. "I've already told you your answer. Why should I say more?"

"Because if you don't, I will be filling the cell across from yours. It is a small cell with only enough room to chain a small man, or a boy, up by his wrists. Typically, I reserve it for spies and traitors. As the blood drains into the feet over the course of several days, I'm told the victim feels an intense agony in his chest and lungs, not unlike a crucifixion. The wails and screams of the prisoner echo through the whole tower for the other prisoner's entertainment. So, hold your tongue then, Elphin, and I will allow you to see your foster son, one last time as he wastes away from across the corridor."

Elphin's eyes blazed listening to Maelgwn's threats. He gnawed the inside of his mouth, attempting to keep from spitting as many curses as he knew at the tyrant. Maelgwn only stood patiently, waiting for his prisoner to decide which option he preferred. Elphin, at long last, bowed his head.

"Alright, O King of Gwynedd," Elphin said with audible venom. "Then listen closely..."

***

Taliesin hated to admit it, but Maelgwn had kept his word. His chamber was lush with the comforts of royalty. The bed in the small chamber was stuffed with goose down and lined with fine fleece blankets. Ornate tapestries covered the rough stonework walls and a simple wooden table stood in its center. On the far wall, an open window looked out over the sprawling field of Anglesey that ended in a thick grove of trees near the edge of the fortress walls.

It was the most comfort and luxury that Taliesin had come across since leaving the Lowland Hundred. It was also the most lonely and miserable the boy had felt. For all that Taliesin knew, only a few feet of stone separated him and his foster father, and yet he still had no idea how to find Elphin. Bryn and Tudno were walking a razor's edge on his behalf, and he had no clue how to communicate with them. What he wouldn't give for Bryn's advice on how to properly perform at a bard's tournament. Meanwhile, everybody else in his life was miles away, about to march off to a doomed battle. His mother must surely be weeping twice as much, both for her husband and now for him. Taliesin heaved a great slow breath to quell the pang of guilt he felt in his stomach.

Taliesin paced back and forth restlessly, his eyes strangely drawn to the bound forest at the edge of Maelgwn's land. He felt isolated and stuck, unsure of how he would survive the next day. He was confident enough that he could recite at least half of the kings from Maelgwn's line, but singing better than twenty-four professional bards while the judge was openly biased against him lay miles outside of what was feasible. If he wasn't afraid of how Maelgwn would retaliate against Elphin and Bryn, he would be tempted to sneak out and make a run for it.

He also wondered just what Bryn had meant when he said that there were things unknown about Taliesin. Things that only his foster family and Bryn knew. That he could perform miracles. Apparently, the bard knew what he was talking about. Taliesin would have never suspected in a thousand years that he was capable of delivering the speech he had made earlier that day. How could his voice call forth such a furious and spontaneous storm and make such an ominous prediction for Maelgwn?

By Dylan, what else have you been keeping from me, Bryn? Taliesin thought bitterly.

Taliesin's musings were interrupted as the latch to the heavy door clanked open and the door swung inwards. On the other side of the door stood a page boy with a small wooden bowl half-filled with vegetable soup.

In one smooth movement, the page boy brought his head up to reveal Tudno's ruddy face. He silently pleaded for Taliesin to keep quiet as he placed the bowl down on the table and cautiously closed the door behind him.

"Tud!" Taliesin whispered. "What news? Were you able to find Elphin?"

"No! And whatever stunt you and our insane bard pulled didn't help in the least either."

"Really? The job should have been easier with a distraction like that."

"In the Lowland Hundred, maybe. But every corner I turned

I ran into guards looking to see what I was up to. I had to steal a bowl and pretend I was shuffling back the same bowl of soup all afternoon."

Tudno jabbed a finger at the soup he had brought in. It looked about as cold as ocean frost.

Taliesin nodded, understanding the risk Tudno was taking. He dug the spoon through the thick mush of cold vegetables.

"You heard what I'm supposed to do tomorrow?" he asked Tudno.

"I caught the tail end of it. What magic spell were you casting earlier that brought the wind down on the castle?"

"I have no idea Tudno, the words just took me and used my mouth to speak themselves. I can hardly even remember what I said, but I know what I saw. Whether Maelgwn wants to believe it or not, he's not well. He thinks that by humiliating me he can ignore it, but the fact is he's dying."

Tudno only stared at his cousin, unsure of how to help.

"Tali, do you know what you're going to do?"

Taliesin placed the soup back on the table and paced aimlessly, allowing himself to gravitate back to the window and in sight of the thick patch of game forest. He shook his head in exasperation.

"I haven't a clue, Tudno. I have a dark feeling that the next time I see Elphin will be from a dungeon cell." He sighed heavily. "I wish Bryn could give me some advice."

Hearing this, Tudno shifted uncomfortably on his feet and seemed to wring something inside his balled hands.

"I should think that it's a sin, but by the savior Tali, it's all I have to help!" Tudno then held out his hand clutching a small, wadded-up piece of cloth.

"Bryn pulled me aside not long after the throne room cleared out. He bade me find you and give you this."

Tudno opened his hand to show Taliesin a small, folded scrap of linen, unremarkable by all measures, except for the rust-red marks where it was stained with blood. The blood smeared the face of the cloth forming a strange symbol. One that Taliesin had never seen before in any of the books that Gilgam had shown him. A long straight red-brown line ran vertically down the cloth. Four shorter lines, all pointed in the same direction, crossed over the first at a forty-five-degree angle, making the symbol look like some strange bastardization of the cross.

"What the devil is this?" Taliesin said, more to himself than Tudno.

"I haven't a clue!" Tudno moaned. "The lout just grabbed me and instructed me to take it to you in secret. I'd say it's some pagan witchcraft. That's his own blood on it, you know!"

Taliesin supposed that was better than someone else's blood, but the note's meaning remained unclear. Did Bryn believe that this would help him during the tournament? A hidden message? Or was it simply a minstrel's superstition?

"I still don't know what that maniac was trying to pull by coming here!" Tudno continued. "Announcing you as a prophet! Maelgwn won't just let us stroll out of Anglesey after that!"

"Don't forget, Rhun already had me by then. If anything, Bryn was trying to save me," Taliesin reasoned. He turned the linen around in his hands, inspecting the strange letter from all angles. Why had Bryn named him as a prophet? Was he just making a desperate bluff? Or did the old bard see something that Taliesin couldn't?

Bryn's words bubbled up in Taliesin's memory.

I wonder if your visions have less to do with the stream and more to do with your thumb.

The boy furrowed his brow, beginning to understand Bryn's intent. He kept his gaze fixed on the strange blood letter and slowly brought his right hand up to his face. He wiggled his thumb between his teeth and gently bit down.

Immediately the lines of blood began to tremble and move. At first, they only squirmed around fruitlessly, like earthworms dying in the summer heat. Then the lines began to expand. The center line grew taller and thicker while the diagonal lines crossing it began to grow and twist. The bottom of the center line split and then split again while the sides of the other lines grew and bent up to the top of the cloth. White teardrop shapes and red dots began appearing on the arms of the symbol as the color of the blood faded to a dark and fearful black. In an instant, Taliesin realized that he was looking at a miniature portrait of a sprawling black bush with white flowers and blood-red berries. The image looked so real to Taliesin that he could swear that it swayed and breathed with the draught that blew in from the open windows.

"Tudno!" Taliesin whispered awestruck. "What can you see? Here on the cloth?"

Tudno reluctantly inspected the cloth in Taliesin's hands before shrugging his shoulders.

"I just see a man's blood making some devil's letter," Tudno responded flatly. "Why? Don't you?"

Taliesin turned his gaze back to the cloth. The image of the tree had transformed back to the brick red symbol etched in dry blood. As Taliesin reflected on this strange vision, he found himself gazing back over the tournament field to the enclosed forest on the far side of the castle wall.

"Tudno," Taliesin called, suddenly inspired. "I think I need to pay a visit to the forest."

CHAPTER 18: The Straif

Eirinwyd yspin.
Anwhant o dynin.

The Blackthorn, full of spines,
how the child delights in its fruit

~ Cad Goddeu, Llyfr Taliesin

The two guards standing outside Taliesin's cell snapped to attention as the door creaked open. A page boy hurried out carrying a chamber pot at arm's length. He shuffled past the guards without acknowledging either.

"You there!" the right guard yelled out. "You're supposed to wait for permission to pass, you dense whoreson!"

The page boy stopped a few steps down the corridor. He half turned his head, keeping his back to the guards.

"Your pardon, Sire!" he called out. "But the southern princeling left an unholy gift from his kingdom in the chamber pot. It smells like all the rotten fish of the sea brought together in one monster turd. Care to admire it?"

The guards broke what small veil of discipline they had and burst out laughing.

"Oi! You sodding brat! Get away then! And take your hellshit with you!"

The page boy smirked as the guards shook their heads and joked with each other, and then descended the stair aisle, keeping the empty chamber pot close to his body.

Taliesin had been reasonably confident he could bluff his way past the guards. Tudno and himself looked close enough alike that they could pass for each other at a distance, so he doubted the guards would question which skinny boy left and which skinny boy stayed in the cell. He only hoped that Maelgwn or Rhun didn't decide to visit while he was out. He had made it clear to Tudno the risk that both boys were taking by switching places. Tudno was willing, but that didn't comfort Taliesin much when he considered that he may not ever see his cousin alive again if he made but one mistake.

Thankfully, now that night had fallen and torchlight illuminated the castle halls, moving about was easy. Once or twice, Taliesin thought he heard Heinin's voice echoing down the corridor, making the boy double back and pass down another hallway. Eventually, he made his way outside the castle through a low window on the ground floor. Once he was away from the castle, the pitch darkness of night gave him all the cover he could want.

Luckily for Taliesin, Maelgwn was vain enough to claim ownership over part of nature itself and had enclosed a portion of the forest within the walls of Anglesey. It was hardly more than an acre or two of greenery connected to its parent forest via several streams that ran under the outside wall. The reserve was large enough to host several families of boar and stag while being close enough that the King could hold tournaments with his emissary guests. Lord Elby of Dyfed, the most experienced huntsman in Gwyddno's court, never spoke well of such tournaments.

"He makes all of hunting about killing and blood-letting! That

Dragon Maelgwn!" he would rant. "The kill is just the end, a sacred God-given moment! The true sport in hunting is the chase, the patient tracking and days of back and forth, all in the majesty of Britain's own forests, not a tyrant's play-garden!"

Taliesin could only hope that Maelgwn's 'play-garden' held whatever Bryn's clue suggested. He hopped over a small hill and discarded the empty chamber pot behind it. His hand clutched the bloodied cloth with the enigmatic symbol. As Taliesin skulked nearer to the eaves of the forest, he also got closer to the city walls that ran along the forest edge. He could see two or three lights from the guards moving along the parapets, but Taliesin judged them far enough away that they shouldn't see him if he moved carefully. An overcasting of clouds obscured the moonlight and, in all logic, the guards up top would probably be watching outside the city rather than within. The thought comforted him as he finally crossed the threshold of the forest's tree line and into the dark abyss.

He crouched low next to the root of a fir tree and waited for his vision to adjust. The forest was well-maintained with several open paths winding their way through the gloomy tree trunks. Taliesin took a careful step, only to find that the way was clear of underbrush. Still, it made the boy wince to think of some low-hanging branch or tree stump he might accidentally walk into in the darkness. Once or twice, a quick rustle and strange noise would sound from almost every direction, turning Taliesin's blood to ice. He wondered, maybe a little post-maturely, if Maelgwn was fool enough to allow wolves to roam his fenced-in forest.

He wouldn't have any reason to do that of course, he thought to himself.

Would he?

He tried to distract himself by taking out Bryn's scrap of cloth. He waited for a thin patch of clouds to let enough moonlight through the trees so he could study the strange mark again. He was reasonably sure the mark indicated a type of tree, but what if he was mistaken? And even if Taliesin were able to find the right tree, how would that serve him? Maybe Bryn meant for Taliesin to club the other bards with one of the branches? Taliesin highly doubted it, but what else was he supposed to do with a tree?

In the dark, Taliesin heard another rustle on his side. From several hundred yards away, a guardsman's voice echoed from the wall. Strolling around through the unfamiliar woods in the dark strained Taliesin's nerves, making him jumpy. The sudden noise caused the boy to flinch, knocking him off balance. The boy stumbled awkwardly for a few steps before tripping backwards and smashing himself into the solid trunk of an oak tree. The fall winded Taliesin and he knelt against the tree trying to steady himself, biting back frustration and fear. He had come so far, and unless he could make sense of this puzzle, he would surely rot in a dungeon cell, maybe one right next to Elphin's.

Under stress and acting purely on habit, Taliesin brought his hand to his face and allowed his thumb to pop into his mouth. He bit down.

In an instant, Taliesin's world exploded into a mishmash of color, sounds, and patterns. He had to fight with his own body to keep himself from panicking. He wished that biting his thumb would at least give him consistent visions. He found, on the contrary, that each vision had its own feeling to it and its own pace, making Taliesin frightened and bewildered. He saw waves of red-brown and deep emerald lapping their way up the trunks of trees that swelled and heaved as if they were breathing. Blues and violets streaked with veins of luminescent orange siphoned out of thin air and dripped down the small twiggy fingers of the outstretched tree branches. The night, which had seemed almost dead silent in the late winter night air, now crackled with strange chirps and growls that came from the eaves of the forest.

Taliesin steadied himself. The simple act of walking had just become a feat of concentration. His own body felt lighter and then heavier from one moment to the next. He wandered from one tree to the other, trying to match each to the image the symbol suggested.

Taliesin could hardly make out what type of tree he was even looking at thanks to the garish colors bleeding out from every plant around him. After a half-hour of fruitless searching, Taliesin sat down on the outgrown root of an oak tree.

Stupefied, Taliesin gave in to studying the intricate pattern on the bark of the oak tree, somewhat amused to see what could have been the shapes of small wiry bent men etched into it. The boy went from amused to dumbfounded when one of the small figures began to move its limbs and crawl over the tree bark like a chattering squirrel. Taliesin gasped out softly in astonishment as the figure hopped straight out of the tree's bark, cartwheeled with inhuman agility down the root, and landed with hardly a sound next to Taliesin's side.

The creature was short, no taller than maybe the height of Taliesin's knee. Its skin was dark and dull looking, like the bark of an old log, but the creature looked angular and splintery. Its long fingers looked like they had been filed down to lethal points. Its eyes were two round plates of amber. Even though it crouched less than a yard or two away, Taliesin couldn't determine what the creature was really made of. It appeared more like a small drawing that had escaped the confines of paper than a natural forest animal. Taliesin couldn't decide if he should be amazed or just terrified by this small spiky creature scurrying across the forest ground and shooting him piercing looks with his eyes.

The creature made a beeline for Taliesin, making the confused boy jump back in fright. The creature crouched low on his haunches and bared razor-sharp teeth.

"Blood," the thing spat out.

"What?!" Taliesin gasped, hoping the creature hadn't said what Taliesin knew he heard. The odd creature pointed his triangular snout at Taliesin's hand holding the scrap of cloth.

"Blood?" the thing said again, sniffing in Taliesin's direction.

Taliesin looked down at his hand, beginning to piece together the thing's intentions. He unfurled the cloth again to glance at the symbol, indeed drawn in blood. As he was distracted, the feral shape darted up to him noiselessly and went to snatch away the cloth from Taliesin's grasp.

"Hey!" he protested and yanked his hand back just in time. The spry creature somersaulted forward and came to rest on a low standing rock, immediately twisting back around.

It crouched low and then fixed its eyes squarely on Taliesin.

The creature's stillness activated a primal terror in the young boy. He could feel adrenaline gurgle up through his body commanding him to run and scream, but he dared neither. Very carefully, he lifted the cloth up and forward, allowing the fabric to unravel and hang free. The bloodstain lay fully visible to the wild creature.

The creature reacted by shifting its weight higher and cocking its head to the side like a confused pup. The impish thing scanned its dark amber eyes up and down the linen.

"Straif," it croaked out. "Straif, Straif!" it insisted and jabbed a thorny claw at Bryn's symbol.

"Huh, do…do you know what it is?" Taliesin asked, suddenly hopeful. "I'm looking for...straif. Can…can you help me?"

The creature looked Taliesin up and down and then turned his darting gaze back to the cloth.

"Straif for blood?" it offered. "Straif for blood?"

"Umm," Taliesin hesitated, wondering how much blood this squirrely thing actually wanted. He eyed the creature's needle teeth warily. "Can you take me to the...straif? I'll let you have the cloth, maybe just a drop or two from my finger, but nothing more, if you please."

The creature grinned menacingly back at him and then jerked its head in a gesture that might have been a nod.

"Straif…follow," it said. The next moment, the creature had nearly disappeared into the gloomy underbrush, leaving Taliesin standing paralyzed in the dark.

"Wait! Come back!" Taliesin shouted. He abandoned all

caution and tore off after the strange creature, hoping that the dense forest would hide any commotion from Anglesey's sentinels. He ran behind the darting shadow, doing his best to hop over roots and fallen tree branches. He kept finding himself on the verge of losing the weird halfling in the underbrush, only to catch sight of his foot as it sprung around one tree and then the next.

Taliesin finally tumbled out of the thickening underbrush into a small clearing, the far side of which ended in the unnegotiable stone wall of the fortress. The adjacent side was sectioned off by a neatly arranged line of bushy plants, the highest branches of which barely covered the height of a grown man. White petaled flowers in the shapes of stars stretched out over the contours of the bushes, while the wood of the plants was a dark, earthy brown. Each branch and twig was dotted with fearsome looking thorns.

"Straif!" the thing called out, hanging from a sturdy branch, evidently not at all bothered by the thorns. Taliesin could almost imagine now that the creature could have been constructed entirely from discarded thorns, given his spiky appearance. It swung back and forth carelessly, like a trained circus monkey.

"This...wait, I know this bush, this is a sloe berry bush," Taliesin said, perplexed. "Sometimes we would go to harvest sloe berries ourselves during the spring. Father would make sloe gin. Well, he would put his best effort into it, anyway." Taliesin always thought people were unfair to scorn Elphin's homemade brew. Crissiant had suggested that Elphin call it sloe berry vinegar. After all, vinegar had many common uses as well. "Blackthorn is what they also called it," Taliesin continued.

"Straif!" the creature insisted. "Thorn for secrets. Thorn for secrets."

"What?" Taliesin asked, feeling like he was walking a knife's edge with this volatile creature.

"Thorns." The creature narrowed its eyes at Taliesin as he pulled his tiny, clenched fist over a tenacious young branch that hung low. It opened its hand to reveal several long black thorns stuck viciously into its splintery palm. It pulled out three of them and offered them to Taliesin. "Thorns. Put them in your tongue. Gives you secrets."

Taliesin accepted the dark thorns, careful not to prick himself on their sharp points, and careful not to get so close to the creature's dangerous looking teeth. He was not entirely sure how three thorns would come in useful for the task he had to face come morning, but he supposed it was better than nothing. He looked up to see the spiny imp creature holding out his empty palm.

"Blood," the thing demanded simply.

Taliesin handed over the piece of linen with the bloody symbol. The spiny creature sniffed at it and then stuffed the whole thing into its mouth, chewing it like a cut of the finest game. After ingesting the whole thing noisily, the creature shook itself and then began to hobble back into the underbrush.

"Wait!" Taliesin called recklessly. "You led me here just for a few thorns? I could have found thorns anywhere, so why this plant's thorns? Why not the leaves, or berries, or the flowers even?"

"Flowers?" The imp looked back to him, his bright glittering eyes shining eerily through the gloom of the forest. "Thorns for secrets," it repeated.

"Flowers for madness."

The small thing disappeared into the woods leaving Taliesin to wonder how much of his strange encounter was real. He collapsed down onto his haunches. He gazed around the clearing, noticing that his senses had returned to normal. Judging by where he could glimpse the moon, no more than an hour had passed since he arrived at the forest. He might have believed that the whole encounter was some mad hallucination he had from biting his thumb too hard, and yet here he stood, in front of a blackthorn bush with several of its thorns still in his hand. He looked at the small, clustered flowers, their snow-white petals practically glowing in the dim light.

He sat down on a nearby rock, nibbled gently on the top of his thumb, and watched an idea begin to slowly bubble in his mind.

***

"Tudno! Psst! Wake up!" Taliesin urged his sleeping cousin. He had returned to his holding chamber to see three people soundly asleep, his cousin within, and the two guards without who had passed out leaning against their own pikes. Taliesin silently thanked heaven for his glimmer of good fortune and carefully slipped back into the chamber as quiet as a mouse. There he found his cousin dozing happily in the down bed intended for himself.

"Quick, Tudno! Before somebody comes and finds you!"

"Hmm? Wha-Tal? Goodness!" Tudno snapped awake. "How long were you gone for?"

"I honestly couldn't say," Taliesin admitted. He had thought he had heard the bell toll two hours after midnight as he was skulking back into the castle, but for all he knew it might have been close to dawn.

"What happened to you?" Tudno shook himself and crawled out of the bed, trading back his page boy robes. "Did you figure out what Bryn's symbol meant?"

"I...well...I have no idea what Bryn might have been trying to say, but I think I found a solution."

"Did you actually get all the way into the forest, in the dead of night?! You know that Gilgam always warned us that the devil stalks the woods by moonlight."

Taliesin bit the inside of his cheek.

"In this particular instance, I might agree with Gilgam!" he said to his cousin's puzzlement. "Tudno, listen. There's not a lot of time and I need you to do something for me."

Taliesin froze suddenly as the two boys heard the metallic clang of footsteps approaching the chamber. By the sound of it, there were a couple of armed men making their way down the hall that led to Taliesin's room.

"Who is walking around the castle at this hour?" Tudno

whispered.

The footsteps couldn't have been made by one person alone, but the steps were so crisp and precise that the boys couldn't discern if there were two people walking or twenty. A rough voice sounded from behind the wood door.

"What ho, you knaves! Is this the kind of discipline that King Maelgwn accepts from his men? I know some sovereigns who would behead a man who falls asleep at his post!"

The guards outside the door suddenly snapped to attention.

"Forgive us, Lord! We meant no harm."

"Fear not, gentles. I am not one who sees any value in punishing the overstrained. Take your leave and rest yourselves. Two of my own men will take your posts until dawn."

"My lord!" one of the guards protested. "We cannot abandon our posts for none but the royal family itself. To do otherwise would mean death!"

"And what would it mean if the King were to hear that his guards had slumbered through half of their appointed time?" The voice paused for effect. "Come! Get some sleep and nobody will speak of it further. I only wish to speak with your captive, nothing more."

"As you wish, my lord," the guard replied. Two pairs of feet noisily marched away. A few seconds later, the metal clang of the door's latch sounded. Whoever was outside was about to enter the chamber.

Taliesin mouthed to Tudno to get behind the backside of the door, out of sight from the late-night visitor. Tudno nodded and leaped over to the far wall just as the door began to swing open, effectively trapping his cousin behind it. On the other side of the open doorway stood Urien of Rheged accompanied by six armed men, two of whom had taken the place of the dismissed guards.

Urien only nodded at Taliesin before stepping over the threshold of the chamber. Taliesin on the other hand bowed low before the northern warlord.

"Lord Urien, hail!" Taliesin said politely. "You've picked an odd time to pay me a visit."

Urien looked down at the boy from his towering height. He sniffed, amused, and then replied.

"A little-known secret. I suffer from bouts of restlessness at night. Sometimes a brisk walk helps put my mind at ease."

"I see, so what has brought you here tonight?"

The lord of Rheged inhaled deeply as if he were trying to suck in every ounce of air in the drafty chamber. His torso seemed to expand like a giant set of bellows.

"First, I wanted to ensure that a boy of such tender age was being treated graciously and not thrown to the rats. Secondly, I wanted to speak face to face with the boy who so blasphemously claims to know God's will. That claims to know when rulers and kings will pass onto the next life."

Urien surprised Taliesin by kneeling down to better look the boy in the face, his commanding height still putting his eyes an inch above Taliesin's.

"I've seen wonders and miracles in my time, but it's been a long while since I've seen such a commotion as you've made today in Maelgwn's halls. Tell me truthfully boy, are you an agent of heaven or of the devil?"

The question penetrated Taliesin to the core. He had never enjoyed Father Gilgam's lectures or self-serving interpretations of the scriptures, yet the boy had always viewed himself as a God-fearing individual, more due to his mother's virtue than anything else. Had he unknowingly entered the devil's service?

"To be perfectly honest, lord, I couldn't say what power has given me this…sight. I have come for one prize only and, although it might damn me, I will use any tool I can to win that prize."

"You speak of your poor foster father," Urien said. He stood up again and crossed his arms.

"Yes. I'd rather die in his arms than live apart from him."

Urien only drilled Taliesin with his gaze for a few tense

seconds and then exhaled sharply, pacing absently across the room.

"You seem sincere enough," the powerful man said, almost to himself. "But sometimes the most sincere of us make the best instruments of evil. How can any of us know for certain that Gwyddno didn't send you with the worst of intentions?"

"Well, for starters, he didn't send me. I came here by my own decision with the help of my bard and...erm...his horse." Taliesin mentally chided himself for nearly giving away Tudno. He couldn't do anything that might jeopardize any edge he had over Maelgwn.

"But Gwyddno rides here any day now. My scouts have confirmed as much. It would be rather cunning of him to send any distraction he could out ahead of him. It's any warmonger's standard tactic."

"My grandfather is no warmonger!" Taliesin protested. "Brash maybe, and proud too, but he has no other option to make war, for his honor's sake."

"Come now, lad!" Urien tersely bit back. "War for appearances' sake is hardly the Christian way. And I should expect no different. Oh, your grandfather was gracious enough with me and mine, but I've seen his enchanted city guarded by that vicious harpy captain of his. I've seen the pagan gods he still worships and then there's his contract with the cursed lot from Annwn. For all his empty talk, Gwyddno is no Christian."

"Why must it always be one or the other?" Taliesin said, beginning to get irritated. "Can't a ruler pay homage to Christ in heaven while respecting the gods of the earth? And, in any case, why should you rush to ally yourself with Maelgwn? His cruelty is hardly Christian either."

"Aye," Urien replied thoughtfully, "but he is more than generous to the abbeys and churches, and there is nothing blasphemous about a shepherd who is stern with his flock. Sometimes that is what is required of a ruler."

"Is it?" Taliesin said. "And where does it say that a shepherd's son can tempt a lady to lust and then cut off her finger when she refuses?"

"What's this?" Urien seemed genuinely surprised. "Whatever are you talking about?"

"Ah! So, you haven't heard the whole truth of Prince Rhun's visit to our kingdom? About how he made to seduce and mutilate my own mother to prove his point? I would ask him next time you see him if I were you."

"Rhun had been unjustly ambushed by your King's men and barely escaped. That is the report that I was given."

Taliesin suddenly looked up at the tall lord with pity and no small amount of shock that such a capable man could be so naive.

"It would seem to me, O Lord of Rheged, that you have been deceived by the Dragon like countless vassals before you."

"That's nonsense!" Urien barked, growing agitated. "The King of Gwynedd has spent the better part of his reign cloistered in a monastery. Half of his treasury is donated to the church. He is a sincere exemplar of the faith!"

Taliesin's tone softened and he chose his words carefully.

"As you so wisely observed, lord, sometimes the most sincere among us make the best instruments of evil."

Urien froze as still as a statue, an incredulous expression plastered to his face. A second later he snapped his head away from the boy and signaled his honor guard to leave. He trailed behind them until he reached the door and turned back.

"You should rest well, young southerling. Tomorrow the whole of Gwynedd will see for themselves how much truth rings in your words. As for me, I would not be surprised to see you flounder before Maelgwn's four and twenty bards. And if you do, I suspect you shall find your infernal master soon enough. Good night, young lad!"

The door closed straight behind him, revealing a pale and gaping Tudno still on the other side.

"Well, he was in a right mood, wasn't he?" Tudno remarked excitedly. "I used to look up to him, I did. How dare he call us a kingdom of pagan heretics?! Is Father Gilgam's church invisible to him?"

"I don't believe him," Taliesin said to himself.

"I know what you mean, the audacity of it!"

"No, I mean I don't believe that Urien is standing by Maelgwn because of religion. His land sits right alongside Maelgwn's and blocks his entrance to the rest of Wales. He *needs* to be allied with Maelgwn, even if he has to lie to himself to do so." The boy stood still, lost in thought. Since fleeing Cantre'r Gwaelod, he hadn't taken the time to consider how the brewing war between the two nations would ultimately play out, aside from inflicting suffering and death on both armies. With Urien's men seemingly entrenched on Maelgwn's side, Taliesin didn't have high hopes for the men fighting for the Lowland Hundred.

"What about tomorrow, Tali?" Tudno asked, snapping Taliesin out of his reverie. "Do you know what you're going to do?"

"Hmm? Oh! Well, in some sense, yes. I just don't know if it will work."

"What is it then? What happened to you outside?"

"Never mind what happened to me." Taliesin didn't know where to begin describing his encounter with the strange sharp-toothed creature in the woods. He wouldn't expect his pious cousin to understand in any case.

He stepped a few paces over and handed Tudno a crumpled bunch of white sloe berry flowers.

"Take these and listen carefully."

CHAPTER 19: The Tournament of Bards

Wyf sarff wyf serch yd ymgestaf.
Nyt wyf vard syn yn aryfreidaw.

I am a serpent; I am love; I will indulge in feasting.
I am not a confused bard driveling,

~ Buarch Beird, Llyfr Taliesin

The first gray slivers of morning light had crested the top of the eastern hillside as Heinin, captain of Maelgwn's bards, strode confidently down the path that led to the palace commissary. The walk was a peaceful beginning to his daily routine. Typically, he would bid each of the twenty-three other bards of Anglesey good morning, brief them on the stories his majesty deemed worthy to hear, which histories were politically convenient to mention, and which foreign guests were presently visiting the King. The orators were expected to work the guests' bloodlines into their stories for the sake of flattering potential allies. Heinin's sharp political savvy in these matters had earned him the position of captain of the bards.

As he rounded the corner, he was hardly surprised to see a large steaming cauldron of porridge already assembled for his company but was perplexed to see a small serving boy, one he did not recognize, stirring the pot with a large wooden ladle. Usually, the bards were left to serve themselves.

"Oy! You there boy!" Hererid called out, "What business do you have with the bards' porridge? You best not be sneaking any yourself!"

The skinny boy started at Heinin's voice but composed himself.

"I wouldn't think of it, master!" He called back and let the ladle drop back into the steamy, watery mush. "I was just sent by the cook to add a quick garnish to the pot."

"Garnishing a pot of porridge?!" Heinin reeled back with disbelief. "What rot! Begone with you already, before I find one of the guards to give your hide a good tanning!"

"M'Lord," the boy answered with a polite bow and then scampered away around the nearest corner.

Heinin shook his head incredulously as he dipped and stirred the porridge with the same ladle. He brought a spoonful up to his lips, allowing a moment for it to cool in the chilly air. He grunted, sipping down a small mouthful past his wiry grey whiskers, and then smacked his lips in approval. He didn't think that porridge needed garnishing, but the mash did have a sweeter, almost floral, flavor to it today.

In twos and threes, the bards trickled into the hall and each helped themselves to their share of porridge. Heinin began briefing the gathering of storytellers on the day's proceedings. One of the younger, more arrogant singers stuck his pale hand up in the air.

"What of that boy from the Lowland Hundred?" he asked. "Isn't he supposed to be our competitor today? When does he get to humiliate himself?"

"The King has decided to put him on after the twentieth act.

It should keep the suspense up a bit. Anyway, that's usually when the comedy act takes place. If Maelgwn wants he can always be brought back on for one final encore before he gets dragged off to the dungeons."

"What!" cried an older, bearded man known as Glem. "I'm to follow the whelp? How insulting!"

"You should be grateful," Heinin shot back, "Your God-awful wailing might sound pleasant for once!"

"What about Bryn?" another voice from the younger bards called. "He won't be representing his own kingdom in the tournament?"

"No, the lout declined to compete, as have every other orator from outside of Gwynedd," Heinin said sourly.

"Understand that we are not the main act today, but rather just the entertainment to an extremely round-about public hanging. Just play your parts so we can be done with the cursed spectacle and spend the rest of the day at the alehouse."

The bards chuckled their agreement and unceremoniously left the dining chamber, their bowls of porridge strewn haphazardly on the tables.

***

"For the entertainment of the court and for the just assessment of the foreign bard, known as Taliesin, by the righteous and one true King of the Britons, Maelgwn of Gwynedd, the tournament of bards shall hereby begin!" The herald bowed deep and then took his leave of the floor, gracious to be away from the King's attention. Maelgwn was grinning smugly from atop his throne. His court of cronies and sycophants mirrored his confidence. Rhun sat in his usual place, equally interested and shooting lascivious smirks at some of the more fetching ladies. Queen Bannon sat on the left of her King, her face a mask of forced tranquility.

Rhun leaned over to his father, whispering out of the corner of his mouth.

"You're not the least worried, are you, Sire?" he inquired. "Elphin's fosterling can be cunning. I've seen it myself."

"He thinks himself cunning, but look how well that served him, eh?" Maelgwn scoffed. "Besides, I know full well that the brat has no idea what he's doing. I spoke with Elphin last night. The boy is a wonder to be sure, but he hasn't a clue to his own nature. He thinks he was picked up at sea from the wreckage of a pirate ship."

"And Elphin told you otherwise?"

Maelgwn fixed his son with a knowing grin.

"Remind me to tell you the whole story later. But the boy doesn't have a clue. He is merely a child swinging a sword blindly in the night. I wouldn't trust a single word of his 'prophecies.'"

"Shall we make a wager on it then, dad?" Rhun suggested, clinging together the same gold pieces he had won off his father only a week prior.

"That's enough! The two of you!" Bannon chided. "How can you even think to gamble on the life of your poor father! The yellow plague has destroyed whole nations. It sealed the fate of the Romans. It's a ghastly curse!"

"For pity's sake, my love!" Maelgwn said with a smile. "Don't let that wretch's lies disturb you. I am King and am under the protection of the Almighty himself. Today you shall see the boy's bluffs fall apart in front of all. Hear me now!"

Lining the sidewall of the throne room stood twenty armored knights with Rheged's standard, the three black ravens, on their breastplates. They held themselves with such discipline that they might have been statues. In the center of the formation, stood Urien, resting his gauntleted hands on the hilt of his sword that stayed sheathed in its scabbard. He took in the spectacle in a controlled and dignified manner, but his bushy eyebrows seemed to crease inward, giving his face a hint of uncertainty. His eyes swept sidelong towards the King and back to the entering crowd.

A staccato fanfare announced Taliesin's arrival. Four brightly armored guards escorted Taliesin into the throne room and boxed him in against the wall opposite Urien and to the right of the throne. They hadn't gone so far as to bind the youth's hands although they each kept a pike on their shoulders at the ready. Taliesin counted it as a stroke of fortune that they hadn't tied back his hands, or they may have found the three sloe berry thorns he was concealing between his fingers. He had to consciously remind himself not to twitch his fingers unless he pricked himself.

The previous morning, Taliesin had been able to walk freely around Anglesey's halls without drawing a second glance. Now, there wasn't a single pair of eyes in the cavernous throne room that could resist gawking at the strange boy. The King and his prince looked down at him with identical sneers, while the queen knitted her brow and pursed her lips. Urien of Rheged crossed his powerful arms over his chest and tilted his head up, like a stern father lording over an insolent son. Every other lord, general, and emissary in the room regarded him with caution, as if they were afraid he would transform into a bird at any moment.

Then the four and twenty bards made their way into the throne room, treating Taliesin to a gallery of sneers and faces as they passed. They marched in, two by two, and took their places in the appointed benches between Taliesin and the King's throne. It was no accident that Taliesin could hear some of their sniggerings as they walked past.

"I wonder what nursery rhyme we'll hear from this one."

"He's about as sickly as his sodding master in the dungeon."

"Maybe Bryn will accompany him on a sheep whistle."

Weren't some of these villains supposed to be friends of Bryn? Taliesin thought with disgust.

Even at that moment, Taliesin caught sight of his friend's head springing up from the back of the crowd. Bryn's clear eyes sought out Taliesin's own dark ones. Taliesin could hardly read the bard's enigmatic expression, but he could feel a steady calm and strength radiate out from him. He only gave Taliesin a sideways smirk, before sinking back down into the sea of onlookers. As usual,

Taliesin was left wondering what the old storyteller really knew.

Taliesin turned back to the bards of Gwynedd with a stony expression. He wanted to project the same confidence that bombarded him from every adversary in the hall. In truth, Taliesin's mind was a maelstrom of uncertainty. He could be reasonably sure that Tudno had followed his instructions, but he had no guarantee that his dreamed-up plan would actually work. In the back of his mind, Taliesin couldn't help but feel terrified that he was wagering his entire fate on a few thorns sticking into his hand and the word of a nightmare creature who may not have even been real.

Finally, Heinin, with vestments of green and silver, and a shaggy beard that tapered into a short braid, took the floor.

"A fine morning to you, O Maelgwn, finest of Kings to the Britons. Firstly, I would have Gendall, junior minstrel of your realm, approach to recite the deeds of your holy ancestors."

Maelgwn nodded his head, squinting his eyes briefly in Taliesin's direction.

"Proceed," he announced.

Gendall looked like he couldn't be more than three or four years older than Taliesin. The feathery orange robe that hung off his diminutive shoulders draped almost a foot lower to the ground than his feet and he had to constantly bat the cloth behind him to keep it from catching under his heels. He held a small lyre in the crook of his arm.

Hopping onto the center of the court floor, Gendall bowed ceremoniously to the King, struck a chord on his lyre, inhaled sharply through his nose-

-but no sound came out of Gendall's open mouth.

Instead, a strange face came over him, like he had been struck dumbfounded by a circuitous math riddle. He gaped his mouth two or three times almost as if he were attempting to dislodge something from the back of his throat. His eyes grew wide and an entire twelve seconds passed without the bard uttering a single sound.

The court didn't dare breathe a single word or murmur, but

the silence was so protrusive that Taliesin could swear he heard the eyes of the nobles brush back and forth. Maelgwn's eyes were glaring at Gendall menacingly as his head tilted forward towards the mute performer. At last, Heinin broke the silence with an embarrassed cough that shook Gendall's voice loose from his throat.

"ehAHHaaaHAAeehhh."

Gendall's eyes widened even more and he snapped his mouth closed. But the sound kept resonating from his voice box.

"bbbrrbbbrr, mmmmnnmlill chit chit chittichhraahh, blat baum bu bloom!"

The bard was sheet pale. His voice rose to a ludicrous pitch and volume. "PllleEEEEE PA PA PIUUUUU! Blooots SPLAAHH MNRuumBUBU!"

Some of the court gasped audibly. Other dignitaries farther away from the throne openly snickered at the terrified fool. The stifled giggling echoed off the stone hallways and found their way to the King, perched on his throne, his face livid with disbelief and humiliation. His body was trembling with outrage as he continued to stare at one of his prize bards babble on inanely. Finally, the King raised his hand. Every mouth in the room clamped shut, except for Gendall's unintelligible sputterings.

"This is nothing short of insulting!" Maelgwn choked. "Surely this poor wretch must be afflicted with madness, or else I would see him beheaded this very moment!"

"MMNoooEEEEEyyaaah!" Gendall made some noise that seemed a mix of groveling and begging.

"This poor child!" Bannon remarked from her seat. "He has obviously lost control of his wits!"

"Forgive him, Sire!" Heinin's voice was shrill. "The boy's been somewhat ill lately. Mayhap it's a touch of the yellow fe-" Hererid broke off abruptly as Maelgwn's face turned a deeper shade of scarlet. "-uhh, I mean, the boy must have taken some bad ale last night. We'll have our next storyteller up. He shall put an end to this regrettable turn of events. Here we have Donhal, the renowned satirist!"

An older, more experienced looking performer stood hastily to his feet. His face was nearly as pale as poor Gendall who, clapping his hands over his mouth, slinked back to the bard's bench, his face held low. Donhal called for his harp, but Taliesin could see the terror in his face stirring beneath the surface of his pores. He scanned over the rest of Maelgwn's praised entertainers, the ones who had crooked their mouths up into rude sneers not more than ten minutes ago. Nearly all of them look stunned and decidedly worried. Taliesin felt his own face contract into a smile. It was his turn to grin at his adversaries.

The spectacle of the bards was only beginning. While tuning his harp, Donhal's fingers began to twitch uncontrollably. He began compulsively striking the same note without the slightest hint of rhythm. His cheeks began to inflate as he willed his lips closed to keep the sound from escaping. The only effect this had was to produce a crude raspberry sound in place of any actual singing.

"This sputtering nonsense again!?" Maelgwn nearly roared. "Get that travesty off my stage. Let's have some actual words for the court!"

The throne room crowd continued to point and whisper their own private jokes to each other. Yet another bard came as Heinin walked Donhal back to the bench, looking like a man bound for the gallows.

One after the other the bards, who only yesterday had been so well versed in histories, satires, songs, and fables, entertained their King and his court with nothing but infantile gurgling and meaningless babble. While the men were clearly out of their wits, it was difficult to discern if they were drunk, insane, or had simply lost control of their tongues and voices. Some seemed genuinely ashamed and humiliated while others reacted to the madness with stark bursts of laughter. One older bard, who normally sang with a rich baritone voice, seemed completely unaware that the sounds coming out of his mouth were hardly words and carried absolutely no melody. He also seemed oblivious to the very loud and crude defecation he made in his pants halfway through the performance. After finishing his unique ballad, the bard bowed deep to his King and then took his place on the bench again, only noticing that something was amiss when he sat down and picked up on the smell.

Maelgwn's face had cycled through several different shades of scarlet, violet, purple, and by the end, a gruesome tone of blue-ish mauve. The faces of the performers who still had their mental faculties, if not their vocal ones, took on the very opposite complexion. Sheer terror had drained their skin of all color and they sat so motionless that they looked like wide-eyed corpses awaiting a mass grave. They had seen what the King does with those that dare insult or embarrass him. Most of the bards had even sung ballads about those very punishments, praising them as righteous victories for their King. Now they were left wondering if they too were due to be the next victims of Maelgwn's righteousness.

The enraged King stood up once more, obviously straining to contain himself.

"And what say you, Heinin?" he asked. "Will you offer any poem, any bit of wit to save us a small scrap of honor?"

Heinin was clearly uncertain of this. Slowly and silently, he drew himself into the center of the stage. He took the time to meet his audience in the eye and planted his feet squarely into the ground. Even the most daring of the crowd that had been so bold to laugh through the morning's embarrassment fell silent. The chief bard's concentration was unshakable. He inhaled audibly, inflating his chest before opening his mouth.

"Bbibibibibibllbibibibi." Heinin's finger was ludicrously flapping his two lips together as he droned on like a spoiled child. Not a single member of the court could hold back as guffaws and bellows of laughter filled the hall.

"WRETCHED CUR!" Maelgwn exploded. A goblet sailed across the throne room and crashed into Heinin's knee, spattering mead across the floor. With a frightened yelp, Heinin rushed off the floor and back to the bard's bench.

"This idiot show is ended! We will hear no more today!" Maelgwn moved to dismiss the court.

"But your Majesty!" Taliesin called out. "Forgive me, but I don't believe that I have had my turn yet."

"I have no interest in hearing another word! The contest is forfeit!"

"Then mine is the benefit of the doubt surely," Taliesin countered. "After all, it was your own decree that I should outperform this band of bards to prove myself. I can hardly be held responsible if your own bards are incapable of competing."

"He's right, Maelgwn, King!" Urien's voice sounded from across the hall. "A king cannot go back on his decree when his words are the very standard of truth. I, for one, would care to hear what the boy can sing."

"These are rather extraordinary circumstances, Lord Rheged!" Maelgwn shot back. "I say it is the devil at work in my halls!"

"Or is it an angel, performing miracles to save us from the yellow plague?" Bannon quietly asked, her eyes fixed into the floor below her.

"Hold your tongue, wife." Maelgwn wheeled to face her like a rabid dog. "This is not your place to decide such things!"

"I am only concerned for you and the kingdom, my Lord," Bannon replied, not daring to meet her husband's face. "If some curse was placed on our poor bards, who's to say that the young Taliesin would not also be afflicted?"

Maelgwn's face twisted and stiffened in his ire. For a moment, it looked as if the great monarch was trying to breathe through one nostril while the rest of his features appeared paralyzed.

"It was your own decree that has placed the boy and your bards against each other," Urien reminded the King. "He deserves to speak!"

Maelgwn methodically unhinged the muscles in his jaw and

even managed to curl his upper lip into a brief smile. He lifted his arms magnanimously for his assembly.

"So, it seems the will of the court that we should continue this farce with one final act. Well, so be it! After all, I am not the kind of host that would deny our lowland guests their fair share of humiliation," Maelgwn announced, drawing a retinue of chuckles. Taliesin begrudgingly admired how the egotistic King managed to save face when necessary.

"Approach, Taliesin!"

He beckoned the young boy forwards and the guards on Taliesin's four sides withdrew. Taliesin stepped into the center of the throne room.

"My first request to you, bard of Cantre'r Gwaelod," Maelgwn sneered. "Recite my lineage starting from the first king of Anglesey's isle"

Taliesin took a long inhale and brought his hand up to his mouth, trying to appear pensive. As subtly as possible, he stuck one of the thorns through his fingers and past his lips, allowing it to prick his tongue.

"Well, fool bard?" Maelgwn prompted.

"I beg of you, your Majesty, just a moment to gather my thoughts."

Taliesin swallowed and could taste his own blood oozing out from the thorn prick. As he pondered how to begin, he suddenly felt a strange twitching coming from his tongue. The slight spasms began to make their way in and around his mouth and then all the way down into his throat and voice box. Startled, Taliesin thought he might indeed start babbling like the other bards. Maybe the whole straif bush was simply cursed.

When he could resist it no longer, he opened his mouth and let the words come as they would.

"First there was Cunneda,
Liberator of Anglesey who hailed from Manaw Gododdin

Of Cunneda came eight sons..."

To Taliesin's great relief, his words came out as anything but babble. Instead, new and strange names escaped his lips, names that he pronounced flawlessly. As the lineage poured out of him, the boy could clearly see the face of each king and chieftain that he mentioned. He could feel the outline of their lives and manner of their rule. Some were wise and just, while others were cruel and tyrannical.

> "Then came the great Arthur Pendragon,
> Scourge of the Saxons and unifier of Britain..."

As Taliesin mouthed the name "Arthur Pendragon," a vision of strength and wisdom flooded his mind. If he had been in control of his speech at that moment he would have stuttered from the majesty of his image. He beheld a king completely selfless and unparalleled in his sense of duty. He was a man who did not see himself in a position of authority or power, but rather in the role of a humble servant. A vessel for divine law and wholly subject to it.

As Taliesin continued to list the kings that had come after Arthur, he felt their compassion diminish respectively. He shuddered as he spoke the name "Vortigen" and could feel the ghost of a heartless, insecure miser, his world filled with enemies.

> "And from Cadwallon came our Lord
> Mael...Maelgwn Gwynedd."

Taliesin stumbled just that once, on the very last and present king sitting before him. As he had said Maelgwn's name, Taliesin saw every deed and crime committed by the devious monarch. In an instant, he realized every act of cruelty and betrayal. And, most shockingly, he saw how he had courted his queen.

Taliesin felt the words cease in his throat like a sea calming after a storm. Maelgwn's hall fell silent as the noblemen exchanged quizzical glances. Rhun spoke first.

"How did the boy speak? What say you Heinin?"

Heinin only shot a frightful glance at the prince and Taliesin, and then nervously nodded his head up and down while staring at the floor.

"Right, so the lad knows his history," Maelgwn announced, managing to compose himself. "But what gifted poem or song can you deliver us? Be forewarned that if you stutter one syllable, I'll declare the contest fraudulent and set you to rot alongside your master in the dungeons."

Taliesin brushed off the threat, knowing full well that it was not the time to debate the contours of the King's original decree. Instead, he merely brought his fist to his mouth, trying to appear nonchalant, as if he were gathering his thoughts.

In a sense, he was.

He stuck another thorn through the knuckles of his fist and scratched it sharply against his tongue for a second time. He inhaled deeply, feeling a spring of visions and inspiration surge up from his guts, and then opened his throat to let it all out.

"Primary chief bard am I to Elphin,
And my original country is the region of the summer stars;
Idno and Hererid called me Merddin,
At length every King will call me Taliesin.
I was with my Lord in the highest sphere,
On the fall of Lucifer into the depth of hell
I have borne a banner before Alexander;
I know the names of the stars from north to south;
I have been on the galaxy at the throne of the Distributor;
I was in Canaan when Absalom was slain;
I conveyed the Divine Spirit to level of the vale of Hebron;
I was in the court of Don before the birth of Gwdion.
I was instructor to Eli and Enoc;

I have been winged by the genius of the splendid crosier;
I have been loquacious prior to being gifted with speech;
I was at the place of crucifixion of the merciful Son of God;
I have been three periods in the prison of Arianrod;
I have been the chief director of the work of Nimrod's tower;
I am a wonder whose origin is not known.
I have been in Asia with Noah in the ark,
I have seen the destruction of Sodom and Gomorra;
I have been in India when Roma was built,
I am now come here to the remnant of Troia.
I have been with my Lord in the manger of the ass:
I strengthened Moses through the water of Jordan;
I have been in the firmament with Mary Magdalene;
I have obtained the muse from the cauldron of Cerridwen;
I have been bard of the harp to Lleon of Lochlin.
I have been on the White Hill, in the court of Cynvelyn,
For a day and a year in stocks and fetters,
I have suffered hunger for the Son of the Virgin,
I have been fostered in the land of the Deity,
I have been teacher to all intelligences,
I am able to instruct the whole universe.
I shall be until the day of doom on the face of the earth;
And it is not known whether my body is flesh or fish."

The words erupted out of Taliesin's throat and, just like the previous day, a great wind blasted through the halls of Anglesey castle, seemingly conjured up by the cadence of the boy's voice. The gale whistled through the cracks in the stone walls causing them to shriek and some of the bard's discarded harps and lyres sang with the vibrations of the rushing air. Some of the ladies in the court clutched at crosses they had around their necks and mumbled prayers of repentance while the men looked on in terror. Maelgwn himself shrank back into his throne while Rhun looked up astounded as he noticed the monstrous wrought iron chandeliers beginning to shake.

Taliesin felt the last of his song escape him as the wind outside began to die. Taking advantage of the confusion, the boy stuck the last straif thorn into his mouth, gashing his tongue once more. He turned to the gaggle of terrified bards. He still had one last poem to recite.

"Minstrels persevere in their false custom,
Immoral ditties are their delight;
Vain and tasteless praise they recite;
Falsehood at all times do they utter;
The innocent persons they ridicule;
Married women they destroy,
Innocent virgins of Mary they corrupt;
As they pass their lives away in vanity,
Poor innocent persons they ridicule;
At night they get drunk, they sleep the day;
In idleness without work they feed themselves;
The Church they hate, and the tavern they frequent;
With thieves and perjured fellows they associate;
At courts they inquire after feasts;
Every senseless word they bring forward;
Every deadly sin they praise;
Every vile course of life they lead;
Through every village, town, and country they stroll;
Concerning the gripe of death they think not;
Neither lodging nor charity do they give;
Indulging in victuals to excess.
Psalms or prayers they do not use,
Tithes or offerings to God they do not pay,
On holidays or Sundays they do not worship;
Vigils or festivals they do not heed.
The birds do fly, the fish do swim,
The bees collect honey, worms do crawl,
Everything travails to obtain its food,

Except minstrels and lazy useless thieves.
I deride neither song nor minstrelsy,
For they are given by God to lighten thought;
But him who abuses them,
For blaspheming Jesus and his service."

Taliesin couldn't exactly say that he had ever had a religious revelation before. He certainly had never felt anything close to divine inspiration sitting in a dark chapel listening to Father Gilgam drone on and on about people who had been dead for thousands of years. Now, in the throes of his ecstatic speech, Taliesin could grasp the shape of Abraham's god, just like he could see the face of the great King Arthur. In this moment, Taliesin could feel, could know beyond any rational doubt, that God was not some fatherly creator or heavenly ruler that demanded worship. Taliesin saw God as a living, breathing entity. A fountain of all thoughts and actions that permeated all that is and ever was. Something that transcended logic, language, and death.

He beheld this vision even as he watched himself chant the final lines of his song and the howling wind subside at last. Then, after gathering himself for a moment, Taliesin turned and addressed Maelgwn with his own voice and words again.

"There. I have successfully recounted all in your line and, without doubt, I have outsung all twenty and four of your bards. Remember your decree now, O King Maelgwn, and release Elphin to me and we will depart and trouble you no more."

All eyes in the throne room turned expectantly to the Dragon King. Maelgwn only sucked on his lower lip as stared back at the young boy. Very few adversaries of the King had ever lived long enough to antagonize him as Elphin's fosterling had, and it was proving to be a frustrating problem indeed. Finally, Maelgwn stood up.

"It cannot be denied that, on *this* day, you have been the worthiest bard, and we salute you, young Taliesin," the King began courteously. "But I would venture to say that your victory was less the virtue of your speech and more the failure of my bards. After much consideration, we remain unconvinced about your gift of prophecy."

"CONSIDERATION?!" An undisciplined voice shouted out from the crowd. "Are you deaf?! There isn't a voice in all the world that's sung like that until now!"

Taliesin didn't need any supernatural gift to know whose voice was defying the King. Inwardly, he felt all his hopes sink into the floor.

The sea of finely dressed noblemen and ladies reeled back from a small boy, as if sharing the same air with him would be cause for execution. Revealed before the whole of King Maelgwn's court stood Tudno wearing the same shocked expression on his face as the onlookers. Clearly, the boy had shared his thoughts without the critical filter of his better judgment.

A cry went out from the throne.

"SEIZE THAT BRAT!"

The commotion that followed would have put the most skilled acrobats and clowns to shame as every guard in the courtroom sprang into action, and into each other, in a mad rush to lay hands on Tudno. Tudno likewise wasted no time in diving headlong into the stunned crowd of dignitaries and dashed his way through the maze of robes and tresses in a wild attempt to elude the guards. Noblemen were jostled and ladies pushed brusquely by Tudno and the guards as the boy raced through the crowd like a spooked pig. He twisted and dodged around stone pillars and lush tapestry, tearing them down off their fixtures in the process, inadvertently giving the guards more obstacles to negotiate as they stumbled after the spry youth. Servants and cooks clutched their dishes as the rabble got pushed over to the serving tables. Standing from the throne, Maelgwn and Rhun barked and yelled out conflicting orders to their soldiers, gesturing frantically at the places Tudno had been or was headed. In their fury, they looked like mad conductors for a symphony of chaos.

In the center of the storm stood the only motionless person. Taliesin's gaze was sunken back into his head. He barely even registered that Tudno was in mortal danger. He had come within an arm's reach of his goal and saw the fruits of his labors hopelessly dashed onto Maelgwn's throne room floor. The considerable amount of mental strength Taliesin had summoned during his performance left him feeling drained, and now his composure almost collapsed entirely.

Finally, after cornering Tudno before he could dive out of the tower window, the guards all but threw him before Maelgwn right beside where his cousin knelt. The head guard kept one heavy foot pressed down on his back.

"How dare you defy your King in his own throne room!" Maelgwn roared. "We shall have to instill some manners into your hide!" Maelgwn waved over a burly guard who carried a deadly-looking whip.

"Hold Sire! I beg you!" Taliesin could keep silent no longer. "Have mercy! This is my own cousin. He accompanied me here as my horseman. He often speaks out of turn when his emotions get the better of him." He made sure to shoot Tudno an icy stare. Tudno only stared at the floor wide-eyed

"So!" Maelgwn sneered, "A piece of the puzzle reveals itself. What other accomplices do you have lurking in my halls?! Where is that overgrown bard of yours?"

"Here, Maelgwn King!" Bryn said, stepping forward. "The boy means no harm. As Taliesin mentioned, his mouth is ever in motion whether it is asked for or not. He is only a child still, have mercy on him, please!"

"Mercy?! Mayhap I shall. Indeed, the boy has done me a service. He's proven that this false prophet of yours can't be trusted and given me full right to deny him his prize."

"Just because my cousin was too cowardly to show himself earlier doesn't make me a liar! Every word I've spoken has been true!"

"What proof do we have of that?!" Maelgwn all but hollered. "So, I'm to die in two years' time of plague? Am I supposed to wait two years until I find out I've been swindled? If you have the gift of second sight, tell us something that I alone could know!"

The command struck Taliesin like a rock. A memory that wasn't his boiled up in his mind. Something that he had glimpsed when he was running through the names of Maelgwn's lineage.

"Very well, King," Taliesin said, deadly calm. "But I would beware of the ghosts of the dead that might still seek revenge. Ghosts, perhaps, of your neighbors of Nant Conwy."

Maelgwn struggled not to react, but it was plain to see that the King had suddenly turned a shade paler.

"And what about your lovely young Queen?" Taliesin pressed. "It's no secret that you courted her after her first husband's death, but does she fully understand what made her a widow? Does any of your court know that?"

Queen Bannon sat straight up in her throne. "What's this the boy speaks of? What of my first husband?"

"It's nonsense, my love. The boy is spreading more lies to try to humiliate us!" Maelgwn said quickly.

"I know the truth just as well as you do, King! And if you won't speak it, then I shall."

"ENOUGH!" Maelgwn's fist thundered down on the side of his throne. His imposing frame radiated fury and, more importantly, fear. Taliesin knew that he was provoking the Dragon's fire and very well might get burnt and devoured for it. But, just as had been the case when he absconded from the Lowland Hundred, he had no choice. Any hope he had of escaping, with or without his father and friends, rested on keeping Maelgwn off balance.

To his surprise, it worked.

"So be it, young bard," Maelgwn growled. "I cannot accept the outcome of this, obviously rigged contest you've won, but neither can I discount your gifts just yet. So, let us have one last contest. A contest that will NOT be tampered with and one that you can only win with the almighty hand of God on your side."

Every set of eyes and ears opened wide to the King. It was unheard of that any soul who had provoked the King of Gwynedd so sorely wasn't locked away in the dungeons. On the contrary, Maelgwn was giving him a second chance to come out of this in one piece. The King continued.

"Tomorrow morning you and your horseman," Maelgwn glared meaningfully at Tudno, "will compete against my prize team of racing stallions driven by my champions, the fastest of which will be ridden by my own son, Prince Rhun. You are to use no other horse but the one that you brought to my keep. If you succeed in beating them around the racing track in the span of three laps, only then will I respect you as a true prophet and allow you to leave my castle with your foster father. If you lose, you both shall be subject to the cruelest forms of punishment at my disposal."

Taliesin could feel his cousin begin to tremble even though he was several feet away. He could sense every set of eyes in the hall bear down on him, treating him to a mix of pity and condescension. Bryn sheepishly cleared his throat.

"By his Excellency's leave," the tall man said quietly. "I, for one, cannot say that I follow the King's logic. How exactly is the sport of horsemanship supposed to tell the worth of a prophet? I don't expect to see-"

"We don't expect you to see *anything* of tomorrow's contest!" Maelgwn snapped. "I've had my fill of your unwelcome, tedious voice in my halls! Bard or not, you are under the patronage of an enemy of war right now and will not stay another hour here. Let all here see for themselves! I am honorable! I will not harm any minstrel during our celebrations! But you are hereby banished from Anglesey and Gwynedd! Go back to your King and tell him his little foster princeling shall be waiting when he arrives at my gates and his ransom will not be at all cheap. Now see him off!"

Within an instant, several fearsome guards caught Bryn by the arms and swept him away. Bryn was only able to call out briefly to

Taliesin.

"Don't worry about me, Tali! Remember why you came! Don't settle for less!"

And then he was gone.

"And finally," Maelgwn continued as if nothing had passed. "To be sure that there is no more tampering, you and your cousin are to spend the time between now and the race under full guard, confined to your chambers. If either of you takes a single step out, I shall have you flayed alive before all here. I suggest you spend the time praying, for only God himself will deliver you now. Begone!"

Taliesin and Tudno were dragged back by their arms. Taliesin allowed his feet to scrape the floor while he fixed the throne with a fiery gaze. He saw Maelgwn's fierce grimace contrasting with his son's cruel anticipatory smile. Bannon stared back at him with shock and fear written on her face while Urien glanced at him sidelong in pity. As they exited the throne room, the court milled about with each other, whispering their astonishment and wonder at the events. Finally, the King, the court, and the thoroughly humiliated bards drifted away, leaving the spacious throne room cold and empty.

Thus, ended that year's tournament of bards.

CHAPTER 20: Seven Stallions

Seith seren yssyd.
O seithnawn dofyd.
seon sywedyd.
A wyr eu defnyd

Seven stars there are,
Of the seven gifts of the Lord.
The student of the stars
Knows their substance.

~ Canu Ygwynt, Llyfr Taliesin

"But can't we just stay a few more days!?" Awena whined at her sister. "Dalia said that she was making me sweet scones for doing such a good job with her at the healer's halls."

"I'll make you loads of scones, but only after we get far away from this fish-festering city!" Mererid replied brusquely to her little sister. She had shirked off her afternoon cleaning rounds and made Awena do the same. Instead, Mererid was spending the afternoon tearing through their cramped, shared servant's quarters packing everything of value they owned into a small cloth sack she had lifted from the kitchen. Their own personal items were sparse, but the frantic girl had used a considerable amount of time tracking down practical items like blankets, clothing, and food. She had made up her mind that very morning. She would leave Cantre'r Gwaelod, her and her sister, by nightfall and trek over the hills and into the forests farther east.

She would not spend one single day in a kingdom ruled over by Seithenyn Ap Gwyddno, even if it was only provisionally.

"Where are you going to do that?" Awena whined. "We don't even know where we're going! Where will I sleep?" Mererid's little sister had dug her heels in at every turn, but the older girl's ire had plowed over any protests.

"I'll keep you warm, that's what the blankets are for. We'll find someone to take us in. Who wouldn't want two cleaning maids willing to work for a few morsels of food and a roof over their heads?"

"But we already have those, sis!" Awena said close to tears. "I don't want to go, Merry!"

"I told you before, I don't much care!" Mererid bit back. "I can't explain it all to you, love, but things are going to be rotten here. Really rotten! You and I are going to be working down to the bone for nothing more than crumbs."

"All day?" Awena asked innocently.

"All day, and for me all night too," Mererid replied bitterly. "Come now, it won't be so bad. We'll hop over the eastern wall once night falls. I know an easy place. Then we just hike down the road, out of sight from anybody, and find new jobs as soon as we can."

Awena sniveled then as thick tears began rolling down her smooth, young face.

"I'm scared, Merry! What if the wolves find us? They're going to eat us, Merry!"

Mererid knelt down and held her sister by the shoulders until the young girl caught her breath and stopped crying. "There are wolves here, 'wena," she told the girl somberly. "Believe me, the kingdom is infested with wolves."

A sharp rap at the door made Mererid start. She fought back her panic and shoved the bundle she was packing into her sister's arms.

"Wena, take this and stay low!" She pushed her sister under the straw mattress they shared.

"Who is it now?!" she called out while straightening out her cleaning gown. "I was just heading out for the afternoon rounds, ma'am, no need to remind me!"

The door creaked open and in poked Crissiant's light-colored head.

"Oh! Why, Lady Elphin?!" said Mererid, dumbfounded. "I...I was expecting the head matron. Is everything alright?"

"Alright?!" Crissiant scowled. "My husband imprisoned, my son and his cousin disappeared, and the whole kingdom marching off to war? Oh, I'm just happy as a clown dear!" The stately lady pushed open the door without waiting for an invitation. On her right arm hung a woven basket with several herbs and sprigs of flowers.

"But I did not come to wail and moan, dear child," she continued. "I've come to see how your poor hand is doing."

Mererid looked down at her left hand wadded in rust-colored cloth. Ever since her run in with Connwn, she had completely neglected it. She could feel the stub of her finger throbbing in anguish.

"It's healing as well as it should, I suppose m'lady."

"Cockle's feet!" Crissiant chided. "I can smell the wound from the doorway. It must be infected with something awful. Come, take off that filthy bandage!"

The Lady Elphin began crushing the herbs and called on her foot servant for hot water. In the meantime, she cleaned away the dry blood and pus oozing from Mererid's wound.

"It looks dreadful! Surely you must have used the mistletoe I left you?"

"That was you!?" Mererid asked, shocked.

"Why, of course, my dear! I thought I told that fool of a waiting nurse to tell you. She's getting a bit senile if you ask me."

The servant returned with an iron pot of water. Crissiant wasted no time soaking the herbs and cleaning around the wound with the infusion. Mererid winced as the hot water and oil from the plants seeped into her flesh and began to burn horribly.

"It stings awful!" she protested.

"It's part of the process, love," Crissiant replied gently. "Healing a wound is never easy or enjoyable but heal we must. If you had used the mistletoe as I thought I instructed, the pain would be much less now."

"I just...I never thought you would have left me anything. Were you not upset with me?"

"Whatever for, you daft thing?" Crissiant sounded almost irritated.

"Well, for the trouble I caused in your home. Wearing your best dress and jewelry and getting my own bloodstains on them. I thought you'd be furious with me considering that Tal...Taliesin has gone." Mererid could feel her face burning red.

"Firstly, you are the least responsible for the commotion in my home, dear. It's that fiend Rhun, King Gwyddno, and my son I blame, in that exact order. If anybody in this fool's kingdom asks me, you were the bravest of the lot of them, and more's the pity that you were the one that had to pay the price for it."

Mererid went back to staring at her hand as Lady Elphin neatly dressed the wound with clean white cloth.

"Since you brought up the subject, you wouldn't have spoken at all to Taliesin before he left?"

Mererid could hear the frailty in the older woman. She shook her head.

"No, I'm sorry, my lady. I have no idea about where he went off to."

"I wasn't asking about that." Crissiant said, rolling her eyes. "Any fool can see he's gone to Anglesey. I suspect he means to either free Elphin or avenge you. I just wanted to know if he said anything to you before he left?"

"Uhm...I'm sorry, m'lady. I didn't see him."

From across the dormitory, a rough wool blanket jumped and Awena stumbled out.

"For pity's sake, sis! Can't you hurry your business up faster?! I can't breathe under this thing!"

Crissiant started in surprise but quickly gave the young girl a warm smile.

"Hello, is this your sister hiding under the blankets there?"

"Yes! I just...I just heard you arrive and didn't know who it was so..."

"Sis didn't want anybody to know that we were leaving," Awena blurted out. Mererid shot her a fearsome look.

"What's this now!?" Crissiant all but cried out in alarm. "You're fleeing? On the eve of war and with an open wound in your hand? That's mad, Mererid dear!"

"I don't see any other choice!" Mererid grabbed back her hand. "Me and my sis, we don't live in the lap of luxury like some do in the Lowland Hundred. And if Gwyddno gets killed in his jolly war things will get far worse!"

"Heavens, dear! Have some faith in our God-given King! You'd be far safer here as a humble maid than outside where the Saxon bands roam. Think of your sister."

"And if Seithenyn was the King?" Mererid asked with venom. Crissiant stared back at her, puzzled.

"What are you talking about, now? What's happened?"

"Oh, my lady! So much has happened."

Crissiant softened her face, her shoulders drew back and out, and she beamed a smile that Mererid had seen only a few times. It was the look of a doting, caring mother. Mererid had seen her use that face with her foster son only a handful of times, and, though she hardly admitted it to herself, it had made her envious.

"Won't you tell me then?"

And Mererid found herself doing just that. She told her everything from discovering Lord Connwn's betrayal to King Gwyddno's stubborn, deaf ears. She told her about the night Rhun severed her finger and how Taliesin had been powerless to defend her. She told her about the afternoon in the gate tower that Seithenyn had revealed himself as a drunken, lust-filled beast. All the while, Crissiant only gazed back at her, absorbing every word, and never once fixing her with that cock-eyed stare she would give when she was suspicious, or when she thought that the maid had wicked intentions for her foster son.

As Mererid finished, her eyes brimmed with tears, but she would not cry in front of the proud woman. Crissiant looked back at her without a trace of judgment.

"You say that Connwn was the one who suggested Seithenyn be left in charge while the men are away at war?" she finally asked.

"Yes, and your dear father-in-law never thought twice about it."

"It's the curse of all parents to be blind to their children's faults. But you should be concerned, we all should." Crissiant stared off into the back wall for a moment and her fine eyebrows knitted slightly.

"Well, we may still be able to right this wrong," she said finally, gathering herself.

"What do you mean, my lady?"

"Seithenyn is a brute, a drunk, a lout, and horribly conceited, but he is not a traitor. He might jump at the opportunity for gold or for status, but he would be just as happy to get those things by doing right by Gwyddno if he can. I think it's high time I had a little word with him."

Mererid gaped at Taliesin's foster mother.

"What...what can you hope to achieve by that?" she asked.

"I'm sure Connwn's been to visit him by now. The company leaves at dawn. I'm curious to see what he offered the gatekeeper. And maybe we can finally convince Gwyddno to see the real traitor right before his eyes."

Crissiant examined Mererid's wound one last time and left the basket of herbs, instructing the girl to change the bandage again before she went to sleep for the night. She bid farewell and made for the door.

"Mistress!" Mererid called out. "Take care. The gatekeeper can be vicious."

Crissiant returned her gaze.

"I know," she replied and then marched out of the dormitory.

Mererid turned back into the crowded maid's room. She realized that several of the other cleaning ladies would be returning soon, and she began returning the blankets and sheets that she had taken for her bundle. Awena was busy on the side of a straw mattress fixing the stringy hair of her rag doll.

"Are we still leaving tonight?" she asked her sister innocently.

"Not tonight, dearest," Mererid replied. "Not tonight."

∗∗∗

"I didn't mean to get caught. You have to know that, Tali!" Tudno protested. Taliesin only turned over in the chamber's one bed to face the wall. Tudno had been pacing the room for over an hour making every excuse for himself. With every whiney explanation Tudno concocted, Taliesin found himself freshly irritated at his cousin for damning them.

"I couldn't let that butcher of a King walk back on his word like that. I had to do something, you know!" Tudno stared down at his feet for a moment before adding. "Granted I didn't succeed in doing much except for landing us in another impossible, rigged, crooked contest, but still some hope is better than none."

Tudno even dared to smile.

The light was quickly fading as the sun approached the western tree line. Taliesin had spent the whole of the afternoon in stony silence with his cousin, neither of them daring to even consider what could be done to escape Anglesey's dungeon at this point. Nobody had even gone to check on Tudno's pony, Stomper, since they arrived at the minstrel camp two days ago. For all they knew their 'horse' was probably stolen. And neither of them was expecting Maelgwn to provide a halfway serviceable horse in good sportsmanship. There was really no need for conversation. The situation was abjectly hopeless.

"Come now, Taliesin, cousin. Speak with me already. You can't still be so upset, can you?"

"Oh, where would you get that idea?" Taliesin's words were dipped in ire. "I'm just not speaking 'cause my mouth's still tender after gashing my tongue three times with a razor-sharp sloe berry thorn!" Taliesin sat up in his bed.

"But please, continue explaining how you screwed everything up without meaning to. It's really doing wonders for my spirits right now!"

"I'd take it back if I could, Tali, you know I would."

"But you can't, can you? And I can't make Maelgwn act any more honorably than you can, so next time, dear cousin, keep your opinions to yourself!"

Taliesin rarely spoke so directly to most people, and least of all to his cousin who had been more like a brother to him. Taliesin could hardly think of a memory from his childhood that didn't include Tudno's companionship. The two were essential to each other growing up. He only wished that Tudno had taken the time to consider his words before he said them, now more than ever.

"What are we going to do tomorrow, Tali?" Tudno asked, his head hanging low. "Are we going to rot in the dungeons until we starve?"

Taliesin pretended not to see the wet spots that Tudno was wiping away from his face, acting like it was dirt.

"We'll do the best we can, Tudno," Taliesin said, showing a little sympathy. "I don't want to be cross with you. You were right, of course. Maelgwn wasn't about to let me walk free. I'm just sorry that now you have to suffer my fate."

The two boys sat in silence as the crisp sunlight inched its way across the stone wall of the chamber. Outside, the acrid smell of torches ascended through the hallways as the page boys placed the lights.

Without warning, the metal latch of the chamber door squeaked. Someone from the other side pushed the heavy door open. The two boys jumped to their feet in an instant.

"Taliesin and his kinsman?" A squat muscular man with two armed guards flanking his sides addressed them.

"Who else?" Taliesin replied. The man nodded.

"Queen Bannon requests that you follow me, now."

***

The burly man escorted the two boys down to the stables. As they walked, one or two passing lords turned their heads twice to regard the now famous young prophet, but none of the guards or pikemen impeded them. They were brought down to the long-covered wooden sheds that housed Maelgwn's prized stallions and dozens of other horses. They were marched into the narrow passageway that ran along the center of the stables. Horses whinnied and stamped their feet as they approached, and Taliesin felt overwhelmed by the stench of manure.

A hooded shape stood patiently at the end of the main walkway accompanied by four men bearing swords. The boys' own escort drew back and stood to attention as Queen Bannon pulled back her hood to reveal her face in the torchlight.

Until then, Taliesin had only known the Queen in the context of her role as royal consort. He had only ever seen her surrounded by expensive silks and fabrics with a small team of servants and waiters in her orbit. Now she stood in a simple robe, her golden headband the only adornment that betrayed her royal status. Taliesin suddenly saw her as the young, sharp-eyed woman that became her reputation.

"Good evening to you, children of Cantre'r Gwaelod." The boys stared back at her awkwardly. "Come then, I know you've been brought up with proper manners. I am a queen, after all."

Taliesin immediately dropped to his knee and pulled Tudno down to do the same. "Forgive us, your Highness. We are just confused at your summons."

Bannon raised her hand, grabbing the attention of the guards.

"Young master...Tudno, was it?" Tudno nodded. Bannon pointed to her left. "You will find your pony in the last stall at the end of this corridor. Go and see that he is healthy and fit to race tomorrow. My men will escort you."

Tudno threw a puzzled look at his cousin. Taliesin only shrugged and silently urged his cousin on.

Tudno thanked the Queen and walked off with the detail of soldiers, leaving Taliesin alone with Bannon and her broad-chested companion. Bannon turned down the opposite corridor and motioned for Taliesin to follow her.

"So, young prophet," she began. "I was hoping to have a word with you privately and that anything we talked about would not be repeated."

Taliesin threw another sideways glance at the queen's attendant, who seemed to have more hair on his body than on the top of his head. Bannon noticed Taliesin's curiosity.

"I pray you, take no heed of Svaron. He was a Saxon prisoner that Maelgwn's war party captured some years ago after we had just married. He was going to be executed, but I pleaded with the King to spare his life, so that I may have him as a servant. The King agreed and now Svaron is utterly loyal to me and quite good at keeping secrets."

"Should I guess that King Maelgwn doesn't know we're here together?" Taliesin ventured.

"He believes you are in your tower chamber, and that I am at church. Although he did consent to having your kin examine his pony. I turned him on that."

"Your Majesty seems to wield a good deal of influence with the King of Gwynedd."

Bannon raised an eyebrow, impressed by the twelve-year-old's eloquence.

"At first King Maelgwn seemed to cater to me out of love, but over the years I think that excitement has gone and now he only listens to me when it is politically convenient for him."

"Most rulers don't stay in power long unless they consider everything from a political view."

"Even a marriage, perhaps?" Bannon asked wistfully. "This brings us to the very reason I chanced talking with you. You mentioned something today during the tournament. Something about Nant Conwy and how my late first husband died. I should very much like to hear what you have to tell on the matter."

The young Queen stopped at a nearby stall to scratch the head of a dazzling white mare. The creature nuzzled Bannon's hand appreciatively. To anybody watching from outside the stables, the queen might have been giving Taliesin a friendly tour, instead of inquiring about long dead secrets.

"I remember what I saw in my visions, but take heed that my words might be...well...upsetting," Taliesin explained.

The queen only continued scratching the bridge of the horse's nose.

"I was not born into royalty, you should know," Bannon said. "I was raised not far from the border of Gwynedd and Powys, near the fortress at Nant Conwy. It was a bonny little village that I shared with so many family and friends. Then the Saxons raided and burned my parents and sisters alive in front of me. I managed to escape and made my way to the fortress with several other survivors. We were taken in by the Lord of Nant Conwy, Afallach ap Maeldaf, who was the nephew of Maelgwn. Afallach was handsome, generous, and so kind. I remember seeing him in Nant Conwy and how joyful he was with everyone, even us poor refugees. He acted like everyone he met was a long-lost brother to him. We fell madly in love with each other, and he made me the governess of Nant Conwy. We had a splendid few years living peacefully and happily together. Then the Saxons returned in greater numbers. Afallach called on the lords of Anglesey to help and so came a band of vicious warriors led by Maelgwn ap Cadwallon."

Taliesin listened intently as the queen continued to speak, her hands brushing back the mane of the horse and her eyes focused someplace beyond Anglesey's walls.

"Maelgwn had a son of his own back in Anglesey, but his eye always seemed to track me wherever I went in the fortress. Finally, the day of battle arrived and Afallach rode out with Maelgwn's men to beat off the Saxon invaders. They succeeded, but my dear Afallach was slain. I must have gone mad with grief because I seized a horse and rode out to the field at once. I found my husband lying face down in the mud facing away from the fortress. There was a single stab wound that had gone in through his back.

"I wept and sobbed my heart out for days. I grieved so strongly for Afallach that I became...numb. When Maelgwn suggested I come back to Anglesey castle with him, I could hardly understand him. It felt like trying to glimpse a deer in thick fog. I allowed myself to be taken back to Anglesey and married Maelgwn merely because I didn't care enough to object."

Bannon looked into the eyes of the magnificent horse she was petting and pressed her head against the animal's brow. She turned herself back to Taliesin, drawing herself up to her full height.

"This is my charge to you, young prophet. You don't need to reveal any more of your vision than this. By whose sword did my late husband, Afallach of Nant Conwy, die? Answer me now."

Taliesin had seen the whole incident flash through his mind in the span of a few seconds that very morning when he had listed Maelgwn's line. There was not a single doubt about it, as far as the boy was concerned.

"By Maelgwn's sword, your Highness. I am sorry."

Bannon stood unnaturally still. Her attendant didn't react in the slightest and Taliesin could swear that the horses themselves ceased their braying and snorting out of respect for their queen. The only thing that betrayed Bannon's emotions was a glistening shimmer that pooled in her eyes and reflected the orange torchlight. At last, the Queen inhaled sharply through her nose.

"Come this way. I will show you something."

Bannon and her stoic companion led the way farther down the corridor and then turned right along the edge of the stable fence. They brought Taliesin to a circular section of the stables ringed by seven stalls plated with brass ornaments on the pillars and gates.

"These are the seven racing stallions of Gwynedd, the horses that you and your cousin will need to beat tomorrow. I've seen the state of your pony and I can assure you that you will not win a typical race with any of these beasts if you raced them every day for a hundred years."

Taliesin walked the ring, carefully peering into the stalls to see tall horses sculpted out of flesh and muscle. Their hindquarters bulged with strength while their coats shined in the dull torchlight. They ranged from inky black to a light cream color, each one a spectacular specimen of racing horse.

"I'm afraid I don't understand your Highness's meaning," Taliesin said after inspecting each horse. "We are well aware of the odds against us. Can you, fair Queen, offer us any help?"

Bannon only paced leisurely around the stalls, taking her time to peer in at the different beasts, occasionally letting her hand graze across the nuzzle of one or two.

"Would it surprise you to know that I have not always been a devotee of the church?" she asked casually. "Can you use your second sight to see my past before I became Queen of Gwynedd?"

Taliesin shuffled his feet awkwardly.

"Well, not just this moment," he admitted "In truth, I am not yet completely accustomed to my gift, nor do I understand the nature of it or from whence it came to me." Taliesin looked the elegant lady

337

up and down. "You seem to be a faithful Christian woman at present."

Bannon smiled at him.

"The men of Gwynedd, both Afallach and Maelgwn, are great supporters of Christianity. I was baptized for my first husband's sake and never regretted it for a second. If the church can inspire great deeds of charity in the rulers of men, and it has even for the King, I would gladly read and live by the scriptures even if I had to be cloistered in a convent.

"But the village that I grew up in had no church, and no priest. Our community was tended to by a wise man, an astronomer. He knew nothing of the savior, but he would perform miracles with the help of nothing more than the trees. He would sometimes tell us stories about a powerful secret held in pieces by the trees and rivers and stars. If anybody could ever find a way to unite these pieces, they would gain access to all the knowledge and histories of the earth. Hidden mysteries that could unlock the secrets of magic and even of life and death itself. He called that secret...*awen*."

Taliesin listened enraptured, the word awen stirring something deep within his gut. Bannon continued.

"Of course, as a Christian, I cannot speak of such things myself. Life and death are only given unto the Lord to understand, and such knowledge has been forbidden to us mortal humans ever since we walked the Garden of Eden. But you, young Taliesin, you can feel that well of knowledge, can't you?"

Taliesin stared wide-eyed before slowly nodding his head.

"Well...yes...It's like an ocean walled in by my head. I could easily dive into it, but the waters are deep and dark, and I don't know if I would ever be able to find my way out once I stepped in."

Bannon regarded the small boy in front of her in awe, making Taliesin blush slightly. She turned and regarded the stallions.

"Our wiseman was brutally flayed by the Saxons when they invaded my village. But I was a young protégé of his and he taught me a small amount of his philosophy. He explained the true names of the trees here in Britain before the Romans obscured the knowledge by using their own names. Our wiseman insisted that every bird, beast, and human had a connection to a certain tree. One that resonates and secretly governs them. They can bestow strange powers to those who know them."

She grabbed Taliesin's right hand and led him over to the first stallion. The Queen puckered her lips and clicked her tongue to call the animal over to the stall door.

"Surely, a miraculous prophet like yourself can see this." Bannon's tone was almost spiteful, teasing. "Simply place your hand on his muzzle and look deep. Look into the depth of his soul. What name can you hear echoing from his very essence?"

Taliesin tried to relax his hand, then he tried pressing harder into the horse's smooth face. He could feel the breath of the animal warming the air between them. He could feel the slightest flick of his ears and tail and faintly, Taliesin could even make out the pulse of the creature's heart.

But no name came to him.

"I'm sorry, your Highness," Taliesin replied, his heart sinking. "I don't hear any name."

Bannon only raised her eyebrow. "Hmmph, maybe your gifts were exaggerated after all," she mused.

"I've never been taught these ancient tree names. I'm afraid I wouldn't know the right name even if I did…" Taliesin trailed off as a vision barged its way into his mind. It wasn't a name, at least not one he could say, but rather a shape. A single straight line with five diagonal lines crossing it. It bore a stark similarity to the symbol Bryn had passed along to Taliesin the other night.

"Hold! I need…something to draw with…a piece of flint! I need a sharp stone. Any at all!" Taliesin demanded, suddenly animated. He abandoned any semblance of formality and began crawling on his hands and knees. At last, he picked up a small, but decidedly pointed gray stone, no larger than his forefinger. Without asking permission he scratched into the oak wood of the stall door.

One straight line, five diagonal crosses.

"Here! This is the horse's name. Its true name and also the name of his kindred tree."

"I see," Bannon said neutrally. "And what is that name then?"

"I know not how to say it, but this is most assuredly the horse's tree!" Taliesin hopped over to the next stallion. The beast brayed at Taliesin. Taliesin carefully stroked the stallion's muzzle, soothingly. He let his hand tarry on the creature's head.

"And here's this one's!" Taliesin said as he scratched a single vertical line and four small straight scratches poking out on the stem's left side.

Taliesin worked his way along the stallions, coaxing out a secret symbol from each one and then marking it on the stable door. Each was composed of the same main vertical line but differed in how many lines crossed on either side or straight through. He marked each stable door with the small cryptic symbols until he arrived at the final stallion, a coal-black, towering horse. The beast lashed out several times, nearly biting Taliesin before the boy finally managed to put his hand on the stallion's brow. After a moment, he pulled it away.

"I'm not so sure about this one here," he confessed. "It's almost as if he doesn't want me guessing his name."

Bannon calmly walked up to the unruly stallion and effortlessly stroked his head tenderly. The stallion whinnied graciously.

"I shouldn't be surprised," she said, gazing into the horse's large dark eyes. "This is Rhun's own racing stallion and easily the fastest of the seven. He is a ruthless runner and won't suffer anybody except my stepson to ride him. All the men in the kingdom simply call him the Wolf's Howl."

"But that can't be his true name," Taliesin pointed out.

Bannon nodded her head.

"No, it is not, and it seems that he will not give you his own true name." Bannon looked at the other stable doors, all decorated with Taliesin's scratchings. "I suppose six out of seven correct guesses is still rather impressive. Certainly, for a beginner. Call this a gift for telling me, at long last, the truth."

Bannon stepped back from the stallion, her gaze growing deeper and farther away than before.

"This is Tinne," she said simply.

The name clicked into place for Taliesin and immediately he carved out a single stem with three small horizontal lines jutting out on the left. He looked back at his works, only truly seeing them for the first time. He glared at them until he could see them on the back of his eyelids when he shut his eyes.

He turned back to the Queen.

"O' Queen of Gwynedd, thank you most kindly for this revelation. But I am afraid I am still full of doubt. As interesting as this all is, I don't see how it's supposed to help me. How will such names stop these stallions from running down our poor pony on the racing track tomorrow?"

Bannon looked back at him, a secret smile hiding behind her eyes.

"You are the miracle prophet, young sir. You'll have to discover that for yourself. And now Svaron will escort you and your kin back to your quarters."

***

Crissiant gripped the banister as she climbed the stairs of the sea gates. She peered inside the guts of the marvelous gate machinery but could only see a grotesque mouth filled with giant teeth, ready to devour helpless victims one by one. The night had brought a stinging chill that whipped the sea gate tower mercilessly, making her clutch her woolen cloak closer to her body. In the past, Crissiant had promised herself to never visit the gloomy tower unless she absolutely had to. After her conversation with Mererid, Crissiant determined that she had no option.

The thought of speaking to the gatekeeper still turned her stomach.

As Crissiant ascended to the gatekeeper's command room at the top of the tower, she passed by a waifish young girl with large eyes and tousled hair. The girl looked no more than fourteen or so and was shuffling around a mop and bucket. She looked pale and anxious, as if she was afraid some horror would emerge from the shadows.

"How now, child?" Crissiant greeted her, holding her candle slightly above so as not to blind the poor girl. "Isn't it a bit late to be cleaning the stairs of the tower?"

"Good evening, m'lady," the girl replied, shakily. "My shift is nearly done...I was asked to come especially by...by Lord Seithenyn."

"Does the head Matron know that you're here this late?"

"No'm," the young girl replied. "I was sent here by Father Gilgam."

"Dreda!" Seithenyn's voice rang out from the top of the tower. "Who are you babbling to?"

"To your brother's wife, Lord gatekeeper!" Crissiant called back up the stairwell. She nodded once more to the young girl and then continued up the steps. "I have something urgent to discuss with you."

"Hang it all!" Seithenyn's irritated voice called out. "Leave it for the morning! I'm closing the tower for the night!"

"This won't wait!" Crissiant said as she barged through the doorway of the operations chamber. Seithenyn wheeled around from the window and practically growled at his sister-in-law. Crissiant only stood tall in the center of the room and glared back at him.

"Well, speak then, dammit!"

"I just thought you would like to hear that the game is up, Gwyddno knows all about the sack of gold that you received from Connwn and he plans to chain both of you up to the dungeon wall at dawn. Grand, isn't it?"

Seithenyn's eyes shot wide open.

"That's impossible! Connwn only just left!"

"Actually, it's a wonder that Gwyddno hasn't twigged on yet, especially with how careless you get after your fourth drink," Crissiant replied, only half-hiding how pleased she was with herself.

Seithenyn moaned and gripped his head. He croaked out, "This doesn't concern you."

"The pox, it doesn't! That's my husband the country is going to war for and your own brother! What is worth throwing your head into a conspiracy for, Seithenyn?"

Crissiant rarely called her brother-in-law by his first name rather than his official title. By the same token, it was rare that Crissiant talked to her brother-in-law at all.

"I have my own reasons," Seithenyn went on. He swung around to face her, noticeably staggering as he did so. "I have to look after my own tower since you keep stealing away my cleaning servants."

"What?" Crissiant had to think a moment before making sense of the drunkard's ramblings. "This is about Mererid?" she asked.

"No, it's about who I care to have in my tower, cleaning my stairs!" Seithenyn all but roared back. "I pay Gilgam well and now…" Seithenyn jingled a bulging sack that was hanging on the side of his belt, "…now I have gold a-plenty to do so."

"What are you talking about? What scheme have you got going on with Gilgam?"

Seithenyn seemed to become aware that he was saying more than he should and pressed his mouth closed. Crissiant noticed the furtive glance he threw past her shoulder. Right where the cleaning girl, Dreda, was working.

"Seithenyn. Listen to me and listen well. It looks to me like you have an important choice right now." She paused to make sure the gate keeper understood her meaning. "You can either sit here with your gold, while I go tell Gwyddno everything and you get thrown in the dungeon by sunup, or you can come with me to the

King, turn over half the gold, and out Connwn as the traitor. You'd still get half your cursed gold, and the King would praise you as a hero."

"Hah! The King is about to lead the country to war in the morning. He won't have time to pester with the likes of me. So... what will you give me in exchange for talking to the King?"

Crissiant's eyes slid backward to point at the stairwell and the young girl working on her hands and knees.

"If you cooperate and stop the kingdom from crumbling to usurpers...then, I'll look the other way. Whatever arrangement you have with Gilgam, I won't intervene."

Seithenyn squinted his eyes, trying to calculate which option would suit his needs best. Finally, he grinned a crooked smile at Crissiant. He began to laugh, a horrid scraping sound

"Hah. In another life, I imagine I would make a fine minstrel. I fooled you plenty just now, pretending to conspire with traitors." Seithenyn stood up straight. "I was waiting for Connwn to approach me. I've been flattering him ever since Maelgwn's prince arrived, hoping to win him over. Well, it's paid off now." He jingled his sack for emphasis. "And now, the King will know who delivered us from traitors. So, let's be off to see dad then, but don't forget what you promised about keeping your blabbing mouth shut."

Crissiant scowled and then gestured for the gate keeper to follow her down the stairs and to the palace. As she exited, the young girl washing the stairs in the icy chill looked up at her once more. There was a pleading desperate look in her eye, and she cowered away from the gate keeper's shadow as he passed. With a grimace, Crissiant kept her gaze up and in front of her, letting the girl and her pleading eyes fade away behind her into the darkness.

***

"It's hopeless Tali! I keep telling you!" Tudno complained far too loudly. "They've hardly fed my poor Stomper, he's in a terrible state! Forget winning any race against the horses, I'll be surprised if I can get him into even a canter!"

"You've said all this before, Tud. We don't have any choice, just hurry up with those blankets already!" Taliesin replied in a hushed voice.

The two boys had been quickly stuffed back into their quarters by the Queen's servant. Taliesin waited until the final hint of sunlight bled out from the night sky before ordering Tudno to make a rope out of their bedding.

"But Tal!" Tudno balked at the idea. "We must be thirty, no, forty feet up! A couple of blankets isn't going to go far."

"Then shred the blankets to ribbons and tie them together end to end," Taliesin instructed. "We'll hide them in the morning so nobody raises the alarm. After then, it won't make any difference for better or worse."

While Tudno busied himself with the make-shift rope, Taliesin stripped off the white cloth of his undershirt and ripped off a sizeable piece, almost the size of his chest. He dug through the folds of his woolen tunic until he produced the jagged bit of flint he had grabbed from the stables. With barely a moment's hesitation, he dug the sharp edge of the stone into his right forefinger until a drop of blood appeared and then immediately set to smearing the blood onto the shred of linen.

"What the devil are you doing?!" Tudno exclaimed.

"I can't really explain. While you were looking after Stomper, the Queen showed me Maelgwn's seven racing stallions. I looked at each one in turn and these are the shapes that came to me." Taliesin held up the first symbol composed of branching lines. Tudno only shook his head.

"Please Tali! Don't start acting insane! How can I manage with you raving like a lunatic, painting nonsense in your own blood?"

"Tud, these are the same type of symbols as the one Bryn gave me. They stand for different trees."

"What good does that do for us against horses?!"

"It's so hard to explain this Tudno. You're simply going to have to trust me. After all, a tree is how we got the better of all those bards this morning." Taliesin went back to transcribing the remaining six symbols, as best as he could remember them.

"So, your plan is to go running into the forest, in the pitch of night, waving a bloody shirt to ask help from trees?"

Taliesin had to confess that, when put into Tudno's words, his actions did appear to be motivated by insanity. He decided not to describe the type of company he hoped to attract in the woods.

"It's not quite as simple as all that," Taliesin replied as he finished the last symbol. "And I'm very curious to hear if you can think of a better plan right now."

Tudno only rolled his eyes and then showed Taliesin the knotted rope made of torn bedsheets.

"Are you ready then?" he asked Taliesin.

"It doesn't really matter if I'm ready or not," Taliesin responded as he carefully rolled up the bit of linen. The two boys checked below if there were any patrols passing below them, and then threw the chord of sheets out of the window. Taliesin tied the other end solidly to the bed leg.

"As soon as I'm down pull up the rope. I'll whistle up to you so you can let it down again when I get back. In the meantime, just stay put and keep a low profile."

"Taliesin?" Tudno asked as his cousin as he leaned his body out of the window ledge.

"What?"

Taliesin turned to face Tudno, surprised to see a mixture of sadness and absolute fear in him.

"You are going to come back?" Tudno asked quietly. In a flash, Taliesin understood.

"I came to Anglesey to rescue my father, my kin back from a tyrant. I didn't come to lose a cousin."

Tudno nodded and then embraced him before watching his cousin slip away into the darkness below.

CHAPTER 21: Fire and Blood

o Brid y bridred:
o Dwr tonn nawved:
o Dan y lluched:
pan ym digoned

from the Mould of the earth;
from the Water of the ninth wave;
from the Fire of the lightning;
from these things was I made.

~ Cad Goddeu, Llyfr Taliesin

By the time Taliesin set foot within the tree line of Maelgwn's private acre of forest, the midnight bell was sounding. Taliesin half worried the ringing bell would crack the very air itself. The weather had turned colder than usual for December and Taliesin could almost feel his blood beginning to freeze. At the very least, he noted there were less guards parading around the borders of the forest. Keeping to the shadows, the boy arrived at the forest reasonably sure that nobody had spotted him.

Once inside the gloomy cavern of tree branches, Taliesin began seeking out the appropriate clearing. He imagined that he could pull off whatever trick he had done the night before when his small, woody, and gruesome companion had shown him to the blackthorn bush. What he was supposed to do with whatever trees the wood imp brought him to this time still mystified him, but he had no choice but to proceed step by step. He somehow doubted that he would be able to slip some magic flower into the horses feeding troughs before the race, like he had done with the bards that morning. Certainly not now that Tudno had been found out. Still, he hoped that some inspiration might strike him at the critical moment and perhaps the night's mission might be far easier than he anticipated. After a half hour of wandering aimlessly, Taliesin concluded that this would not be the case.

Finally, the boy came to a small opening with a jagged boulder sticking up from one edge, like a giant tooth. He scanned the edge of the clearing hoping, and dreading, to see any small rustle or otherwise sign of the wood imp. He wondered if he could call out to it, but then realized that he had no idea what to call it. He clamored up the side of the boulder and sat, waiting to see if anyone or anything appeared. The stone felt like a slab of ice. He took a moment to inspect each root and branch of every tree in sight. When no obvious solution presented itself, Taliesin sighed heavily. It was time to try his last resort.

Taliesin raised his right thumb to his mouth and bit down hard.

Immediately, a faint ripple flitted around Taliesin's field of vision, but otherwise almost nothing about the clearing changed. Taliesin feared that his charm had failed him, but then he noticed a profound silence had suddenly come over the forest. It seemed like the blustery winds had paused. More astonishing still, Taliesin discovered to his great relief that he no longer felt the bitter cold of the night.

That's when he began to see them.

For all Taliesin could tell, they might have been part of the very tree trunks, hiding in plain sight and peering at him since he had set foot in the clearing. They were the same type of creature from the night before; small, twiggy, impish things with bright amber eyes and needle-sharp claws and teeth. Only now, instead of one strange wood imp, he counted twenty or twenty-five, at least. He noticed them one by one as they started to twitch and scuttle from one camouflaged position to another. What unnerved Taliesin the most was how they would burst into a flurry of silent motion and then freeze absolutely still. The more that Taliesin looked at them, the more pairs of beady amber eyes stared back at him. Their bodies looked like they had been ripped out of the wood from the trees and were sharply angled at the joints. Sharp spines that could have been a spread of wooden splinters jutted out from their shoulders, backs, and crowns. Taliesin scanned the throng of knee-high fey folk but couldn't immediately recognize which one had assisted him the night before. It either wasn't there at all, or it was every one of them at once.

Finally, one of the small creatures tumbled its way to Taliesin and crouched low next to Taliesin's boulder.

"Human," was all it said, making an almost rude grimace.

"Uhm...Yes. I am called Taliesin. And I need your help." Taliesin felt completely out of his element addressing the strange creatures but didn't know how else to proceed.

"Want. Straif?" Another small creature snarled next to him.

"Uh, no." Taliesin was very certain that blackthorn was not on the list of symbols. "Listen, all of you, I need help racing against the King's horses tomorrow. I'm pretty sure I need to find these."

Taliesin unfurled the bit of linen with the symbols he had drawn out in his own blood. The group of imps leapt closer, studying the seven shapes and sniffing at the linen in anticipation.

"Blood?" one of the creatures asked.

"Yes. The blood is for you when you bring me what I ask for." Taliesin stated as clearly as possible. The imps twitched uneasily.

"Blood, blood before favors," another of the imps said, taking a quick step towards Taliesin.

"I must have what I need first, then you may take the whole sheet and do what you will with it," Taliesin insisted. He held the linen high out of reach of the spry creatures, wondering what would happen if they collectively decided not to participate in the deal. The creatures scanned the symbols and then began to flash their needle-sharp teeth.

"Beith."

"Fern."

"Nion."

"Ruis."

"Onn."

"Tinne."

"Coll."

The creatures sounded off one after another as if they had rehearsed a performance. Taliesin stared back at them, dumbfounded.

"You know what these are? Can I use them to win against the King's horses?"

"King?" one of the meaner looking creatures spat. Its coloring was slightly darker and its eyes contorted into glowing slits at the mention of the King. "King hunts, King chops, King takes. Blood for help."

"I told you already, I'll give you the blood after you get me what I need." Taliesin didn't want to give away the only bargaining chip he had too soon.

One of the creatures let out a shrill cry, like a warbling nightingale, and the crowd of wood imps dispersed. Taliesin did not have to wait long before they started coming back one by one. In turn, they brought seven straight branches, each no bigger around than Taliesin's forefinger and about as long as his arm. Taliesin looked at each one carefully.

"What is this? Birchwood?" Taliesin asked.

"Birch." The creature holding the wand repeated. It sounded as though the word itself tasted bad in its mouth. "Beith. Beith, Fern, Nion, Ruis, Onn, Tinne, Coll." The thing pointed at each of the branches as he said each word. A puzzle clicked in place for Taliesin.

Beith
Fern
Nion
Ruis
Onn
Tinne
Coll

Birch
Alder
Ash
Elder
Gorse
Hazel
Holly

Satisfying as this revelation was, it brought little comfort to Taliesin. What exactly was he supposed to do with seven different tree branches? He gathered up the small boughs taking care to remember which was which.

"Blood." A voice jostled Taliesin back from his thoughts. One of the wood creatures was crouching besides him, looking at the bloodied fabric in his hands like a begging dog.

"Oh, of course." Taleisin held up the symbols. "Here, then. Take it with my thanks."

The creature snapped at the fabric with lightning speed and eagerly shoved it into his mouth. Several other creatures lashed out at the cloth and tore off hunks of it with their strong claws. They began snarling and gnashing at each other in a riotous frenzy. In their ferocity, they reminded Taliesin more like hungry wolves than...whatever they were. He decided that the deal was concluded and began to silently retreat from the grove when one of the creatures, the first one to get a good mouthful of Taliesin's blood, picked his head up with wide eyes.

"Ceridwen...Ceridwen's mead!"

The other creatures immediately stopped fighting over the shreds of cloth and began sniffing and licking the smears of Taliesin's blood.

"Ceridwen's mead...Ceridwen's mead!" They began to echo. Taliesin noticed more and more of the amber orange eyes turning his way, fixing him with predatory stares. Taliesin did his best not to look afraid but couldn't resist taking a mincing step backwards.

"I...I already gave you what you wanted." Taliesin couldn't keep the fear out of his voice. "I have nothing more for you. We're done."

"No." The creatures began to creep over to him. "Blood, Ceridwen's potion in blood. Enough for all. All knowledge. All Awen. We take blood!"

Taliesin spotted the haunches of the closest wood creature tense up like a spring. Without thinking, Taliesin dropped his head back as the murderous creature dived passed him, swiping at his throat with razor sharp splinters. That was all the invitation Taliesin needed to turn on his heel and race away, the throng of demons flying after him.

Taliesin weaved through the low hanging branches and scrambled over discarded logs and stones at a breakneck pace, all the while hearing the scampering and howling of the ravenous creatures behind him. Taliesin dared not look back. He could feel the bloodthirsty creatures' teeth snapping at his calves. His lungs burned and his muscles ached. Several desperate swipes of wooden claws drew a few drops of blood from his leg. If Taliesin had looked over his shoulder, he would have seen several of the spiny creatures rush over to where his dripping blood had landed to eagerly suck down the red liquid like it was the sweetest wine.

Taliesin had only one thought on his mind; to burst out of the woods as quickly as possible, secrecy be damned. At that terrifying moment, the boy would rather subject himself to the cruelties of Maelgwn than get torn apart by those ferocious beasts. The imps were more coordinated than they appeared. Several of them cut ahead of Taliesin and would swoop in from the side whenever the boy thought he could see an exit in the tree line. The group of bloodthirsty devils were corralling Taliesin around, keeping him trapped in the cover of the trees, where, he supposed, they could wait for him to drop from exhaustion. Fear pounding through his veins, Taliesin suddenly understood the horror a deer must feel during a kingly hunting party.

Out of the corner of his eye, Taliesin thought he saw the flicker of torchlight. Maybe some of the castle guards heard the commotion and were coming to investigate. Maybe Taliesin would be spared a violent death for a longer torturous one. The thought distracted him long enough that Taliesin didn't see the tree root ahead of him until his foot caught it. He was thrown tumbling forward and careened solidly into an oak trunk.

He turned to see twenty hungry grins flash at him in the night, teeth drizzled with thick foam. Then, with a blood curdling shriek, they surged at him.

The lead creature lunged, then collided headlong into a blazing fireball.

The twiggy imp bounced backwards, clawing madly at its own face as parts of it smoldered and threw off stray cinders. The other creatures immediately halted and drew back as they all glared and hissed at the tall man bearing a roaring torch. The man planted himself squarely between Taliesin and the creatures who snarled back defiantly. Taliesin gaped.

The torch bearer was Bryn.

The bard waved his torch at the encroaching horde and yelled out. Several of the small twiggy things began to scurry off back into the woods fearful of the bright fire. A couple of the larger ones stayed, keeping only as close as the range of Bryn's swinging arm.

"Blood! Boy offered us blood for secrets. We want his blood!"

"Come a hair closer and you'll get a blast of hell fire instead," Bryn threatened. "Get back to your festering holes, you won't be taking another drop tonight!"

The creatures let loose a chilling howl and then gathered themselves together into one powerful mass, like a Roman phalanx. Bryn drew himself up to his full impressive height and brought a clay pot up to his lips taking a deep drink in. Taliesin noticed his cheeks puffed out slightly as he placed the jug down behind him. The intimidating flock of wood imps inched their way forward, ready to break formation and swarm over the two humans as soon as they got the chance.

They never did. In a swift fluid motion, Bryn brought the torch right next to his lips and spewed out a fast jet of liquid that burst into a torrent of fire. He swept his head quickly from one side to the other, like a dragon, sustaining the stream of fire all the while. Light, noise, and heat filled the clearing and several of the foremost wood imps yelped and leaped backwards, batting at their arms and faces. Bryn took one more swig from his clay mug and blew out another long fireball. The wood imps shrieked again and then fled back into the safety of the underbrush. Bryn waited until the last one was out of sight before lowering his torch.

"Bryn?!" Taliesin gasped out, surprised he could even breathe.

"Are you alright, lad?" Bryn said, whipping around. "I thought you were going to be torn to shreds!"

"I'm...I'm fine. A little scratch, but I'll be okay." Bryn helped pull the boy to his feet. Taliesin felt like he wanted to blurt out a million questions at the bard all at once. "How did you find me out here? How can you still be here in Anglesey? What were those things?"

"Those?" Bryn asked pointing to where the wood imps had vanished. "I thought I've told you the story about those things hundreds of times. Those were Lunantisidhe."

"Lunantisidhe? The faeries that guard trees from people who chop down too many? But, that's just a faerie story."

"Yes! And those were the faeries. Just because I tell stories about things most people never see doesn't make them false!"

"You've seen them before?!"

"How else did I know how to best get rid of them?" Bryn smirked. "But come along, they may come back soon with more. And you shouldn't be found out here by yourself."

"What about you? I thought you were banished, why are you here in Maelgwn's forest in the middle of the night?"

Before Bryn could answer, a stark yell echoed through the trees. Taliesin could see several torch lights making their way through the forest. Bryn immediately crushed out his own torch and pulled Taliesin with him through the underbrush.

"We've run out of time for explanations. You need to get back to your chamber. Now! While the guards are distracted in the forest."

"Not until you tell me why you're here!" Taliesin insisted. He held up the small bundle of wood. "Do you think I'm out here to gather firewood? Those faeries gave me these seven branches, just what am I supposed to do with them to win a race?"

"By Dylan, how would I know?" Bryn said, getting agitated.

"Didn't you follow me into the woods to guide me? I thought you would know."

"I had no idea you would be foolish enough to go offering samples of blood for the Lunantisidhe to taste. I heard you yelling and all the commotion, so I lent you a hand."

"You didn't follow me?" Taliesin said, genuinely confused. "I don't understand Bryn, what would be worth defying Maelgwn just to hang around his private forest for?"

"Bryn?" The voice came a few yards over and it didn't belong to any soldier or minstrel. Queen Bannon, clad in a long velvet robe rose from the forest floor. She had no attendants or servants accompanying her.

"Bryn, the soldiers are closing in. We won't be able to escape them now," Bannon whispered.

Taliesin began to wonder if he was hallucinating. How was it that Maelgwn's own wife and Bryn the bard were out in the forest alone? The gravity of Bryn's predicament began to dawn on him.

"Tali!" Bryn chastised him as he dragged him to the tree line. "It's crucial you get back unseen. I don't know why the Lunantisidhe gave you what they did, but you'll have to live to figure that out for yourself. Now go!"

"But...they'll catch you!" Taliesin protested.

"Better me than you!" Bryn struggled to keep his voice low. "The game is up for me as it is. You can still liberate Elphin. You can still get yourself and your family out in one piece and stop a war before it begins. Remember that!"

"They'll kill you!" Taliesin bawled.

Bryn peered at the young boy in the darkness. Taliesin could see the bard's brilliant blue eyes shining in the gloom of night, like twin stars in the sky. Bryn spoke softly and deliberately.

"You were willing to risk death to find somebody you loved. I did the same and I found her. Death has no power over me now, lad. You'll understand someday."

With those words, Bryn shoved the boy as hard as he could, knocking Taliesin backwards and sending him tumbling down the small hill that creased the edge of the forest. Taliesin tumbled onto his back and prepared to jump up and rush back to his friend when he heard the soldiers shouting.

"Oy! The villain is over there!"

"Halt! You wretch!"

"By Christ! Tend to her Majesty!"

Taliesin dared not move an inch and could only watch as the

castle guards swarmed over his friend. Bannon was hollering out orders for the soldiers to desist, but they paid little attention to her. Within five minutes, Bryn was led away with his hands wrapped in shackles and a pike aimed at his back. The soldiers tried to escort Bannon out of the woods, but she would have none of it. Finally, Svaron, her swarthy attendant, arrived and accompanied the Queen out of the forest and back to the castle. Taliesin waited until the light of the guards had faded behind the thick wall of trees before finally picking himself up and darting back towards the castle.

***

Earlier that afternoon

The Queen of Anglesey typically did not stray from her usual daily routine of bathing, dining, praying, facilitating mundane castle business, more praying, and finally sleeping. So, when she told her attendants, after the memorable tournament of bards had concluded, that she wished to visit the forest, understandably there were questions.

"This ghastly tournament has put me in such a state!" she explained. "I only wish to collect some winter berries before the season passes. I would find it most peaceful after such a terrifying display."

Once Bannon arrived at the forest with her two maidens in waiting, she wasted no time occupying them by ordering them to strip some of the towering bushes of all the pale green berries they could find. When the Queen silently stepped back and disappeared into the forest, the two serving maids could only shrug and continue to do their Queen's bidding, at least until she returned.

Bannon walked down a narrow path flanked by tall ash trees until she came to a small clearing with a single bare boulder in the center. She only had to enter the clearing before Svaron poked his head out of the low-hanging branches. Bannon quickly crossed the clearing to where Svaron was waiting.

"Did you do as I asked?" She hardly dared to bring her voice above a whisper.

"I did, your Majesty. I met the rogue outside the castle gates. He didn't believe me until I showed him your Majesty's brooch, as you suspected. After that, it was no difficulty bringing him back here."

"Where is he then?"

"At the Queen's service, your Majesty!" Bryn the bard dropped down from the overhanging branch, landing gracefully with his cloak of many colors draped over his shoulders. "To think that I was afraid I would have to leave Gwynedd without a proper reunion yet again."

"Why are you so sure that I brought you here for a reunion?" Bannon returned. "Maybe I don't trust you any more than my husband and feel you should stand trial as a heretic?"

"And resort to such betrayal? No, the girl I chased back in my village couldn't have changed that much. I'm not mistaken, am I?"

"I'm not sure you could ever appreciate how much I've changed." She stared daggers back at Bryn. Then she turned to Svaron.

"Wait for me by the edge of the clearing. Make sure that nobody interrupts us."

"My Queen, should this vagabond try to do you any harm…"

"I will call if I need you, now be off please!" Bannon said, making it clear she didn't want to repeat herself. Svaron tossed Bryn a suspicious look before stalking off to the clearing's edge.

"Maybe I could appreciate how you've changed," Bryn said. "You've certainly taken on the authority of a Queen, it appears."

"You, however, have hardly changed at all," Bannon replied without humor. "Still the same lanky boy that swings around in trees peeping on any girl that passes by."

"Not ANY girl!" Bryn protested. "And I should also think my musical talents have progressed quite since we last met."

"It's a pity that you didn't think to compete in the tournament. Or were you afraid of babbling like an idiot like the rest of them?" Bannon said knowingly.

"If you're wondering if I had anything to do with that, I can assure you I was as surprised as the rest of the court."

"But you knew about the child, about Taliesin. You told the whole kingdom he is a prophet. How true is that Bryn? Did your King send him as my husband believes?"

"No." Bryn creased his brow in a rare display of seriousness. "The boy took it upon himself to come here, for the sake of his foster father. I caught him first and then decided to accompany him. I figured he could use all the guidance he could get. But I had my own reasons for returning back to Gwynedd."

Bryn held the Queen's gaze, silently willing her to understand his intent and the risk that he had taken. She stared back into the piercing blue eyes that had followed her everywhere when she was hardly more than a child. Finally, Bannon turned her brown eyes towards a small snowdrop flower pushing its way out of the winter ground.

"What of that bit of Nant Conwy the boy mentioned?" Bannon asked. "Did you teach him to say that?"

"I had nothing to do with anything the boy has said! I can only guess what power speaks through him."

"And I should just take your word for it?"

"You know me for being many different things, Bannon. Have I ever been a liar to you?"

"No, but you've been spiteful." The Queen glared up at the taller man. "We grew up together, we lost everything to the Saxons together. We were taken in by Afallach without conditions. And then as soon as he courts me, you break with him and wander off to God knows where. Was my company worthless to you if you couldn't have me for your own?"

"Hardly!" Bryn went to grab Bannon's wrists, but she batted him away. "I honored Afallach. He was a wise and just king, which are few and far between. I was jealous maybe, and yes, heartbroken. Nothing I could offer could measure up to him. But you were happy and deserved it. I left so I wouldn't be a distraction."

"Is that all?" Bannon cocked an eyebrow at him.

"...and yes, so I wouldn't have to see you on his arm every sodding day, but I never held spite for either of you!"

Bryn stepped backwards until his feet searched out a fallen log. He crumpled and sat down. Bannon softened her tone.

"What is your...prophet alluding to, about the death of my first husband? What can he possibly know that I don't?"

Bryn lifted his hands in exasperation.

"As I said, I have no clue what Taliesin knows nor how he knows it. But whatever it was, it certainly seemed to trouble your current husband. What do you imagine it could be?"

"How should I know?" Bannon replied. "Maelgwn and Afallach rushed into battle in our defense. Plenty can happen on the battlefield, so who can say except God himself?" Bannon began to tear at the small flower in her hands, her fingers shredding into the soft petals while she peered through the winter foliage.

"That's another change I've yet to appreciate," Bryn said, leaning forwards on his knee. "I was hardly surprised to see Afallach turn you to the church. I wasn't pleased with it, but I could hardly blame you. But then, to become the consort to a man like Maelgwn, that hardly seems in keeping with the teachings of the church."

"Maelgwn was a man of the church, don't forget. He still is!"

"Emphasizes the Old Testament, does he?"

"How many monasteries, churches, missions has he funded? How many of the hungry and poor have been fed and sheltered, by his own hand? My husband has his faults, but he is generous!"

"Generous to those who will return the favor. To everyone else that dares to defy him, how much Christian charity does he bestow upon them? You've seen better than anybody what cruelty he is capable of. Would he be pious enough to spare Afallach that cruelty, even if he had something he so desired?"

"I don't like what you are implying!" Bannon said, taking a furious step forward.

"Why not? Unless you've thought about such things yourself?" Bryn said, as gently as he could. Bannon's face went from livid indignation to hopeless desperation. She squeezed her eyes shut, and then let herself sit down on the same log as the bard.

"I pray, every morning and night, for forgiveness for joining with...with that man." Bannon seemed close to tears. "I have no love for him. I know he has no love for me, just a beastly lust that fades a little more every day. We swore before God that we would be faithful to each other, that we would love and honor each other. But, God help me, how can I love a monster like him?!"

Bannon dissolved into quiet sobs. Bryn hesitated and then, as tenderly as he could, reached out to hold her hand in his. She did not recoil.

"What's worse!" Bannon continued. "When your small prophet first appeared in our court and he told Maelgwn he would die in two years, I acted horrified, but something inside of me...I was actually hopeful. How wicked is that? I was hopeful that my husband would be dead in two years."

"You were glad to think that you might be free in two years," Bryn suggested. "Not that he would die of the plague."

"I will never be free from this," Bannon answered. "I will always be Queen of Gwynedd, but maybe I can live with just a little less horror in my life."

"You don't have to wait for two years," Bryn said as he sank off the log and knelt before the Queen. "I love you, Bannon. I always have. And I am here now, nobody needs to know. I can make you feel loved and beautiful once more."

Bannon looked down at her childhood sweetheart through swollen eyes. By assuming the throne of Nant Conwy and then Gwynedd, she had done all in her power to help those in need. Those that had lost their villages to invaders, or to the plague, or to mere cold and starvation had all been helped by her commitment as

Queen. Because of this, Bannon never felt as if she had any regrets. But as she looked into the face of the young boy that had teased her and chased her and brought her countless bouquets of flowers week after week, she found herself wondering what might have been different.

Bannon composed herself and stood up, brushing dirt off her velvet robes.

"How can you be so sure the boy is a prophet?" she asked, blatantly dodging Bryn's proposal.

"It was the day that we found him. Elphin, Gwyddno and I all saw him behave as no ordinary babe should. We decided to wait for thirteen years to see what miracles or mischief the child was capable of. And here we are, a few months shy of thirteen years and the young bud has finally started to bloom."

"But why now? How can you be so sure that he has the gift of second sight and isn't just stringing us all along?"

"You remember our old master, back in the village? You remember what he taught us?"

"What?...well...yes, about the ancient names of the trees? I had to renounce all of that when I joined the church."

"He knows them, Bannon!" Bryn crowed. "Nobody in Cantre'r Gwaelod knows anything about them, excepting myself and maybe Gwyddno. How could he possibly have learned that? And yet there he was on the way to Gwynedd, almost drowned in a river and calling a birch tree Beith! I took a chance yesterday and wrote down the rune for Straif, wondering if the boy could piece it together, and there he was with sloe berry flowers this morning!"

"Sloe berry? So, he did cheat," Bannon accused.

"Only enough to make his victory undeniable. No one can sing poetry like that or shake a castle to its foundations with only a voice. The lad claimed to understand Cumbric, a language he has never studied. It's as the wiseman in the village said. The boy has achieved the gift of Awen."

Bannon looked up at the grinning bard suspiciously. "How?"

"Pox on it if I know how! Maybe the boy is favored. Maybe he's a changeling from Annwn. What does it matter? I am certain, even if he isn't, that he has knowledge of all things. And he can reveal all, past and future."

Bannon paced back and forth across the forest floor for a minute, her thoughts churning inside her head.

"I suppose you mean for me to ask the boy to reveal what actually happened to my Afallach, the day he was slain?" she demanded.

"He claims to know the truth, and he hasn't disappointed us so far."

"Very well," Bannon said with finality. "But if my worst fears are realized, if I have to be told that Afallach was betrayed, I would ask one thing from you."

Bryn cocked his head in anticipation. Bannon stepped in close

"Promise me that you'll find me here tonight," Bannon said, pressing her warm weight against the bard's chest. "Promise me that you'll show me love like you say and make me forget the last fifteen years of my life. Just one night is all that I ask."

"I would give you love enough for the rest of time if I could, my dove," Bryn said, embracing her. "As it stands, one night might be the end of my time if things go wrong. But I would risk all of it and more for you. You have my word."

Bannon nodded without smiling.

"If Taliesin convinces me, I shall arrive here by myself by candlelight and then I will light a single torch so you may find me. Until then, do not leave the forest or the guards will surely seize you."

The two gazed once more into each other's eyes before Bannon slipped away and began walking back to her silent escort.

"One more thing, my lady!" Bryn called out. "If you come, do me this favor and bring a small jug of distilled mead, the rare strong stuff."

Bannon looked as if Bryn was making the worst joke in the world. "You wish to show me love in a state of inebriation? I've had my fill of that sorry dance with Maelgwn."

"Hardly," Bryn scoffed. "But tonight may be my last and most beautiful night in this world. I only wish to pay homage to the old gods for a glorious life well spent."

Bannon couldn't help but smirk. "You are far more pious than you let on. So be it, love."

CHAPTER 22: The Race

Wyf kerdolyat. wyf keinyat claer.
Wyf dur wyf suw.

I am a harmonious one; I am a clear singer.
I am steel; I am a druid.

~Buarch Beird, Llyfr Taliesin

The bells from Caer Wyddno rang out at the very first hint of sunlight from the Eastern hills. The Lowland Hundred was a vast kingdom, but every soul heard the crying bells that morning. Every household knew what the coming day would bring. The bells signaled the start of war.

The palace of Caer Wyddno soon erupted in activity like an anthill. Knights and warriors organized themselves, calvary men inspected their horses, and the top of King Gwyddno's generals assembled themselves for one final meeting in the King's war room.

Connwn marched down to the meeting, crisp and punctual as ever. As he approached the war chamber, he was surprised to see Lady Elphin exit through the chamber's massive doors and walk right past him.

"Good morning, Lady Elphin!" Connwn said politely. "You are up rather early to be visiting the King before daybreak."

"Good morning, Lord Connwn," Crissiant returned. "I merely stopped by to give my blessings to my father-in-law."

"Fear not, Gwyddno is still strong. Surely he will lead us to a swift and glorious victory."

"And bring my husband, Prince Elphin, home to us at last," Crissiant added.

"Yes, of course. Nothing less would count as victory," Connwn hastily agreed.

"I'm glad you think so. Well, I won't delay you any longer, my Lord. I'm sure that our King has a lot to say this morning." Crissiant left with a strange enigmatic smile. Connwn carried on into the war room, wondering why Lady Elphin's smile had unnerved him.

As it turned out, Gwyddno's briefing was nothing so out of the ordinary. One thing that did surprise Connwn was the King's sudden shift in transportation.

"And lastly, I've decided that for the purposes of keeping our tactical advantage, the company will travel by sea rather than land," Gwyddno announced to the assembly of generals.

"Sire, is that at all possible?" Lord Elby asked. "We have many horses and warriors from outside Cantre'r Gwaelod. Will we have the capacity?"

"My own galley can hold two hundred steeds if we fill it to the brim. And we still have *The Hand of Lir* that Prince Rhun forgot to steal," Gwyddno assured him. "We should have no problem with space, and it's a short trip remember. This way we will be within sight of Anglesey before sundown. Cut off that worm Maelgwn from any reinforcements he might have coming."

"What of our own supplies, Sire?" Connwn spoke up. "Without a clear path out of Anglesey we run the risk of being trapped ourselves."

"We can carry a great deal more supplies on a boat than we

can on horseback. And, yes, we may have some trouble getting anything from Ceredigion or Powys for example -" Connwn might have imagined it, but he could have sworn he saw the King shoot him a sidelong glance laced with hidden meaning, but in the next instant it had disappeared. "- but with our fleet, we can easily send for more supplies from Cantre'r Gwaelod and Maelgwn will be powerless to hinder us. Our armies may be near equals, but we have the superior navy. Let us use that to our advantage."

Gwyddno finished up the briefing and sent his team along to make ready their troops. He expected to pass through the sea gates for Anglesey no later than an hour past sunup. As the knights and generals were exiting, Gwyddno quietly called Connwn to join him at the balcony from where they could observe the departing ships.

"Have you set up your contingent that will stay behind as we discussed?" Gwyddno asked.

"Yes, Sire! Everything is prepared."

"And you left instructions for Prince Seithenyn? He will be equipped to handle the command until we return?"

"I spoke with him last night, your Highness. I am confident he will take command eagerly."

Gwyddno nodded, apparently satisfied. He turned his face towards the sea gate, whose towers were just catching the early morning sunlight and reflecting it back to the palace of Caer Wyddno. The King wore a grim expression.

"Is there something troubling you, Sire?" Connwn asked cautiously.

"Many things, but one, in particular, concerns me at present."

Connwn casually looked around the war room checking that he and the King were alone.

"Your Highness?" Connwn pressed.

"I'm just worried about Seithenyn's ability to lead," Gwyddno finally said. "The whole kingdom knows his weakness for the drink. I'm worried about coming home to a great big mess thanks to him."

"You give him too little credit, my liege!" Connwn insisted.

"Seithenyn is far more capable than you think. After all, look how diligently he performs his duties as gate master."

The King only shook his head dismissively. "Opening a gate is one thing, but managing an entire kingdom at the height of war is another. Maybe we should have Enid stay in my stead."

"Oh, surely not! We would be sorely disadvantaged in battle!"

Gwyddno continued to pace restlessly. "There's no denying that too...But a pox on it! I'd wager ten gold pieces that Seithenyn brings shame on me when this whole mess is over."

"In truth?" Connwn asked. "Very well, I would take your wager, your Highness. I should only hope that we take a good haul of spoils from Gwynedd. I would hate your Highness to dip into the royal treasury for a simple wager on my behalf."

"Hmmph. You really do put a lot of faith in my second born," Gwyddno said with obvious amusement. "So be it! If Seithenyn does me proud by our return, then ten gold for you, Lord Connwn."

Below the balcony, a river of men, swords, and horses began to flow into the two dozen ships specially designed for battle. The King and his advisor readied themselves and took their place on the fleet of ships. By now the sun was blazing down from over the hills, igniting the great harbor and lighting up the sails and banners on the ships like a fire. The great sea gate opened, and the war fleet departed north, their bright sails a wall of flame drifting on the sparkling blue sea.

***

A brusque knocking woke Taliesin from his black sleep.

"Get up, lowland sea scum! Your 'horse' awaits!" The guards' cackling echoed through the stone room as Taliesin pushed himself out of bed. Tudno woke up flailing his arms and legs in shock. The boy hadn't gone to sleep until Taliesin managed to return from the forest, well past midnight. Even then, Tudno refused to go to sleep until he heard all of Taliesin's story in detail.

"So, Bryn was in the forest with Queen Bannon!? And he breathed fire to save you from a gang of wood faeries?"

"Yes, and then he was captured by the castle guard. He risked everything for me," Taliesin answered.

"The poor old clown. He should have settled for banishment. I would trade whatever mess we're in now for banishment in the wink of an eye."

"I guess he thought there was something worth coming back for," Taliesin said, thinking about the vision of Queen Bannon in the woods. "Now it looks like he'll hang for it."

"Did you at least find whatever it was you were looking for in the forest?" Tudno demanded. "If not, we may be reunited with Bryn faster than we think."

Taliesin wished he knew how to answer his cousin. He only held up the seven small branches from the different trees he'd be given. Tudno looked at each one in turn, trying his best to piece together what they meant.

"We're going to…shoot the horses with arrows from this wood?" Tudno guessed. Taliesin was about to chide him for being foolish but realized he had no better suggestion.

"I don't think so," Taliesin said neutrally. "I know which rod goes with which horse, but I still have no idea what I'm supposed to do with them."

Tudno stared at him, his face a mix of shock and hopelessness.

"Well then, O mighty prophet, let's pray that it comes to you in your dreams by morning, or we'll be in the same cell with Bryn until we rot, surely."

Now morning had arrived, but no solution for how to win the race passed by in his sleep. The two boys were quickly rushed out to the stables to pick up their pony. Taliesin took the seven sticks and bundled them together with a piece of fabric and then hid them under his tunic. He realized how lucky he was that the guards weren't out to search him for weapons, or else he would have a lot to explain. By pinning the bundle with his left arm against his body, he could carry the rods of wood with little difficulty.

The pungent odor of horse traveled along on the breeze as the group neared the stables. The guards shoved the two boys inside, growling orders to get their pony ready without delay. They found Stomper looking tired from the frigid night but seemingly well-fed.

"I think he ate the whole feedbag of oats. And he's picking his head up a bit more. He might have a little more spunk than usual today," Tudno announced with a cheerful note.

"Let's pray so," Taliesin replied. "We're going to need all the advantages that we can get to beat the King's stallions."

"You haven't thought at all about how those twigs in your pants are going to help us, have you?" Tudno said as he began to adjust the reins and saddle. "It won't matter if Stomper races like a champ today or not, there's no matching a pony against a stallion."

Taliesin only grimaced and stared out across the field that led to the racetrack. He could see the magnificent dark stallions being led out to the racing field by their riders. Most of the riders were light, lean boys that couldn't have been much older than him or Tudno. Then there was Rhun riding upon his stunning twenty-hand horse, by far the largest horse and rider in the race. Rhun hardly showed the slightest empathy or kindness to the animal that would bear him around the racing track and kept a firm hand on the reins, yanking the horse this way and that. Whenever the poor horse objected or shied away, Rhun would raise up a thin stick with a patch of leather on the end and savagely flog the horse into obedience.

As swift as lightning, Taliesin caught a flash of inspiration.

"Tudno! What is Rhun doing to his horse there? What is he using?"

"That?" Tudno looked like he was going to break out laughing. "By the saints, cousin! That's a riding crop, to spur on the horse. Maybe you're not the all-knowing prophet Bryn said you were."

Tudno's words opened a door inside Taliesin's mind. In the span of an instant, he suddenly knew why he had to visit the forest last night, why he had to collect the seven wands from seven different trees. He understood what the sticks that were digging painfully into his ribs were.

"Tudno, quick. Can you tie up a sling onto the saddle?" Taliesin demanded.

***

The guards escorted the two boys and the pony over the race field where Rhun and his six fellow riders awaited their King patiently. From several hundred yards away, Taliesin could already make out the fanfare of people marching out from Anglesey castle to the racetrack. Rhun wasted no time hurling around insults to pass the time.

"Lovely weather we're having this morning, eh whore's sons?" he called out with a sneer. "I was worried there might be too much mud on the field. I would hate to fling such filth on you as my horse passes."

On cue, the six other riders joined in the chorus of laughter. Taliesin staunchly ignored them. His eye was fixed on the approaching train of people. Maelgwn was easy enough to spot, riding on his portable throne carried on the backs of four unhappy slaves. The silver flags to the side of Maelgwn marked Urien's company, the old warlord walking in the center, his face somber. Taliesin was mildly amused not to see any of the King's squadron of bards. Maelgwn had only brought along Heinin, who looked bound and determined not to talk to a single soul that morning.

Then came a sight that almost made Taliesin shout across the field. Surrounded by six armored pikemen and bound in a thick silver chain, trudged Elphin. His red and silver head stood out even from halfway across the field. He looked pale and worn, like a hermit that hadn't seen the sun in months. He walked with a slight limp but with his head held high and proud. Taliesin wasn't sure if he felt like laughing or crying.

"Happy to see your imbecile patron, are you?" Rhun chided. "You have me to thank for that kindness, you know. I insisted that your foster father should be there to see your defeat and your punishment. What father would miss out on such a milestone?"

"What would you know about a loving father?" Tudno hissed back. "I'm surprised Maelgwn didn't feed you to his dogs when you were little!"

"Ha-HA! This one has spirit in him!" Rhun hollered to his men. "We may have to be careful with him. Maybe his cousin and pony can ride on top of him!"

Taliesin could feel his cousin simmer at Rhun's jokes. He could hear his breath get quicker and sharper. He grabbed him by the shoulder.

"Tudno, they're braying asses, no more. It's not worth fighting with them any more than is to argue with a mule. Ignore them."

Tudno scowled and then looked back at the approaching crowd. His face widened in surprise.

"Tali! Look! They have Bryn! They're leading him out to the racetrack!"

Taliesin wheeled around to see the tall bard being escorted by four guards, his hands bound behind his back and his head hung low. The guards kept their pikes trained on Bryn's chest, as if they expected him to escape at a moment's notice. Taliesin felt a flash of relief that gave way to dread. It was unthinkable that Maelgwn would show Bryn mercy, so what purpose did the King have for bringing him to the race? Would he torture the poor bard, or simply execute him, merely to demoralize his friends?

Taliesin also noticed that the Queen was auspiciously absent.

The crowd of people arranged themselves on the close side of the racetrack, with the King occupying a large wooden viewing box. Trumpets sounded, announcing the beginning of the event. Maelgwn stood and saluted his guests from his court and the neighboring kingdoms. A magnanimous smile shone from his broad face. He might have been opening the festivities to a picnic rather than a trial to determine whether two boys lived or died. After catching enough of the crowd's eye, Maelgwn turned his broad frame to the racetrack and his adversaries.

"So, it shall be officially recorded, here begins the final test for the youth Taliesin of Cantre'r Gwaelod. The youth who infiltrated my country and castle and who names himself 'Chief of Bards.' He who seeks to bring his hapless foster father back to his squalid kingdom and he who has sought to scare me with prophecies of my untimely passing. Well, I say, by my divine authority, that only one being has command over life and death, only one before whom I shall ever humble myself. If this boy before me is a true soothsayer, let God Almighty prove him so. Oh, heavenly father! By your grace and wisdom, reveal to us the truth in these matters, so that we may guide our fair country in righteousness." A dull roar of two hundred people calling out to the heavens followed the King's invocation.

"So, you are familiar with the terms," Maelgwn went on. "You are to ride your horse around the fairground track three times against my seven racing stallions. If you are faster than all of them and complete three laps before any other horse, we will grant you your freedom."

"And my countrymen and father," Taliesin wasted no time in reminding him.

"On my honor, it shall be so." Maelgwn resumed. "You will be permitted to leave without obstacle. However, should even one of Gwynedd's stallions complete the track first, your kinsmen will be executed, and you and your foster father will be kept in the great tower until death takes you or you are sold off for ransom. You are not to injure any of my prize horses or otherwise use sabotage as a means of winning. Have you any questions?"

Taliesin was not expecting the King to throw in this last

caveat. The plan Taliesin was finalizing in his head may not be considered strict sabotage, but he didn't want to leave Maelgwn the smallest hole to wriggle out of his agreement.

"Only one question, your Majesty," Taliesin said respectfully. "If your horses are too slow, would you like me to whip them for you, just to keep things interesting?"

A nervous laugh bubbled through the crowd. Maelgwn grinned like he was listening to a drunk man telling a bad joke.

"If you can even get close to the ass of one of my horses, you may whip as hard as you like, fishmonger's brat!"

Jeerful laughter rained down. Taliesin nodded slightly.

"Much obliged, O King."

"TALIESIN!" Elphin's voice rang out. "My boy! Don't do this!" Several of Elphin's guards jabbed the older man in the ribs with the butt of their pikes, but Elphin carried on. "Take your cousin and fly! Fly home! Don't give yourself over to this butcher!" Another hit to the gut finally forced Elphin to stop his ranting.

"Father!" Taliesin called back. "Father! I will not abandon you! By the end of this day, we will be free together! Take heart, father!"

Elphin finally ceased his fruitless struggling and fell briefly on his knees before getting up. He fixed his clear blue eyes on Taliesin, pleading silently with the boy. Taliesin then turned to Bryn, noticing for the first time a strange piece of cloth lining his mouth. The cloth was soaked a dark red color.

"Will you to the starting position, prophet?" Maelgwn prodded the young boy.

"What did you do to our bard?" Taliesin asked back.

"Beg pardon?"

"What did you do to our bard, Bryn?!" Taliesin demanded. "He will not speak, and he does not lift his head. What did you do!?"

"We only enforced the law, boy," Maelgwn explained. "Your bard was banished and yet returned. He was caught in conspiracy against the crown just last night. Bard or no bard, he is still subject to the law."

"So why the gag then?" Taliesin asked, fearing that he could guess the answer.

"Gag?" Maelgwn asked, amused. "Why, he has nothing of the sort. That, my dear boy, is a bandage."

"No!" Tudno gasped, arriving at the same conclusion Taliesin had.

"It was within my power to kill the wretch, but I decided to be merciful and spare this degenerate bard's life. Instead, I only took his bastard's tongue."

Maelgwn nodded and a guard grabbed Bryn by the jaw and squeezed, forcing him to open his mouth. Taliesin could clearly see a gaping hole where Bryn's tongue had been. The bard winced and writhed in pain, but he did not cry out. He turned his pitiful eyes towards Taliesin and then looked away in shame.

"You monster!" Tudno called out reflexively. Maelgwn paid him no heed.

"Let's be done with this already. Riders, to your marks!"

***

Within minutes, the riders from Gwynedd lined up the fearsome-looking stallions at the top of the racetrack. Rhun, as the favored rider, took the outermost ring. Before lining up, Rhun flattered the crowd by trotting his stallion along performing frivolous tricks and maneuvers. Tudno walked his pony to the innermost ring and motioned for Taliesin to join him. Taliesin had never learned much about horsemanship and sat awkwardly behind Tudno. He felt like he could fall off the back of the saddle at the slightest bump.

Taliesin ran his hand over the leather sling pinned to the side of the pony's saddle. By feel, he counted the seven switches of wood that had previously been in his pant leg. No one had objected or had even given any inclination that they noticed the bundle of sticks. From where the crowd looked on, Taliesin hoped they would appear as any other rider's crop.

As the King's herald brought his horn to his lips, Taliesin suddenly found himself praying. He couldn't remember exactly when he had started but he found himself praying silently inside the walls of his head. There were no words, no chants, or mantras as Father Gilgam had taught him. He wasn't even sure to whom he was praying. A barrage of people, places, and ideas swarmed through his mind. The face of his grandfather, King Gwyddno, Mererid's lips, and the spray of the ocean. The taste of the strange water in the river and the fearsome cackle of the Lunantisidhe. He could feel the hard steel of his father's manacles and the painful ache in his back. He thought of Bryn's empty, mutilated mouth. He poured all his soul, all his hopes, his fears, his very spirit into every one of them.

His silent prayer was cut short as the herald sounded a great blast on his horn and the seven black stallions beside them surged forward. Tudno's old pony only looked around in confusion, clopping its hoofs idly, until Tudno yelled out.

"Go, STOMPER! GO!"

Stomper let out an annoyed bray and trotted forward. With much encouragement from Tudno, he finally moved into a gallop, though it hardly matched the speed of the stallions, most of whom were already on the other side of the racetrack and were beginning to creep up on the pony and his two riders from behind. The crowd hooted and jeered raucously.

"This is as fast as I've ever seen him run!" Tudno shouted to Taliesin. "There's no way he'll overtake the stallions. What are we going to do?"

"Pull him to the left and hold the inside track!" Taliesin commanded. "And keep him close to the stallions when they go to pass us!"

"What? They could knock us flat over!"

"Do it, just the same!"

Tudno pulled the pony towards the shorter inner lane of the racetrack. Taliesin could see Rhun break away from the pack and charge ahead, eager to overtake his slower rival. Taliesin watched him carefully, and then bit down hard on his right thumb.

The world shifted like it had been revealed from behind a thick pane of glass. Taliesin could see the essence of each stallion trailing behind them. He studied the horse thundering down on them and looked for his secret name.

Tinne. The hazel branch.

Taliesin reached into the sling and pulled out the slender shoot of hazel. He waited, not daring to take his eyes off the stallion for a second as Rhun proudly galloped closer. Taliesin yelled for Tudno to pull a little farther to the right and bring Stomper as close as he could to the stallion.

"It's no use blocking me, you whoresons!" Rhun hollered. "I'll run you down into the dirt if I have to!"

Finally, with a cacophony of beating hooves, the stallion sprinted forward and passed within an arm's reach of Tudno's pony. With one swift motion, Taliesin whipped his arm around in a wide arc and brought the crop of hazel down on the stallion's hindquarters. The horse let loose an unearthly cry, almost like it was in pain, but not quite, and then did something extraordinary.

Swinging his neck around towards the right, the horse trotted aimlessly through the track and then began a series of cantering steps that everyone watching that day would only ever be able to describe as a horse dancing. Chasing himself in circles, the stallion cantered and hopped to an unheard rhythm. Rhun cursed and hollered at his mount, beating it with his crop to no effect. The crowd's previous laughter came to an alarming halt as everyone gaped at the bizarre sight. The great black horse reared up on his two back legs, nearly throwing off his irate rider. The horse shuffled backwards as the other stallions rushed past him.

Taliesin's hand flew into the sling and pulled out the birch and ashwood sticks, one in either hand. He saw the names like they were branded on the side of the horses as they ran up

Beith, Nion

"Pull him a bit more left! Can't you get him any faster?!"

Taliesin called out.

"I'm amazed he's made it once around the track, count your blessings!"

As the silver-coated stallion charged past, Taliesin lashed out cruelly with the birch branch, striking the horse across the neck, then twisted his body wildly to whip the hindquarters of the light brown contender on his left with the ash. Both horses veered off the track bucking and prancing. Their movements looked so well-rehearsed, many in the crowd began to anticipate that the horses would join for a duet. There was an explosion of shouts, laughter, incredulous cries, and desperate prayers for God's deliverance. One of the two riders fell off his mount and ran off the track for fear of getting trampled.

"Tali! Easy!" Tudno reached back and grabbed Taliesin by the back of the collar. He had nearly lost his balance watching the scene behind him. As he steadied himself, the fourth racing horse went charging past them. With a roar of thundering hoof steps, two more shot past the boys.

"They'll have finished up their second lap when they catch up to us again!" Tudno exclaimed in frustration. "Where's the last one?"

Taliesin looked back to see the slowest in the pack surging forward. He looked carefully for the hidden symbol radiating from the horse.

Onn.

Taliesin grabbed the splintery gorse wood just as the horse pulled up to their side. He planted a swift blow on the competing horse's backside sending him cantering around in a tight circle.

Sheer chaos bubbled from the throng of spectators. Taliesin could see men pointing and jeering. He could see Maelgwn's dominating figure stand up yelling at any poor servant that made his way too close to him. Bryn, openly defiant of the King, was standing tall clapping his hands high over his head and laughing through a tightly shut mouth. For the briefest moment, Taliesin caught a glimpse of Elphin looking on, his eyes gleaming with tears.

"Tali, on your right!" Tudno shouted back to him. The three

horses that passed them earlier had already completed their second lap and were fast approaching from behind. Taliesin studied them carefully and pulled out the Alder, Elder, and Holly branches.

They shot by at double speed, but Taliesin was ready.

Fern.

Ruis.

Coll.

He landed each blow in succession as the horses charged past. One after the other, they began leaping and cantering directionless around the track, joining the other dancing horses. Most of the riders were now off their horse's backs and wrestling with the reins, trying to get a hold of the mad animals. Tudno shook Stomper's reins violently as the tired pony lumbered into his third and final lap as the front runner of the race.

With a loud snort and a cloud of dust, Rhun's horse, Wolf's Howl, bolted past them.

"Out of the way, sea scum brats!" Rhun cursed from atop the horse. Evidently, the horse had finished its magic dance and had resumed the race.

"He's running his second lap!" Tudno observed. "If he passes us again before we cross the finish line, there'll be no hope for us!"

Rhun, enraged to fall victim to Taliesin's sorcery, was pounding across the racetrack with a vengeance. Taliesin saw some of the other horses were beginning to shake themselves loose from whatever spell the switch of wood had placed them under. Now, Rhun's determined stallion had already completed his second lap and was closing in on the two boys and their enfeebled pony.

"He's going to pass us again, Tal! Give him another hit when he comes past!"

Taliesin had no idea if a second blow would work. He looked back down for the sling and the switch of hazel. Suddenly, a wave of panic coursed through his veins like an electric shock. It flooded his nerves and paralyzed his mind. He knew what hazel should look like, but on the bouncing horse amid so many other rods of wood, he couldn't locate the hazel, literally to save his life.

"Taliesin, he's gaining!" Tudno's warning only further alarmed him. He tried with all his might to find the one hazel stick in the bundle of seven. He could hear the stallion's deafening footsteps get louder and the hot air of the horse's breath. Stomper strained in effort trying to keep apace of the stallion but Taliesin could feel the poor animal's energy draining away from its stringy muscles. The stallion pulled his head and neck past Stomper.

"Taliesin!" Tudno cried out. Taliesin looked up to see Rhun's powerful arm swing his riding crop viciously at the young boy's head. Taliesin leaned back, almost making his body flat on the back of the horse. He dodged the blow but nearly lost his balance in the process.

"I'll see you rot next to your fool master!" Rhun yelled at them, slowing down. He swiped his riding crop at them again, but only managed to graze part of Taliesin's arm. "Then when your kingdom is burnt to the ground, I'll take sport feeding you to my dogs!"

Rhun spurred the creature on, slipping past the two boys on the pony. In a final act of mad desperation, Taliesin grabbed all seven of the rods in his fist and brought the whole bundle whipping down on the passing stallion's rear.

The horse brayed like it had been stabbed with a pike and leaped impossibly high into the air, only to crash back down onto the track, shaking his head and bucking around in circles wildly. Rhun hollered at the animal as it flung him loose from the saddle. The prince of Gwynedd sailed through the air before landing in a puddle of horse dung.

Keeping a wide berth of Rhun's convulsing horse, Tudno brought Stomper past the stallion and cantered their way forward. In the brisk mid-morning sun, on a muddy horse track, the most powerful men in all of Britain, not the least of which being King Maelgwn himself, watched a half-lame pony and its two novice riders trot across the finish line while their competition danced stupidly in the background.

The crowd buzzed with disbelief, confusion, and sheer excitement as Tudno drove the pony up to Maelgwn's booth. Some of the court members lifted their arms to the sky, asking God above them for mercy. All noise faded to silence as Taliesin carefully swung his leg over the pony and dismounted. Maelgwn glared down at the boy who only returned the stare with resolute eyes. Before either could speak, Elphin's voice rang out.

"You saw it! You ALL saw it! You wanted proof from God that my boy is blessed? Well, what more do you want!?" Elphin's hoarse voice squeaked as he hollered out his question.

"My foster father is right," Taliesin said. "You asked me to complete three laps around the track before any of your horses. You promised that I and my countrymen would go free if I did. You called on the Almighty to bear witness over the race. Now you can clearly see the divine will. Release us and we will depart and trouble you no more, O King Maelgwn."

Every set of eyes trained themselves on Maelgwn, who sat unmoved in his throne. The King looked down at the boy and ran his tongue over his teeth. Finally, he hefted his bulk up to his feet and signaled to the guards closest to him. He stabbed his ruddy finger at Taliesin.

"Gouge out his eyes," Maelgwn commanded casually. "Then break his bastard cousin's legs."

CHAPTER 23: Revelations

Oni vallwyv, yn hen
Yn ygn, angheu anghen
Ni bydiv un dirwen
Oni volwyv Urien

Until I fall into old age
into my dire inevitable end
I shall take no pleasure
but in the praise of Urien

~ Dadolwch Urien, Llyfr Taliesin

Two pairs of hands clamped down on the boys' shoulders. Maelgwn's court stood silent. The only sound was Elphin's pitiful wailing and pleas for mercy. Bryn struggled against his captors, but with his hands tied, it was a pointless effort. One of the chief soldiers next to the King unsheathed a lethal-looking dagger and began walking towards Taliesin.

Taliesin did not struggle or try to escape. He only watched the soldier's blade get closer and closer. It might very well be the last thing he'd ever see. He expected to be terrified, but only felt calm

dispassion as the knife drew nearer. It was like watching a storm
marching towards him with no shelter. He had done what he could
and was out of options at last.

Then, from the crowd of shocked onlookers, a hoarse voice
cried out.

"ENOUGH! Maelgwn, put an end to this now!"

All eyes turned towards Urien of Rheged as he barreled his
way onto the field, making a beeline for Taliesin even as the
Gwynedd soldier closed in. Urien arrived first. He drew his sword
mid-step and aimed the point at the chest of the Taliesin's would-be
mutilator.

"Take one step closer, cur, and I'll stick you straight through
the heart!"

"Lord Urien of Rheged!" Maelgwn called out. "What is the
meaning of this intrusion?"

"This is no fitting punishment for winning a race. Indeed,
this is no decent act whatsoever, blinding a child of his age?
Horrific!"

"We are in Anglesey and I am King here!" Maelgwn shot
back. "I will punish those who speak against my kingdom as I see
fit!"

"So be it, but as Lord of Rheged I have the authority to
decide who my soldiers and I support, and I am not willing to back a
bloody tyrant! If you will not act honorably as King, I would just as
soon take my knights to King Gwyddno's camp."

Taliesin scanned the crowd. He estimated that there were at
least two dozen of Urien's knights standing at attention on the
racetrack alone and then there was a field full of tents with the black
raven standard.

An ugly glare broke through Maelgwn's calm composure.

"I assure you, Lord Urien. I rule justly! I am a descendant of
Arthur himself!"

"So is Gwyddno, which makes him kin to you. And just look
how you've honored your own blood. You've imprisoned and

tortured his son, mutilated his bard, and have used his foster grandson for sport. Time and again the lad here has risen to your challenges and for this you would take his eyes? These are not the actions of Arthur's lineage. These are the tantrums of a child!"

"I will not tolerate defiance, Urien!" Maelgwn sputtered. "Do what you will with your men, but the boy and his band of spies are mine!"

"Then you'd best think carefully." Urien barely lifted his voice, but his baritone timbre resonated across the field. "I will, here and now, depart from Anglesey with my knights. The word from my messengers is that Gwyddno is riding towards you as we speak. I will either escort Gwyddno's family to him and ask him to turn back, or I will leave the boy with you and go to join the Lowland Hundred's army. How will your prospects of winning the day look after that alternative, O King of Gwynedd?"

"Traitor!" Rhun's voice yelled out. He had finally picked himself out of the foul mud and cleaned himself up. "You swore your allegiance to us less than a week ago!"

"Under false pretenses, so I hear," Urien said. "You never mentioned the souvenir you brought back with you from Prince Elphin's house."

"We'll butcher every last one of your poxy men before we let you join Gwyddno's lot!" Rhun shouted, enraged. "Death to traitors!"

In a flash, Rhun's sword was in his hand as he lunged straight at Urien. The older man moved with the grace of a cat, side-stepped the lunge, and brought the hilt of his sword down on the back of Rhun's shoulders, sending him reeling forward. For the second time that morning, the Prince of Gwynedd found his face buried in a pile of mud. At the provocation, every single man wearing Rheged's symbol pounded their shields against their armor and drew their swords in perfect unison. The noise sounded like the clang of an unstoppable, terrifying machine built for war.

"You may butcher us," Urien remarked, unphased by Rhun's

attack. "You can train every fighting man in Anglesey against us until we drown in our own blood. But how many men will you have afterward to fight off Gwyddno's army? If you fight us now, you doom yourself to certain defeat within the day."

He turned to look straight at Maelgwn.

"Tell me, then. What choice would a wise king make?"

Maelgwn's face remained motionless, his beady eyes staring dead into Urien's face. Only the flushed hue trickling into Maelgwn's pudgy face betrayed his inner fury. Taliesin could also see something hidden working through Maelgwn's head. A cold and steady calculation as he mentally took stock of the number of men and horses he would command without Urien. Judging by the flare of his nostrils, it wasn't a favorable sum.

"You do me a great disservice, Urien," Maelgwn said at length. "One that the throne of Gwynedd won't forget. We see now how you've allowed yourself to be so manipulated by Gwyddno's charlatan prophet. Are you really going to desert Anglesey, who's treasury helps fund countless abbeys and monasteries throughout Britain? All for the self-serving, pagan kingdom of Cantre'r Gwaelod?"

"Britain needs fewer monasteries with full coffers and more rulers who can act justly. My decision stands."

Maelgwn may have snarled. At last, he clenched down on his teeth and spat out his ultimate decree.

"Take him then and leave our kingdom. Throw him back to his master along with his pathetic foster parent and silent bard. Tell Gwyddno there shall be no battle today, but that he should take care not to test the might of Anglesey, unless he should like to pay a very steep price for victory."

Maelgwn signaled with a wave of his hand. Elphin's sentinels exchanged looks and then unlocked the shackles around his bruised wrists. Bryn's own rope bindings were cut and the two men were unceremoniously shoved away from the crowd towards the two boys.

Forgetting all forms of demeanor, Taliesin rushed past his own cadre of guards and threw himself into his foster father's arms. For a moment, Taliesin feared that he was only dreaming. He held on tighter.

"Whatever happens to us after this," Taliesin said quietly, "I am just glad to be able to hold you again."

"Let's save our celebration for when we're out of this hell pit," Elphin whispered back. The two of them separated. Urien had one of his men sound a silver horn, signaling to every fighter bearing Urien's crest to make ready to leave. The Lord of Rheged brought out a beautiful young horse to carry Taliesin and Elphin.

"I'm sure that marvelous pony of yours will appreciate carrying half the weight," Urien said good-naturedly to Taliesin.

As the company readied themselves to leave, Taliesin walked cautiously up to the King's booth as Maelgwn looked on with a sour expression. Part of Taliesin wanted to leave without a single word spoken and never return to the island of Anglesey if he could help it. Still, another part of the boy felt closure was necessary. Whether he was a murderous tyrant or not, Taliesin had foretold Maelgwn's death date. He felt the Dragon King should know that it was not Taliesin's will that he should die by plague. He only told the truth as simply as he could.

Taliesin approached and stooped to his knee.

"King Maelgwn, on behalf of the Lowland Hundred, I thank you, for granting my family liberty." Maelgwn made no reaction, so Taliesin continued. "It is understandable that you may be suspicious of my gifts and predictions, but, with all sincerity your Highness, I would not take my prophecy lightly. I wish you health and long life, so that our two kingdoms may prosper together in peace."

"Your words are noted," Maelgwn replied through his frown. "But I will take the counsel of my own physicians before I listen to any of your lot. As for the prosperity you speak of, I now see the scope of your naivety, boy. The only prosperity a kingdom can gain does not come from peace. No, prosperity only comes from the spoils of conquest and the great business of war. We may be at a stalemate today, but don't think that the kingdom of Gwyddno has escaped its doom for good."

"Let providence reveal the scope of our naivety, O' King," Taliesin replied with a respectful bow. "We shall take our leave with Urien, your Majesty." He then turned on his heel and marched back towards the black-haired Lord of Rheged, praying that the humiliated King Maelgwn wouldn't change his mind.

After the knights of Rheged and the four from Cantre'r Gwaelod were mounted, they began their march out towards the gate of Anglesey. The King's court watched them go with muted tones of bitterness, derision, and wonder. Never had anyone from Anglesey or without defied the King and walked away. They eyed the Dragon King, perched on his throne, expecting him to boil over with fury and outrage. The King scowled at the entourage of knights leaving the field, but he did not dole out any orders to Rhun, who sat waiting at his side, nor did he finger the jeweled dagger sheathed in his belt. He only exhaled heavily and rubbed absently at his chest. He brought out a linen handkerchief and coughed into it. The King called for his physician and then rose from his throne and retired to his chambers where he stayed with no visitors until the next morning.

***

The train of warriors and horses marched from Anglesey palace and exited through the great gates that separated Maelgwn's keep from the rest of the island. Taliesin and Elphin rode alongside Urien. Tudno and Bryn trotted along just behind them with the pony, Stomper, in tow and unburdened. They had barely passed over the first hill when they saw two people standing expectantly underneath a lone oak tree, a large built man and a smaller person concealed in a dark cloak. As they approached, the man held up his arms, indicating that he wanted Urien's army to stop. Taliesin looked closer and was surprised to see that the man was Svaron, the Queen's servant.

"Lord Urien!" Taliesin called. "By your leave, let us speak with those two."

Urien nodded and signaled the company to halt. Svaron stepped into the road.

"Hail, Lord!" He addressed Urien in a weathered voice. "My mistress bids you well and safe travels. She has a gift she would like to bestow on Bryn, the Lowland Hundred bard."

"So be it," Urien said simply.

The woman in the cloak stepped forward carrying a fair-sized bundle. She walked straight up to Bryn, who remained sitting on the back of Tudno's horse. She lifted her hood back and all the men around her gasped in shock to see Queen Bannon's smooth face.

Bannon looked up at Bryn with love and pity gleaming from her eyes. He looked back mystified and tired. They stayed like that for the span of almost five minutes, simply watching each other's faces. Bannon once or twice reached up and caressed Bryn's swollen jaw, resting her fingers on his lips. Finally, she took her bundle and raised it up to the bard, closing his hands around it. Bryn bowed his head and held Bannon's hand tenderly for a moment more before finally letting go. Bannon raised her hood once more and walked back to her valet.

"Thank you, lords," she said to Urien and Elphin. "I will not detain you any further. Farewell."

One of the knights just behind Urien raised his voice.

"That's all? You delay us and don't even offer a word to the minstrel there?"

Bannon turned towards the soldier.

"Where I come from, it is horribly rude to speak a language that a guest cannot. My love can speak no more languages at all now and so, to him, neither will I. But there are more ways of speaking than plain words."

Bryn pressed his lips into a thin line and appeared to choke back tears.

"I bid you all safe travels and that you remember what has

been sacrificed today for your liberty. Will you meet with King Gwyddno?"

"Aye, my Queen," Urien replied. "I have sent scouts ahead to locate his train and intercept him as he comes. Hopefully with Elphin freed we can avert a pointless war."

"See that you do," Bannon replied. "It would truly be a shame to see more innocent lives lost over a contest already decided."

Bannon brought up her hood over her head and waved to dismiss the company. Urien nodded respectfully and then spurred his company forward. After marching out of sight of the Queen and her serving-man, Tudno turned around in his saddle to address Bryn.

"What was it the Queen gave you then?" he asked with childish impatience. "Won't you open it?"

Bryn worked off the leather bindings of the package and pulled away the cloth. He held up something that looked like a large square harp but with six strings. The strings ran lengthwise down the instrument which had two square holes cut into the top, allowing Bryn's hand access to the strings. Bryn also held up a small bow strung with horsehair.

"By the saints!" Elphin remarked. "A crwth! I can hardly remember the last time I heard one of them. Beautiful instrument, that is. And a tricky thing to play as well."

Bryn held the crwth in his arms preciously, like a newborn. Taliesin only then realized that the bard's usual harp must have been lost or confiscated since Bryn's arrest. Now the crwth was the only thing that Bryn had that could make music, a true gift worth treasuring.

The company swiftly left the isle of Anglesey and traveled at a brisk canter down the road south. Taliesin and Elphin rode alongside Urien, who kept the conservation sparse and practical.

"We will ride straight to Cantre'r Gwaelod with all haste," he explained. "But we must first intercept King Gwyddno. He should be en route to Gwynedd right now. He'll be impossible to miss."

Taliesin and Elphin took turns relaying their gratitude to Urien. Neither was particularly sure about who had the authority to speak on behalf of their kingdom. Elphin was the eldest prince, but Taliesin had proved himself worthier a dozen times over. Taliesin did his best to uphold his foster father's status while filling in Urien on details that Elphin missed.

The sun was approaching its zenith and the company of fighters was passing the town of Llanllfyni when Elphin started breaking into inconsolable sobs.

"It's the dungeon of Anglesey," Taliesin explained after Urien gave him a concerned look. "I'm sure my father is haunted still by that foul place."

"He should have never been locked away in the first place," Urien said, shaking his head. "The hubris of it all! And there I was behind that scoundrel Maelgwn simply because I believed he was a man of God."

"Maelgwn would not be one of the most powerful kings in Britain if he didn't know how to keep allies with him," Taliesin offered.

After it became clear that Elphin would not stop crying, Taliesin asked permission to seek out privacy for a few moments.

"Very well!" Urien agreed. "We shall take a small recess here!"

"Thank you, my Lord!" Taliesin gingerly eased his horse off the trail and into the small grove of trees nearby.

"And, uh…I have to take a piss myself!" Tudno announced unceremoniously and urged his horse after Taliesin's.

The horses trotted over a small hillside dotted with sheep and swept into the tree line of an oak grove. Since the Lunantisidhe attack, Taliesin couldn't help but feel a little anxious among the trees, but he wanted to provide Elphin with as much solitude as possible for a while.

"Tudno, go on a little bit farther with Bryn and give my father and me a few private moments," Taliesin explained gently.

Tudno only nodded, trying his best to hide his discomfort at seeing his uncle's tears. Bryn only looked on pitifully, the absence of the bard's normally cheerful voice echoing throughout the grove.

"Just give us a shout when you're ready, cuz," Tudno replied, and took his horse farther on to a pool of water.

Taliesin helped Elphin down off the horse and sat him down on a rock, bare except for a few patches of moss. The bulky man's features were pulled wide in grief as he moaned softly into his chest. Taliesin knelt beside his guardian's knee.

"Father...Dad!" Taliesin said, trying to turn Elphin's gaze. "Please, what is wrong? There is nothing to fear now. We will go back to Cantre'r Gwaelod. You won't be held prisoner any longer, you can see mother again."

"Oh, Tali!" Elphin cried. "That's just it, she's not your mother!"

"I know that dad. I know you found me."

"Oh, boy! You don't...you don't know at all." Elphin buried his head again in his trembling hands. "It's what I told him...that's why...he was torturing you...playing with you! Just to see if what I told him was true!"

"Told who, father?"

"Maelgwn!" Elphin wailed, "Who do you think? Julius Caesar?"

"Father, please, compose yourself and talk sense!" Taliesin insisted. "When did you talk with Maelgwn, and what exactly did you tell him? It can't be of any consequence now."

"Oh, it's all come true! Every bit of it," Elphin continued, oblivious to his foster son's bafflement. "Oh, I know I should be happy, you've saved us all, boy! Ohh... I just can't understand it, I am not worthy to have you, son! I was never worthy to have found you!"

"But why on earth not Father?!" Taliesin began to lose his own composure. "You are the kindest and most gentle in all the Lowland Hundred! What should we care about what anyone else says of you! There's no one else in all the world I would rather call father than you!"

Taliesin's invocation shook Elphin just enough to put an end to his ranting. The graying man gulped in several deep breaths and wiped away his few remaining tears with his beard.

"Now would you please tell me?" Taliesin pressed gently. "What did you tell Maelgwn?"

Elphin squeeze his lips together and stared pensively into the ground. For a moment, Taliesin thought his guardian would dissolve back into tears again.

"This is a conversation that I hoped I would never have with you, Taliesin." He heaved a great sigh. "But I knew I would...I knew.

"I was alone in the tower for however many days it was, I lost count, when suddenly Maelgwn himself shows up saying that you had barged in on his halls and served him up a death sentence. He said that Bryn had told him that you were a prophet and capable of seeing into the future. Maelgwn wanted me to say whether it was true. I couldn't just keep my mouth shut, he would have chained you up and tortured you. So, I told him the honest truth.

"I told him about the day that I was charged by Gwyddno to bring in the annual catch of salmon from the weirs and nets that we string up around the shores of Ceredigion. I had just returned from a rather unlucky hunt, you see, where the only animal I brought back was one of the King's prize horses that ran off a cliffside while chasing down a boar. Gwyddno thought that the sea would give me better fortune than the land. So, I set off with my boat and crew. We checked trap after trap. Usually, the first haul of the season is enough to fill an entire boat with big fat salmon, but in every spot we checked we only found empty nets. Finally at our last stop of the day, when we found no fish waiting for us, my crew began to despair and curse out loud. I wasn't in a particularly jolly mood myself. That's when I looked down and noticed a small leather bag that had been submerged in the net since Lord knows when. I lifted it out of the water knowing not what else to do. My first mate then turned to me and said:

"'Truly you are the unluckiest soul alive. These weirs should have brought in salmon by the thousands, and you will return home with naught more than a water-logged bag.'

"That's when I heard it, boy. A voice that came straight out of the bag.

"'But inside the bag is a treasure worthy of millions of salmon!'

"The whole of the boat stared as I lifted back the cover. Poking up from the bag was a small forehead that shone like a brilliant star in the sunlight."

Taliesin felt the hair all along his spine stand up on end as he recalled the meaning of his name.

Taliesin

Radiant Brow.

"From the bag," Elphin continued in reverie, "I took out a small newborn baby boy. And then this little babe, no more than a month old at that, told me this:

'Fair Elphin, cease to lament!
Let no one be dissatisfied with his own
To despair will bring no advantage
No man sees what supports him;
Never in Gwyddno's weir
Was there such good luck as this night
Although I am but little, I am highly gifted.
Weak and small as I am,
On the foaming beach of the ocean,
In the day of trouble I shall be
Of more service to thee than three thousand salmon.
Elphin of notable qualities
Be not displeased with thy misfortune
Although I recline thus weak in my bag
There lies a virtue on my tongue

While I continue thy protector
Thou hast not much to fear
Remembering the names of the Trinity
None shall be able to harm thee.'"

Elphin paused to look up at his foster son. The boy was pale with shock.

"Dad," Taliesin said at length, "You told me that you found me adrift on a piece of jetsam after a pirate attack, when I was already four years old. Why did you keep this from me?"

Elphin bowed his head.

"There's more. After finding you, we had no choice but to return to Cantre'r Gwaelod and report our discovery to King Gwyddno. I can still remember his miserable look when I walked into his hall carrying only the bag and you and not a single trace of salmon from the weirs. He asked me, 'Is this another case of your rotten luck? That you return here with nothing to show for it but a useless old bag?'

"'But contained within is a treasure only the superbly lucky could find,' you said from the crook of my arm. Understandably the King and court were surprised.

"'You can speak, and one so little?' Gwyddno asked you.

"'I am more suited to speak than you are to question me!'"

"I said that to Granda?" Taliesin interjected.

"Yes! It was the only time I can recall that you talked back so fresh. Anyway, the King was more intrigued than offended. He then said to you, 'Let me hear what you have to say to us, then.'

"And so again, this miraculous child in my arms spoke.

"'Three times have I been born, I know by meditation;
It were miserable for a person not to come and obtain
All the sciences of the world, collected together in my breast,
For I know what has been, what in future will occur.
I will supplicate my Lord that I get refuge in him,

A regard I may obtain in his grace;
The Son of Mary is my trust, great in him is my delight,
For in him is the world continually upholden."

Taliesin stumbled backwards, his backside instinctively
seeking out a flat root to sit on. A flood of memories from growing
up in the Lowland Hundred invaded his mind. Memories of school
lessons that he already knew by heart, of church sermons that he
somehow knew were inaccurate. He remembered the strange and
curious looks he would attract in his grandfather's halls. Hearing
Elphin's words was like feeling someone open a lock in the back of
his brain.

"I remember being inside the bag." Taliesin's spine tingled at
the visceral memory of the ice-cold water and the suffocating
darkness. "I remember hearing your voice as you pulled me up out of
the weir and your face in the sunshine when you opened it and freed
me."

Taliesin followed his reverie as far as he could, until a nagging
question forced him to speak.

"Why did you keep this from me? Why did everyone tell me I
was found on a piece of driftwood out at sea?"

Elphin rubbed his clammy forehead with his hand and kept
his gaze squarely in front of him.

"After you appeared before the King, I gave you to my wife.
We were never able to have a child of our own, you know, and not
for lack of trying. After you took to her breast, you ceased making
such grand statements. If it weren't for a keen look in your eye, as if
you could understand everything being said around you, we would
have taken you for any other newborn babe. For all your wisdom,
you certainly weren't housebroken for another two years. Numerous
wisemen, priests, and physicians visited us trying to identify exactly
what you were and asking you various questions, but you gave no
reply, no word, not even a cry.

"Gwyddno called me for a council the night I brought you

back. He had been troubled by many in the court who thought you might be a curse, or a faerie changeling meant to bring ruin to us. He told me that there were some that wanted to cast you back into the sea or leave you out in the wild for the wolves and beasts to find. I argued to the death against it. To Crissiant and me, you were a godsend, clear and simple.

"In the end, it was Bryn that came up with a compromise. He suggested that we let you prove for yourself if you were bane or boon. He crafted a cover story to explain your origins plausibly so that neither you nor any other outsider would be swayed by supernatural expectations. We would raise you as a mortal boy and see what promises you would bring us of your own accord. And here you are, thirteen years later and you've done just that!"

"So, Bryn knew all along that I had second sight?" Taliesin wondered out loud.

"He heard you speak to the King. He understood your potential. He took one hell of a gamble calling you out on the spot when he did though!"

Elphin's voice wavered before breaking down into another series of sobs. Taliesin sat still as a statue, his head boiling over with memories and long-lost dreams. Overwhelmed, he absently chewed his thumb and watched the world around him melt away. In place of the Welsh landscape, Taliesin could see the contours of his own thoughts, all of them. He only needed to bite down a little harder on his thumb, push through the paper-thin walls of his distractions, and he might just be able to move through, to master those thoughts. Every question could be answered; where he came from, how to win over friends, allies, how to triumph in any battle, even what lay on the other side of death. He could know all of it if he only willed himself to go a little bit further.

Taliesin glanced once more at his guardian. He saw a cloud of blue-black miasma pouring off Elphin's body. The color reeked of shame, loneliness, and utter self-hatred. Taliesin knew his father as a loving, humorful man. Somebody that could whether the worse life had to throw at him by virtue of his sheer optimism. Confessing his deception to Taliesin had broken Elphin open far more effectively than any dungeon or torture could and revealed all the pain that his foster father worked so hard to conceal. It was the first time that Taliesin, despite his father's lackluster reputation, truly saw Elphin as misfortunate.

Taliesin let his thumb drop from between his front teeth. He felt his thoughts fold back from the horizon neatly into his head and into his heart. He knew that the knowledge was there like a complicated puzzle, complete but now obtuse and hidden, waiting for him to open it again. He waited for the feeling to return to his feet and then picked himself up and walked over to Elphin. He sat down beside him, draped an arm around his shoulder, and together the two of them wept.

CHAPTER 24: The Horn at Sea

Aennadeu dodyt
Mor-hynt anvonawg
Dy'gawn i'n letcynt
Meilynt yn ceudawd

The envoys, sent on a
sea expedition, have come
We shall obtain news
that shall sustain our hearts

~Glaswawd Taliesin, Llyfr Taliesin

Tudno and Bryn crept back into the clearing as Taliesin and Elphin were climbing back up their borrowed horse. They began to trot back to Urien's train of knights who were waiting for them on the ridge.

"Did you know, Tudno?" Taliesin asked his cousin quietly as they passed over the wide barley field.

"Know what, Tali?"

"Did you know that I could speak when I was just a babe? And that I was found inside a bag out at sea?"

Tudno's face screwed up in confusion.

"What are you talking about, cousin? They found you on some driftwood after a pirate battle. That's what I was told."

Taliesin looked over at Bryn sitting just behind Tudno. The bard's eyes had gone wide with shock.

"You knew though, didn't you?" Taliesin asked the tongueless man.

Bryn lowered his gaze but shook his head affirmatively.

"Then, you weren't bluffing when you told Maelgwn that I was a prophet. You knew what I could do," Taliesin said softly. Bryn again only looked down at the backside of the horse.

"You knew that Taliesin could do all of that?!" Tudno asked, looking back. "Why didn't you just tell us then?"

Taliesin watched his friend with downcast eyes. He could practically see the pain roll out of Bryn's face like a running brook.

"What use would it have been, Tudno?" Taliesin asked his cousin. "Could he have told me how to use my gift? Or what prophecies to make? No. You wanted me to discover the gift for myself, didn't you?"

Bryn nodded, slow and painful.

"I understand Bryn, and I don't hold it against you."

Tudno snorted.

"I say it might have been nice to know that we had a seer with us throughout the whole thing," he said rudely.

"Telling somebody they have a sword isn't the same as showing them how to use it. Who on earth could have helped me make sense of having all the world's knowledge locked in my head?"

Tudno only shrugged and at last kept his mouth shut. Bryn smiled weakly. Taliesin was still getting used to the idea of never hearing the bard's voice again. If any of the four from Cantre'r Gwaelod had paid too steep a price for their boldness, it was the silenced bard. Taliesin would never forget that he owed Bryn his life.

As the group approached the train of knights, they found Urien frowning over the reports of several messengers that had freshly arrived. Urien listened attentively to each report, his thick eyebrows knitted together, perplexed.

"How now, my Lord?" Taliesin asked. "You seem troubled."

"I thought for certain that we would meet Gwyddno on his way up to Anglesey. But none of the scouts I've sent out can find him on any road. If Gwyddno left this morning, he should nearly be upon us by now."

"Has King Gwyddno called off the attack, maybe?" one of Urien's men suggested.

"That's not so likely," Tudno said. "Grandad didn't like Rhun's little stunt one bit and there were a lot of lords pressing him to attack."

Elphin lifted his head. "Something might have gone wrong? Maybe Gwyddno had to delay the attack?"

"Perhaps," Urien said, scratching at his beard. "But if we press on to Cantre'r Gwaelod and find it empty, we'll be powerless to stop the war."

As the debate continued, Taliesin set his gaze out on the horizon. The small ridge provided a sweeping view of the Welsh countryside's rolling hills and creeping forests. Taliesin brought his thumb to his mouth and gently bit down. In an instant, he could see the rolling hillside sail past him as his view stretched beyond to the village behind the hill, and then to the river beyond that, and then the mountains again. Taliesin willed his sight farther and farther until the gates of Cantre'r Gwaelod appeared. Taliesin could see the castle as if he was a soaring bird flying over it. He could make out gross details, like the flow of fishing boats and skiffs in the harbor, or a train of peasants riding from market. He could also scry the training field and the barracks for Gwyddno's soldiers, all empty. So was the war room and Gwyddno's wing of the palace.

"King Gwyddno is neither riding towards Anglesey, nor is he still in Cantre'r Gwaelod," Taliesin announced to the group of men.

All debate immediately ceased.

"You can...see that?" Urien asked, aghast.

Taliesin nodded.

"But how can that be?" Urien's second-in-command asked. "Where is King Gwyddno, then?"

With another bite of his thumb, Taliesin scanned the roads in every direction from Cantre'r Gwaelod, searching for any sign that would give Gwyddno away. All the land around the Lowland Hundred appeared peaceful and empty. Taliesin thought carefully for a minute and then turned his gaze west, out near the coastline of Wales. He could see the edge of Cantre'r Gwaelod's great sea wall in the northern side of Cardigan Bay. He followed the churning blue water up to the rocky cape that capped the border of the bay. There, right on the tip of the cape, Taliesin could clearly see a fleet of ships, the head flagship bearing the unmistakable turquoise sail of Gwyddno Garanhir.

"They are coming by boat!" Taliesin yelped. "Gwyddno's taken his whole army to sea and just now are rounding Bardsey island!"

"Of course!" Elphin threw his hands towards heaven. "I should have guessed it! The Lowland Hundred have the better navy, why wouldn't they use it?"

Urien, on the other hand, found the news far more concerning.

"If they are at sea, we'll never be able to stop them! Gwyddno and Maelgwn are doomed to destroy each other!"

"They aren't there yet!" Taliesin said, his eyes riveted to the horizon. "Quick! That path to the west there! There's a fishing town nearly ten miles down the path, we can stop them if we move now! Hurry! Please!"

Urien shook his head in disbelief.

"This is a most unusual detour for my men and horses, but I'll put my faith in our prophet for now. Sound the call, we move west at all haste!"

A knight by Urien's side blew loudly on his horn, calling every armored man to attention. "Lead the way then, young Taliesin!" Urien commanded.

Taliesin prayed that his mediocre horsemanship skills would be enough, and then drove his horse down the path at a gallop. Elphin had to grab fast to the saddle to avoid getting thrown off the speeding animal. Tudno and Bryn followed just behind while Urien's forces lumbered forward, powerful yet slower than the two agile horses. Taliesin spared all caution as he raced the horse down muddy and overgrown paths. The fishing village lay on the north side of the Llyn peninsula, meaning that Taliesin had to wind his way down from the steep mountains that ran through the countryside. More than a few times Taliesin nearly lost control and Elphin had to grab the reins to steady the horse.

Within an hour, the fishing village came into view, nestled between a gap in the mountains and Caernarfon Bay. Taliesin and Elphin careened through the small wooden gates and clattered up a shambled dockside that lined the shore.

"Stop already, lad!" Elphin cried. "The horse will tumble right through the boards!"

Taliesin took the advice and pulled the horse to a standstill. Urien's train and Tudno were still racing down the hillside above. Villagers from straw-work huts began congregating and pointing towards the oncoming train, some yelling that they were under attack.

"Please!" Taliesin called out to the crowd. "We don't mean anyone harm, but we need to make use of a boat and fast! King Gwyddno of Cantre'r Gwaelod is sailing up the coast. We have an urgent message for him!"

"King Gwyddno Garanhir! Of Cantre'r Gwaelod?" A swarthy fisherman with a grey beard and sun-tanned skin stepped forward. "Heh! That'd be a bold move, these are Maelgwn's waters, he's in for a monster of a fight if he heads much farther. You sure about that, boyo?"

"We're sure to offer you a fair reward if you take us out to intercept him," Elphin chimed in. "I am Elphin, the first-born prince of the Lowland Hundred!"

"Elphin! The luckless prince?" the old man replied, eyeing Elphin up and down "That's a laugh! Look at you! Starved half to death, pale as a ghost? You look more like the victim of the most ragged misfortune in all of Britain."

He took a moment to consider what he had just said.

"Egad! It IS Prince Elphin!" The fisherman stumbled back in shock. "Right yeh are then, your Majesty. This way! I've a skiff of a vessel ready here. Let's just see if Gwyddno is on his way then!"

The grey-haired man ushered them to a small but sturdy fishing boat sporting a drab, patchwork sail. Tudno and Bryn galloped down the dockside and joined them.

"No more passengers!" the fisherman said after the four of them had shuffled into the boat. "It'll be a miracle if she stays afloat as it is. We won't be sailing at top speed with a load like this, you know."

"We'll run the risk, now please hurry!" Taliesin said.

The fisherman hauled up his rope and kicked the rickety vessel away from the dock.

"Make sure we have a horn!" Elphin declared. "We'll need one to signal the fleet."

"If you say so, your Lordship. I've one there on the mast." The man jabbed a pudgy arm at a small tin horn tied onto the ship.

A violent winter gale was whipping along the bay which helped the small boat gain speed but also pushed up chaotic waves that slapped rambunctiously at the boat. As they moved farther out, a dozen tall ships appeared on the southern edge of the bay. Bright crimson and teal banners streamed behind the masts announcing battle. The navy of Cantre'r Gwaelod was nearly in sight of Anglesey.

"Gad zooks!" the fisherman cried. "You were right! King Gwyddno's come to bring war to us all! Oh gracious!"

"We can stop him!" Taliesin shouted over the waves. "We

must get close enough to hail the ships!"

"There's not a chance that we catch them in time. Those are the swiftest ships in Christendom, those are!"

"Just get us as close as you can!" Taliesin pleaded. Inwardly, he conceded that the fisherman was right. The royal navy would hardly trouble themselves with a fishing boat, and they were still too far away to call out. If they missed the King now, they might follow in their wake until they reached Gwynedd and the start of a truly apocalyptic battle. They waited anxiously as the ships drew nearer and nearer. Even from several hundred yards away, Taliesin could make out the brilliant turquoise sail of his grandfather's flagship. Any farther now and the ships would pass them by.

"We have to try to hail them now, they're as close as they're going to get!"

"Aye then!" The fisherman grabbed the horn and blasted out several long calls.

The ships continued sailing. The sailor tried the horn again. Then a third time.

"It's no use, boy!" the fisherman called out. "The wind is too strong today!"

In an instant, Bryn side-stepped around the man and snatched the horn out of his hands. He grabbed onto the mast to steady himself and then unleashed a thunderclap of sound from the fishing horn.

BLAAAAAAAAAAMMH, BLAAAAMH, BLAAAAAAAAAAMMMHH!!!

Another minute went by. The ships continued their course to Anglesey.

Until finally, Taliesin's ears heard the signal echoed from the distant ships. The rest of the group heard the same. One by one the tall ships began to reverse course and tack towards the shore. They moved their formation like a flock of monstrous birds and began charging towards them. Everyone on the fishing boat cried and cheered for joy.

As the ships loomed closer, Taliesin became unsure about their reasons to celebrate. Instead of intercepting the fishing boat, the warships maneuvered around the small skiff, as if they were afraid of its passengers escaping. Bryn had clearly used a horn signal specific to the Lowland Hundred, yet he could see archers and pikemen lining up on the surrounding ships, acting like they were rounding up a group of spies. Taliesin could feel the tips of hundreds of arrows trained on him.

Gwyddno's flagship sailed forward directly in front of the skiff. It veered starboard and stalled in front of the fishing boat. From the deck of the ship, Enid stood and called out to them.

"AHOY! Who goes there?! Announce yourselves now or we'll send out a volley!"

"AHOY! CAPTAIN!" Taliesin called out. "It's us! Taliesin, Tudno, and Bryn!"

"TALIESIN!?" Enid yelped. "You three are wanted for abandonment and treason!"

"Call us traitors if you must, but we have Prince Elphin here!"

"You jest!?" Enid demanded.

"ENID! BY THUNDER!" Elphin practically roared. "IT'S ME! NOW LET US UP TO TALK WITH GWYDDNO!"

There was a moment's pause and Enid disappeared over the bow of the ship. She returned and ordered that everybody aboard the fishing skiff be brought onto Gwyddno's ship and then warned the group not to draw a weapon or act outside her directions. A ladder was thrown down over the hull and the fisherman warily brought his vessel about to the side of the ship.

"Oh saints! I'm not out for trouble!" the fisherman mumbled nervously. "They're not going to kill me, are they?" He was looking anxiously at the drawn archers perched on the prow of the ship.

"Nobody's dying today, take heart!" Taliesin said, although he could have used some reassurance himself. Why the heightened security for just a handful of fishing passengers?

Taliesin motioned for Elphin to climb up the ladder and then Tudno and Bryn. He shuffled up the rope ladder last and hoisted himself onto Gwyddno's deck.

On board, he was greeted with no less than four pikes aimed squarely at his neck. Elphin, Bryn, and Tudno had received similar welcomes and the four were roughly hustled together in one clump flanked on either side by a line of soldiers. Standing center deck, looking on passively, stood the captain of the guard.

"Enid!" Taliesin called out. "Enid, there's no need for this." He indicated the armed squadron. "We've freed Elphin. Maelgwn and all of Gwynedd have been hobbled. There's no nee-"

"You three have abandoned your countrymen during a critical time of war!" Enid cut Taliesin off. "You went, without permission, into the camp of the enemy, made unsanctioned promises on your kingdom's behalf, and are now interfering with a military action!"

Taliesin had hardly ever seen the captain so upset before. He had seen the verbal abuse she could dole out to the new cadets in order to instill respect, but this was far different. Tudno dared to talk back.

"We didn't make any promises to Maelgwn, we beat the Dragon at his own game!"

"You are to be tried for high treason at the earliest possible moment," Enid announced, ignoring Tudno. "That is the mandate of the King!"

"Hear me now, you tin-coated pigeon!" Elphin stepped forward, having the guts to push aside one of the pikes aimed at his chest. "I've been through three fat weeks of hellfire and the only person that pulled me out is my foster son here and this lot. My own father must be going senile to accuse his own family of treason!"

"Senile, am I?" Gwyddno walked onto the deck with his entourage of generals accompanying him. "With all the commotion you've caused, it's a wonder I still have any wits left at all!"

Gwyddno stood squarely in front of the group of four, his

face steely and cold. The other generals looked at each other tensely. Lord Connwn bit the inside of his cheek.

Taliesin finally stepped forward.

"Granddad, please. Tudno, Bryn, and I...we didn't take our decision to leave the kingdom lightly. We were willing to risk our lives to save Elphin because we knew that anything less would bring horrible suffering. You knew that too, Sire, but what choice did you have but to go to war? Now we have Elphin back and our kingdom's honor is restored. There is no longer any need to attack Gwynedd."

"The wheels of war don't grind to a halt because of one man, no matter his title." Gwyddno replied.

"If they can start turning for one man, I don't see why they can't stop for him."

Gwyddno smiled softly, despite himself. He wiped his grin away quick enough and returned to his generals.

"What say you lords?" he addressed them. "Shall we turn back with our prize in hand and nary a man slain? Or should we press on and dole out our vengeance to Maelgwn and his swine?"

Connwn wasted no time speaking up.

"Speaking for Powys, we are too close now to stop the storm that Maelgwn has brought down on himself. I say we press on and every man here wins his share of glory! Death to tyrants!"

Nearly half of the assembled generals cheered while the other half only stood still looking grim. Gwyddno paced to the prow of his ship and looked north towards Anglesey.

"Lord Connwn of Powys, you seem rather eager to arrive at battle."

"Well, yes. There is much honor to it, your Highness," Connwn responded.

"Honor...yes," Gwyddno said thoughtfully. "I suppose we would know, old ally. We've both seen many wars, we fought the bastard Saxons, threw their brats against the rocks to rid the land of them. How many children have we mutilated so that they can't swing a sword when they grow? We've seen such honor, haven't we? We've seen maybe a thousand honorable sights in our time." Gwyddno's tone never wavered from the friendly casual note he started on. He could have been talking to an old cousin of his.

The King glanced at the half dozen other lords on deck before continuing. "Well, if no one dissents, that seems like wise enough counsel for me."

Gwyddno took three steps away from Taliesin and then gave the order.

"*Ma rai or hwareli!*"

Connwn snapped into step and went to grab Taliesin by the scruff of the neck. He froze halfway through his walk, suddenly realizing that he was the only person on deck that had moved.

"Lord Connwn…" Gwyddno said amiably. "I wasn't aware that you understood orders given in Cumbric tongue."

Connwn looked noticeably shaken.

"I had…had heard a lot of the wet nurses back in Powys speaking nursery rhymes and such, I must have picked up more than I thought."

"Is that so?" Gwyddno asked, stepping towards Connwn with a leisurely gait. "And that was one of the things your wet nurses taught you? 'Ma rai or hwareli,' 'Seize the prisoner?' You must have had some very strict matrons indeed."

Out of view from Connwn, Gwyddno threw Enid a knowing glance. The captain's hand drifted to her sword.

"Lord Connwn, do you remember the wager that we made, just this morning? Regarding my son Seithenyn?"

"Well…uh…naturally, Sire."

"Whether I could trust him with the reins to the kingdom while away? That he would comport himself honestly and loyally and refrain from debauchery while I was gone?"

"Yes, Sire."

"Well, then. It appears that I owe you, Lord Connwn, a gold piece." Gwyddno approached the baffled warlord and placed in his hand a single gold coin. Connwn closed his hand around it warily and then turned pale as he inspected the coin. Inscribed on the gold disc was the sigil of Gwynedd.

"Seithenyn may have his faults to be sure, but he is no traitor," Gwyddno went on. "It was just before dawn this morning that my second born came in with my daughter-in-law, lady Crissiant. They reported a very disturbing incident of one of my closest generals laying the groundwork for mutiny, including trying to bribe the gate master himself into usurping the kingdom. Now I'm sure, by nature, that Prince Seithenyn must have been sorely tempted to keep this bribe and use it for his lecherous ways, but alas, Prince Seithenyn has more honor than you give him credit for. He handed over every piece of your traitor's gold and made it well clear who gave it to him. And how surprising it was to hear that the scoundrel trying to buy Seithenyn off was the same cur that suggested he be put in charge."

Gwyddno smiled warmly and clapped his hand on Connwn's shoulder. Connwn only stared blankly at the gold coin, his expression opaque.

"Don't be sour about it, Connwn," Gwyddno went on. "You're not the first to lay a scheme against me, I'm just happy for you that we caught you in time. Do you really think Maelgwn would have left all of Cantre'r Gwaelod for you?"

The dagger flashed into Connwn's hand, seemingly from nowhere. Taliesin saw it first while Gwyddno's back was turned. He yelled out as the traitor lunged for the King in a blind rage.

King Gwyddno had not remained king for so long by being slow, however. In an impressive act of grace, the old and powerful man pivoted on his heel and brought his hands down on Connwn's arm and neck. In one fluid motion, Gwyddno swung his adversary around once and then slammed him against the deck. Gwyddno brought a heavy boot down onto Connwn's hand, effectively disarming his dagger.

"Seize the traitor," Gwyddno ordered as if he were selecting his lunch. Every general on the ship immediately laid their hands on the lord of Powys who thrashed and threatened them. After some struggle, they had Connwn's hands bound and led him below deck to await justice back in Cantre'r Gwaelod. King Gwyddno watched them lead Lord Connwn away, absently wondering what the conniving man might have done in the fray of battle to secure his treachery.

After the commotion had settled down, Enid approached the King.

"Sire, what are your orders?"

Gwyddno turned to look at his beleaguered family and bard. The King dropped his grim facade and allowed himself to radiate his warm, ferociously caring self yet again. Taliesin felt he was only now seeing his grandfather for the first time that day.

Gwyddno looked at each of his fellow countrymen in turn before replying.

"Well, I'd say that we've gotten all that we came for!" he said, smiling brilliantly at his son. "Tell the captains to reverse course! We return home victorious!"

A cheer rose from the relieved soldiers, many of whom started the day wondering if they would ever return home to their families alive. Gwyddno stepped forward and embraced his foster grandson.

"You had me most worried, you know," he said to the boy. "But I had a feeling you would do something extraordinary."

"I said as much when we first met, didn't I?" Taliesin said with a grin. Gwyddno stared back in shock.

"You were told?"

"Just a few hours ago. I guess now, we know what in heaven's name I was talking about."

The two shared a warm laugh together. Then Gwyddno turned to see Elphin, standing silently in the ocean sun.

"Elphin, my boy!" Gwyddno ran and pulled his misfortunate son into a tight, possessive embrace. "I had to play the grim father just now, for the sake of smoking out a rat. But, oh what comfort it gives me to see you again. You're starved, exhausted, and look ten years older than me, but you're home and safe again. The gods bless you, lad!"

"Uhm...Sire!" Taliesin said, not wanting to interrupt the King's reunion. "Before we head back to Cantre'r Gwaelod. There is somebody ashore that would want to speak with you."

"And that would be?"

"Lord Urien of Rheged. It was thanks to him that Elphin and I were able to seal our escape. He and his men are waiting for you at the fishing village yonder."

Gwyddno blinked in surprise. "By the winds, lad! This is a lucky day indeed. Right, get a skiff ready. Take us to shore!"

The sailors wasted no time getting a boat prepared. Meanwhile Gwyddno embraced Tudno and then turned to Bryn. He held the bard tight to him and then stepped away, looking the taller man up and down like he was searching for something. Finally, he noticed the bard's swollen jaw and his uncharacteristic silence.

"Bryn...what in God's name happened to you?"

***

Gwyddno's loud cursing and rambling threats filled the air on the short ride back to the village. After Taliesin relayed to the King how Bryn had helped them, risked his life and reputation, and then lost his tongue for Taliesin's sake, the King turned beet red and hurled a bewildered soldier's pike out to the sea. It took the pleas and reasoning of Taliesin, Elphin, and Enid to dissuade the King from pressing on with the attack.

"With Urien's help or not, it will take weeks to lay siege to Anglesey!" Enid reminded him. "Our bard did not sacrifice his voice to see you go off to slaughter!"

"And in any case, Maelgwn's rule is finished!" Taliesin cried out. The whole deck stood still. "I told him myself, and it's the truth! Maelgwn of Gwynedd will die of the yellow plague in two years' time. We would be fighting a condemned ruler."

"What?!" Gwyddno asked, astounded. "You're certain?"

"It was a hot topic of controversy for most of my stay in Anglesey but, yes, I am quite certain."

Gwyddno tensed his jaw and glared at the sea northwards. "This is hardly justice," he said. "I love you like a son, Bryn. It grieves me to no end that we shall not hear your laughter and songs in my halls. We should have vengeance!"

"The greatest injury we could do to Maelgwn now is to prosper and live on while Maelgwn grows sick and dies," Elphin remarked. "We won't accomplish that by going to battle in vain."

In the end, it was only Bryn's pleading look and self-satisfied smile that finally convinced the King to contain his wrath. Yet, by the time they reached the docks of the fishing village, Gwyddno was still muttering all forms of insults and curses. Urien had already assembled his men into parade formation. The knights of Rheged saluted the King of the Lowland Hundred as he hopped onto the rickety fishing dock.

"That arrogant toad!" Gwyddno continued. "It's just a code of human decency, no more! You don't harm a maiden's face, a painter's hands, or a bard's tongue, by the spit of the sea! You put him to death, maybe, if he's deserved it, but you leave him with his bloody tongue!"

"Hail, King Gwyddno," Urien approached and offered a respectful bow. "We are much relieved to see you."

"The same, Lord Rheged," Gwyddno said, composing himself. "My son and foster grandson tell me that I owe you a world of gratitude."

"Not at all. I only made the decision that was best for my kingdom. Nobody gains when you support a bloody tyrant. You're not still planning to attack Anglesey, are you?"

"I am tempted," Gwyddno admitted. "Except a man in my own council was just charged with sedition and pushing the kingdom to war for personal gains. I won't grant him the satisfaction. Besides," Gwyddno turned to look at Taliesin. "I've been told that Maelgwn will be dead soon enough, and that you witnessed the prophecy that foretold so."

"It's true, your Majesty," Urien spoke. "I saw the lad here speak such words that shook the walls of Anglesey and I saw him stand firm against the most bloodthirsty king of Britain. He is truly a prodigy worthy of legend."

"Oh, yes?" Gwyddno replied. "And did this prodigy of my kingdom cause you to reconsider our offer? I take it you didn't consider Maelgwn an honorable ally?"

"Very true, but that had more to do with his lies and cruelty than Taliesin himself. No, Maelgwn has been revealed as the heartless Dragon he is, but that does not mean that I can pledge my kingdom's allegiance to Cantre'r Gwaelod for nothing."

This drew a wry smile from Gwyddno. Taliesin smelled negotiation in the air.

"I never expect to have allies for free," Gwyddno replied innocently. "The offer still stands, several wagons full of the sea's bounty, mussels, sealskin, salted salmon and such every month, and naval protection for any ship of Rheged's that anchors in Cardigan Bay."

"I'm sorry to say that still won't cut it, O King," Urien politely returned. "Even if Rheged could anchor in Cardigan Bay, we'd have to pass through parts of Gwynedd, hardly a simple matter after today." Urien held up his gauntleted hand. "I am interested in another prize for an alliance, however."

"Well," Gwyddno raised his eyebrows curiously. "Let's hear it, then."

"I would ask you to allow me to take young Taliesin here as my own bard. His extraordinary gifts of prophecy can be shared between our two kingdoms, but he shall reside in my court and keep his counsel primarily with me. If you can give me this, Rheged will pledge loyalty to the Lowland Hundred as long as our two kingdoms stand."

Gwyddno face was set like stone carved with a plain, neutral expression. Taliesin was the only soul that afternoon who saw a small dimple form on the corner of Gwyddno's mouth where he was sucking his cheek. The King was quietly at war with himself.

At length, Gwyddno answered.

"That is a steep price indeed, Urien. What's more, my people are not used to treating others like property. We have servants and peasants in our land to be sure, but none are really mine to give away, least of all my foster grandson. If you ask him, and so long as he is never brought to harm should he go with you, his choice will stand."

Urien inclined his head towards the twelve-year-old boy. "What say you, Taliesin?"

The question blindsided Taliesin and presented him with a personal dilemma. He had just rescued his father and saved the kingdom a world of trouble and sacrifice. He may be treated as a glorious hero who brought fame and glory to his people. Word would spread like lightning about his deeds and talents, and he would automatically have fame and status for the rest of his long life. Why should he trade that to be another master's bard?

Another thought pulled at him. Many in the kingdom would seek his advice for their problems. How could he really trust his visions of the world without experiencing it firsthand? How could he say for sure that his visions were true and not just a spell of madness? Would he be satisfied dwelling in the palace of Caer Wyddno for the rest of his life, ignorant to the physical world outside?

Everyone's attention was pinned to Taliesin as he finally picked his head up and turned his grey eyes to Urien.

"Give me a month to prepare, and I will go with you to Rheged."

And so it was.

EPILOGUE

The sun was just beginning to push its way up through the mountainous eastern skyline of Ceredigion as Taliesin secured his bag of possessions to his pack mule. Enid and a handful of knights were due to accompany him on the long and perilous road to Rheged. In all the previous month, news from Gwynedd had been quiet. Whatever was happening in Maelgwn's kingdom now, the Dragon King seemed content to keep it within his own borders. Still, as the road to Urien's castle passed straight through Maelgwn's territory, Enid insisted on providing Taliesin with an escort.

"I suppose that there is no serious cause for concern," Enid joked as they were planning out the journey. "If there is any attack in store for us, our soothsayer here will surely give us warning."

The news of Taliesin's gifts preceded his return to Cantre'r Gwaelod. Back in the great harbor, Taliesin stepped off the King's ship with Gwyddno on one side of him and his father on the other. Maidens from across the walled kingdom draped flowers and ornate jewelry around his neck and the knights receiving them saluted Taliesin with newfound respect and awe. Hardly anyone in the whole Lowland Hundred could bring themselves to look the enigmatic youth in the eye. Throughout the welcoming crowd, Taliesin could hear different whispers.

"...the boy foretold Maelgwn's death! Really shook him up too..."

"...saying that he can work magic right? How does he beat the fastest horses in... "

"...I heard he's made a deal with the Fae. He'll be no..."

Taliesin felt that all the adoration and reverence was misguided. One smiling face did lift his spirits, however. Lady Elphin was the first to greet her foster son and husband the moment they stepped onto the dock. She embraced her son first, feeling that his shoulders stood a little taller than they once did.

"Something has changed with you," she whispered to him through joyful tears.

"Perhaps, but nothing can change that I am your son," Taliesin said as he gripped her tighter. Then the Lady Elphin saw her husband, frail and ragged, step off the ship. She ran her eyes over him once before throwing her arms around him and weeping unabashedly on his shoulder. Taliesin could see the horrors of his father's imprisonment wash off him in her tender embrace. At long last, he was home.

Once they had been received, Taliesin took his mother aside to explain his arrangement with Urien. Lady Elphin was confused and distraught at first, but Taliesin's confidence and sense of purpose eventually mollified her.

"I should have known you were meant to fly away. I'm just surprised you never grew any wings, angel that you are to me," she said through sniffles.

For the most part, the whole kingdom shared Lady Elphin's shock. Several knights predisposed to be suspicious of Rheged raised objections. They voiced concerns that Urien might use Taliesin's apparent supernatural abilities against Gwyddno and the kingdom. The King was quick to dismiss such objections.

"If Urien wanted me dead, he could've just allowed us to march off to war with Gwynedd. What's more, if Rheged does turn hostile to us, I'd be very glad to have a family member working inside his court."

With the King's express permission, Taliesin spent most of the last month he had in Cantre'r Gwaelod sharing bittersweet moments with his parents and visiting Bryn when he could get a chance. The King, while forced to search for another orator, kept Bryn in his service as a musician of the highest honors. Bryn quickly developed a pleasing repertoire on his new crwth and offered Taliesin lessons on the harp. Since his awakening, Taliesin had little difficulty mastering the fingering and timing needed for the harp. Now, most of the instruments that Taliesin touched felt familiar, like something that he performed artfully dozens of times in his dreams.

Keeping Bryn company felt both comforting and heartbreaking. The world was a darker place now that Bryn's songs and stories had been silenced forever but Taliesin actually appreciated Bryn's presence even more now that both had no use for unnecessary talk. Most of the time, the two of them would speak through their music and the few lucky souls that passed close enough to Bryn's tower would hear the most breathtaking notes and chords than ever was played in any hall of Britain.

Tudno also received high praises from the King and nobility. Even Seithenyn pardoned his youngest son for taking his old pony without asking. With so much to do and prepare, Taliesin saw little of his cousin after returning home until the last week before his departure. Tudno showed up at Elphin's estate dressed in the plain, utilitarian attire of an apprentice monk. His hair was cut short and conservatively. He explained to Taliesin that watching him perform miracles, however they may have been performed, had galvanized his faith in the Almighty and that he decided to devote himself wholly to the church. He handed Taliesin a modest book bound in tanned leather.

"We're not supposed to take these from the abbey," Tudno said, "but I figured that we already have so many copies, the Lord would have you take it. It's a copy of the holy bible. I'll be sure to copy down several more in my time anyway. Surely, you'll need to study it, now that you're a bard to a Christian king."

Taliesin accepted the gift with warm thanks. However, he did not have the heart to tell Tudno that he already had the whole book committed to his limitless memory.

After Tudno's visit, Taliesin's days seemed to hang in suspended animation, feeling both timeless and fleeting all at once, until the morning he found himself gazing out at the roaring sea from Elphin's doorstep for the last time. He had long since confirmed that his belongings had been packed, but he wanted to appreciate the sweeping view of Cantre'r Gwaelod before he left. As the sun broke over the clifftops on the eastern hills, a slender figure appeared out of the radiant air. Even though Taliesin had spoken with just about every person that he would miss from his home kingdom, there was still somebody he sorely wished to see.

Mererid's face came into view, haloed by wisps of her bronze hair backlit in the sun. She walked towards the tower with an even, determined gait. She stopped several yards away from Taliesin, who stood at attention in front of her. He was afraid to move or to speak, thinking that the smallest twitch might send her running like a deer. That or possibly flying at him like a hawk.

As it turned out, she was the first to speak.

"I heard that you will be leaving us for Rheged," she said without a hint of a smile. "You're not going to turn traitor to us, I hope."

"No," Taliesin replied. "You were the one that caught the true traitor. Thanks to you, Connwn's been found out and exchanged for ransom. We can share this victory, Mererid. We both saved the kingdom from catastrophe."

"But I wonder who they'll remember as the hero," Mererid spoke without mirth. "Did you see Rhun while you were in Gwynedd? Did you run him through with a blade?"

Taliesin inhaled purposefully.

"Rhun doesn't have any happy days ahead of him. Maelgwn will be dead in two years' time. Then Rhun will either be slain for the throne, or he'll have to put together the pieces of the mess his father made. I do not envy him."

"I envy you for having the chance to claw out his eyes," Mererid countered. "And I'm disappointed you didn't take it." The tall girl turned her head out to sea slightly giving Taliesin a glint of her elegant neck. "The men all say that you now have the gift to see the future. Can you do it, then?" She turned her face back to Taliesin and peered into him. "Can you tell me my future?"

Taliesin only shook his head.

"The men do not quite understand what they are saying," Taliesin tried to explain gently. "Sometimes I see visions of the future. Other times I see enough of the present to make very accurate predictions. But I am not a deity. Trying to look at one person's specific future, even my own, is like trying to find a root of a tree without digging."

Mererid only scoffed quietly. "I didn't think you would. But I'm sure I could tell my future better than any fortune teller." Mererid picked up her head like she was announcing a decree to the seaside. "And the maid, Mererid, lived forever cleaning the chamber pots and mopping the floors of Caer Wyddno until she became an old gray spinster. Because even though she was very beautiful, she found no one to marry her. Because after all…" For the first time, she held her left hand up to show her stump of a finger. "Who would marry a maiden that couldn't bear the ring of her betrothed?"

Taliesin's stomach clenched painfully at the sight of Mererid's hand, not from physical revulsion, but from guilt. He couldn't bear the thought that his own recklessness put her in harm's way and that she had been wronged so brutally.

"Mererid," Taliesin said at length, "I cannot offer any apology that will undo the evil I've done to you. And I truly can't give you any comforting glimpse into the future for you. But, by all the sight granted to me, I can tell you this: that you are the most virtuous, intelligent, and beautiful maid in all of Britain, and any suitor that cannot see past a missing finger is not worthy of you by far."

If Mererid was even slightly moved by the young seer's words, she hardly showed it except maybe but for the bat of an eyelash. She covered her hand up with her glove.

"That may not do me any good if there are no worthy men in Britain," she said softly. "I am happy to see Prince Elphin back safe with your mum. I am glad that the traitor was caught and that we saved the Lowland Hundred from ruin. But you," Taliesin thought he might have seen the sheen of tears in her stoic eyes. "Sometimes I wish that we had never met, dear Taliesin."

The words stung Taliesin more sharply than the blow he had received from Rhun or the nip of the wood imps in Gwynedd. Still, he did not begrudge her in the slightest for saying so.

"I wish you farewell, bard," Mererid said as she pulled her shawl tightly around her soft shoulders. "May God guard you on your path here and forever." She turned and began to walk back down the stone causeway towards her daily chores.

"And may He bless and keep you as well," Taliesin said softly after her. She did not look back.

Taliesin watched her leave until she was out of sight, and then gathered himself up and stepped back inside to bid farewell to his foster mother and father. Then, with Enid and four men on horseback, he set out for the northern kingdom of Rheged.

***

It was the first night of May in Maelgwn's private forest. In a patchy clearing close to the center of the woods, a single, pointed boulder jutted out of the earth. As the last light faded from the eaves of the forest, a stark *crack* caused the birds and smaller animals to scatter. In the center of the grove, the boulder shifted, and a pale thin hand grasped the rock's surface, followed by the dark shape of a man. He lifted himself up through cracks in the rocks that no passer-by would ever find, squeezing himself through impossibly small doorways that would amaze even a mouse. The figure finally gathered himself and stood upright in the crisp evening air. The moonlight reflected off the figure's shoulder and chest, sending silver glints throughout the grove. The man lifted his arms and breathed deeply, inhaling the scent of every tree, bird, and fish.

With the man's entrance, dozens of other shapes began to scurry out from the bushes and roots of the trees. The Lunantisidhe usually kept themselves out of sight of men and beasts alike, but tonight the grove swelled full with the jagged creatures. They cackled and hissed at each other as they crowded the base of the pointed boulder. The tall, ghostly figure sat down in the hollow of the boulder, like a prince sitting on a gloomy throne.

One of the Lunantisidhe hopped up the boulder and crouched low next to the man's ear.

"How now, you forest guard?" The man spoke in a clear dark voice, like the bottom of a mighty river. "Does that fool king of Gwynedd still pretend he rules these woods?"

The imp next to his ear began chattering softly to him. The man kept as still as stone while he listened.

"In two years' time, is it?" the man repeated. "So Maelgwn's line finally begins to wilt. And how did we come by this happy bit of news?"

The throng of creatures began jumping and chattering with excitement. In a hundred different voices, they all began crying the same words.

Bright Brow!

Boy from Gwyddno's kingdom.

Radiant Brow.

Awen.

Ceridwen's Brew!

The man listened to the chorus of sharp voices and swept the crowd with his grey eyes.

"So, the brew of Awen has been consumed, and by a human boy from Gwyddno's country, eh?"

The Lunantisidhe shouted in affirmation.

"That is an interesting report to wake up to." The man rested his chin in his hands while he turned the information over in his silver head.

"It's been many years since we've had cause to consider Gwyddno Garanhir, but he knew such a day would come." The tall man stood up, stretching himself like a young sapling oak. "I think it's time we pay Gwyddno a little visit. Methinks the time has come to collect our tithe."

ABOUT THE AUTHOR

Alexander Corby is an American author with Welsh heritage on his father's side. Taliesin, Chief of Bards is his first full-length novel. He holds a bachelor's degree in both Theater and Physics from Vassar College of Poughkeepsie, NY, and has also studied at the Dell' Arte International School of Physical Theater in Blue Lake, CA. For much of his life, Corby trained as a circus artist developing repertoires in juggling, acrobatics, unicycling, and balloon sculpting. Some of the most rewarding experiences of his life thus far have been volunteering with social circus projects such as the Dreamtime Circus and Performers Without Borders. While participating in these programs, Corby traveled to several countries including India, Perú, and Nicaragua where he helped offer free circus shows and workshops to underserved communities. Corby now resides in Puerto Rico with his wife and daughter. Enchanted with the art of storytelling, Corby hopes to continue writing and giving voice to more tales in the future.

Printed in Great Britain
by Amazon

78970415R00249